PRAISE FOR PATRICIA MORRISROE'S
THE WOMAN IN THE MOONLIGHT

"An intoxicating novel about love, art, and life. Just as Beethoven's *Moonlight* Sonata moves one from tears to hope, so does Patricia Morrisroe's story of the woman who inspired the sonata, Countess Julie Guicciardi."

—Lara Prescott, author of *New York Times* bestseller
The Secrets We Kept

"I was utterly absorbed in this beautiful novel of the brilliant, impossible Beethoven and the lovely countess who inspired one of his greatest sonatas. The story is so moving I was sorry to come to the last pages. I read them with tears in my eyes."

—Stephanie Cowell, author of *Marrying Mozart*

"Sensual, witty, and deeply researched, *The Woman in the Moonlight* vividly captures the tumultuous romance between volatile genius Ludwig van Beethoven and his 'enchanting girl,' Countess Julie Guicciardi. In a love story ripe with decadence and court intrigue, Patricia Morrisroe transports readers on an unforgettable romp through nineteenth-century Europe. Brava!"

—Sally Koslow, internationally bestselling author of
Another Side of Paradise

"Captivating and emotionally compelling. Morrisroe writes with intelligence and great wit. Her spirited heroine is simply unforgettable. A must-read for music fans and anyone in search of a gripping love story. I could not put it down."

—Sheila Weller, author of the *New York Times* bestseller *Girls Like Us: Carole King, Joni Mitchell, Carly Simon—and the Journey of a Generation*

"*The Woman in the Moonlight* shines a light into nineteenth-century Europe's political and cultural history, revealing lives that are just as nuanced, tortured, and decadent as any we might read about in the tabloids today. Morrisroe's touching debut novel is a tribute to the focus, tenacity, courage, and sacrifice demanded by both art and what is commonly called true love."

—Barbara Quick, author of *Vivaldi's Virgins*

The
Woman
in the
Moonlight

ALSO BY PATRICIA MORRISROE

9 1/2 Narrow
Wide Awake
Mapplethorpe

The
Woman
in the
Moonlight

A Novel

Patricia Morrisroe

Little

Text copyright © 2020 by Patricia Morrisroe
All rights reserved.

Published by Little A, New York

www.apub.com

Amazon, the Amazon logo, and Little A are trademarks of Amazon.com, Inc., or its affiliates.

ISBN-13: 9781503903753 (hardcover)
ISBN-10: 1503903753 (hardcover)

ISBN-13: 9781503903746 (paperback)
ISBN-10: 1503903745 (paperback)

Cover design by Jarrod Taylor

Cover image: Johan Christian Clausen Dahl, *View of Dresden by Moonlight*, 1839. Heritage Image Partnership Ltd/Alamy Stock Photo

Printed in the United States of America

First edition

To Dr. Clarice J. Kestenbaum

Cast of Characters

Alexander I—tsar of Russia

Andrey Razumovsky—Russian diplomat, art collector, and music lover

Anna von Brunswick—Julie's aunt and Susanna Guicciardi's sister-in-law

Anton Schindler—Beethoven's secretary

Armgard von der Schulenburg—Friedrich von der Schulenburg's wife

Babette Keglevich—Beethoven's pupil and Julie's friend

Baron Franz von Hager—Vienna's chief of police

Carl Czerny—pianist, composer, and piano teacher

Caroline Murat—Napoleon Bonaparte's youngest sister, wife of Joachim Murat, and queen of Naples

Catherine Bagration—Klemens von Metternich's Russian mistress, mother of his child, and salon hostess

Christiane Lichnowsky—Karl Lichnowsky's wife

Christoph von Stackelberg—Josephine von Brunswick's second husband and father to three of her children

Count Sedlnitzky—Vienna's chief of police during the Congress of Vienna

Daniel Steibelt—pianist who engaged with Beethoven in a musical "duel"

Domenico Barbaja—Italian impresario

Eleonora von Fuchs—Robert von Gallenberg's sister

Ferdinand IV—king of Naples, married to Queen Maria Carolina (Marie Antoinette's sister)

Francis I—emperor of Austria

Franz Guicciardi—Julie's father

Franz von Brunswick—Julie's cousin and Josephine and Therese von Brunswick's brother

Friedrich von der Schulenburg—Saxon diplomat

Friedrich von Gallenberg—Julie's youngest son

Fritz von Deym—Josephine von Brunswick's son

George Polgreen Bridgetower—Afro-European violinist

Gerhard "Trouser Button" von Breuning—Stephan von Breuning's son

Gioachino Rossini—Italian opera composer

Hugo von Gallenberg—Julie's oldest son

Ignaz Schuppanzigh—violinist

Isabella Colbran—Spanish opera singer and Gioachino Rossini's wife

Joachim Murat—French cavalry leader, king of Naples, and Napoleon Bonaparte's brother-in-law

Johann van Beethoven—Beethoven's brother

Johanna van Beethoven—Beethoven's sister-in-law (married to Karl), nicknamed the "Queen of the Night"

Joseph Bonaparte—king of Naples and Napoleon Bonaparte's brother

Joseph Müller, a.k.a. Count Joseph von Deym—Josephine von Brunswick's first husband and proprietor of Müller's Art Gallery

Josephine von Brunswick—Julie's cousin and close friend of Beethoven's

Julie Guicciardi—Beethoven's piano student

Karl Lichnowsky—Beethoven's powerful patron

Karl van Beethoven—Beethoven's brother, husband to Johanna, and father to Karl

Karl van Beethoven—Beethoven's nephew and "son"

Kitty Caldwell—Julie's cook and Lucy Caldwell's niece

Klemens von Metternich—Austrian statesman

Louis-Antoine Duport—French ballet dancer and coadministrator of the Kärntnertor Theater

Lucy Caldwell—Julie's maid

Ludwig van Beethoven—piano virtuoso and composer

Maria Julie "Jülchen" von Gallenberg—Julie's daughter

Matthäus Stein—Nannette Streicher's brother, built Beethoven's "hearing machine"

Michael Umlauf—conductor

Moritz von Fries—Austria's richest man and patron of the arts

Nannette Streicher—piano manufacturer and musician

Napoleon Bonaparte—French military leader who crowned himself emperor

Ramo—Neapolitan fisherman

Robert von Gallenberg—composer and Julie's husband

Stephan von Breuning—Beethoven's old friend from Bonn

Susanna Guicciardi—Julie's mother

Therese van Beethoven—Beethoven's sister-in-law (married to Johann), nicknamed "Fat Lump"

Therese von Brunswick—Julie's cousin and Josephine von Brunswick's older sister

Victoire von Deym—Josephine von Brunswick's daughter

Wilhelmine, the Duchess of Sagan—Klemens von Metternich's German mistress and salon hostess

PART ONE

1

H is hands terrified me. They were strong and muscular, broad at the fingertips and flecked with coarse black hair. As he played a fantasia—an improvised piece that reflected his mood and imagination— he pummeled the keyboard with a bestial force that made the instrument tremble. Sliding a hand up and down two octaves, he delivered the equivalent of a double slap. My cheeks stung in sympathy. He scowled and grunted, the shadow of a beard eclipsing the lower part of his face. Was the great Ludwig van Beethoven turning into a werewolf?

My mother and I had been waiting for my Hungarian relatives at the Golden Griffin, a modest inn not far from the Kärntnertor Theater. Through charm and sheer persistence, Josephine and Therese had managed to persuade the greatest pianoforte virtuoso in Vienna to give them music lessons during their holiday. Aunt Anna had even rented a Walter pianoforte, which barely fit through the door, receiving numerous scrapes and an ugly abrasion that ran down its leg like a knife wound. I'd been living in Vienna for the past year but had never heard Beethoven perform. With my relatives' tardiness and Beethoven's unwillingness to converse, I had asked if he'd play a little something for us.

This, in retrospect, was a serious breach. People who asked him to play anything did so at their peril. Beneath a vaulted ceiling, with hunting trophies on the walls, he unleashed the musical equivalent of rage, teasing us with multiple climaxes and playing louder and faster until I feared my heart would burst. The pianoforte groaned and swayed; its maimed leg crackled. The innkeeper, covering his ears, fled the room.

I started to follow, but Beethoven, lifting his burly hands, paused for a few seconds. I knew what was coming next. He was going to kill us. But he suddenly played a melody that was so tender, so exquisitely sensitive that I couldn't believe that it flowed from the same surly individual. I looked at his hands again. They had now assumed the graceful contours of a gentle lover caressing his innocent bride. I felt light headed, imagining those hands around my waist, warm, still vibrating with passion.

Beethoven's hands . . . the last thing I remembered.

Looking back, I can still see Beethoven tugging at his right ear while gazing down at me from the foot of a burled walnut bed. As the room came into focus, I noted that it was large, with a cheerful fire and a window that faced a busy street. "Here, drink this," my mother said, handing me a glass of water. "The innkeeper has called a doctor."

Beethoven continued to stare. Away from the pianoforte, he resembled less a supernatural creature than any number of mortal men strolling down the Graben. He wore a gray morning coat, matching trousers, and a white cravat tied three times around his neck. The cravat was wrinkled as if he'd tugged at it too strenuously while attempting to knot it. At twenty-eight, he still didn't have a wife, and his woeful cravat signaled his marital status in a way that touched me.

People often described him as ugly, but I didn't find him so. He was short, about five feet four, with a peasant's stocky build. A broad nose marked a square-shaped face and balanced a prominent cleft chin. His dark hair was coarse and closely cropped, his ruddy skin stippled with smallpox scars. He rarely smiled, but when he did, he showed off straight, remarkably white teeth. His deep-set brown eyes were his best feature. Like his music, they communicated a full range of emotions.

When my aunt and cousins finally arrived laden with pastries, they looked at Beethoven and then at me.

"What is Julie doing in my bed?" Aunt Anna asked sharply.

"She fainted," my mother explained. "Herr Beethoven had to carry her upstairs."

"And she called me a werewolf," Beethoven added. His eyes twinkled as if he relished the role of mischief-maker.

"A werewolf!" my aunt said, glaring at my mother. "Julie is hardly a child. When I invited you to sit in on our lesson, I didn't expect your daughter to insult Herr Beethoven and make him carry her to my bedchamber."

With the doctor's appearance, Beethoven quickly excused himself, chastising my cousins for their tardiness and ignoring the pastries they offered. "I hope you feel better, Countess," he said to me. "Perhaps Mozart is more to your taste."

"Not at all," I replied. "It's just that I hadn't . . ."

By then, he was out the door.

The doctor, after checking my vital signs, attributed my fainting spell to overstimulation. "Herr Beethoven is right," he said solemnly. "You should listen only to Mozart, and then only to his comic operas. Someone of your delicate nature shouldn't be exposed to Herr Beethoven's music. In my experience, only the strongest females can handle it, and they usually make poor wives."

It was true that I'd fainted upon hearing it for the first time, but I hadn't eaten breakfast and had been feeling woozy even before he started to play. Now the doctor was prescribing an elixir of comic operas. If I needed to strengthen my "delicate" constitution, shouldn't I listen to more of his music? The doctor made no sense.

"Herr Beethoven does have a reputation for violence," my mother said. "He once struck a pupil with a knitting needle, and he used to give Babette Keglevich music lessons in his dressing gown and nightcap. He lived across the street, but still."

"Susanna, you listen to too much gossip," my aunt chided. "In all the time we've known him—"

"That would be three days," my mother countered.

Aunt Anna was plump and pragmatic, a woman more comfortable assisting one of her cows birth a calf than chitchatting in Vienna's salons. Knowing that springtime was breeding season, she had come to the city to find a mate for one of my cousins. Procuring Beethoven as a teacher was an inspired first step.

Musical connoisseurship was a vital part of pleasing the opposite sex, and the pianoforte was one of the few instruments appropriate for ladies. Strings required too many quick, powerful movements, giving the impression that the female player might suffer from a choleric temperament. The violoncello sat between a woman's legs, arousing male listeners in ways not in keeping with music's higher purpose. The pianoforte had elegant lines and a keyboard that emphasized a woman's graceful fingers and dainty wrists. Many a marriage proposal followed a recital, as long as the music was pleasing to the ear and didn't rattle the gentleman's composure.

In the calculating world of arranged marriages, Aunt Anna was betting on Josephine over Therese, whose handsome face couldn't compensate for a deformed spine. A self-proclaimed "priestess of truth," she saw the world through a prism of gloom, and her frequent Cassandra-like pronouncements left even the cheeriest individuals in despair. Josephine was even more complicated, but her beautiful face and lissome figure went a long way to compensate for her easily excitable nature.

"I'm afraid I have a bit of bad news," Aunt Anna announced. "We won't be joining you tonight." We'd been planning to see a performance of Mozart's *The Abduction from the Seraglio*. "The plot is really quite barbarous," she went on. "Two women are abducted from a ship and sold into slavery to a Turk. The pasha keeps a harem, and the heroine is expected to have conjugal relations with him. Hardly a suitable subject for Julie in her weakened condition."

"Let me understand," my mother said slowly. "You're not going to the opera because you object to the plot."

"I do object to the plot and for Julie's sake, so should you. But that's not the reason we're canceling. We have something better to do."

"Better than listening to Mozart?" I asked.

My aunt thought for a second. "Not necessarily better but related. We're meeting Herr Joseph Müller, who made Mozart's death mask. He's invited us to see it."

No matter how much Aunt Anna disliked *The Abduction from the Seraglio*, it seemed an affront to Mozart's memory to prefer his death mask over his music.

"Is this the same Joseph Müller who owns that strange cabinet of curiosities?" my mother asked.

We'd visited Müller's Art Gallery when I was small, and it gave me nightmares for weeks. Among its gruesome attractions was an anatomical model of a pregnant woman with a see-through stomach and detachable parts. Considered pornographic, the woman was carted off by the police just as a tourist was pulling a half-formed baby from the womb. Why would Aunt Anna want to spend an evening with someone who made death masks and obscene women?

"Herr Müller is a man of great wealth," my aunt said in response to our skeptical looks. "His cabinet of curiosities is Vienna's top tourist attraction. And he's an aristocrat."

"Wasn't he stripped of his title?" my mother asked. "I'd heard that he left the army over an illegal duel. And then he became a fugitive."

"Mama, why are we visiting him?" Therese asked nervously. "He doesn't sound appealing at all."

"Herr Müller has shown an interest in our dear Josephine," she replied. "He spotted her while we were out walking and was charmed by her old-fashioned clothes."

"Old fashioned!" Josephine objected. "I packed my best dress."

Unlike my mother, whose bible was the Parisian fashion magazine *Journal des Dames et des Modes*, Aunt Anna was a notorious skinflint with no sense of style. For their Viennese holiday, Josephine and Therese were allocated only one silk dress apiece, and Josephine had a noticeable hole in her right sleeve.

"I would imagine Herr Müller might know a thing or two about being old fashioned since he is very old," my mother stated.

"How old is he?" Josephine asked.

"The issue is totally inconsequential," Aunt Anna replied.

"How old *is* he?" Josephine repeated.

"Nearing fifty," my aunt admitted. "But that shouldn't matter. A man his age can still reproduce."

"But that's nearly thirty years older than I am," Josephine protested. "I don't want to meet him."

"You don't have a choice, Pepi," she said, addressing Josephine by her family nickname. "The lower classes can afford to marry for love. You don't have that option."

At the opera that night, I kept thinking of the similarities between Josephine and Mozart's heroine. Religion aside, I didn't see much difference between being sold to a pasha or the proprietor of a wax museum. One could argue that Mozart's heroine was in the better position, for at least she could talk to the other women in the harem, while Josephine would have only wax figures for company.

Preparing for bed, I relayed the day's events to my maid, Lucy. British by birth, she was fluent in several languages and a chatterbox in all of them. Her last employer had been committed to the Narrenturm, nicknamed the "Gugelhupf" for its resemblance to the popular Bundt cake. Lucy was always telling me that if I didn't watch out, I'd wind up there.

"I met Herr Beethoven," I told her as she brushed my long dark hair. "I was afraid he was going to kill me, but I was drawn to him. I've never experienced anything like it before."

"If you don't mind my saying, milady, you've had very little experience with men."

Lucy was ten years older and had lost her husband—"my beloved Bertie"—at sea. She'd always been vague on the details, leading me to suspect that Bertie's disappearance had little to do with water, but curbing my natural curiosity, I didn't pry. She was right about my lack of experience, though. At sixteen, I'd never been in love and had been kissed only once, by a young baron who lost his balance while attempting to reach my mouth. I was taller than average—five feet eight—with a reputation for speaking my mind. Most men of my acquaintance preferred smaller women with larger bosoms, a sweet manner, and the ability to bear as many children as possible without dying in childbirth. Even if they did, there was no shortage of women to replace them.

My mother had lost four babies, disappointing my father who had longed for sons. I was an only child, with all the obligatory pressures to look beautiful, become proficient at the pianoforte, and marry well. My parents' marriage had been arranged, but at one time they'd been deeply in love. Now they were separated—he was in Trieste—but he'd recently secured a position as a court counselor at the Austrian-Bohemian chancellery and would be joining us soon. I didn't, however, expect much to change.

On paper, the union between the Brunswick and Guicciardi families was everything one could hope for. My mother was of Hungarian nobility, my father an Italian count whose own father had been a distinguished field marshal in the army. My mother had expected much from her marriage. She loved beautiful things—clothes, jewelry, furniture—but my father hadn't achieved the kind of success that afforded her great luxury. He'd worked his way through a series of middling jobs in the government, resulting in numerous moves that took us to Galicia, Reggio, Laibach, and finally Trieste, where my mother said, "Enough!" She had a beautiful voice and had longed to be an opera singer, but that option wasn't available to a woman of her class. Consequently, she felt defrauded on all fronts. "I might as well have disgraced the family and become a singer," she often complained. "At least that would have been exciting."

Lucy didn't like my mother but was careful not to criticize her. It was the one area in which she showed restraint. Her bright-red hair seemed to catch fire whenever she became annoyed, and despite the difference in our status, I tried not to cross her.

"I wonder if Herr Beethoven would teach me," I mused.

"Teach you? You told me that you thought he was going to kill you." Lucy yanked the brush through my hair for emphasis.

"But he didn't. After I fainted, he carried me upstairs."

"You fainted? So you're telling me you want a teacher who caused you to faint but at least didn't kill you? I'm sorry, milady, but you're going to wind up—"

"Yes, Lucy, I know."

I didn't see much of Josephine and Therese for the rest of their holiday. They were too busy with Beethoven and Herr Müller. One afternoon, however, Therese and I took a stroll through the Prater, the former imperial hunting grounds that had been turned into a public park and playground. It was May, the trees bursting with pink and white flowers, the cafés and taverns full. Therese was wearing an artfully arranged shawl to disguise her crooked spine. When we sat down for coffee, she showed me Beethoven's calling card. She was extremely proud of their budding friendship.

"Louis van Beethoven," I read. "Don't you think it's a little pretentious? His forename is Ludwig."

"It's the fashion for all things French," she said, adding that Beethoven had composed a song for them, "I Think of You," based on a Goethe love poem. "I fear Louis is thinking far too much about our dear Pepi."

"Is she thinking of him?"

"I believe she is, but we haven't spoken of it. She glows when she's with him. A bad sign indeed."

Beethoven was infatuated with Josephine? How could this be? I was the one who'd fainted. I was the one he'd carried in his arms. Couldn't he write a song for me?

Before returning to Hungary, Aunt Anna invited us to a celebratory dinner in honor of Josephine's engagement to a man named Count Joseph von Deym. Though I'd never heard of Count Deym, he was undoubtedly a better choice than the mysterious Herr Müller.

"How wonderful!" I whispered to Therese. "Herr Müller seems to have fallen out of favor."

"The count *is* Herr Müller," she replied.

Aunt Anna had agreed to the engagement on the condition that Herr Müller successfully petition Emperor Francis for the return of his former title. Once that was done and Josephine's dowry had been agreed upon, she saw no need to delay the nuptials. The couple would be married at the Brunswicks' country estate in Martonvásár at the end of July.

Josephine appeared to be in shock. She hardly said a word during dinner and kept picking at the hole in her sleeve. Though I now viewed her as my rival, I felt nothing but pity. She was being sold like a slave to a strange old man.

"Don't worry, Pepi," I whispered, reaching out to hold her hand. "Everything will be all right."

"What do you know?" she said, slapping my hand away. "And don't call me Pepi! You aren't my sister."

I looked over at Therese. She mouthed the word "doom."

My mother and I had been planning to take the waters at Karlsbad. Now we had to go to Hungary for a hastily arranged marriage between my beautiful but troubled cousin and a former fugitive who fashioned death masks.

Therese was relieved that I'd be joining them, telling me that Josephine needed everyone's support at this "dark, perilous time."

"You know how she gets," she added.

I did know, which was why I wanted to leave as much distance between us as possible, but several weeks later, I found myself in a carriage traveling more than two hundred miles toward Josephine.

2

Martonvásár, Hungary

A massive stone lion with a flowing mane and downcast eyes guarded the entrance to Martonvásár. It was a proud symbol of the Brunswicks' connection to Henry the Lion, who had ruled parts of Prussia in the twelfth century. During the next six hundred years, my ancestors had lost much of their land and noble titles, but after my grandfather quelled a peasant uprising, he was made a count and awarded several hundred acres of barren fields and swamplands. He drained the marshes, built dams, and set about creating Arcadia for the next generation of Brunswicks.

Curving pathways took visitors past colorful flower beds and around the perimeter of a man-made lake lined with weeping willows. A circle of lemon trees, each named for a relative or intimate friend, was planted near the house. Josephine and Therese frequently talked to the trees, a ritual that cemented their sisterly bond and underscored their peculiarities. Josephine made sure that my tree was planted outside the magic circle, on an island in the center of the lake. "You're not one of us," she'd explained, a comment that was both hurtful and mildly reassuring.

We'd never been on the best of terms. Lonely and precocious, I'd spent much of my childhood reading books. Since my family had moved so much, Martonvásár was the only place that felt like home. I used to pretend it was mine and that Josephine was a benevolent older sister. Her repeated attempts to relieve me of that fantasy assumed many forms. When we were younger, she used her extra weight to overpower me, once dragging me into a gardening shed, securing the door, and leaving me there. Hearing my screams, one of the gardeners let me out, but Josephine threatened to break my arm if I told anyone. As I grew taller and she could no longer physically overpower me, she relied on snide remarks. This strategy wasn't as successful, for I was smarter and quicker, but aware of my status as an interloper, I held my tongue.

Josephine anticipated her upcoming wedding with all the enthusiasm of someone about to be exiled to a penal colony. For the next week, she remained in bed, complaining that she'd been felled by one of the chronic fevers that had afflicted her since childhood. Aunt Anna had previously consulted with numerous doctors, but no one could arrive at a proper diagnosis. Due to Martonvásár's marshy location, one speculated that it might be "swamp fever," which evoked both the River Nile and the smell of rotten eggs. Josephine and Therese, finding the term suitably exotic, adopted it.

While Josephine thrashed and moaned, Therese sat by her side reading from Goethe's *The Sorrows of Young Werther*, a popular tale of unrequited love that ends in the hero's suicide. I didn't think it the best choice—it had never been one of my favorites—but it was folly to come between the sisters.

"'It is night,'" Therese recited while Josephine started to wail. "'I am alone, forlorn on the hill of storms. The wind is heard on the mountain.'"

With Josephine indisposed and Aunt Anna and Therese caught up with the wedding arrangements, I amused myself with my cousin Franz. A portly young man with receding brown hair, a double chin, and sweet blue eyes, he had the serene personality of someone who, with my uncle's death, had inherited an estate and didn't have to worry about being married off to the proprietor of a wax museum. He played the violoncello, and when he wasn't practicing, he and Aunt Anna were looking for ways to improve the breeding capability of the estate's livestock. Being a gentleman, he steered clear of that salacious topic, preferring to discuss Beethoven.

"Therese and Josephine described him as extraordinary," he said. "Do you share their sentiments?"

"Extraordinary wouldn't be an exaggeration."

Franz confided that Therese had received a letter from him inquiring about Josephine's welfare and asking if he might pay a visit. "Mama didn't think it wise. She was afraid he'd contract swamp fever. A ruinous thing for a genius."

Franz, like most men, was extremely obtuse when it came to understanding a woman's motivations. Aunt Anna didn't want Beethoven anywhere near Josephine for fear she'd run away with him. I advised Franz that Beethoven should be kept at a distance. I certainly didn't want competition from a wailing but still beguiling Josephine.

When Count Deym arrived the following evening, Aunt Anna placed me in charge of entertaining him, advising me to steer clear of any controversial subjects, such as why he had killed a man in a duel and fled Austria. "Ah, what a beauty!" Count Deym said upon greeting me. "Your face is as classically proportioned as Athena's. And that alabaster skin! How it sets off your blue eyes and dark Grecian curls. You, my dear, are truly a goddess. A tall one at that! I would love to render you in wax."

The count wasn't as dreadful as I'd imagined. Though nearly bald, with a stomach that bulged from his waistcoat, he had roguish blue eyes, sensual lips, and a hearty laugh. Despite being a foot from the grave, he was still attractive, and I thought Josephine could have done much worse, though no immediate examples came to mind.

"Have you been to my art gallery?" he asked, polishing off a third glass of wine.

"Yes."

"And did you find it amusing?"

"Somewhat."

There was silence for a few seconds. I thought I heard Josephine screaming.

"Do you like music?" I asked quickly.

"Mozart wrote several pieces for my mechanical organ. I would love Herr Beethoven to compose something. Have you made his acquaintance?"

"In a manner," I said, thinking of the embarrassing incident at the Golden Griffin.

"I had the honor of doing Mozart's death mask. The story is quite thrilling. Would you like to hear it?" Without waiting for a reply, he continued. "At the time, I employed people—spies, if you will—who would tip me off whenever someone famous was in the last throes. When I heard that Mozart had died, I ran as fast as I could to his lodgings at Rauhensteingasse. You can't wait too long to take an impression. Rigor mortis distorts the features. While his wife, Constanze, was handling the funeral arrangements, I quickly put wax on his face and made the death mask. I also took a set of his clothes."

"You stole clothes from Mozart's dead body?"

"No, no, my dear. Constanze gave them to me. She was out of her mind with grief, but I put them to good use. I created a replica of Mozart, inviting the Viennese people to see the great composer 'in his very own dress.' Most weren't music connoisseurs, but they'd all heard stories of the boy prodigy and knew he was famous. It was a great success."

I smiled and nodded.

"Josephine hasn't come downstairs," he said. "Is it because she doesn't want to see me before the wedding?"

I was tempted to add "or ever," but I thought it best to explain the situation in medical terms. "She has swamp fever."

"I have never heard of such a thing. Is it—"

"Contagious? Do not fear. It's specific to Josephine."

A few minutes later, Aunt Anna greeted her future son-in-law, attributing Josephine's absence to a mild headache brought on by the excitement of the wedding.

"It's not swamp fever, then?" he asked.

"Of course not! Do not listen to Countess Guicciardi." As one of the servants poured more wine, she whispered to me, "I told you to watch your tongue!"

"You told me not to bring up the duel," I said under my breath. "You didn't say anything about swamp fever."

We heard loud noises from upstairs.

"It sounds like a woman screaming," Count Deym said. "Is everything all right?"

"It's mating season," Aunt Anna explained.

"For the sheep," I added.

On the morning of the wedding, Aunt Anna sent me to check on the bride while she went over last-minute details with the servants. Josephine, whose eyes were bloodshot and puffy, was still in her bedgown and seemed disinclined to remove it unless forced at gunpoint. I wondered if Count Deym had brought his dueling pistol.

"Pepi hardly slept," Therese said. "She kept having nightmares."

The nightmare, I feared, was her future husband, but it was too late now. The bishop was already downstairs mingling with our relatives from Korompa, the other Brunswick estate to the north.

"Dearest Pepi," Therese implored, "you must be strong and confront your fate."

Josephine, collapsing on the floor, began screaming, "I cannot do it, I cannot do it."

Therese cradled her head. "Oh, Pepi, my dearest Pepi," she whispered.

"I'm going to kill myself," Josephine said. "Promise me that you will talk to my tree."

"You don't have a tree," Therese reminded her. "The trees are only for people who live somewhere else."

"I *will* be living somewhere else," Josephine screamed. "I will be dead!"

In the interest of soothing her nerves, Josephine had consumed a substantial amount of wine, which failed to have the desired calming effect, for she kept screeching, "Let me die! Let me die!" Luckily, the music muffled her voice. Preferring death over marriage wasn't an ideal way to begin wedded life.

Finally, Aunt Anna and my mother came upstairs to see how the situation was progressing. Not well by the looks of Josephine, who was in the midst of having a real or fake seizure. Aunt Anna's experience with livestock had given her little patience for human weakness, and, grabbing Josephine by the shoulders, she slapped her hard across the face.

"Pepi, you stop this right now," she ordered. "Today is your wedding day and the guests are waiting. If Count Deym finds out about this, he will return to Vienna."

"But I cannot marry him," Josephine pleaded. "I do not love him. He is too old." Turning to Therese, she begged her to marry him instead.

"Dearest Pepi," Therese said. "You don't know what you are saying."

Josephine knew exactly what she was saying: she was willing to sacrifice Therese to avoid marrying Count Deym.

"I've had enough!" Aunt Anna said, pulling Josephine to her feet. She and Therese helped her into her wedding dress, tying the laces of her bodice and then attaching the veil to its embroidered crown.

Wiping Josephine's tearstained face, Aunt Anna dabbed some rouge on her cheeks, proclaiming her "the most beautiful bride."

I'd never seen a more miserable bride in my life, but somehow Josephine regained her composure, and before God, the bishop, and the extended Brunswick family, she became Countess Josephine von Deym. As the newlyweds headed to Prague for their honeymoon, storm clouds rolled in and it began to pour. We stood outside waving goodbye as the carriage disappeared into the rain-soaked forest.

"She is facing a difficult fate," Therese intoned. "As black as the sky!"

For once I didn't think she was exaggerating. The very thought of their wedding night was almost enough to induce swamp fever in me. I'd run away or join a convent before I let that happen. Thankfully, I had only a small dowry and was taller than most men. Only one towered over me—and he was four inches shorter.

3

Decorating our new apartment in the Hoher Markt, Vienna's oldest square, gave my mother purpose. She wanted to have it all set
up before my father arrived. Our old pianoforte, which had survived
multiple moves, needed to be replaced, so we visited Frau Nannette
Streicher at her warehouse in the Landstrasse suburb. It was rare for a
woman to succeed in a male-dominated profession, but Frau Streicher
had learned the craft from her father, whose pianofortes Mozart had
played. She now worked with her husband, Andreas, and brother
Matthäus, producing some of the finest instruments in Europe.

Frau Streicher, who had a kind face and nurturing manner, apologized for her wan appearance, explaining that she'd been up all night
with a seriously ill son. My mother suggested that we return later, but
Frau Streicher smiled and said, "I would hate to lose a sale. Besides, the
distraction will do me good."

She explained that her chief competitor, Anton Walter, made
sturdy instruments that produced a big sound. In contrast, the Frère et
Soeur Stein pianoforte had a sparkling brilliance and light action. She
encouraged me to try it, and I played the first movement of Mozart's
Pianoforte Sonata in C Major. It was a relatively easy composition, but

I was nervous and made several mistakes. My mother, as usual, was quick to point them out.

"What do you think?" Frau Streicher asked when I'd finished.

"I like it very much," I said. "My fingers practically flew across the keyboard."

"I wouldn't exactly go that far," my mother added, sitting down to perform Haydn. She would have played for the next hour—she craved an audience—but before she moved on to Mozart, Frau Streicher asked her opinion. My mother told her that we'd like to purchase one but that she needed her advice on something important.

"Yes, please," Frau Streicher said. "Since I build the instruments, I know everything about them."

"What color wood do you think would go best with my complexion?" my mother asked.

"What color . . . wood?" Frau Streicher repeated.

I assumed she'd been expecting a question about hammers or dampers or strings, but after we engaged in a lively debate over the pink hues in my mother's skin, we settled on a warm cherry.

"Herr Beethoven has frequently borrowed our instruments," Frau Streicher told us. "He's always suggesting ways to improve them."

"What does he want?" I asked, eager to hear anything about him.

"Everything." She laughed. "He'd like them to be louder and stronger. More notes. He complains that he's composing to the limits of the instrument and keyboard. He's always frustrated."

She told us that she'd recently heard his First Symphony at the Burgtheater. "It's undoubtedly a masterpiece, but there was some grumbling about the opening adagio. Too shocking. But the final movement was so delightful that people came away smiling. Naturally, Herr Beethoven wasn't satisfied. He had to select the program, rent the theater, hire the musicians, and sell the tickets himself. I don't think he made much money."

"I'm sorry I missed it," I said.

"Next week he's engaging in a duel with Daniel Steibelt. It's being held at Count Moritz von Fries's."

Duels were the equivalent of gladiatorial combat, pitting one virtuoso against another for the pleasure of the aristocracy. Beethoven, a veteran of these battles, had engaged most notably with Josef Wölfl, whose subtle, delicate playing appealed to traditional tastes. Despite their aesthetic differences, Beethoven respected Wölfl, while he disliked Steibelt, who often performed with his glamorous tambourine-playing wife.

"You must attend," Frau Streicher urged. "The concert is a rematch, and if it's anything like the last one, it will be unforgettable."

In a city known for its sumptuous baroque architecture, Palais Fries was a masterpiece of elegant understatement, the enormous caryatids flanking the entrance even more imposing when set against the plain façade. As we climbed the staircase with its latticework handrail, a servant in knee breeches, silk stockings, and powdered hair guided us to the music salon. An enormous crystal chandelier dangled from a gilded ceiling. Count Fries, heir to a banking fortune, was rumored to be the wealthiest man in Austria, and *tout* Vienna was there.

My father had just arrived from Trieste, and he agreed to join us. I was happy we were all together again, but the old tensions between my parents flared. My father preferred the solitude of his library, while my mother adored any kind of soirée. She had voiced her unhappiness even before we'd left our apartment, describing the type of man she *should* have married—enormously wealthy, influential, a charming conversationalist, the owner of a palace and country estate, a true partner in social advancement.

Opposites in personality, they were equally dissimilar in appearance. Though both were extremely attractive, my mother was light to his dark, with blonde hair, ivory skin, and exquisite cheekbones that rendered her perfect from every angle. My father's black hair and flashing eyes were set off by a brilliant smile that could quicken the heart. I knew from an early age that other women were attracted to him, but for whatever reason—love, duty, routine—he was devoted to my mother.

Countess Maria von Gallenberg nearly knocked over a servant in her enthusiasm to greet him. We'd known her from Laibach, where the Gallenbergs enjoyed immense status as one of the city's oldest families. She was overweight, with an enormous bosom that preceded her by at least two feet, pitch-black hair, and chalky skin heavily dusted with powder. I sneezed as she approached.

"Franz, how wonderful to see you," she said warmly. Glancing at my mother, she added, "And you too, Susanna."

"How is your husband?" my father asked.

"Ill, possibly dying," Countess Gallenberg said dispassionately. Before my father could respond, she introduced us to her daughter, Eleonora—"engaged to an imperial chamberlain"—and her son, Robert—"in search of a suitable bride." Count Gallenberg was about my age, with brown hair, long eyelashes, a Cupid's-bow mouth, and a prominent cleft in his chin. Though I peered down at him from a vantage point of several inches, he was not easily intimidated.

"Do you have a favorite in this match?" I inquired.

"Herr Steibelt," he replied. "Herr Beethoven's playing lacks finesse and control. It's nothing but fireworks."

"Robert is a composer too," Countess Gallenberg informed us. "He studied counterpoint with Herr Beethoven's teacher Johann Albrechtsberger. Robert was the better student. You should hear his work. It's brilliant."

Taking it upon herself to point out Beethoven's most influential patrons, Countess Gallenberg kept up a running commentary: "There's Prince Lichnowsky. Herr Beethoven would be nothing without him. Over there is Prince Lobkowitz. Such a sweet-looking face. What a shame about the clubfoot. Then there's Prince Razumovsky, the Russian ambassador. His wife is Prince Lichnowsky's sister-in-law."

Prince Karl Lichnowsky and his wife, Christiane, began walking in our direction, stopping every so often to greet friends. Countess Gallenberg accelerated the process by waving them over. She related the tale of her husband's illness, explaining that he could die at any moment, which prompted Princess Christiane to ask if it was a love of music or indifference to her husband that brought her to the duel.

"Well, I . . . I . . . do love music," she stammered. "And the doctor assured me that my husband's death probably wouldn't occur tonight."

"My dear Countess Guicciardi," Prince Lichnowsky said, cutting in. "How nice to see you again. And this exquisite creature must be your daughter?"

"Yes, this is Countess Julie Guicciardi," she replied as I curtsied.

Prince Lichnowsky and his wife held frequent musical soirées at their palace, where they maintained their own string quartet. The Lichnowskys were both fine musicians, though their devotion to the arts hadn't appeared to elevate their spirits. The prince's sharp nose and hooded blue eyes gave him the look of a bird of prey, his powdered hair accentuating his ashen complexion. The princess might have been pretty if she hadn't carried herself with the knowledge that she could destroy anyone in the room. It hardened her face, turning it into a premature death mask. She stared at my mother as if searching for a physical flaw. Finding none, she and the prince moved on.

They greeted Beethoven, whispering words that I presumed were of encouragement, but from his haughty expression, I doubted he needed much. The man radiated confidence. It had nothing to do with smart clothes or noble titles. He knew that he'd been given a great gift, and that powerful, intoxicating belief drew people toward him.

On the opposite side of the room, Steibelt, a handsome man with a mound of dark Medusa-like curls, stood next to his comely wife. The previous week, he'd listened to Beethoven present a trio for pianoforte, clarinet, and violoncello before playing a showy fantasia that brought down the house.

"Ladies and gentlemen, may I have your attention," said Count Fries, whose extravagant curls surpassed Steibelt's. "You are indeed fortunate to be witnessing a duel between two great champions. A duel to the death! Who will survive? Who will perish? We will see. First up is the very charming, very talented, and I am sure you ladies will agree, the very handsome Herr Daniel Steibelt—straight from successful tours of London and Paris."

The count led the audience in a prolonged stint of boisterous clapping as Steibelt presented one of his own compositions. Beethoven, ever the diplomat, rolled his eyes. In keeping with the traditional format, Steibelt then played a fantasia, incorporating his hallmark quiver— the tremolo. The crowd gasped. "He's improvising a theme from Herr Beethoven's trio of last week," Countess Gallenberg whispered. "He's thrown down the gauntlet!"

It was indeed a daring move and the crowd, hoping to provoke Beethoven's ire, which needed little goading, exploded in wild applause. At the end of the performance, the audience began shouting, "Beethoven! Beethoven! Beethoven!" After the count introduced him, he sauntered over to the pianoforte, picked up the cello part of Steibelt's composition, and mimicked ripping it up. He then placed it upside down on the music stand and played what sounded like a nursery tune. He didn't stop there. Elaborating on the theme, he mocked Steibelt's use of the tremolo before launching into an improvisation, making the original piece larger, better, a work that defied description, a work that was uniquely his own.

I had never heard anyone play with such passion and fire. Vengeance too. I couldn't imagine more drama if they'd been dueling with actual pistols. Beethoven finished to cheers while Steibelt stomped out of the room, his wife and her clattering tambourine following behind. Prince and Princess Lichnowsky rushed toward Beethoven, along with a cluster of female admirers, who, contrary to the doctor's opinion, didn't appear to be suffering any ill effects from his music. They looked exhilarated, in a state of almost passionate arousal.

"I was not impressed," said Count Gallenberg, who suddenly appeared at my side as I waited with my parents for the carriage. "In my opinion, Herr Steibelt won the duel. Herr Beethoven played like a madman. It's impossible to maintain that intensity. He's merely a passing fancy. A curiosity, that's all. Who will even remember him five years from now?"

"I will," I said as the footman helped me into the carriage.

4

When I was younger, my father and I often read books together, usually in separate rooms, with both doors closed. We read in German, French, Italian, and English, with Shakespeare our mutual favorite. Sadly, we never discussed our love of literature, and the only time it came up was when my father seized all four volumes of *Les Liaisons dangereuses* by Pierre de Laclos. Even then, he didn't say anything. Just took them away. Later, my mother told me that the novel was unsuitable for a girl my age—I was then fifteen—and that if I wanted something scintillating, I could borrow one of her Parisian fashion magazines.

My father preferred the written word over the spoken one, and it was impossible to engage him in sustained conversation. He kept his thoughts and emotions to himself. He never told me that he loved me or that I was pretty or intelligent. He never told me much of anything, so I became an expert at reading meaning into silence. I learned that people expressed love in different ways. One just had to work hard at divining it.

Love was definitely not on Aunt Anna's mind when we visited Josephine in the fall. Josephine had now been married for over a year and had a five-month-old baby and an eighty-eight-room residence that spanned the entire block from Rotenturmstrasse to Schwedenplatz.

Josephine had been spending much of her time in Martonvásár, so it was the first time we'd seen Palais Deym and heard Aunt Anna's firsthand account of the marriage. "Poor Pepi has been suffering from melancholia and swamp fever because her husband is a liar and a cheat," Aunt Anna said.

"And let's not forget the murderer part," my mother added. My mother was jealous of Aunt Anna because she'd married into the Brunswick family and was reaping all the rewards, though in this case it came with its troubles too. Count Deym—Herr Müller—was mired in debt. He had been counting on Josephine's dowry to help defray the costs of his new building, which also housed his cabinet of curiosities. Not only had Aunt Anna refused to give him the money, she had also initiated annulment proceedings.

"In the eyes of the church, lying about money is a legitimate reason to end a marriage," Aunt Anna fumed. "It's worse than discovering your husband is a murderer."

"He *is* a murderer," my mother reiterated. "He killed a man in an illegal duel and had to flee Austria." My mother looked askance at her sister-in-law's clothing. While my mother was wearing a stylish gown, Aunt Anna had on a simple peasant dress that smelled of hay.

"Who cares about the stupid duel?" Aunt Anna shouted. She was in no mood for my imperious mother. "It's about the money! But Pepi refuses to get an annulment. She says that she's in love with the old fool."

She continued to list all of Joseph's faults as we made our way through one cavernous room after another. Most were empty, except for large chandeliers hung with glass prisms that intensified the candlelight, creating a dramatic sparkling effect. "Joseph's idea," Aunt Anna said. "People now call it the 'fairy palace.' Too bad the fairies can't pay for it."

Two young children ran by, footsteps echoing down the endless hallways. Joseph claimed he had adopted them on his travels, but no one, least of all Aunt Anna, believed it.

When we finally reached Josephine, she was holding Victoire on her lap.

"Victoire?" my mother asked. "I don't recognize it as a Brunswick name."

"She's named after my sister-in-law," Josephine explained.

"Victory indeed!" Aunt Anna said bitterly.

I tentatively asked Josephine if I could hold the baby. I didn't know if the combination of motherhood and melancholia had blunted her hostile temperament. Clearly, it had not. Before she relinquished the baby, she warned me not to drop and kill her. "She's beautiful," I said as she wrapped her little fingers around mine. "Hello, little one. Hello, *ma petite* Victoire." I burrowed my face into her neck, sniffing her sweet baby smell.

"She doesn't like that," Josephine said, taking her back. "It's clear that you haven't spent time around babies. In case you haven't noticed, I'm with child again."

"Could the situation get any worse?" Aunt Anna asked.

"It could," Therese warned.

"Have you heard from Herr Beethoven?" I asked. I hadn't been able to get him out of my thoughts, but with Josephine at Martonvásár, I hadn't had the opportunity to see him. Though I'd asked my mother if I could take pianoforte lessons from him, she told me that I needed someone calm and sedate like my previous teacher, Herr Pichler, who had snored during my lessons.

Joseph suddenly appeared in the doorway and began arguing with Aunt Anna. "You promised me a substantial dowry," he said. "I was deceived."

"*Deceived?* This from a man who pretends to have money and then expects us to bail him out."

"Joseph, why don't you show Aunt Susanna and Julie downstairs," Josephine said. "I'm sure they'd love to see your museum. Mama, why don't you accompany them?" Josephine gave her a hard stare. "I will join you shortly."

Once again, we walked through the maze of rooms, glittering lights dancing on bare walls. The children were attempting to play hide-and-seek, but without any furniture and no place to hide, they ran around in circles. Climbing down several flights of stairs, we finally reached the museum's entrance. It was closed for the night, so Joseph unlocked the large door. It took time for my eyes to adjust to the dim light. The last time I'd seen Müller's museum, it had been located in a smaller space near Saint Stephen's Cathedral. Now it was vast and even more unsettling.

"After I left Vienna, I eventually wound up in Naples," Joseph explained.

"He fled Vienna," Aunt Anna mumbled. "Who'd end up in Naples voluntarily?"

He continued: "Maria Carolina, the queen consort, gave me permission to make plaster casts of the finest sculptures in the Naples Art Gallery. They formed the basis of my first gallery." He gestured toward a hundred ancient Greek and Roman statues, including one that depicted giant snakes killing the Trojan priest Laocoön and his two sons. "It was so successful that Emperor Francis awarded me the title of 'imperial court statuary.' I added to the collection with wax figures of famous people." He pointed to Frederick the Great; Louis XVI and Marie Antoinette; and numerous Austrian generals. Joseph was unquestionably skilled at his craft; the figures were remarkably lifelike, right down to the eyes and hair.

"Where did you get the hair?" I asked.

"I have friends at morgues," he replied.

"If only you had friends at banks," Aunt Anna said.

Joseph showed us his pièce de résistance—the huge mausoleum that commemorated the heroic field marshal Ernst von Laudon. Two grieving soldiers, along with Mars, the Roman god of war, overlooked Laudon's wax effigy encased in a glass coffin. Benches were set up for visitors to listen to different funeral music on a mechanical organ. That night, it was Mozart's Fantasy in F Minor.

Joseph kept talking, comparing himself favorably to Madame Tussaud, who had plied her trade by making death masks of guillotined heads plucked from the Parisian gutters. I'd heard enough, so I wandered away. In the Bedroom of the Graces, Venus looked down upon a sleeping young girl, her innocent pose hinting at some future violation, perhaps at the hands of one of the deviant criminals whose masks lined a wall. In another corner, I saw the figure of the pregnant woman, innards exposed. Joseph had obviously retrieved her from the police. Several fetuses floated in clear jars right behind her.

I was beginning to feel ill even before I saw Mozart's death mask. A wax figure was positioned to its right, facing away from me. It looked so real that I reached out to touch it. The figure whirled around. *Beethoven.*

"Forgive me," I said. "I thought you were a statue."

"I will be one day." Gesturing toward the death mask, he added, "I suppose I'll be that too. Poor Mozart! The Viennese quickly grow bored of their geniuses, but I've always considered myself among his greatest admirers."

"I'm sure you don't remember me, but I'm Countess Guicciardi."

"How could I forget? To my knowledge, I've never caused anyone to faint, and I've certainly never carried an unconscious woman to her bed."

Josephine, holding Victoire, interrupted us. Beethoven made funny faces, causing the baby to gurgle and coo. When Josephine casually handed Victoire over to him, he seemed perfectly comfortable, laughing when she swatted him in the face. "Ah, you're a feisty little one," he said. "That's good. You'll need to have spirit to fend off all the rascally devils who will chase after you."

It was sweet watching him with the baby. I wouldn't have expected him to have any interest in children at all. I couldn't imagine one crawling at his feet while he indulged his penchant for fiery fantasias.

"Louis visits all the time," Josephine explained. "He's been very kind to give me music lessons."

"She's improved a lot," he said, "but she's always had a great feel for music." They exchanged warm, admiring looks. I sensed something between them and I felt a pang of jealousy, though I realized I had no right. He was her teacher, while I was merely the cataleptic young woman he'd deposited on a bed.

"I see that you have found Countess Guicciardi," Joseph said, putting his arm around Beethoven. "Louis has given me several pieces for a musical clock, and I'm deeply honored to have him represented here."

"Do you play an instrument?" Beethoven asked while Aunt Anna and Joseph were in the midst of another squabble, and Josephine brought the baby upstairs.

"I've been taking lessons on the pianoforte since I was seven. I'm looking for a teacher if you'd be willing."

"You don't think I'd present a danger?" he said, smiling.

"Only to the pianoforte," I replied.

"I'd be happy to offer my services."

My mother, overhearing the conversation, walked over and jabbed me in the ribs. "How kind of you, Herr Beethoven, but we're still waiting for our pianoforte from Frau Streicher. Her son died and orders are backed up. We only have an old one that's falling apart. Besides, I'm not sure if my daughter is up to your standards. She makes a lot of mistakes."

"Mistakes?" he said derisively. "Who doesn't make mistakes? You may come to my apartment: 241 Tiefer Graben. I'm free tomorrow at noon. Please be on time."

5

Lucy accompanied me to Beethoven's apartment, which was located off the Graben, where the city's monied classes displayed themselves for their own pleasure and the pleasure of watching others. Normally, I would have loved the fashionable parade—Hungarians in short-sleeved dolmans, Poles in sleeveless waistcoats and woven sashes, Romanians in silk boyar shirts embellished with seed pearls and gold thread—but I couldn't be late for Beethoven.

"Milady, do you think he'll play for us?" Lucy asked, struggling to keep pace.

"No! And whatever you do, don't ask."

"I would never take such liberties. I simply thought it would be memorable."

"It would be."

We climbed three flights to Beethoven's apartment, where a harried-looking servant answered the door. After we announced ourselves, she let us in. I'd never seen such an untidy place, every inch covered with loose papers, haphazardly arranged books, dirty clothes, half-eaten food, and mysterious rolls of cotton steeped in sweet-smelling oil. The creator of all this chaos was sitting at the pianoforte. He was so caught up in his playing he didn't even notice us until a servant tapped him on the shoulder.

"Countess Guicciardi is here for her lesson," she announced.

He stared at Lucy. "Who are you?"

"Lucy Caldwell, lady's maid and companion."

"I cannot teach with an audience. Go away."

I'd expected that Lucy would stay with us, and I wondered if Beethoven had overturned the entire apartment in a fit of rage during a previous lesson. *Do not show fear,* I reminded myself. It's what Aunt Anna told me when I first mounted a horse.

I walked Lucy to the door, stepping over a pile of unwashed shirts. "With all respect, milady," she whispered, "I don't feel comfortable leaving you with that man. He strikes me as strange and filthy." She lowered her voice. "Remember, I worked for someone who went insane. I'm not saying I'm an expert but—"

"Thank you, Lucy. I will be fine."

She knitted her orange brows together. "If you don't answer the door in exactly one hour, I'll contact the police."

When I turned back, Beethoven was retrieving a cup of half-spilled coffee from the floor. The servant attempted to wipe up the excess, but Beethoven directed her to leave too.

"Distractions," he muttered. "To create, one needs order and discipline."

I thought he might have been joking, but he was serious. There was nothing ordered or disciplined about anything. Even his hair stood up in every direction. He wore it *à la Titus*, a short, spiky style that had originated in Paris as a reaction to the elaborate powdered wigs of the *ancien régime*. It suited him, accentuating his strong features and aligning him with Napoleon and the democratic ideals of the French Revolution. After he caught me staring, he tried to smooth it down. I noticed that his ears were shiny, as if he had applied oil to them. He smelled of almonds, the same fragrance I detected on the cotton.

"You've been to Frau Streicher's," he said. "She makes an excellent instrument, although I do wish it sounded less like a harp."

"How would you like it to sound?"

"Like me." He laughed. "I would like to produce my own tone. Her pianofortes are still too delicate. I need something capable of withstanding—"

"Violence?"

"At times." Then he said abruptly, "What will you play for me today?"

"One of yours. I hope you don't think me too bold."

"Ladies usually find my music too difficult. I commend you for your boldness. As for your talent, we will have to see."

I'd been practicing his Sonata in F Minor on my old pianoforte. It was badly out of tune and it was almost painful to hear the sounds it made. I'd managed only the first movement, which began with an ascending note pattern that required a player to speed up, propelling the music faster, louder, and higher. It lasted less than seven minutes, but I was nearly breathless by the time I'd finished.

He didn't comment, and I was afraid to look at him.

"You have talent," he said finally. "If you didn't, I wouldn't waste my time, but you're holding your fingers all wrong."

I'd been taught to play with my fingers flat, but he insisted they should be bent and held close to the keys in order to produce a singing tone. He had me run through some scales, bending my fingers whenever they lapsed into the familiar horizontal position. He wasn't shy about using excessive pressure.

"You're not going to hit me with a knitting needle, are you?" I asked.

"You've been listening to the gossips. I would never hit someone who plays as well as you do. I did strike a student once, but he deserved it."

"I can't imagine why anyone would warrant such punishment."

"No, I suppose you can't," he said. His dark tone warned me not to pry, so I quickly changed the subject by asking why he had dedicated the sonata to Haydn. He explained that Haydn had been one of his first teachers when he arrived in Vienna, so he felt obligated. "But then he wanted me to add 'Pupil of Haydn' to the sonata's title page, which I refused to do. I didn't learn anything from him."

"Do you use your dedications to settle obligations?"

"I dedicated my first three pianoforte trios to Prince Lichnowsky, a true friend. He recently agreed to give me six hundred florins a year so I don't have to scrounge around like poor Mozart. Shall we get back to the music?"

He asked me to play the first movement again, keeping in mind the new finger position.

After I'd finished, he admonished me for being distracted.

"You're right. I kept thinking, *Fingers, fingers.* And then I remembered the time I traveled with my mother to Venice. I was seven or eight. The streets were very crowded and we got separated. I began running up and down trying to find her. I was afraid I'd never see her again."

"But you did. You're very lucky."

"Is your mother not living?"

"Countess Guicciardi, you ask a lot of questions. Didn't *your* mother ever tell you that it's annoying?"

"All the time, but I don't ask a question unless I'm sincerely interested."

He glanced over as if he had never really noticed me before. "Countess, are you serious about music, or are you simply using it to acquire a husband?"

"What a rude question! Are you using music to acquire a wife?"

"If that were the case, I'd have one already. I do believe I'm the finest musician in Vienna." He paused. "Perhaps in the world."

"Your mother?" I pressed.

"She died when I was sixteen," he said slowly. "I raced home to Bonn as fast as I could. Along the way, I kept receiving messages from my father that she was failing, so I hurried faster and faster. I managed to reach her in time, but she died a few days later. Consumption. She suffered greatly."

As he told the story, I heard the first movement, the hurried arpeggios, the breathless quality.

"She was an honest, good-hearted woman," he continued, "but I don't believe she was happy. She often said that marriage was a chain of sorrows and that if given the choice, a woman should remain single."

"Based on the marriages I know, I don't think your mother was entirely wrong, but one must hold out hope."

"Hope," he repeated softly.

We returned to the sonata, Beethoven occasionally correcting my hand position or calling out legato to remind me that I should play in a smooth, flowing manner. He disliked the staccato style, which he dismissed as "finger dancing." The hour went by so quickly that I was disappointed when Lucy arrived. I didn't know how I should approach the issue of his fee.

"I'm sorry," I said. "I don't have money with me right now, but my father—"

"Money?" he shouted. "I don't give lessons for money. Or at least I won't take money from you. I'm not a servant."

"I didn't mean to imply that you were. I just wanted to show my appreciation in some way." I felt myself blush.

"You may give me a hand-embroidered item."

"I'm afraid I don't embroider or sew, but I like to draw."

"Then you may present me with a sketch, but only if the subject inspires you. I'll see you the day after tomorrow. Noon. You should buy Bach's *Essay on the True Art of Playing Keyboard Instruments*. I recommend it to all my students."

When I returned home, my mother said, "I hope you didn't embarrass me with your playing."

"He says I have talent."

"No matter. He's the wrong teacher for you." She was all dressed up, ready to take the carriage to meet a friend.

"I like his hair," I added. "He wears it *à la Titus*."

"His hair? Who cares about his hair? I hate to use the word 'repulsive,' because connoisseurs like Prince Lichnowsky have proclaimed him a genius, but I do think his looks detract from his music. If only Count Gallenberg had his talent."

"But he doesn't."

6

"Cut it off!" I said.

Monsieur Collet ran a brush through my long dark curls while Lucy buried her head in her hands. "It's beautiful, Countess," he said. "Are you sure?"

"Yes," I replied as he fetched his leather hairdressing kit. Collet had trained under the famous Parisian coiffeur Monsieur Duplan and was much in demand. "It is too bad that wigs are now *demodées*," he said. "You could have made a healthy sum selling your hair. During the Revolution, wigmakers preferred the hair of the recently guillotined. It was considered healthier."

"Why?"

"It was fresh. Some people refer to *la coiffure à la Titus* as *la coiffure à la guillotine*." He made a chopping gesture. "Without hair, it was easier for the blade to *couper le cou*."

My hand flew up to my neck.

"There are no guillotines in Vienna. Do not worry."

"Were you there during the Revolution?" I asked. "Did you see—"

"Heads roll? Yes, it was terrible. Poor Marie Antoinette. The things they said about her. Even if she acted like a silly girl, she didn't deserve the lewd comments and pornographic cartoons. And then to be accused of bedding her own son."

"I didn't know," I said.

"I hope I haven't upset you. Today is a day for beauty." He took his scissors and began snipping my hair, long strands drifting off my shoulders and onto the floor. After he had cut off about twenty inches, he offered several styling options. I could either wear it spiky or accentuate my curls with a touch of pomade.

"Curls, I beg you," Lucy cried. Monsieur Collet began twirling my hair around his fingers, fashioning ringlets so that they framed my face and nestled at the back of my neck.

"*Je l'adore!*" Monsieur Collet exclaimed after he had finished. I turned my head in the looking glass to admire my profile. The effect was very *gamine*. Even Lucy had to admit the coiffure was flattering, though she did worry about the effect it might have on my mother. We didn't have long to find out.

"What have you done?" she screamed.

"I've cut my hair."

"And destroyed any chance of finding a husband!"

"I wouldn't want a husband who would judge me solely on a hairstyle."

"Do you realize that when women are sent to the Gugelhupf, they wind up with shaved heads?" she said.

Lucy nodded. "It's true, milady. I saw it with my own two eyes."

"Wait until Countess Gallenberg finds out," my mother continued. "The poor woman recently lost her husband and now this!"

"I'm not sure what my hair has to do with the recently deceased Count Gallenberg."

"Did we raise you as a peasant? Her son will inherit everything, and she'll want him to marry. He's very popular with the young ladies—all of whom have hair."

I arrived for my second pianoforte lesson with a copy of Bach's book. A tiny smile crossed Beethoven's face when he saw my new hairstyle, but he didn't say anything. He seemed preoccupied and didn't make any comments as I played my scales.

"Herr Beethoven," I asked, "is something wrong?"

"I'm feeling melancholy today. There's so much work to do and so little time." He sighed. "I will be thirty in December."

"That's not old. Not like Count Deym. I'll be eighteen in a few weeks and already I'm unsatisfied with the little I've accomplished." I stopped there. "I understand it's not the same."

"No, it's not."

"I can go if you'd like. I'm sure you have better things to do."

"It's true," he said, mentioning the string quartets he was trying to finish. "But I enjoy the company, and I'm not sure how much longer I'll be able to do that."

"Why?" I asked. "Are you going somewhere?" He brushed off the question.

Beethoven was such an unusual man that I assumed music flowed out of him with little or no effort, but with prodding, he explained that it wasn't the case. "I carry my thoughts in my head for a very long time before I commit them to paper. I change many things, discard some, keep others, but the fundamental idea never abandons me. It keeps growing and developing."

"Where do your ideas come from?"

"Everywhere! I could be walking in the woods or gazing at the night sky and something strikes me. A poet translates his moods into words. I do it with tones. They race and roar and storm until they cry to be let out."

"Like a baby about to be born."

"In a way."

He was nervous about the string quartets, fearing he would be compared unfavorably to Haydn and Mozart, masters of the form.

"I struggled with the String Quartet in F Major," he said. "I was rereading *Romeo and Juliet*, and while writing the second movement, I kept thinking of the tomb scene. I enjoy Shakespeare. My formal education was limited, but I've always tried to better myself."

"I know *Romeo and Juliet*," I volunteered. "I've read all of Shakespeare's plays, even *Titus Andronicus*, though I can't say it's a favorite. I used to act out scenes from *Romeo and Juliet* in my bedchamber. 'Give me my Romeo; and, when he shall die, / Take him and cut him out in little stars, / And he will make the face of heaven so fine.'"

"I don't believe that's from the tomb scene, Countess."

"It isn't but—"

"The tomb scene is unbearably sad, as you undoubtedly know from having performed the play in your bedchamber. It was my task to capture that feeling in music. Now let's proceed with your lesson. You're very easy to talk to, but we're not here for that."

While playing the first movement of the Sonata in F Minor, I made several mistakes and kept repeating, "I'm sorry."

"Stop apologizing!" he ordered. "Mistakes are due to chance. The real mistake is when you don't play with expression."

"My mother always points out my mistakes. It's made music very difficult for me."

"Music is difficult. That's not an excuse."

Starting over, I kept hearing Beethoven's stomach gurgle, and then he burped and emitted gas. I laughed nervously and couldn't stop.

"Countess Guicciardi, is music amusing to you?"

"Opera buffa is amusing."

"But this isn't opera buffa. It's my sonata."

"Would you play it for me? I'd love to hear what it really sounds like."

"I don't like this one anymore. The more progress I make, the less I'm satisfied with my old work."

I clasped my hands together. "Please."

44

"Countess Guicciardi, do you always get what you ask for?"

"No, when I was little I wanted a pony for Christmas."

He tried to stop himself from laughing but couldn't. He then confided that Count Browne had given him a horse in appreciation of the works he'd dedicated to the count's wife. After Beethoven put the horse in a stable, he'd completely forgotten about it. I was tempted to ask how could anyone possibly forget about a horse, but with Beethoven, such questions were unnecessary.

"You'll play the movement for me?" I asked again.

"In light of your tragic pony story, I suppose I must."

Beethoven started the music as written but then veered off into a fantasia. Listening to him was both inspiring and dispiriting, for he had the ability to wrench basic emotions from the most technically complex material. I knew that I'd never reach anywhere near his level. Few would. I suddenly felt compassion for this strange, brilliant man. A tear trickled down my cheek. Quickly, I wiped it away, but he saw it and grew angry.

"You're a very silly girl," he scolded. "Tears—from music!"

"Why silly? Because I thought it was beautiful? Because you touched me deeply? Didn't you just tell me that the most important element was to play with expression? Isn't expression meant to touch the emotions?"

"I'm sorry. I'm in a bad temper because I didn't take my daily walk. If you'll excuse me, I will get some air."

"I'll accompany you."

"That wouldn't be proper."

"Is it proper for you to leave me alone in your apartment? What if a robber attacked me? Lucy will be here any moment, and we'll all go together."

No sooner had Lucy arrived than Beethoven was out the door. It was a lovely afternoon, clear and crisp, and I hoped it might be easier to talk without the distraction of my lesson. Beethoven walked very quickly, and soon Lucy was lagging behind. As I struggled to keep up, I made a few passing comments about the weather. He didn't seem interested in conversing and instead began humming, jotting down things in a notebook. He was so preoccupied that he bumped into several people without bothering to apologize. Before long he was way ahead of me, and I felt like Count Browne's abandoned horse.

"Herr Beethoven," I called out. "When will I see you again?"

He didn't answer.

7

My short hair turned me into a daring woman with all that implied, and soon I was known as "La Bella Guicciardi."

"Seize the opportunity," my mother advised. "Next month there will be a new girl with a new hairstyle and you'll be forgotten."

In preparation for the Winter Season, which began after Christmas, we had purchased a beautiful selection of silks so that Lucy could make several new gowns for me. Fashionable women, in addition to cutting their hair, were now shedding their corsets in favor of the neoclassical *chemise à la grecque*. While appropriate to the Greek climate, it didn't translate well to Vienna's bitter-cold winters, especially when the gowns were made of lightweight mousseline. Women feared "mousseline sickness," a serious inflammation of the lungs, but it didn't stop them from adopting the trend.

I was swaddled in silk and riddled with pins when one of the servants announced that Beethoven was at the door. "I'll tell him to go away," my mother said. "I'll explain that you have mousseline sickness. Since Josephine suffers from swamp fever, he'll think it's related."

"I'm sure he won't," I said, telling Lucy that I'd meet him in the music room.

My new pianoforte had recently arrived and he was playing a few chords, frowning as if he didn't like what he heard.

"Is there something wrong with it?" I asked.

"No, no," he replied distractedly. "It's nothing."

"Forgive me for keeping you waiting, but I wasn't expecting you."

"It is I who seek forgiveness." Beethoven wore a pained look that was the opposite of his customary defiant one. "I've treated you in the most wretched manner. I'm sure you know what I'm referring to."

During our previous encounter, he'd berated me, made me cry, and then abandoned me on the street, so I had no idea what he considered the most grievous.

"I forgive you for leaving me on the Graben," I guessed.

"When did that happen?" he asked incredulously.

"After our last session . . . we took a walk together. Or at least I attempted to walk with you."

He shook his head in frustration. "Ah, raptus!"

"I'm not sure what you mean . . . *ouch!*"

"What happened?" he asked, alarmed. In my haste to get dressed, a pin had attached itself to my chemise and was now pricking my bosom. I suggested we sit down and as I took a chair, I plucked at my gown to remove the pin. He gave me a quizzical look.

"A flea," I explained. He immediately accepted the account since his own apartment was probably filled with them. "Please go on . . ."

"When I lived in Bonn, the Breuning family were my great supporters," he said, glancing at my gown for further evidence of vermin. "Whenever I got lost in my own thoughts, Frau Breuning would say, 'He's in his raptus again.' I must have been in a raptus."

"I'm totally confused. Why are you seeking my forgiveness, then?"

"Your hair! You cut it, and I didn't even have the decency to comment on it."

"Do you like it?" I asked, twisting one of the curls at my neckline.

"No, I prefer it long."

"Oh."

"But I should have complimented you anyway. I'm hopeless at playing games."

I told him that I wouldn't want him to lie for the sake of social convention and that he must tell me the truth. Always.

"In that case, Josephine asked if she could use your lesson time."

"We didn't set up a time," I said.

"Even better. She'll be playing at a soirée in my honor, and she's nervous and needs me."

"I completely understand," I said, trying not to show my resentment. "Of course, you must be with her. Hold her hand. Do whatever you must." I rose from my chair. "If you'll excuse me, I'm in the process of being fitted for my ball gowns. You may find it hard to believe, especially with my short hair, but I'm very much in demand."

Beethoven stared at me with a look of total incomprehension. "I don't find it hard to believe at all. You are the most enchanting woman I've ever met. And that is very much the truth."

I sat down again. I couldn't keep up with the man.

"Countess, are you having a raptus?" he teased.

Before I could answer, he was out the door, leaving me so elated I couldn't focus on my gowns. Lucy showed me one shade of white after another, but what did I care about ivory versus alabaster? Beethoven thought me enchanting—no, not only enchanting, but the most enchanting woman he knew. I'd never met anyone like him. He wasn't the easiest of men. He was rude, unpolished, mercurial, with a bad temper and no tact. Yet he combined virility with vulnerability, brilliance with simplicity, haughtiness with compassion. He wasn't one thing but all things. And the worst part? I was utterly infatuated with him. I didn't know if I could call it love, having never been in love before, but I was becoming increasingly obsessed. Even when he exasperated me, which he did often, I couldn't stay angry.

"Enchanting, he called me enchanting," I practically sang as Lucy told me to stand still. "I've bewitched him." I didn't think it was possible that I could bewitch anyone, let alone Beethoven. I wondered whether he thought Josephine was enchanting. He certainly had feelings for her. I heard it in his voice when he said, "She needs me," but I refused to let Josephine spoil the glorious moment.

The Deyms' fairy palace glittered with the reflected glow of hundreds of prisms, its massive size more than compensating for its minimal décor. Josephine was flushed with happiness, the kind that could easily turn into hysteria if circumstances went awry. Like Beethoven, she had difficulty sustaining a steady mood, and I wondered if their similar temperaments were part of their mutual attraction. When they were aflame, they could illuminate Palais Deym, but when they were not, darkness fell and everyone suffered.

Despite the restoration of his title, Vienna's aristocrats still viewed Count Deym as Herr Müller, the proprietor of a vulgar museum. If not for Beethoven, most would have declined the invitation, but with Prince and Princess Lichnowsky leading the way, they filed into the music room, careful not to collide with Joseph's adopted children, who were turning cartwheels on the ornate parquet floor.

I was dressed in one of my new silk gowns, my bared arms turning to gooseflesh. Beautiful women in similar garb floated around the massive room like Greek goddesses. Beethoven was deep in conversation with Josephine, who wore a yellow gown and gold cap that accentuated the blonde glints in her light-brown hair. Despite their money woes, Joseph had encouraged her to purchase an elaborate wardrobe, and her clothes equaled those of the finest ladies.

"Joseph is wildly jealous of Louis," Therese told me. "Last night he and Pepi got into a terrible fight, and I heard him say, 'Then go to your beloved Beethoven!' Pepi immediately professed her love to Joseph and then . . ." Therese blushed, lowering her voice. "Pepi says that Joseph is very knowledgeable in the ways of love."

I wanted to hear more, but Frau Streicher introduced me to another one of Beethoven's pupils, Countess Babette Keglevich. She was about my age, with a pretty face, lively demeanor, and a fiancé who was not only a prince but also related to a pope.

"You are quite the avant-gardist," she said, referring to my hair. "I'd love to cut mine, but my fiancé doesn't approve. I'll have to wait until after the wedding." She laughed in a most infectious way.

"Did Herr Beethoven really show up at your apartment *deshabillé?*" I remembered my mother mentioning her name at the Golden Griffin, telling us that he had worn his dressing gown and nightcap to her lessons.

"Yes, many times. He looked totally foolish, especially in his floral robe. Such a strange man, but I admire his boldness. Prince Lichnowsky's mother-in-law once asked him to play for her, and he refused. She actually got down on her knees and begged. She was a major patron of Haydn and Mozart and quite a skilled musician herself, so it seemed rather sadistic. But the whole family is *très excentrique.*"

The concert was about to start and people began taking their places. "One day soon you must pay a visit," she said. "We can gossip over pastries and chocolate." She laughed her delightful laugh and then went off to join her prince.

"Now that is a good match," said Aunt Anna. "Why couldn't my Pepi have married someone like that? It's important to maintain the highest breeding standards. Otherwise, the best characteristics are lost."

"Such as a dowry?" I asked. Therese giggled, and before Aunt Anna could reply, the music started. Beethoven presented his Violin Sonata in E-flat Major with Josephine at the pianoforte and Ignaz Schuppanzigh, who performed regularly with Prince Lichnowsky's string quartet, on the violin. Josephine played beautifully. Beethoven had turned a good musician into an excellent one. The concert ended with Beethoven's String Quartet in F Major, its second movement alluding to the tomb scene in *Romeo and Juliet*. Merging the sound of grief with the sweet music of young love, Beethoven pushed the movement toward its fateful star-crossed ending.

After the concert, I congratulated Josephine and then found Beethoven. "You have made 'the face of heaven so fine . . . ,'" I said.

"'That all the world will be in love with night,'" he answered. "Thank you, my dearest Giulietta."

That night I told Lucy that Beethoven had called me Giulietta. Was he simply having fun with my name? Or was he equating me with Shakespeare's Juliet?

"Pardon me for being so forthright, milady, but with Herr Beethoven, it could mean anything. I wouldn't take much stock in it. Besides, you've told me that you think he's in love with Josephine."

He did seem enamored of her, but she was married and pregnant with her second child. I knew from Therese that she was happy with Joseph, and if she'd wanted an annulment, Aunt Anna had given her ample opportunity. Perhaps there was a chance for me.

I was too excited to sleep, so I took out my sketch pad, drawing a sky with dozens of stars, each illustrated with Beethoven's face. It was four in the morning when I finally finished, and I still wasn't satisfied, so I added a full moon. At the bottom of the paper I wrote, "And all the world will be in love with night." I drew a little heart before signing it "Forever yours, Giulietta."

8

Babette Keglevich greeted me in an ivory gown, a blue enamel choker accentuating her long neck. She kept glancing at her betrothal ring, a cluster of rose-cut diamonds that added an element of grace to her surprisingly pudgy fingers. We sat in a sunlit salon, where the butler poured hot chocolate from a painted porcelain pot and then set out a tray of pastries—punch cake, apple strudel, various tortes and éclairs, glacé cherries, and the ubiquitous gugelhupf.

"I love sweets, but I shouldn't be eating them," she said. "My wedding is in two months, and I won't be able to fit into my gown." She laughed and bit into an éclair.

"Your fiancé is very handsome," I remarked.

"He is, isn't he? He was named after a distant relative—Pope Innocent XI—but church history really isn't my specialty." She laughed again. "Everybody says it's an excellent match, but I hear that his love-making skills are merely adequate." She sampled the punch cake and shrugged. "One can always take a lover. And what about you? Is there anyone you desire? I hear that Count Gallenberg is quite taken with you."

"Can I tell you a secret?"

"You may tell me anything. I am famous for my discretion."

I doubted that, but I was so bursting with excitement I had to share it with someone. "I find Herr Beethoven very appealing."

"Louis? Appealing? He is beset with so many problems I cannot even begin. I hate to be indelicate, but he has terrible indigestion, and not just his habit of emitting burps at the most inopportune times. How could you possibly bed the man? He'd be running back and forth to the chamber pot the whole time. No, he is not for you. It's rumored that he proposed to the contralto Magdalena Willmann, but she turned him down. She called him ugly and half-crazy."

"I don't find him ugly at all," I said defensively.

"He does possess a certain *je ne sais quoi*, but I would hate to be the woman he marries. Frau Beethoven? Can you imagine such a life? Trust me, Louis will never marry. He's constantly falling in love with women above his station."

"He is above everyone."

"In talent, yes, but not in ways that really matter. He has no title and no money."

"He has Prince Lichnowsky."

"The prince is a true lover of the arts, but a very gross and perverse man. Do you know what they call him? 'The enlightened patron of music and the patron saint of bordellos.' Very clever, no?" The butler poured more hot chocolate into our white demitasse cups. "I trust you will keep this *entre nous*," she continued, "but have you ever wondered why his wife looks so unhappy? The prince can't keep his britches on. It's whispered that she's enamored of Louis, but I don't think the feelings are mutual. It is rather sad."

I nodded and sipped my hot chocolate. It was hard for me to summon feelings of empathy in light of the unfolding narrative.

"Princess Christiane was so desperate for her husband's favors that she once dressed up as a prostitute and surprised him in a brothel. He keeps a regular room at Madame Violette's, where he brings his mistresses. From what I understand, their only child is a bastard. The prince also likes young girls—and boys. He has extreme tastes, but you didn't hear that from me. I suppose it's offset by the good he does for music."

She sampled a strudel. "This is delicious. You must try one!"

"Herr Beethoven strikes me as a very moral man," I said. "I can't believe he would take money from someone like that."

"Musicians need money. They take it wherever they can get it. I'm not sure Louis knows the whole story. I only know it, because, well . . ."

She ate another piece of strudel, washing it down with hot chocolate. It left a stain on her upper lip, which she daintily removed with a serviette. "My fiancé thinks he's marrying a virgin, but he's not the first or the second."

"Not Prince Lichnowsky?" I said in disbelief.

"Yes, but only once. He's had his way with many young aristocrats. I was fifteen—not as young as the others. By the way, he is merely adequate, not as nimble as Count Deym."

I realized that in comparison to Babette, I'd lived in a convent, but I couldn't conceal my surprise. "You have lain with Count Deym?"

"Oh, my dear, everyone has. But now that he has finally married, I hear he's very loyal to his wife. Please, you must sample the gugelhupf. Oh, yum! It is totally divine. I've always thought it quite sad that they nicknamed the insane asylum after this delicious cake. The shape is quite similar, but why should a wonderful dessert be associated with a bunch of lunatics? It's so unfair to the cake."

I was starting to feel dizzy, the pastries swirling around like pastel-colored kites. Babette kept eating and talking. I didn't want to be rude, so I stayed a proper length of time and then took my leave.

"I probably shouldn't tell you this," she said, "but if I were in your position, I'd want to know."

"Know what?" I asked, my heart sinking.

"Your mother is Prince Lichnowsky's mistress—or one of them. I hope you won't hold it against me for being so forthright."

I couldn't believe what I was hearing. *Mother . . . mistress . . . Lichnowsky.* A word game in which the words didn't relate. *Lichnowsky . . . mistress . . . Mother.* No matter what order I placed them in, they still didn't make any sense.

A servant retrieved my cloak and I thanked Babette for the delicious sweets and conversation. I didn't recognize my own voice. It was a child's voice. *Mama!*

Out on the street, I took in large gulps of air. I wanted to clear my head so that the words would disappear, but they'd lodged themselves in my ears like furies shouting curses. Poor Papa. I wondered if he knew. I wondered if all of Vienna knew. In aristocratic circles, it was hardly considered a scandal to take a lover, but to choose someone so vile . . .

I began to walk with no idea of where I was heading. At some point, leaning against a building, I vomited the gugelhupf. Perhaps I'd gone mad and imagined the whole conversation, but then I remembered the way Princess Christiane had looked at my mother at Beethoven's duel. There had been hatred in her eyes.

It was growing dark, and snow had begun to fall. I found myself at the Christmas market at Freyung, where vendors sold everything from bratwurst and thick goulash soup to cardboard figures of Saint Nicholas and Krampus in his devil mask and horns. I loved visiting the market, with its sweet-smelling chestnuts, gingerbread, and mulled wine, but now I wandered around in a daze, trying to ignore the lewd comments of drunken men who assumed that a woman walking alone, even a properly dressed one, was a prostitute.

"How much to get between your legs?" one shouted.

"She doesn't look like an asphalt swallow," another said, referring to a common term for a streetwalker.

"She's no lowly whore, that's for sure," the first man said. "She's high class. Probably too dear for your pocket."

I felt a hand at my elbow. It was Beethoven, who looked totally amazed to find me at a Christmas market being propositioned by several ruffians.

"Don't you realize how dangerous it is for a woman of your stature to be wandering alone after dusk?" he scolded. "I'm going to take you home."

We passed through the rest of the Christmas market, stopping to glance at the carved wooden toys. "Oh look, a pony!" I said. It brought me back to the innocent days before "Mama" turned into "mistress."

"Countess, your behavior is exceedingly strange. You didn't imbibe too much mulled wine, did you?"

"I did not. I'm just very weary and confused. Have you ever learned something so terrible that it suddenly changed the way you view the world?"

"Yes," he replied. "I have."

I was too distressed to ask what he meant.

We spent Christmas in Vienna with members of my father's family. Talk immediately turned to the ongoing war with France. Several weeks earlier, Napoleon's forces had crushed the Austrians at the Battle of Hohenlinden, leaving the French army only fifty miles from the city. "He won't be stopped," my father warned. "We will have to sue for peace."

"Franz, it's Christmas Eve," my mother said. "Please stop talking about war."

Later in the evening, I accompanied my mother on the pianoforte while she sang "Dove sono" from Mozart's *The Marriage of Figaro*. In the aria, Countess Almaviva reminisces about the tender times in her marriage before her husband cheated on her. As my mother sang, "'Where have the promises gone that came from those lying lips?'" I thought I was going to be ill again. My mother was cheating on my father, yet in her "art," she imagined herself the aggrieved party. How could she sleep at night?

Afterward, we exchanged presents. I gave my father a book of Shakespeare's sonnets and my mother a bottle of Galimard perfume. I wished that my father had picked out a book for me, but he left gift-giving to my mother. She presented me with one of the necklaces that she'd consigned to the bottom of her jewel box. "It is perfect for you," she said. "Try it on." It looked terrible, but I pretended to like it. One gift remained. It was wrapped in torn newspaper and tied with string.

"Who in the world would give you a present like that?" my mother said. "It's a disgrace!"

After I unwrapped the newspaper and unknotted the string, I opened the box. Inside was one of the hand-carved ponies I'd seen at the Christmas market. The enclosed note read: "Now you have your wish. Your most devoted servant, Ludwig van Beethoven."

"It's a pony," I said.

"I can see that," my mother replied. "Who would give you such a cheap, childish gift?"

"An admirer."

"I certainly hope it's not Count Gallenberg. If so, I am going to have to rethink this whole alliance."

My mother's obsession with Count Gallenberg was troublesome, but in my excitement over the gift, I put my concerns aside.

"It's from Herr Beethoven, Mama. He knew I wanted a pony."

"A pony? Fine, if it were an actual pony. But this is a cheap wooden version. Julie, I worry about you. No common sense."

I wanted to reciprocate with a present, so the next day, I had one of the servants deliver my drawing of the moon and stars to Beethoven's apartment. And then I waited.

9

A week went by without a response. I was an idiot, a fool. How could I have been so presumptuous? The gift of a wooden pony could be interpreted in multiple ways, but a drawing that referenced *Romeo and Juliet* had only one meaning. If that eluded him, my valediction— "Forever yours, Giulietta"—would not. And I'd drawn a heart. *A heart!* I'd declared my love and he had rejected me.

I was sitting at the pianoforte staring at the keyboard when my mother casually mentioned that Beethoven had just returned from Martonvásár. If he'd been away, he might not have seen the drawing. I needed to get it back.

"It's in a brown envelope with my writing on it, remember?" I said to Lucy on the way to his apartment. On the pretense that we'd set up a lesson, I planned to distract him by inquiring about Martonvásár while she snatched the gift.

"I remember full well, milady. I also remember his apartment. I mean no disrespect, especially knowing your feelings for him, but he's not one for orderliness. Finding the envelope won't be easy."

"Then you'll have to be especially observant."

We knocked on the door, and Beethoven opened it himself. It appeared that we'd caught him in the midst of composing.

"I'm here for my lesson," I said.

"I don't remember setting up one for today, but as you know, I can be absentminded."

"Did you enjoy your time at Martonvásár?" I asked, nudging Lucy to begin searching.

"Yes, yes," he said distractedly.

"And Josephine and Victoire? They are well?"

"Yes," he said, turning to stare at Lucy. "May I ask what you are doing? Auditioning for the role of housekeeper? I'll be happy to teach the countess, but I won't have you scavenging around like a ravenous dog. I'm sure you have more productive things to do."

"I could organize the letters on your desk," Lucy said, her eyes darting toward a pile of papers that included my envelope.

"I'm capable of organizing my own letters," he said, pointing toward the door.

After she'd gone, I thanked him for the little wooden pony, telling him that it was my favorite Christmas present of all.

"I presume you didn't get many presents."

"It's true. I didn't. But that didn't make yours any less precious."

When Beethoven began clearing things off the pianoforte, I grabbed the envelope and was in the process of hiding it in my cloak when he caught me. "Countess, are you stealing my letters? First, I find you on the street being mistaken for a prostitute, and now you've become a thief."

"This is my letter."

"Then will you please explain what it was doing on my desk?"

I told him that it had been delivered by mistake and if he opened it, I would suffer great humiliation. I began to cry. I suspected that Beethoven hadn't had much experience comforting tearful women, because he just stood there. As a result, I cried harder while he tried to find a clean handkerchief. Failing to do so, he wiped my eyes with the ruffles of his shirt and then cleared his throat as if signaling an end to my congested music. Having already forfeited my dignity and facing the prospect of Beethoven's continued silence, I thrust the envelope into his hands. He looked at me for assurance that it was all right to open it. I nodded.

Beethoven studied my drawing for what seemed like a long time. I watched his eyes move from star to star, stopping to gaze at the moon, and then, finally, to Shakespeare's quote and my valediction.

"Did you want to take this back because you no longer feel this way?" he asked hesitantly.

"No. I was afraid."

"You placed my face in all the stars. You've made me better looking than I am."

"I drew your likeness the way I see it."

"And you've added a little heart? I can't draw at all. It's a gift I admire. I only draw notes." He showed me a composition he was working on, and I immediately felt pity for his music publishers. The notes were impossible to discern from the numerous ink blotches, cross-outs, and amendments. When he turned away to put the letter back on his desk, I whispered, "I love you." He didn't respond and I felt foolish yet again. I had gone too far. But then he took my hands in his.

"May I call you Julie," he asked. "Or would you prefer Giulietta?"

"You may call me Julie, but on special occasions, I will be Giulietta. And what shall I call you?"

"I was Ludwig in Bonn. Now in Vienna, I am Louis or Luigi." He shrugged. "They are just names."

"Then I will call you Beethoven. It is more than just a name."

Everything was different after that day. I met Beethoven at his apartment or he came to mine, but music lessons were no longer the primary focus. We discovered each other as people do when they're courting, but we were still very formal and didn't even share a kiss. I wanted to know everything about him, but conversing with Beethoven was like learning to play the pianoforte. One needed to practice and perform with great sensitivity, for he was easily riled and would break off a conversation in midsentence. He would then make amends for his boorish behavior, begging for forgiveness in such a dramatic fashion that I would wind up soothing him. We repeated this pattern so often that I came to believe that being soothed was his primary goal.

Week by week, I learned a little more about his childhood. He was more forthcoming after he had indulged his fondness for wine, but nevertheless, it took all my skills to extract even the slightest tidbit. I knew that he had two brothers, Johann and Karl, but that he didn't think highly of them. He spoke movingly of his paternal grandfather and namesake, an affluent kapellmeister who conducted operas and masses and possessed a fine bass voice. If he'd lived, Beethoven's life might have been different, but he died right before Beethoven's third birthday. Beethoven's father, Johann, was an exceedingly strict teacher who beat him in order to get him to practice and beat him even more whenever he failed to adhere to the written music and indulged his penchant for fantasias. He admitted that his father, a heavy drinker, would sometimes lock him in the cellar or deprive him of sleep so he could spend more time practicing. Beethoven's mother, Maria Magdalena, suffered from melancholia, having lost four children, including her firstborn also named Ludwig.

"I tried to make up for the other babies," he said, "but I was just one boy. My mother wept all the time. Whenever I think of her, I hear mourning music. I'm not sure my father ever appreciated what she'd gone through. But I did. I felt it to the depths of my soul."

Beethoven relayed his story without a shred of self-pity. When I commented that his father sounded like a brute, he denied it, telling me that when it came to the pianoforte, he had been doing only what he thought was right. By discouraging his fantasias, his father taught discipline to his son.

He did admit that he practiced best when alone. "Sometimes I think I do everything best alone. In Bonn, I was friendly with a family that had two telescopes in their attic. You could see for twenty miles! I loved secluding myself with that telescope, staring at the Rhine or the night sky. I was happy—well, if not exactly happy, then filled with joy."

"What's the difference?"

"Schiller's poem 'Ode to Joy' is one of my favorites. I've always wanted to set it to music. One day I will."

"I know the poem. It's in my father's library."

"Joy connects us to something larger than ourselves," Beethoven explained, "while happiness is something more personal, something a little more selfish perhaps."

"And how do you feel now?" I said, kissing him on the lips.

"Filled with happiness. And joy."

10

I couldn't wait for the end of the Winter Season and its insufferable balls. My feet ached from dancing, my head from conversing with so many dim-witted young men. There was one ball I dreaded the most. The host and hostess were Prince and Princess Lichnowsky, two people I couldn't think of without tasting regurgitated gugelhupf. I tried to come up with a socially acceptable reason to decline, but my mother told me that if I failed to attend, it would blemish her reputation. It was all I could do to keep quiet.

My father looked very handsome in his crimson and gold-braided uniform, shiny black boots reaching above the knee. It pained me to think of him as a cuckold. My mother was arrayed in her best jewels, a diamond tiara crowning her blonde curls. I wore simple pearl earrings with a cameo tied around my neck. I was in no mood to be placed on display.

"Do you think you're going to the market?" my mother asked. "Here, put these on." She handed me a pair of long diamond earrings that I refused to wear, and we didn't say another word on the way to the ball.

Dozens of torch-bearing lackeys were stationed outside as one carriage after another rolled up to the entrance. Tapered pilasters flanked a large portal, next to which two wooden doors were crowned by large urns. High above the pediment, putti held aloft the Lichnowsky coat of arms. A footman, in violet and gold, extended a gloved hand to ease us onto the red carpet that protected our dancing slippers from the snow. Moving through the vaulted vestibule, we ascended the grand staircase, with its Hercules caryatids, to the *piano nobile*, with its splendid halls and galleries. The ballroom floor was inlaid with a sunburst pattern, and gilt-framed mirrors on the walls reflected the men's jewel-toned waistcoats and the women's gleaming diamonds.

After greeting the prince and princess, I said hello to Babette Keglevich, who wanted me to meet a family friend. "I've always found him very attractive," she confided. "He's married, but I hear that he and his wife have certain difficulties." Taking my arm, she brought me over to a tall, elegant man who was conversing with Countess Gallenberg. He seemed relieved when Babette interrupted.

"Count Friedrich von der Schulenburg, I would like to present Countess Julie Guicciardi," she said.

The count was indeed very handsome, with thick blond hair, a long straight nose, and sparkling blue eyes the color of the sea on a sunny morning. His features were so perfect that I expected him to be arrogant, but he had a charming smile and equally captivating manner.

I wasn't surprised to learn that he was a diplomat.

"Count Schulenburg was the envoy to Copenhagen," Babette explained, "and is now heading to Saint Petersburg. Is your wife with you?"

"I'm afraid she's indisposed," he said as Babette nudged me.

I looked around for Beethoven but didn't see him. I knew that he despised such affairs but wouldn't want to disappoint his most important patron. The insufferable Count Gallenberg had requested the first dance, and the orchestra struck up a quadrille, ladies and gentlemen forming two long rows of squares, each couple creating a single side of a quadrangle.

"You look particularly lovely tonight," the Count Gallenberg said as we met in the center and passed each other.

"I trust your composing is progressing well," I said, taking his right hand and returning to the center.

"It is indeed," he said, moving past me again. "I have no trouble finding subjects that inspire me. Right now, you are stimulating my senses so much that I long to be at my pianoforte."

"Please don't let me keep you," I replied, catching sight of Beethoven. He looked at me, frowned, and then stared at Count Gallenberg before retreating to an adjacent salon. He had recently composed the music for *Creatures of Prometheus*, a new ballet that drew on the myth of Prometheus and his quest to bring enlightenment through art and knowledge. In a few short weeks, Beethoven had written fifteen numbers, and I attributed his aloofness to exhaustion.

Several other men asked me to dance. I kept looking for Beethoven but didn't see him. As the orchestra began to play a waltz, Count Schulenburg requested the honor. I wasn't a particularly graceful dancer. Being taller than most of the boys at dancing school had made me self-conscious, but I'd attended enough balls to know the basic steps. Unlike the quadrille, which kept couples at a relatively safe distance, the waltz, which had recently been introduced, was considered almost scandalous. Not only did it bring couples in closer proximity, but the twirling motion was said to cause dizziness and swooning. The count was exceptionally skilled; he had obviously had much practice during his diplomatic career, and as we spun around the room, I felt airborne, the other couples receding into the blurred background. When the dance was over, I was breathless and giddy.

"You, Countess, are an excellent dance partner," he said.

"You, Count, are an excellent diplomat—and liar."

He laughed, his face breaking into a wide smile, unleashing creases around his blue eyes.

"I'm sorry to leave so quickly," he said, "but I'm traveling to Saint Petersburg tomorrow."

"I wish you a good journey. Perhaps we'll see each other again."

"That, I would most enjoy." He bowed and walked away.

The waltz had unnerved me, and I was looking for a place to sit down when I confronted Beethoven's glowering face.

"I was wondering where you were," I said.

"Why talk to me? I'm just a lowly musician."

"You're being ridiculous! Everyone loves you. You're the resident genius."

"I'm the monkey in the zoo."

Count Gallenberg had claimed the next quadrille, and I had no choice but to accept. Beethoven talked to Princess Christiane, and I noticed that she put her hand on his arm, as if attempting to soothe him. When it came time for the "lady's choice," I found Beethoven and asked if he'd partner with me. The orchestra started to play a waltz, and Beethoven looked as if he wanted to run away. For someone with his musical talent, he was a terrible dancer, every movement strained and awkward. This time I was definitely earthbound and acutely aware that I had unwittingly placed him in an embarrassing position. After he caused a near collision with another couple, several people, including Count Gallenberg, laughed loudly.

"It doesn't matter," I whispered. At the end of the dance, Beethoven bowed and left the ballroom.

During my next lesson, Beethoven was cold to me. I knew he was embarrassed, and I wanted to ease his concerns. "I don't much care for dancing myself," I said.

"Then it's lucky I'm not giving dancing lessons," he replied sharply. "Now shall we begin where we left off—at the pianoforte."

I'd been lax with my practicing, but after some warm-up scales, I began playing a Clementi sonata but kept hitting wrong notes.

"No, no, no," he shouted. "You are playing like a child. An untalented one at that! You don't have a feel for the music today."

"You're right. I'm upset."

"I don't think I can continue to teach you. You are an impossible girl!"

He tossed the sheet music on the floor, toppled a chair, and then threw a pair of candlesticks at the wall. Moving over to his desk, he sent papers and letters flying before pounding his fists against a nearby windowsill.

"Stop!" I cried. "Your hands! Don't injure your hands!"

"My hands?" He sneered. "You're worried about my hands?"

"Please tell me what's wrong? I'm sorry for hurting you. I didn't mean it. I will never do it again. Please—"

"Leave!" he shouted. "Get out and go! You are stupid and shallow like all the others."

"I'm not like all the others, and I'm not leaving. What is wrong?"

"Wrong? You want to know what's wrong? Then I will tell you. I am going deaf! Beethoven, the musical genius, is losing his hearing!"

"It can't be true," I said, though I suddenly remembered our conversation at the Christmas market. I'd asked if he'd ever learned anything so terrible that it changed his view of the world, and he'd said yes. He had known it then. It also partially explained his absentmindedness, some of which could be attributed to raptus, but not all. Thinking back, I realized he seemed especially uncomfortable in crowds. A few times I caught him staring at my lips, which in my vanity I interpreted as desire. Now I realized he was only trying to decipher my words. I let out a small cry.

"I am the most wretched of men," he said. "A deaf Beethoven! Can you imagine the ridicule?"

"How bad is it?" I asked in a loud voice.

"You needn't shout! I'm not totally deaf—yet."

"I'm sorry. I just simply wanted to find out . . ." I kissed his hand and held it up to my cheek. The simple gesture calmed him.

"It started maybe three or four years ago," he explained. "It wasn't bad at first. I assumed it would go away, but it has only gotten worse. Now I have difficulty hearing the high tones of voices and instruments. And the buzzing! Sometimes I fear it will drive me mad. When it disappears for a time, I rejoice that I am healed, but it always comes back. Like a swarm of bees. Sometimes I hear ringing as well. Ringing and buzzing . . ."

"You should see a doctor," I suggested gently. "Perhaps there's some help."

"I fear there is none. I've stuffed my ears with cotton steeped in almond oil. I've tried strengthening medicines, cold baths, tepid baths, and yet I cannot rid myself of this fiendish malady. People think me a misanthrope, and it's true. I'm not always the most convivial of men. But I enjoy social intercourse. Now I'll be isolated and alone."

"You have many friends. I'll be here for you."

"How am I to live?" he asked plaintively. "It would be bad enough if I were a printer or an innkeeper, but musicians are expected to have superior hearing. What will they think when they discover that poor, pathetic Beethoven is deaf?"

He slumped down on the floor, put his head in his hands, and wept. I had seen him rage. I had seen him throw furniture, but I had never seen him cry. I had never seen any man cry. Tears trickled down his ruddy face, moving in and out of the pits and crevices of his skin, until they lingered for a second at his strong jaw before dripping onto his wrinkled cravat.

I didn't know what to do, but instinct took over. I held him and kissed away his tears, and then we were kissing with the kind of passion that I imagine happens before husbands are called into battle. I kissed him to counteract the sickening silence he faced. I kissed him to erase the specter of death. We moved over to his bed. He laid his head on my chest and continued to weep. I quickly undressed and offered my body to him. He began to suckle my breasts as if he were a baby, gentle at first, and then with a desperate hunger. He removed his britches and then looked at me to see if I wanted him to stop. I shook my head no. I didn't know what to expect, but as he entered me, I was swept up in his passion and despair, a waltz that was both airborne and earthbound, dizzying, dangerous, defiant. The dance ended with several powerful thrusts and he whispered, "Giulietta."

I don't remember how long I lay next to him. Eventually, I heard him breathing deeply and looked over to see that he'd fallen asleep. I didn't want to disturb him, so I got dressed and let myself out. As I walked down the street, I could still feel him inside me, as if all his pain and fear had been released into my own body. I wept as I walked down the Graben, not over my lost virginity, which in light of his terrible news mattered little. I wept for him, my dear Beethoven. I wept because I knew he would always be part of me, and I wasn't sure that I had the strength to bear it.

I woke up to the sound of ringing. Was I going deaf too? My heart raced as I threw off the coverlet. I'd been awake most of the night, and in my few hours of sleep, I'd had terrible nightmares.

"I'm sorry to have disturbed you, milady," said Lucy, holding a small silver bell. "But it's nine o'clock and Herr Beethoven is downstairs. He's talking to your mother."

"My mother! I'll get dressed. You distract them."

"How, milady?"

"Anything! Play something."

"I don't know how to play."

"Then pretend."

Beethoven's honesty often got the best of him, and for all I knew, he was telling my mother everything. I quickly put on a gown, ran my fingers through my hair, and pinched my cheeks. Walking down the hallway, I heard the most awful sounds coming from the music room. Beethoven and my mother were staring stupefied as Lucy banged away at the keyboard.

"I had no idea she was so gifted," my mother said derisively.

"It's a new kind of music," I explained.

"Whatever the case, I've heard enough," my mother said. "I have many things to do today and I'm already late. Goodbye, Herr Beethoven. I hope Julie is progressing with her lessons."

Once we were alone, Beethoven turned to me with a look of total fury. "Did you concoct that little charade to make me feel even worse? Do you think that's how I will play if I lose my hearing completely?"

"It wasn't a charade. I wasn't expecting you, and I wanted to do something to distract my mother. She's a difficult woman."

"It runs in the family."

"Please, I can't get into a fight with you. May I ask why you are here?"

Beethoven was still debating whether he should yield to his suspicious nature or whether he should follow through on his original intention. His better nature won out, for he suddenly dropped to his knees and begged my forgiveness.

"I consider myself a moral man. I have a good heart. I didn't act out of malice or depravity. And yet my behavior was bestial and now you are ruined."

"I'm not ruined at all, and since I was the one who instigated my own 'ruination,' who better to judge?" I led him over to a chair.

"I preyed on your pity by announcing my hideous malady and you had no choice but to—"

"Lie with you? Do you think me so unimaginative that I couldn't have come up with another option?"

He was quiet, as if trying to think up other reasonable possibilities. "You could have made bread soup. It's a favorite of mine. I like it with ten drowned eggs."

"You are the most ridiculous man! Don't you understand? I love you."

"No, you don't. It's pity."

"I know my own heart. I believe I've been in love with you from the first time we met at the Golden Griffin."

"And I fulfilled your fears by turning into a beast! Where is your father?" He began looking around as if he were about to go on a room-by-room search.

"At the chancellery."

"I'll wait for him to come home, and then I will ask for your hand in marriage."

"You will do no such thing. I don't want a husband whose only reason for marriage is that he mistakenly thinks he stole my virtue."

"I love you," he said quietly.

"I think you love Josephine. I'll always be in second place."

He lowered his head. "I was in love with Josephine. But she is married, and I would never come between a husband and wife. It is immoral."

He'd been in love with Josephine. I'd known it all along. But how could he be in love with her and also with me? We were as different as day and night. Is that why he was able to shift moods so seamlessly in his fantasias? He could play both Julie and Josephine with equal passion.

"I'm in love with *you*," he said fervently. "But I tried to quell my feelings because I feared you didn't share them. I couldn't believe such a beautiful girl would want someone like me. Especially now." He glanced longingly at the pianoforte.

Realizing the obstacles that we'd face, I advised caution, telling him that my parents would undoubtedly oppose the union and that he needed to concentrate on his music. "Please promise to keep everything a secret," I said. He nodded, kissed my hand, and then made me promise not to mention his hearing loss. "People will know it soon enough," he said, "but I cannot bear for them to know it now."

11

Beethoven and I continued to see each other, but it was no longer about my music lessons. It was all about him. After *Creatures of Prometheus*—dedicated to Princess Christiane—opened in March, he was busier than ever. He was receiving more commissions than he could handle, and between negotiations with his music publishers and consultations with doctors, he had little time.

He didn't take me to his bed, though I would have gone willingly. Instead, we talked, kissed, held each other, but he always made a point of stopping whenever things became too passionate. Until we were married, he said, we would enjoy a union of souls, for there was nothing more noble or better.

He discussed the possibility of having to give up his performing career but was determined to continue as a composer. His strength and resilience amazed me. In some ways, he was so thin skinned that I sometimes imagined him as one of Joseph's anatomical figures, with the vessels and arteries exposed. He was easily hurt by poor reviews, calling them the work of "scoundrels" and "rascally dogs," but nothing stopped him. I loved that about him. I also loved his sense of humor. He made me laugh, often unintentionally. Though his apartment was in a constant state of disarray, he was meticulous about the strangest things, such as counting out exactly sixty beans for his coffee. He told me that once we were married, he'd trust me to count them. I remembered Babette Keglevich's remarks about the drawbacks of being Frau Beethoven, but quickly forgot them.

When I didn't bleed for two months, I wasn't overly alarmed. My menses had always been irregular. By the third month, however, my breasts were swollen and I felt queasy in the morning. Lucy was the only person who knew that I had lain with Beethoven, and she urged me to marry him. "It's the only sensible thing, and at least Herr Beethoven won't disappear at sea like my beloved Bertie."

I knew that he would marry me, but it would create a scandal at a time when he was struggling to cope with his hearing loss. I couldn't do that to him. Babette had once told me that several of her friends had induced miscarriage with certain botanical preparations, such as the root of worm fern, known as "prostitute root." I debated asking her where I could buy it, but I couldn't forget Beethoven's sadness when he recalled his mother's miscarriages and his joy at being around Josephine's children. I didn't know what to do, so I did nothing.

In the middle of April, my parents went to visit my mother's brother in Korompa. As the oldest son, he'd inherited the bulk of the money, and he and his family lived in a grand art-filled estate. He controlled the quarterly dividends that were apportioned to the Brunswick siblings, and my mother was seeking an advance on hers. After convincing my mother to let me stay behind, I visited Josephine, who'd recently had a baby, Friedrich, and was on the verge of collapse.

"This is all too much," she said, handing the baby to Lucy. Not knowing what to do, Lucy gave the baby to me on the assumption that since I was pregnant, I was better qualified. Fritz attempted to clamp onto my breast, and I had to keep switching positions so his gummy mouth didn't hit its target. Finally, he stopped squirming, and I stared at this little creature, with his barely there eyebrows and lashes, fingernails no bigger than a fairyfly and skin so soft it felt as if it could melt. Something shifted inside me. It hurt at first but then subsided.

"Please get my husband," Josephine said, breaking into loud sobs. "I'm feeling feverish. It's all too much. I shouldn't have had children. I'm afraid I'll hurt Friedrich. Get Joseph—now!"

I gave Friedrich to Lucy, warning her to keep him away from Josephine. Then I ran half the length of Palais Deym, until a servant told me that Joseph was downstairs in the museum. He was closing up for the night, extinguishing all the candles. I caught sight of the anatomical figure of the pregnant woman, and my hands reflexively went to my stomach.

"Joseph!" I cried. "Your wife needs you. She's very upset."

In the murky light, the figures appeared to come to life, Mozart opening his eyes, Marie Antoinette clutching her neck and staring at me as if to say, *Why?*

Joseph looked old and tired, the stress of dealing with Josephine and his dwindling finances reflected in his sagging posture. "Pepi has been suffering from melancholia since giving birth," he explained. "It happened with Victoire, but it wasn't as bad. I know that her temperament is unpredictable, but sometimes she frightens me."

As I followed Joseph out of the museum, I felt a dull cramping in my stomach and something wet between my legs. I didn't say anything and waited to get upstairs, where an agitated Josephine informed her husband that she wanted to give Friedrich away. "I'm a terrible mother," she cried. "He deserves better."

Joseph was in the process of reassuring her when I doubled over in pain. Lucy's eyes immediately went to my light-colored shoes. Droplets of blood were forming around the toe tips. "Milady, you must lie down," she said, helping me into an adjacent bedchamber. My condition was enough to shock Josephine out of her hysterics, and she and Joseph immediately came to my side.

"Are you having your courses?" Joseph asked with the bluntness of someone with two mysterious children running about.

I didn't want to admit the truth, but blood continued to flow between my legs and the cramps were becoming sharper. My mother had suffered several miscarriages, and I remembered the blood and her anguished face.

"I am losing my baby," I said.

"You are . . . what?" Josephine replied. "I don't understand."

"She is with child," Lucy explained. "Three months."

Joseph called for one of the servants, who had previously worked as a midwife, and she gave me willow bark tea to ease the pain. I realized that a miscarriage would solve my problem, but I couldn't bear to think that a baby conceived in loss would in turn be lost.

For the next five hours, I bled and cramped and cried while the midwife watched over me. There was little she could do. I passed several large blood clots and then something slightly bigger. The midwife immediately picked it up, telling me not to look, but I demanded to see it. Turning her back, she gently wiped off some of the blood and then presented me with a tiny luminous creature that resembled a baby but also any number of fantastical things that could take wing and fly away.

"No," I cried. "It cannot be. No, no, no."

I continued to sob while Josephine took my hand, and when I finally had no tears left, I saw that she'd been crying too. She climbed into the bed and held me. When I woke up, I was still in her arms.

"We must get you out of these clothes and into something clean," she said. "You can wear one of my bedgowns."

"Thank you," I replied. Nothing felt real, especially Josephine's kindness.

"I'm so sorry," she said. "But perhaps it's for the best? I presume it was Count Gallenberg's. Everyone knows he's enamored of you."

"I cannot say."

"It wasn't Joseph's?" she asked desperately. "I'm sure you've seen these strange children in the house. I don't know who they are or how they came to be. Please tell me you didn't sleep with Joseph."

"I thought you were in love with Herr Beethoven."

"I am—was. But Joseph is my husband. People think I refused an annulment to get back at my mother, but that's only partly true. I began to fall in love with him. Joseph is everything to me, so please tell me, did you sleep with him?"

"I did not."

She was so relieved that she began to cry, and I was so happy that she was no longer in love with Beethoven that I cried too.

"We must never speak of this again," she advised. "It is too troubling."

"You promise not to say a word about what happened to me?"

"I promise," she said.

At this point, I'd made so many promises that I felt like a spider plaiting a web, one silk spiral at a time. I knew from playing with them as a little girl that each lustrous circle had a remarkable degree of flexibility and strength. I also knew that when stretched too far, the whole complex structure would collapse.

I rested at Palais Deym for the next ten days. Josephine treated me as a wounded younger sister, caring for my every need. Even Joseph showed a generosity and compassion that I hadn't noticed before. He entertained me with amusing tales of his travels and wax-sculpting career.

"I hope you don't think I'm overly inquisitive," I said. "But did you really flee Vienna on account of an illegal duel?"

"That's the question everyone wants to know, isn't it? The truth is that I was having an affair with Countess Thun and her husband found out."

"Isn't she Prince Lichnowsky's mother-in-law?"

"The very same."

"And her husband challenged you to a duel?"

"Hardly, my dear. He was twenty years older, and I was an army officer and very fit. No, I made up the whole story about the duel because it was romantic and served as a distraction. I've always believed that the best diversionary tactics should employ exaggeration. Otherwise, people will focus on the obvious. In this case, Count Thun appealed to the emperor, and I was sent into exile. Among Vienna's aristocracy, it's the way things work."

Josephine interrupted to announce that Beethoven had arrived for their usual lesson but left in a huff when she refused to let him visit me. "Louis seemed extremely worried about you," she explained. "I told him you had contracted mousseline sickness but were recovering nicely. He then wanted to see you, which I found very strange. I explained that an indisposed lady would never allow a gentleman into her bedchamber, and he kicked over the music stand and left. Do you have any idea what this is about?"

I could see Joseph fitting the pieces together. "I hear that he's having another duel," he said quickly. "Perhaps he's overwrought."

"I know nothing about an upcoming duel," Josephine said. "Surely he would have told me. With whom? Herr Steibelt?"

"I believe that's what I heard," Joseph replied.

"I find this very odd. *Steibelt?* The last time he was in Vienna, he said he never wanted to see Louis's face ever again."

"Shall we look in on the children?" Joseph said, taking Josephine's arm and escorting her from the room.

When I recovered my strength, I went to Beethoven's apartment to assure him that I was in fine health. Once again, he was in the process of moving to new lodgings.

"You don't look right," he said immediately. "Something has changed."

"I was ill, but I'm much better," I said, trying to pacify him.

"People have accused me of being unobservant, but in matters close to my heart, I have very keen eyes. The last time we met, your skin had a rosy flush and you looked like an angel. I wondered if you might be carrying my child. The mere thought filled me with such hope that it lifted my black despair, but now I'm afraid."

I hadn't planned on saying anything, trusting that Josephine and Joseph would keep my secret. It wasn't something he needed to know. He had dealt with so much loss: his siblings, his mother, and now his hearing. How could I cause him more pain?

"You are not a good liar. I will ask you again, did you lose our baby?"

I stood there not saying anything until I suddenly cried, "Yes, it is gone."

He put his hands to his ears, as if attempting to block out the single word: "gone."

I expected him to smash things, to shout and scream and rage at the god that was slowly robbing him of his hearing and now had taken his child, but he just looked at me, his dark eyes welling with tears. I wanted him to fold me in his arms, tell me everything would be fine, but we just stared at each other. No words could express how desolate I felt. All I could do was hold my hand over my heart.

Beethoven turned his back on me and I thought, How cruel! How horribly insensitive! Why couldn't he comfort me? Instead, he went over to the pianoforte and began to play, tentatively at first, as if trying to recreate bits and pieces of a theme he had once heard or imagined. Slowly, it began to coalesce, unfolding in a series of poignant triplet arpeggios that progressed into a melody that was plaintive and achingly sad. I couldn't bear to listen, and yet I couldn't leave. I was totally under his spell. He was playing *Trauermusik*—mourning music—a hymn for a dead child. When he had finished, neither of us spoke. He had said everything.

I left him at the pianoforte, and as I walked down the staircase, I felt pity but envy too. He could transform his grief into art. When I first started my lessons with him, he'd told me that his thoughts swirled around his head until they were ready to come out. I'd replied, "Like a baby about to be born." His baby had died but also lived, while mine, mine was gone.

12

Beethoven spent the next four months in the country. I'd written him a letter expressing my enduring affection, but he'd returned it with the seal unbroken. He couldn't even bother to read it. I was heartsick. I tried to remember the melody he'd played, but it came and went as if in a dream. What did I expect? It was a fantasia, and perhaps my relationship with him was a fantasy, a fancy, an illusion.

I was preparing to leave the city as well. To be caught strolling the Graben in the heat of July was to announce that one didn't have a country estate, the money to travel, or relatives who were tolerant enough to endure an extended visit from less-affluent kin. Before we imposed ourselves on our relatives in Korompa and Martonvásár, my mother and I went to Abano Terme, a popular cure resort outside Padua. Emphasizing its connection to the ancient Roman art of bathing, it was decorated with classical mosaics and a few scattered ruins. The guest accommodations bore the name of famous emperors.

After moving into Villa Julius Caesar, my mother and I had separate appointments with the spa's director, Dr. Mario Scarlucci, author of *The Effects of Waters, Warm and Cold, on Aches, Pains, Fevers, and Other 19th Century Diseases.* "Countess Guicciardi, I am honored that you have chosen Abano for your rest cure," said Dr. Scarlucci, whose book was prominently displayed on his desk. "So, what is bothering you?"

What, I wondered, was not? I had suffered a miscarriage, and the man I loved no longer loved me.

"I'm fine," I insisted. "I'm only here to keep my mother company."

He picked up his book and began reading from it. "Do you suffer from convulsions, palsies, numbness, trembling, swellings, distempers of the bowels, inveterate headaches, barrenness, vertigoes, cold affections of the womb, flux of the menses, gout, scabs, stones . . ."

"I am in excellent health, thank you."

"In addition to the waters, I would recommend a *fango* regimen. I refer to it as our 'magical mud.' It stimulates the skin and draws impurities to the surface. Since a woman's organic functioning is easily activated, we must be careful not to induce violent congestions. But all in all, I think this is a perfect plan."

For the next week, my mother and I rose at six in the morning to drink the vile-tasting waters before soaking in the thermal baths and submitting to *fango* treatments. Afternoons were spent drinking more water, perusing the shops along the colonnade, attending a concert or sitting in a coffeehouse. At four o'clock, we dressed in our finest clothes for another promenade before an extravagant dinner, which ended with yet another promenade, and then dancing or gambling.

By the third week, I was so bored and bloated that I told Dr. Scarlucci that I felt a "violent congestion" coming on, and he gave me permission to take a respite. I started to read *Candide* but put the book down after too many bad things kept happening to the hero. Unlike Pangloss, Candide's eternally optimistic tutor, I didn't necessarily believe that all was for the best "in this best of possible worlds." Was it for the best that Beethoven was losing his hearing? Or that I lost our baby? Picking up my sketchbook, I did a drawing from memory of a woman who wore a diamond tiara over her bathing bonnet. I saw her again at the thermal pool. This time she was wearing even more jewelry. She must have been in her late seventies, with a diamond ring for each decade. I overheard her tell another woman that she was looking for a young husband, which partly explained the glittering charade.

I was about to get out of the water when another woman sidled up to me and asked how I was enjoying my stay.

"I cannot wait to leave!" I said. "It's like being in a thermal prison."

She laughed, showing off a set of dimples. With her body submerged up to her neck, I couldn't judge her full appearance, but she had a pretty face, almost doll-like, with large blue eyes, pale skin, and two front teeth that protruded ever so slightly from a full mouth.

"May I ask why you're here?" she said.

"A heavy heart."

"I'm sorry," she replied.

"And you? I hope you are not suffering from anything too burdensome."

"It's more of a physical nature. My husband thought the waters might make me fecund. He wants children very much. I've tried many remedies, but it's been three years now."

"You mustn't give up hope," I said, sounding like Pangloss.

"I love my husband very much and pray he doesn't leave me." She began to cry but regained her composure. "I thought I might meet someone that I could introduce him to." She looked at me shyly. "Our encounter wasn't purely coincidental. I've been watching you. You're very beautiful. You read books. My husband is a man of great intellect, and I thought—"

"That I would bear his child?"

"Naturally, I would introduce you first. But I thought that if he knew he had a son, even if he saw him only occasionally, it would ease the strain in our marriage."

"I appreciate the offer of an introduction," I said, "but I'm not sure how I'd benefit. One day I hope to marry and have children of my own."

"Why, I would pay you, of course. I'm sure we could work out a satisfactory financial arrangement."

I looked over at the woman in the diamond tiara. She was flirting shamelessly with the type of young man who frequented such cure resorts for non-medicinal purposes.

"I'm sorry," I told my new acquaintance, "but I wouldn't consider such a thing."

"I hope I didn't offend you." She appeared on the verge of tears again.

"No, not at all. I'm sorry, but I don't even know your name."

"Forgive me . . . I am Countess Armgard von der Schulenburg. My husband, Friedrich, is the envoy to Saint Petersburg. He'll be joining me here shortly."

Friedrich Schulenburg—the man who waltzed with me at Prince Lichnowsky's ball, the man whose elegant dancing had stood in stark contrast to Beethoven's. I had put him out of my mind because the events that followed—Beethoven's hearing loss, the miscarriage—had destroyed all pleasurable memories. Now I felt light headed at the thought of seeing him again. I told myself it was the magical *fango*. Nothing more.

A few days before our departure, my mother and I decided to take a sightseeing trip along the Brenta River. We rendezvoused with a small group of hotel guests at Padua's Porta Portella before boarding a *burchiello*, an ornate wooden barge once popular among the Venetian nobles. I spotted Armgard among the people waiting to embark. She immediately came over to us.

"Julie, I want you to meet my husband, Count Friedrich—"

"You've met before!" my mother interrupted. "At Prince Lichnowsky's ball."

"It's nice to see you both," he said pleasantly. His hair and skin were burnished from the strong sun; the fine hair on his graceful hands had turned golden as well.

Armgard gave me a curious look, and after we had settled into the *burchiello*, she asked why I hadn't mentioned our previous acquaintance. I explained that in Vienna, one dances with so many men that it was impossible to remember names. She seemed to accept the excuse, and before long we were floating down the Brenta, past villas in varying degrees of disrepair. Most were built in the sixteenth and seventeenth centuries at the height of the Republic of Venice's grandeur, when the nobles flitted from villa to villa in a frenzy of feasts, parties, and theatrical games. The guide explained that Venice had been in decline since the mid-eighteenth century, but with Napoleon's army seizing key territories, the Republic had fallen in 1797. As part of the peace treaty with France, Austria gained control of Venice and its outlying areas, but the days of the *villeggiatura*—the hedonistic country holiday—were over.

"How depressing!" my mother remarked as we toured the threadbare Villa Pisani, once the most splendid residence on the Brenta. On the ceiling of the grand ballroom, Tiepolo had painted a fresco illustrating *The Glory of the Pisani Family*. Not wanting to hear their sad narrative from pomp to poverty, I left to explore the large hedge maze outside. A statue of Minerva stood atop a central tower, reachable only by a double staircase. In medieval times, a masked lady would have occupied that perch, waiting for a knight to make his way through the labyrinth and rescue her.

The hedges were so high that I couldn't see over them and lost my bearings. Wandering down various pathways and around concentric rings, I confronted one dead end after another. I began to panic. I turned right, then left, then right again. Another dead end.

"Is anyone there?" I yelled. When no one replied, I wondered if they'd boarded the *burchiello* without me.

"Help!" I screamed. "Please, someone—*help!*"

I heard a man shout, "Hello!" I recognized Count Schulenburg's voice.

"I'm trapped in the maze," I shouted back.

"Keep talking. I'll follow the sound of your voice."

"Talk about what?"

"Anything. Begin counting."

"One, two, three, four . . ."

I heard him cursing. He too was hitting dead ends, but by the time I'd reached thirty, he had found me.

"Thank you," I said, embarrassed. "I shouldn't have entered the maze alone."

"You have spirit. It's not such a bad trait in a woman."

"How will we get out?"

He pulled out a leather journal. "I marked the path by wedging paper into the hedges."

"How very clever!"

I started to follow until he suddenly wheeled around, looming even larger than the hedges. He had the most penetrating blue eyes, and for a moment I thought he might kiss me.

"I understand that my wife has suggested that you become my mistress," he said. "I hope you won't think poorly of her. She's been under much strain. It's been difficult."

"I don't think poorly of her at all. On the contrary, I'm envious. You are lucky to be married to someone who loves you that much."

"Yes, I am very lucky." He gave me a wistful smile as he led me out of the labyrinth. Heading toward the *burchiello*, we suddenly fell in step as if we'd been walking together for a long time.

"What happened?" Armgard said as we neared the boat. "I thought you'd both disappeared."

"I was lost in a maze," I explained. I didn't tell her that Friedrich had rescued me. He didn't tell her either.

We arrived in Martonvásár a week early because my mother had picked a fight with my uncle in Korompa. He had purchased a second major Titian, which my mother thought the height of profligacy, especially since she didn't even own a minor one. Josephine didn't seem to mind the intrusion, making a point of telling me that she had supervised the replanting of my lemon tree. It was no longer on an island in the middle of the lake but in the grove with a select group of Brunswick friends and family.

"Your tree is right next to Louis's," she said, "but you must promise not to eavesdrop when I talk to it."

"I wouldn't dream of it," I replied, trying not to smile, because she and Therese took communing with vegetation very seriously.

"Louis is coming tomorrow," she said. "He has written two new sonatas and promised to play one for us."

I suddenly felt ill. Did one of the sonatas arise from the fantasia he'd played for me? I wasn't ready to hear it. In recent days, I'd found myself thinking more and more about Friedrich. Though I had refused to bear his child, he helped temper my obsession with Beethoven.

While Josephine went inside to see the children, Joseph joined me in the lemon grove. "It was my idea to plant your tree next to Herr Beethoven's," he said. "After what you've been through, it felt appropriate. Not that a lemon tree is any compensation—"

"You don't have to explain," I interrupted. "It was a kind gesture."

Joseph drew on his pipe, exhaling a spicy-scented smoke ring. "How long have you been in love with him?"

"Is it that obvious?"

"To me it is."

"Thank you for helping that evening," I said. "You could have told Josephine everything and you didn't. I'll always be grateful."

"This family is complicated enough without adding another layer." He smiled, and then, extinguishing his pipe, assumed a somber look. "I would like to request a favor. I'm much older than Josephine, and there may come a time when I won't be around. You are strong and have common sense. Josephine is mercurial with a frail constitution. If she ever needs you, please look after her."

I told him I'd try.

The next afternoon, hearing a carriage pull up, I looked out a window to see a scowling Beethoven climb out. The footman took his battered valise and led him into the house, where Josephine and Therese rushed to welcome him, little Victoire screeching, *"Lou-lee, Lou-lee."* Since I couldn't avoid him, I decided to come downstairs to prevent any awkwardness. He was holding Victoire, her face nestled in the crook between his neck and shoulder. He wasn't expecting me, and, having been the recipient of a small child's unabashed affection, his expression changed from sheer delight to apprehension.

"It's good to see you looking so well, Countess," he said tentatively.

"And you, Herr Beethoven."

We didn't have a chance to talk during dinner. Having found a common enemy in Titian, my mother and Aunt Anna monopolized the conversation by criticizing my uncle's wasteful spending. Occasionally, I looked over at Beethoven, but he was focused on his pork stew. After dessert, we retired to the music room, where a mahogany Walter pianoforte sat beneath an inlaid ceiling adorned with the Brunswick crest. The room was sparsely decorated, the red velvet chairs frayed, the gold wallpaper peeling and stained, but a large triple-paned window offered a glorious view of the grounds.

Beethoven looked nervous, but Josephine, who was very adept at handling him, asked if he might tell us something about the new sonata.

"It is in C-sharp minor," he said gruffly.

"Can you give us a little more? What inspired you to write it?"

"Waking up from a dream."

Beethoven began to play the first movement, the adagio. Though I'd heard an earlier version on the terrible day he'd learned of my miscarriage, I couldn't have anticipated the overwhelming effect it would have on me. He had indeed written a song without words: wistful, mournful, hushed. The rhythm was unrelenting, a funeral march with no ending or beginning. By performing the work without dampers, he allowed one note to blur into the next, creating an impression of listening from a distance. Was he anticipating the day when he might not be able to hear at all? The melody was doleful but so beautiful that it made me happy to be alive, which made it even more poignant, for it simultaneously conjured the shadow of death. I feared that he was saying goodbye to me, along with the world of sound and laughter and life. *Trauermusik.*

But then, without pausing, he moved directly into the second movement, the allegretto, creating a light, fetching atmosphere in the form of a scherzo. Was he recalling happy moments from the past—ones he'd never be able to duplicate?

If the first movement was sorrowful and contemplative, the third—the presto—was powerful, defiant, and ferocious in its rapid shifts in volume and pace. Though the underlying motif was an expression of profound grief, he answered it with a display of dazzling virtuosity that made it abundantly clear that he would rise above his anguish. Whenever I thought he'd reached the climax, he unleashed a series of explosive arpeggios that ran up and down, until the final ascent and three thunderous fortissimo chords.

It was such a bravura performance that no one even applauded. We just sat there dazed, until Josephine initiated the clapping and we all joined in. I was exhausted, but Beethoven, energized, announced that he wanted to take a walk. Therese volunteered to go with him, and Joseph suggested I accompany them. He knew that Therese wouldn't be able to keep up, allowing us to be alone. Therese was heartier than I expected, though we both trailed Beethoven. Therese finally gave up and headed back to the house.

I caught up to him as he was about to enter the path that encircled the lake. "Wait!" I cried. "Please!"

He turned around, still wearing the look of defiance that he'd brought to his new sonata. His face relaxed when he saw me. I threw my arms around him, holding him tight in case he pushed me away. Gently, he took my face in his hands, caressing my cheek with his fingers. We walked arm in arm until we came upon a bench facing the island in the middle of the lake.

"The sonata—it's magnificent," I said. He sat next to me and took my hand. "It made me very sad but also hopeful," I continued. "I feared you were saying farewell."

"I would never say farewell to you, but yes, I suppose it's a farewell of sorts. Even before you told me the wretched news, I'd been contemplating what might be a lasting malady and a life of solitude."

"But the third movement . . . something changed," I said.

"You ask too many questions, but yes, I am not a man who easily accepts his fate."

"Why didn't you open my letter?" I asked. "That was cruel."

"I didn't feel strong enough. If you'd said goodbye, I wouldn't have been able to bear it."

A lock of hair had fallen into my eyes and he brushed it away with his strong fingers. It was such a simple gesture, but coming from him, it felt unbearably intimate. "Your face is luminous tonight," he said. "I want to absorb all of it." He pulled me closer to him. "Have you given more thought to my proposal?"

Seeing him again, I knew that I would never love anyone as much. I thought of Armgard and her selfless love for her husband. I wanted to act in his best interest, whether or not it was best for me. "The timing isn't right," I said. "Marriage would bring so many undesired complications that it would ruin your health and your music. Save your energy for what you've always described as 'the noblest' part of you. I will wait."

I expected an argument, but to my surprise, he agreed. "I'm working on another sonata and a cycle of six lieder and perhaps even an opera." His dark eyes flashed at the very thought of resuming his work.

"We'll see each other come fall, and we'll cherish our moments together," I said.

He kissed me gently on the lips and then, cupping my face, told me that I sparkled like the brightest of stars.

"Do you love me only because you think I'm beautiful?" I teased.

"I love you because you are the beautiful together with the good."

13

"Countess, please turn to your right." Emile de Guerard, the aristocracy's favored miniature portraitist, was attempting to recreate my likeness so he could later copy the painting onto a sliver of ivory. Guerard was particularly adept at capturing bright colors, so I'd worn a crimson shawl over a white gown tied with a matching crimson bow, tinting my lips the same brilliant shade. Lucy accentuated my *coiffure à la Titus* by strategically placing my dark-brown curls on my forehead and cheeks, and at the nape of my neck. She added two dramatic curlicues at each cheekbone.

When Guerard presented the miniature to me several weeks later, I was very pleased with the result and immediately showed it to my father, who agreed that it was flattering. He was currently amassing the required genealogical information for my mother's acceptance into the Order of the Starry Cross, the equivalent of knighthood for noble Catholic women. My mother was adamant that she be awarded the coveted medal, hoping it might improve her social stature in light of her perceived penury.

My mother advised me to save the miniature for my betrothed, comparing it to my virginity—a "precious commodity." Since I was neither a virgin nor betrothed, I immediately went to Beethoven's new lodgings on the Wasserkunst Bastei so I could present it to him. I found his habit of changing residences disconcerting. As someone who had moved from place to place as a child, I prized domestic stability, but he thrived on turmoil.

He greeted me with tourniquets strapped around his upper arms. "I would like to hold you," he said, "but it's too painful."

"Did you hurt yourself?"

"The doctor is trying a new treatment for my ears. He straps the bark of the daphne plant around my skin, and the sap causes redness and swelling."

"And then what happens?" It seemed very cruel.

"The skin erupts, and the doctor lances the blisters."

"Oh, my poor Beethoven."

"I wouldn't mind the pain if I could play the pianoforte, but I am encumbered by these straps."

Beethoven was skeptical about the treatment; he claimed the buzzing and humming had lessened somewhat, but his hearing continued to fail, especially in the high registers. Nevertheless, he was in unusually good spirits, showing me the open views from his windows. They looked west over the city's medieval ramparts to the glacis, with its vast expanse of green lawns, tree-lined alleys, and tumult of autumn leaves.

"And look at this," he said, pointing to a portrait of his grandfather. "My childhood friend Franz Wegeler sent it to me from Bonn."

Beethoven's grandfather looked every bit the affluent kapellmeister; he was dressed in a fur turban and a rich velvet robe, his right finger pointing toward a musical score spread out on his lap. I immediately saw the resemblance in the dark eyes, the cleft in his chin, and the shape of his hands. His expression was a gentle one, betraying none of the alarming intensity that marked his grandson.

"It is very fine," he said proudly.

"It is indeed."

While we were on the subject of portraits, I thought it a good time to surprise him with mine. "I have something for you," I said, hiding the miniature behind my back. Lucy had wrapped it very prettily, tying it with a crimson ribbon that matched the color of my shawl.

"The package is so delicate—like you," he said, tearing the paper to shreds. He opened the box and then, putting on his spectacles, held the miniature up to the light. "It is quite good, although no artist can capture your true beauty." He continued to stare at it. "He has caught the fullness of your lips and your hair, of course." He reached out and touched my curls. "He's also captured your stubbornness. It's right there in your eyes—see!"

"Stubborn? Then I'll take it back and give it to someone else."

"It wasn't meant as an insult. You are willful and determined. I can't imagine anything stopping you. It's a quality I admire." He kissed the miniature and then put it inside his shirt. "I will keep it close to my heart."

"I'd advise you to keep it in a safer place." I imagined him hurling his clothes on the floor, the miniature disappearing in a stack of soiled laundry.

"You are right. I'll put it in my desk drawer and cherish it until the day I die." He looked slightly embarrassed. "I have a present for you as well. I was going to wait for a special occasion, but since you've given me a gift, I would like to give you something. I'm dedicating my Sonata in C-sharp Minor to you. Perhaps you would prefer pearls but—"

"My dearest Beethoven," I said, kissing him.

"I was afraid it might bring back too many sad memories, but I couldn't imagine dedicating it to anyone else."

I was so moved I began to cry, and Beethoven said, "See, I knew it would upset you."

"No, I'm happy that you were able to create something beautiful from so much pain. Now our names will be linked forever, although I'm not sure I deserve such an honor."

Beethoven grunted. "That's what Prince Lichnowsky said. He wanted it for his sister, Henriette, but I refused. Although I'm indebted to him in many ways, he's not my master. I gave the Countess Henriette my Rondo in G Major, which I wrote several years ago. This placated the countess, but not Princess Christiane. She was extremely agitated when she found out I was going to dedicate it to you."

"It's rumored that she's in love with you," I said.

He seemed totally surprised. "No, she's more like a mother, and I certainly don't have feelings for her, except those of a dear friend."

I didn't tell him that one possibility for her antagonism might be my mother's position as Prince Lichnowsky's mistress, but if Babette Keglevich was right, the prince's licentious behavior was nothing new.

"But everything has been resolved, and the sonata will bear your name," Beethoven said. "I recently wrote to Wegeler and told him that we are in love. Don't worry! I didn't reveal your identity. I simply called you 'a dear, enchanting girl.'"

14

1802

The year began with an irate letter from Beethoven addressed to my mother. "The man is quite mad," she fumed. "Listen to this: 'I am not exaggerating when I say that your present gave me a shock. What else could it have done? It immediately put the little I had done for dear J. on par with your present, and it seemed to me that you wanted to humble my pride . . . But I shall plan my revenge.' He signs it 'Your greatly upset Beethoven.'"

"What did you do?" I asked.

"I gave him a shirt Lucy had made. It was originally intended for your father, but it didn't fit properly, so Lucy reworked it for Herr Beethoven. I also shoved a few florins into one of my old purses."

"You gave him money . . . in a purse?"

"It was quite a nice one. I thought he might present it to a lady friend, although he's so ugly I cannot believe anyone would ever be attracted to him."

"What would prompt you to do such a callous thing?"

"Your sonata! After you told me that he planned to dedicate something to you, I had to reciprocate, especially since he refuses payment for your lessons. I wouldn't want him to think we were on equal footing.

I *was* trying to humble his pride, although that would take more than an old purse and a few florins."

"You deserve every bit of his scorn."

"The dedication bothered Prince Lichnowsky very much," my mother continued. "There are certain rules one needs to play by, and clearly you don't understand them."

"Mama, what are these 'rules'? That it's acceptable to meet Prince Lichnowsky in a brothel? I know that you are his mistress—or one of them."

My mother blanched and immediately denied it. "How can you make such a preposterous accusation? You're as crazy as Herr Beethoven."

"How could you do it to Papa?"

She pretended she didn't hear me and sat down at the pianoforte to vocalize. *"Oh, eh, a, ah . . ."* She moved her jaw in an exaggerated manner. *"Oh, eh, a, ah . . ."*

"Would you please stop that?" I said. "How could you do it to Papa?"

She stopped singing and turned around to face me. "How could I do it? How else do you think we're able to live the way we do? On his meager salary? On my dividends from the Brunswick properties? We needed money, and I had to do whatever was necessary. Karl provides me with three hundred florins a year."

"So that's your price?" It was half of what he provided Beethoven. I was tempted to tell her, but she quickly replied that we all had our prices. Three hundred florins was hers.

"Did you ever love Papa?"

"Yes, I did love him, and that was my mistake. He turned out to be a failure. Did you know that he was fired from his job in Galicia for taking bribes?"

"Yes, you've told me many times. I'm sure he only did it because of your complaints about money."

"I spent my marriage following him from one place to the next, hoping that he'd become a success."

"I think you were hoping he'd become a prince."

"I found my own prince, using my beauty as a bartering tool. I did what I had to do, and I won't have you criticizing me. You wouldn't be living in this apartment or wearing such beautiful clothes or playing such a fine pianoforte if it weren't for Karl."

"Does Papa know?"

She shrugged. "Probably not. He's too caught up in his books."

"You paint a very ugly picture of the world."

She returned to the pianoforte. "It is ugly."

I was too much in love to accept her bleak philosophy. Though I'd experienced misfortune and wasn't as overly optimistic as *Candide's* Pangloss, I also believed that wonderous things could happen. In Beethoven's case, he made them happen, and I was the fortunate recipient.

When the Sonata in C-sharp Minor was published in March, the title page bore the inscription "Sonata after a fantasia, for harpsichord and pianoforte, composed and dedicated to Contessa Giulietta Guicciardi by Luigi van Beethoven, op. 27, no. 2." I had never felt so proud. People wondered why he'd dedicated it to me. I wasn't the daughter of a wealthy patron, merely a pretty young countess who took pianoforte lessons from him. No one knew that I was his "dear, enchanting girl." It was our secret.

The sonata immediately resonated with the public, particularly the atmospheric first movement, which, unlike the third, was well within the reach of talented amateurs. People found it haunting, enthralling, enchanting. Perhaps that's why it eventually became known as the *Moonlight* Sonata. Decades after the composition was published, the poet Ludwig Rellstab wrote that the first movement reminded him of moonlight shimmering on Lake Lucerne. At first, I was offended. Neither Beethoven nor I had ever been to Switzerland, and who was

Ludwig Rellstab to describe any part of the sonata? In time, however, I began to think differently. What was moonlight but the absence of clarity? It provided something for everyone, stories embedded in shadows.

I saw Beethoven again at one of Josephine's musical soirées. He was suffering the aftermath of another painful bark treatment. He flinched every time someone accidentally bumped into him. We greeted each other cordially, careful not to betray our furtive relationship, but if one looked closely, it was obvious—the way we gazed at each other and quickly glanced away, the blush I felt rising to my cheeks, the affection in his expressive dark eyes.

Josephine had invited Robert Gallenberg to present one of his own compositions. Before he sat down at the pianoforte, he told me that one day he'd dedicate something to me and it would be far superior to Beethoven's sonata. "It's almost an insult," he said loudly.

Beethoven, growing red-faced, might have assaulted him if Princess Christiane hadn't placed a restraining arm on his. He cringed as much from the blistering attack as from his blistering skin. "Swine," Beethoven muttered as the princess led him away.

Afterward, she walked over to me and whispered, "You're playing a dangerous game—*Giulietta*."

Count Gallenberg's sonata in the style of Mozart was neither dreadful nor very good. It was simply forgettable. Indeed, I'd practically forgotten it before he'd reached the finale.

Josephine asked Beethoven to perform, and I knew he would have liked nothing better than to erase the already distant memory of Gallenberg's music, but his painful arms prevented him.

"Count Gallenberg is going to ask for your hand in marriage," my mother said on the way home. "I was speaking to his mother, and we both think it's an excellent match. You're already nineteen, and you can't count on your beauty lasting forever. He's young, handsome, and comes from a noble family with a sizable fortune. Your father agrees that it's a fine union."

Now I knew how Josephine had felt when Aunt Anna had married her off to Joseph. In her case, she had grown to love her husband, but I couldn't imagine even liking Robert Gallenberg. I found my father in the library and begged him to reconsider. "Papa, I don't love him," I pleaded. "Don't you want me to be happy?" He didn't know what to say. Like Beethoven, he couldn't cope with a surfeit of emotion. "Please!" I cried. "I'm in love with someone else."

"Do I know this man?"

"Yes, it's Herr Beethoven, but please do not tell Mama."

"You cannot marry Herr Beethoven. Your mother is being considered for the Order of the Starry Cross, and it would ruin her chances. He's not suitable for a girl of your class. I'm not sure he's suitable for anyone. But I will speak to her about Count Gallenberg. Perhaps the process can be slowed down until your mother finds another worthy candidate."

I wanted to wrap my arms around him and smother him with kisses, but I knew that would make him feel uncomfortable. So I simply said thank you and left him to his genealogical research.

The news that La Bella Guicciardi would soon be affianced to Count Gallenberg made the rounds of drawing rooms at the same time that Babette Keglevich, now Countess Odescalchi, began inquiring about Beethoven's possible hearing loss. If Babette knew, all of Vienna did.

Beethoven had canceled two of my lessons, and when he didn't come for a third, I went to his apartment, where I found him packing. He explained that a new doctor had recommended moving to the country in the hopes that a peaceful environment might soothe his nerves and help his hearing.

"Where will you be going? For how long?" I felt ill at the thought of being apart from him.

"Heiligenstadt," he said, referring to a village in the Vienna Woods. "I'll be gone for six months." He walked over to his desk and retrieved my portrait miniature from the drawer.

"Give this to Gallenberg," he said angrily. "Your betrothed."

"Do not believe rumors!"

"Are the rumors about my deafness false as well?" he replied bitterly. "I'm a laughingstock. People pity me."

"Nobody pities you. How could they? You soar above them all."

"I'm a deaf musician who will no longer be able to play the pianoforte. Marry Gallenberg. He's a fool and a bore and a man of no talent or imagination, but at least he can hear. Please go—my lacerated heart can take no more!"

"I will marry you if you'll still have me."

"Now you're playing tricks."

"I am not! You won't be acquiring a sizable dowry, but I can promise that I'll be a loving wife—one who understands your needs."

"My needs?" he scoffed. "Will you be my ears?"

"Now you are being cruel. Perhaps you will see things more clearly once you are in the country."

"You don't want me as I am now."

"Do you think you're the only one who is suffering?" I said, my voice cracking. "Have you forgotten what I went through?"

"Of course I haven't forgotten! I can barely listen to that damned sonata without feeling the pain all over again. Now everyone is playing the first movement. Fools!"

He was impossible to reason with when he was in one of his black moods. I returned the portrait miniature to its rightful place in his writing desk and left him to pack for Heiligenstadt.

15

I didn't bother to write. I knew he wouldn't respond. Beethoven had the ability to wall himself off when it suited him, and I was now on the opposite side of the barricade. From time to time, he communicated with Therese, who told me that he was enjoying the fresh air, the walking trails, and much-needed solitude. He was experiencing a surge of creativity, working on multiple violin and pianoforte concertos, and perhaps even a new symphony. I worried about him. Often these bursts of energy presaged a bout of melancholia similar to Josephine's, but there was little I could do.

When he returned to Vienna in October, I summoned the courage to visit him at Wasserkunst Bastei, only to discover that he'd moved once again, this time to Petersplatz, between Saint Peter's and Saint Stephen's churches.

"I think you're making a very big mistake, milady," said Lucy. "Herr Beethoven is lost at sea—if you don't mind the comparison to my dear Bertie. He will never give you what you need."

"He's already given me a sonata. If I have only that, I'll be happy."

"No, you won't. Ultimately, you'll want more. Look at you! He's only just returned to Vienna, and you're chasing after him like a madwoman."

I instructed Lucy to return home, and as I climbed to the second floor, I passed a man who bore a resemblance to Beethoven. It turned out that it was his brother Karl, who was acting as his publishing agent. When I knocked on the door, Beethoven screamed, "And tell those archvillains that if they ever try to swindle me again, I will ruin them!"

"Hello," I said.

Before he could respond, the bells from both churches began ringing so loudly that the building vibrated. He motioned for me to come inside.

"I had not counted on . . ."

"What?" I yelled.

"The bells, the bells."

"I cannot hear you," I said.

"I had not counted on the bells!"

He took my hand and led me over to his walnut writing desk, where my portrait miniature was still tucked away in the drawer. He picked it up, holding it to his heart, and by the time the bells had stopped chiming, we were in each other's arms, kissing with an intensity I hadn't experienced since the afternoon we had lain together.

"I didn't think I would ever see you again," he said finally.

"I made my intentions clear during my last visit."

"That's not what I mean," he said, glancing away. "I didn't know if I could go on living. My hearing—it has not improved. *My hearing!* The one sense that should be superior to everyone else's. I felt such despair that I thought of ending my own life." He looked at my portrait. "But my art saved me."

"I'm glad," I said softly. It was naïve of me to expect that my love could compensate for his devastating loss—he had already confessed that he "lived" in his music—but I was hurt.

"You look sad, my dear Giulietta. Would you have preferred me dead?"

"Of course not! What a terrible thing to say. It's just that—"

"I love you. My feelings haven't changed. When I thought of taking my own life, I did think of you. I'd carried your portrait with me and looked at your beautiful face every day. It helped lift some of my desolation, but it wasn't enough to ward off my terrible despair. I'm sorry."

"I understand." How could I not? He had dedicated a brilliant sonata to me. I might have been the inspiration, but I wasn't its creator. "Where do we go from here?" I asked.

"A walk," he said, grabbing his felt hat and racing toward the door.

16

Vienna's salons were vibrating with gossip about the newly arrived twenty-four-year-old George Polgreen Bridgetower, a celebrated violinist who was rumored to be the son of a white mother and an African prince. He had lived for many years in London, where he'd played before the king and queen of England and had received guidance and support from the Prince of Wales. Beethoven found him so fascinating that the two men developed a close friendship, and Beethoven began writing a sonata for him.

With her weakness for titles, my mother had invited both men to dinner at our new apartment, furnished and paid for by Prince Lichnowsky. They arrived drunk, bantering back and forth like two naughty schoolboys. At one point, he and Beethoven placed the serviettes on their heads and attempted to fashion them into bunnies. Beethoven then confided that he hadn't had time to write out the pianoforte part for a concerto he'd recently performed and that most of it was a fantasia. "Someone turned the pages purely for effect," he said. Bridgetower found this so amusing that he laughed so hard he nearly fell off the chair.

My mother peppered him with questions of his life as a young African prince. He seemed to have little knowledge of the continent, and I wondered if he'd ever been there. He was tall and thin, with pale-brown skin, large expressive eyes, and a certain elegance in spite of his inebriated condition. After dinner, Beethoven clumsily knocked over a crystal vase that had been in the Brunswick family for years, and my mother gave him a scolding. This escalated into a shouting match, and Bridgetower and I retired to the music room, where he began running his hands over the pianoforte's rich cherry wood. "What a beauty!" he said, grabbing me around the waist and kissing me on the mouth.

I tried to slap him, but he grabbed my wrist and held it tightly. When he wouldn't let go, I bit his hand, causing him to immediately jerk it away. "Are you mad?" he said. "I'm a violinist! You could ruin my career!"

"If your career is ruined by two small teeth marks, then you don't have the stamina for it," I said, returning to the drawing room.

"What happened to your hand?" Beethoven asked when he saw Bridgetower cradling it.

"A dog bit me," he said.

"We don't have a dog," my mother replied.

Bridgetower suddenly remembered that he had a pressing engagement and left with a bewildered Beethoven, who staggered out the door.

For the next several weeks, Beethoven and Bridgetower spent much of their time carousing in taverns. It was a side of Beethoven I hadn't seen before, and it worried me. I knew that after Heiligenstadt, he was a different man, one who had seemingly accepted his hearing loss and was determined to push ahead. He had every right to enjoy himself, but I couldn't help feeling that I'd been replaced. Between drinking and writing his sonata for Bridgetower, he had little time for me.

The two men were set to perform the sonata at a joint concert at the Augarten at the end of May. A staple of the city's musical life since Mozart's day, the morning concerts attracted a large crowd despite the early hour. I'd arranged to meet Josephine and Therese, who confided that Beethoven and Bridgetower had been up all night, and Beethoven hadn't even finished the sonata. When the two men appeared, they looked drunk or in dire need of sleep.

The first movement began with a slow introduction, Bridgetower's violin making screeching noises like that of a lusty cat. Beethoven answered and Bridgetower responded, each flaunting their virtuosity. At one point, Beethoven executed a series of spiraling arpeggios, prompting Bridgetower to respond with his own improvised runs. Beethoven, relishing the spontaneity, jumped up to embrace him before they resumed playing. They continued to go back and forth in a fiery musical dialogue that mimicked the give-and-take of two lovers in the midst of a heated quarrel. The concert was a huge success, the sonata lauded for its passion, exuberance, and overt sensuality. Beethoven dedicated it to Bridgetower, referring to him as a lunatic on the manuscript's title page.

Several days later, Beethoven appeared at my apartment just as I was finishing my lesson with my new teacher. I'd decided that it was better if I studied with someone else. Beethoven was too preoccupied with his own music to pay attention to mine. I'd been attempting to learn the third movement of the *Moonlight* but kept tripping over the lightning-quick arpeggios.

"I've yet to meet a woman who can play it," my new teacher said.

"Countess Guicciardi is more determined than most," Beethoven replied.

After the teacher left, Beethoven told me that he was no longer speaking to Bridgetower. "He said something rude about someone I love."

"Please continue."

"He told me that you flirted shamelessly with him and that you pushed yourself on him and then kissed him. Since everyone knows that you're going to be married to Count Gallenberg, he described your behavior as that of a—"

"Say it."

"Common whore."

Why was it that a man felt the need to impugn a lady's reputation when he was free to foist himself on her without fear of retribution? I'd told no one about Bridgetower's advances, yet he'd decided to attack first. I waited anxiously to hear what Beethoven would say. If he sided with Bridgetower, it would be over for us.

"I didn't believe it, so I called him a pig and a filthy wretch," Beethoven said, "and then I threatened to exterminate him."

I couldn't have loved Beethoven more at that moment. He didn't need an explanation. He believed me without question. And yet I felt the need to explain:

"Herr Bridgetower pushed himself upon me. That's why I bit him."

Beethoven roared with laughter. "He told me it was a love bite. The man is a lunatic."

"Yes, I believe that's what you called him in your dedication."

"The dedication—I took it away. Such a scoundrel doesn't deserve my sonata. But that isn't why I'm here. I wanted you to know that I think you have the most beautiful voice. It's warm and rich and harmonious. I hear it in my dreams."

"Thank you, that's a lovely compliment."

He stared at me without saying anything, fidgeting with his cravat.

"So . . . you paid me a visit to tell me that you like my voice?"

"No! Well, yes. I do like your voice. That's why I want to marry you while I can still hear it. I want a few years before it's lost to me forever."

He got down on one knee and took my hand. "Giulietta, will you be my wife? I hope I haven't waited too long. Except in my music, my timing is not always what it should be. Will you have a deaf composer as your husband?"

I sank down on the floor next to him. "Yes," I said, tears springing to my eyes. "Yes, yes." We huddled together beneath the pianoforte, both laughing and crying, our emotions rising and falling in tandem.

Beethoven said he was tired of Vienna and within the next year wanted to move to Paris. He was already plotting ways to make his mark. He greatly admired Napoleon, whose liberal ideology reflected his own, and he planned to call his third symphony *Bonaparte*. He'd already gathered a list of musicians who might help him in Paris, the first being the celebrated violinist Rodolphe Kreutzer. "I met him five years ago when he came to Vienna," he explained. "He was modest and unassuming—the total opposite of that scheming Bridgetower."

"I have an idea," I said. "You could dedicate the violin sonata to him."

"Excellent!" he replied. "People would probably refer to it as the *Kreutzer* Sonata. In Paris, he's more famous than I. But if it helps me win a favorable position, it will be worth it."

Beethoven suggested that we marry immediately, forgetting that he was leaving for Baden the following day. After that, he was staying in Oberdöbling for several months to work on *Bonaparte*. I recommended that I speak to my father to smooth the way. All would be settled once Beethoven returned from the country.

"And if he refuses to give me your hand in marriage?" he asked.

"I will marry you anyway. You have my word."

My father was in the library with a volume of Shakespeare plays. When I asked what he was reading, he replied, "*Macbeth.*" I'd been hoping for a comedy, perhaps *A Midsummer Night's Dream*. I needed him to be in the right frame of mind when I delivered my news.

"Papa," I said tentatively. "I have something to tell you. I'm marrying Herr Beethoven. It would please me very much if you would give us your blessing."

"Oh, Jülchen," my father said, using my childhood nickname. "You've picked a difficult path. Is this what you really want?"

"Yes, I'm sure of it."

He put down the book and looked at me. "You've always been different. At times, I don't know what to make of you. A part of me has always longed for a son. We could have done things together, related in ways that fathers and sons do. I never knew how to handle a daughter."

"Then let me tell you," I instructed. "Give me your consent to marry Herr Beethoven."

"If that's what you truly want, I'll give my consent. But we must wait for your mother. She'd be very angry if we didn't at least pretend to consult her."

My mother was at a cure resort in Piestany, where her devotion to the waters bordered on religiosity. Beethoven, meanwhile, was taking the waters in Baden. I wrote to him immediately, telling him that my father had approved of the marriage but that we couldn't make a formal announcement until my mother's return. "My heart is bursting with joy," he wrote. "We will be happy together. I promise you! Work is going extremely well on *Bonaparte*. Erard, the Parisian manufacturer, is sending me a new pianoforte. For once I feel as if the fates have smiled on me. I love you, I love you, my dear, dear Giulietta, angel of my heart."

I was happy too. Though I realized it wouldn't be an easy life and that my role would be to comfort and support him, I couldn't imagine a worthier man. I knew there might come a day when he couldn't hear at all, and I did worry about the impact on his career, but he had already demonstrated his strength and resolve. Nothing, even total deafness, would stop him from making music. And if he could no longer hear my voice, he'd feel the beating of my heart and see the love in my eyes. We'd already endured loss. If we had to, we'd endure it again as man and wife.

When my mother returned, my father waited a few days before bringing up the delicate topic. She was in a bad temper because she still hadn't received word about her acceptance into the Order of the Starry Cross. Her mood didn't improve when my father announced my intentions.

"You want to marry Beethoven?" she asked incredulously. "Beethoven of the hairy hands and dark pock-marked skin? Beethoven, the man you called a werewolf? Beethoven who cannot hear? You will destroy me if you marry him. Why not marry George Bridgetower? At least his father is a prince."

"Papa has given his consent," I said. "It is done."

"You have disgraced me—and your father! I am being considered for the Order of the Starry Cross, and if word leaks out that my daughter is marrying an ugly, deaf composer, I will never be allowed in. Your father has spent an enormous amount of time conducting genealogical work, locating obscure Brunswicks and Guicciardis in all corners of the globe. If you do this, I will never set eyes on you again."

"You don't have to worry," I said. "We're moving to Paris."

"Paris isn't far enough away," she screamed. "You should move to Africa!"

I was so upset I started to cry, and afterward my father came into my room and assured me everything would be all right, and I believed him.

17

My father was at the chancellery when Prince Lichnowsky paid a visit. He'd never come to our apartment before, and I was surprised to see him. My mother had put on her favorite gown, rouged her cheeks, and applied her Galimard perfume. She had obviously been expecting him.

The prince had little time for idle chatter. "Your mother has informed me that you intend to marry Herr Beethoven," he said in a high, tinny voice. "I'm sorry to tell you that it's not going to happen."

"I don't mean any disrespect, Prince Lichnowsky, but you are a patron of the arts, not a marriage broker," I replied.

"You think you are very clever, Countess Guicciardi, but that tongue of yours will get you in trouble."

I looked to my mother for the slightest show of maternal support, but she stood firmly with her lover.

"Speaking as Herr Beethoven's friend, perhaps his best friend, I can tell you that you'll ruin his life. Do you think you can possibly make someone like Beethoven happy?"

"Yes, I do."

"That's just as bad, isn't it?" he went on. "Who wants a happy Beethoven? He thrives on misery and discontent. Just because he dedicated one sonata to you, do you think you're his muse? Do you think a man like Beethoven even needs a muse?"

I saw Lucy hiding in the hallway watching me. I wanted to show that I wouldn't be cowed by this hideous man's bullying.

"I am marrying him," I said firmly. "You cannot stop me."

"Oh, dear girl, you are so naïve." He turned to my mother, tweaking her left breast between his thumb and index finger. "My darling Susanna, you haven't taught her the ways of the world."

"Mama, I beg you," I said. "Help me! For God's sake, help me!"

"If you go ahead with this ridiculous marriage," he continued, "I will make sure your father knows that your mother has played the whore for countless years. I'll tell him what I've done to her, each and every sordid detail. But obviously you care nothing about preserving the Guicciardi name."

I felt ill, placing my hand on a chairback to steady myself. The prince began pacing up and down the room as if he owned it, which, to a large extent, he did. "If you don't care about your parents," he continued, "you obviously care about Herr Beethoven. Let me tell you what will happen. I'll cut off his stipend of six hundred florins a year. I'll make sure that Lobkowitz, Kinsky, Razumovsky—every aristocrat in Vienna—shun him. He'll be left to scrounge for money like poor Mozart, but unlike Mozart, he's losing his hearing. What is more pathetic than a penniless, deaf composer? It's up to you. You can marry him—and destroy his life. Or give him up and let him fulfill his destiny."

I looked at my mother, but she refused to meet my eyes. "You give me no choice," I said weakly.

"You had no choice the minute I walked into the room."

I turned to go, but he wasn't finished yet. "It would be very unwise to have you unmarried, and since Countess Gallenberg is desperate for a match, you are to wed her son."

"Robert Gallenberg? You want me to marry *Gallenberg*?" I cried. I knew that I shouldn't have been surprised. Our names had been linked together for several years, but were Beethoven and Gallenberg the only two men in the Hapsburg empire?

"My dear, there is no need to become so emotional," he said. "This is the way matches are made. He's not a musical genius, but geniuses can be so fickle. Women are like musical compositions to Beethoven. He falls in love with one, grows discontent, and falls in love with another. You, my dear, will eventually be an old melody he no longer wants to hear. Or should I say *can* hear."

As Prince Lichnowsky took his leave, he brazenly kissed my mother on the lips and then told me that Princess Christiane sent her regards. "She loves him, you know, so I was hardly going to let him go to Paris. I've been such a bad husband that I wanted to do something nice for her. And now I have."

Joseph was at the foot of the Laudon mausoleum, looking every bit as bereft as the wax mourners. He and Josephine were planning to move to Prague, and he was preparing to sell his possessions in order to settle his debts. "I've spent my life accumulating objects and now what?" he asked. "I had hoped to keep my collection together, but it seems as if I'll be selling it piecemeal. It will be worth it, though, if it brings in enough money. Josephine and I are looking forward to a fresh start."

I'd wanted a fresh start too, but it was now impossible. I told Joseph what had happened, asking if there was any way around the prince's ultimatum.

"No," he said. "And don't be surprised if you are exiled. He won't want you anywhere near Louis." He embraced me. "I'm so sorry, Julie." I left him staring at his treasures—the lifeless bodies of gods and goddesses, geniuses and deviants, kings and paupers—and then I made my way to the Theater an der Wien. As a composer in residence, Beethoven had been given a small apartment there, and he'd traveled from Baden to celebrate the good news.

How could I explain my change of heart? If I told him the truth, he wouldn't tolerate such an abominable injustice. He'd cut off ties with the prince and lose everything. Or would he? I'd made peace with the knowledge that as Beethoven's wife, I would be second to his music. But what if the situation never progressed that far? What if given the choice between me and his stipend, he chose the stipend?

When I knocked on his door, Beethoven immediately opened it, drawing me into his arms. "My Giulietta," he murmured.

He looked so happy I couldn't bear to deliver the bad news, but he saw it written on my face. "What's wrong?" he asked anxiously. "Your father has consented. We're to be married. You gave your word."

"I cannot marry you," I said softly. I hoped he would not hear it, never hear it.

"Why? *Why?* Did your father go back on his pledge? I will speak to him. I will straighten things out."

"It's not my father. Or my mother."

"Then, please, tell me, what is it? Are you ill? I know plenty of doctors."

How could I do this to him? How could I even say the words? I'd practiced in my bedchamber, but now he was right in front of me, the man I longed to marry.

"I do not love you," I whispered.

"Please speak louder."

"I do not love you!" I shouted.

He looked confused, shaking his head as if his poor hearing were playing tricks on him.

"You do not love me?" he asked. "Then why . . . why?" He slumped down in a chair, looking up at me with his expressive eyes. They conveyed hurt and anguish, even despair. I didn't know if I could continue, but I couldn't leave him in this state. I remembered Aunt Anna and

Franz shooting a horse whose leg had gone lame. "Better this way," Aunt Anna had said. "Why let the poor animal suffer?"

"I love Robert Gallenberg," I stated loudly and clearly.

"I don't believe you!" Beethoven said. "You don't love him. You wouldn't last five minutes having to listen to his frightful music. Something happened. Tell me!"

I wanted to tell him everything, but what good would it do? He needed the prince's stipend, and he was experiencing a surge of creativity. What would happen to *Bonaparte* and every other brilliant composition swirling around in his head?

"I do love him," I insisted.

"No, you don't," he said, rising from the chair. "You don't want to marry me because I'm not of your station. I'm not good enough. I thought you were different, but I was wrong. Get out! *Get out!*"

"Please, no!" I stood in front of him, tears coursing down my cheeks. I didn't want it to end this way.

He turned around and began smashing things and hurling books, nearly knocking his grandfather's portrait off the wall. His eyes lit on my drawing. He had framed it and kept it on his desk. "Oh no! Please!" I said. He threw it to the floor and stomped on it. Breaking the glass, he ripped it out of the frame and tore it into little pieces, the stars fluttering to the ground. The words "Forever yours, Giulietta" landed at my feet. When I bent down to pick it up, a shard of glass pierced my hand. Beethoven kicked the paper and then, grabbing my shoulders, shook me so hard I thought he'd kill me. Pushing me toward the door, he shoved me onto the landing, where I fell on my hands and knees, the glass digging deeper into my palm.

"I never want to see your face or hear your voice again," he shouted. "Damn you! Damn you to hell!" He slammed the door.

I was so distressed that I had to steady myself before I could climb down the staircase. I heard him sobbing, a sound I never forgot, a sound that even Beethoven with all his genius would never be able to replicate in his music.

I was still trembling when I went outside and climbed into the waiting carriage.

"Milady, you're bleeding," Lucy said. "What did he do to you?"

"It's what I did to him," I cried. "What I did to him."

18

I once read about the phenomenon of the stigmata—the manifestation of wounds that reflected those of the crucified Christ. People who had received them were thought to feel Christ's suffering so much that his pain became incarnate. Whenever I looked at the red mark on my palm, I was reminded of Beethoven's pain—and mine.

For the next week, I barely ate or slept. Beethoven had damned me to hell and I deserved it. I had caused him nothing but unhappiness, this great composer who was struggling with an affliction that would have felled a lesser man, and I had added to his suffering by lying and breaking his heart. When my father expressed his concern over my well-being, my mother explained that I was secretly pining over Count Gallenberg, Beethoven being a temporary infatuation.

"Jülchen, is this true?" my father asked.

"Yes, Papa. I was only using Herr Beethoven to make Count Gallenberg jealous."

"That isn't like you," he said. "You don't play games."

"Franz, you don't understand women at all," my mother lectured. "Julie has been talking about Robert Gallenberg since the first time they met. If you ever got your head out of your books, you would have known that."

He still wore a dubious look but didn't want to contradict my mother, especially now that she was in a good mood, having recently and not purely by chance been inducted into the Order of the Starry Cross. She wore the insignia—an oval medallion with an enamel cross—pinned above her left breast, the same one I'd watched Prince Lichnowsky pinch.

While Beethoven worked on *Bonaparte* in Oberdöbling, I tried to muster enthusiasm for my new fiancé. Familiar with the ways of aristocratic marriages, Robert didn't seem at all surprised to discover that I was to be his wife, and after receiving my father's consent and presenting me with a sapphire betrothal ring, he became a frequent visitor. Though he cut a handsome figure, possessed a noble title, and was reasonably intelligent, he didn't grasp the limits of his talent, and it was painful to hear him expound on his musical aspirations. At the very least, he would give me fine-looking children.

A month before the wedding, my father called me into the library to advise me to break off the engagement. He had recently learned that Robert had far less money than Countess Gallenberg had led him to believe, and he told me that it was folly to marry a struggling composer. My mother walked into the room to announce that the issue had already been resolved. "Prince Lichnowsky has secured Robert a position with Count Fries."

"At his banking house in Vienna?" my father asked.

"Better than that," my mother replied. "At the office in Naples."

Joseph had been right. I was being exiled.

"Julie, do you love Robert this much that you're willing to make this sacrifice?" my father asked.

I looked over at my mother, whose eyes were as cold as the Starry Cross.

"Yes."

In mid-November, I married Count Wenzel Robert von Gallenberg at Saint Stephen's Cathedral. Lucy, in between crying, had made me a beautiful tulle wedding gown embroidered with seed pearls and gold thread. People told me that I looked beautiful, but I had seen my haggard face, and it reminded me of Josephine's on her own wedding day. Yet she was now six months pregnant with her fourth child and excited about moving to Prague.

"I'm surprised Louis isn't here," she said. "After all, he did dedicate that beautiful sonata to you. We saw him for dinner several nights ago. He seemed very melancholy and imbibed to excess." She turned to Joseph. "Didn't his behavior trouble you?"

"That's Louis," Joseph said. "Comedy, tragedy—he wears them equally on his sleeve."

"My heart aches whenever I hear his name," I whispered to Joseph. "I have destroyed him."

"You must take care of yourself," Joseph advised. "Louis will survive."

"I didn't like you when we first met," I confessed, "but I will miss you very much."

He kissed my hand. "Don't suffer too much, dear Julie. Naples is a beautiful city."

Robert and I spent our wedding night at Palais Gallenberg so he could be close to what he loved most: his pianoforte. When the muse struck, which it did with alarming frequency, he couldn't be without it. Countess Gallenberg had decamped to her daughter's home to give us privacy. Robert spent most of the time reworking his one-act opera, *The Little Page or the State Prison*. "It's a 'rescue' opera, like *The Abduction from the Seraglio*," he said excitedly. "The main character is named Julie—just like you!"

I waited in the bedchamber while Robert finished the aria in which Julie cried, "Help!" to the little page boy. Wearing my new silk bedgown, I worried how he'd react when he discovered I wasn't a virgin. When he finally came in, he seemed exceptionally nervous. He didn't remove his clothes or attempt to take off mine. He didn't even kiss me. I tried to put him at ease by inquiring about his opera. "Who will play the little page? A young boy?"

"I wanted a dwarf," he said. "Can you imagine what a sensation that would create! But I couldn't find one who could sing well enough, so we cast the woman who was in Beethoven's *Christ on the Mount of Olives.* I've given her a far more challenging role."

"Didn't she play the angel who comforts Jesus prior to his crucifixion? You consider playing a page boy more challenging?"

"It's all in the music! If you continue to compare me to that pretentious man, I will leave right now. He's going deaf, you know."

"I didn't know. How very sad."

Despite the chill in the room, Robert was perspiring and acted as if he wanted the small page to rescue him. We sat around making polite conversation until he suddenly announced that he had something important to tell me. "I am impotent!" he blurted. "I cannot lie with you or have children."

"Are you relating a scene from the opera? Who is impotent? The small page?" I couldn't imagine how an opera about a small, impotent servant could have any chance of success.

"No, it's not the opera! I'm discussing my own situation."

The events of the past few months had been so disorienting that it took me several minutes to comprehend what he was saying. "Are you certain?" I asked. I didn't even know the full consequences. Did this really mean we couldn't have children? "I'm sure there's something you can do." I remembered saying the same thing to Beethoven when he revealed his hearing loss: "I'm sure there's something you can do."

"I've tried every treatment to incite the nerves and provoke lust," he explained. " I've consulted with healers. They've given me mandrake root, Spanish fly, rocket seed."

"And doctors?"

"They believe that I have too little fluid flow within my body."

Before the wedding, my mother had taken me to Madame Violette, who ran the high-class brothel where Prince Lichnowsky maintained a regular room. My mother explained that it was common practice for young noblewomen with little or no experience to be given a lesson in the art of pleasing a man. Madame Violette was reputedly an excellent teacher. "The virile member can sometimes be very *capricieux*," she'd explained during my tutorial. "It is up to you to make it happy."

Robert wouldn't even let me try, reacting angrily at all suggestions. "No," he said vehemently. "It would only end in humiliation. It is fate. I must save my precious fluids for my music. I trust that you will keep this private. I wouldn't want to be thought of as less than a man."

"Did my parents know about this?" I asked, feeling betrayed.

"No. But I'm not sure it would have mattered."

"Robert, why don't you just get into bed and hold me. We can still be intimate."

He shook his head. "I'm bringing in a substitute. We must have children."

"Robert, isn't this a little premature? We could see doctors together. I'm sure there is some solution."

"There is none," he said sullenly.

I heard a knock on the door, and Prince Lichnowsky walked in.

"The prince has kindly offered to father our first child," Robert explained. "I'm very grateful to him."

"No," I said, backing away. "No, please! No! Robert, do not do this to me!"

He shut the door behind him, leaving me to face Prince Lichnowsky, who still smelled of my mother's perfume. I couldn't believe this was happening. Was I dreaming? I quickly reviewed my options. There were none.

"My dear, if I can please your mother, I'm sure I will be able to please you," he said.

"Please me? *Please me?* How could you possibly please me?"

He looked genuinely wounded, as if he actually thought he was performing a good deed, the equivalent of charity work for the Ladies of the Starry Cross.

"I am known to be an excellent lover," he said, pouring us both a glass of wine. "Here, this will make you relax."

I threw the wine in his face and began looking for a sharp implement, a letter opener, a pair of scissors, a knitting needle.

"My, you are feisty," he said admiringly. Did he think it was a game? I was ready to kill him.

"You have ruined my life, you vile, debauched swine," I shouted, grabbing a hairbrush.

"I see that you have picked up Beethoven's way with words. At least he has left you with something." Pushing me down on the bed, he grabbed the brush and began spanking me with it. "So, this is what you like? I thought so."

"Stop that!" I screamed. "You're hurting me."

"But it feels good, doesn't it?"

"It does not!"

The prince stopped immediately. "I do apologize. I misread the signs."

I asked him to leave. In case he misinterpreted my words, I pointed to the door, shouting, "Go—now!" I stood up and straightened my gown, my buttocks stinging from the bristles.

"I'm afraid that's not possible," he replied. "Don't forget that your family's livelihood depends on me. As for Beethoven, I could still withdraw his stipend."

"You could not!" I said, trying to steady my shaking voice. "We made a bargain."

"I don't think you're in a very strong bargaining position, my dear."

Shoving me down onto the bed again, he pulled up my gown and thrust his way into me. "I would have kissed and caressed you," he murmured. "But you ruined it. You really missed an opportunity. I'm quite the lover, and I do find you very beautiful." Gratefully, it was over very quickly. As he hoisted up his britches, he glanced at the bedsheets. "My, my," he said. "No blood. And I thought I was getting a virgin. Don't worry. I won't tell your husband. It will be our little secret. With luck, you'll have a noble in your belly, although I'm not sure you deserve it."

I heard the door close behind him, feeling his stickiness between my thighs. Using the bedgown Lucy had made for my wedding night, I began to wipe it away, scrubbing so hard that my flesh burned. I wanted to leave Robert right then. I wanted to run out of the house and seek help—but from whom? The Deyms? They were preparing to leave for Prague. My friend Babette would never go up against the Lichnowskys. The police would never arrest the prince. Rape within marriage was not considered a crime, and getting an annulment based on Robert's inability to have children not only was difficult to prove but what if I did become pregnant?

I poured myself a glass of wine, and then a second and a third. When Lucy found me, I was passed out on the floor.

19

Robert and I spent our honeymoon in Rome, staying in a friend's apartment near the Piazza di Spagna. We never spoke about our wedding night. Lucy was the only one who knew the details, but I told her that I never wanted to talk about it again. Repeating the story gave it additional power, and I needed to bury it deep inside me. Otherwise, I couldn't go on.

When Beethoven had confessed that he'd contemplated ending his own life, I hadn't understood. How could anyone choose not to exist? Now I appreciated his suffering. Whenever I thought of what the prince had done to me, I felt humiliated and racked with guilt. I should have stabbed him with a pair of scissors, sunk my teeth into him, kicked him, jabbed him—anything. But I hadn't, and I hated myself for it. Thoughts of suicide flitted through my head. I could take a potion and drift off to sleep. I'd leave instructions for my requiem Mass, requesting that someone—not Robert—play the first movement of the *Moonlight*. But I didn't have the courage for suicide, or perhaps I was too sensible. I'd never had much patience for the suicidal hero of Goethe's *The Sorrows of Young Werther*. My punishment was to live.

While Robert spent his days putting the final touches on *The Little Page*, Lucy and I went sightseeing. Walking around in the persistent rain, we followed the typical tourist route, visiting the Colosseum, the

Forum, the Capitol, the Arch of Constantine, the Pantheon, the Vatican. I lit candles in countless churches but didn't offer up any prayers. I no longer knew what to ask for. I didn't know if I even believed in God anymore.

We returned to Vienna in January 1804 for the premiere of *The Little Page* at the Theater an der Wien. Beethoven still kept a room there, but I didn't expect him to be in the audience. Robert's opera ran for only four performances, with critics disparaging his slavish imitation of Mozart and Salieri. Unfortunately, he wasn't discouraged.

After the last performance, as Lucy and I were packing for Naples, my mother rushed into my bedchamber. We'd hardly spoken since my honeymoon, and my first inclination was to tell her to leave, but she didn't give me a chance.

"Joseph is dead!" she announced. "I just received word from Anna."

"How?" I asked weakly. It didn't seem possible. I had just seen him at the wedding in November, and he had appeared to be in good health.

"He caught a bad chill bringing his two boys to Prague. His symptoms didn't appear dire at first, but then he developed consumption. Josephine was with him at the end."

Joseph had helped me through my miscarriage, kept my secret safe, and shared his experience of being expelled from Vienna. That he would die seemed a fitting coda to this excruciating period of my life.

"Whenever you feel sorry for yourself," my mother said, "just think of poor Josephine. She has no money, and she's about to give birth to Joseph's child."

I thought of the other "adopted" children running wild through Palais Deym and asked what would happen to them.

"An orphanage probably," my mother said. "Josephine has enough problems."

I remembered my promise to Joseph that I'd watch over her if anything happened to him, but I couldn't do that from Naples. I left Lucy to finish packing and took the carriage to the Theater an der Wien. I knew that Beethoven, even without my encouragement, would happily serve as her guardian angel and perhaps more, but I wanted to be certain. Besides, I needed to see him one final time.

When I knocked on the door, he shouted, "Who's there?"

"Julie," I shouted back. I was no longer Giulietta.

"Who?" he yelled.

"Julie . . . Julie Guicciardi."

"Don't you mean Countess Gallenberg? Go away!"

"I'm not here for myself, but for Josephine," I said. "She needs you."

"You need me? Ha! All of Vienna is laughing about your husband's wretched opera. Perhaps poor Beethoven doesn't look so bad to you anymore. I won't take you back no matter how much you beg."

"I'm not begging for myself."

"Perhaps the 'little page' can help you—if he hasn't been already confined to the state prison on charges of musical malfeasance!"

He was silent for a few moments, and then I heard him at the pianoforte, playing the first movement of the *Moonlight* as if Robert had written it. His skill at mockery was unrivaled.

"Won't you ever forgive me?" I implored. But he couldn't hear my voice above the pianoforte, and I couldn't listen to him desecrate my sonata. I pressed my lips to the door and said goodbye. The following day, we left for Naples.

PART TWO

20

O ur house overlooked the Bay of Naples, where fishermen in small open boats cast their nets into the glimmering sea. When the winds quieted down, I could hear them sing "Trippole Trappole," an old folk song about a white butterfly that nipped someone's heart. The words didn't make any sense, but then nothing did. I was nearly eight months pregnant with Prince Lichnowsky's child, married to a man I despised, and separated from the one I loved. The view was my sole pleasure.

Beyond the fishing boats, the tiny island of Megaride, with its hulking Egg Castle, captivated me with its tragic tale of love and loss. It marked the spot where the body of the mythical siren Parthenope washed up on the rocks. She had tried to seduce Odysseus with her sweet voice, but he'd instructed his sailors to stuff wax in their ears and tie him to the ship's mast. He sailed right past her. Distraught, she threw herself into the sea. Who could blame her? She'd been rejected. A white butterfly had nipped her heart.

Robert spent his days as a banker at Fries & Co. He hated the work—passionately. That and his music were the only things that aroused him. After dinner he would immediately sit down at my pianoforte and compose for hours. I put wax in my ears and fantasized about running away with my favorite fisherman. He was young, not more than sixteen, with lustrous black hair and skin the color of copper. He often fished without his shirt, and whenever he cast his net, I admired his sinewy arms.

I did whatever I could to take my mind off Beethoven. Nights were the hardest. He frequently appeared in my dreams, hurling angry insults, smashing precious objects, pushing me through endless doorways. Other times he'd look so vulnerable that I'd wake up gasping for air. Sometimes I'd hear his music, tossing and turning on the tide of his notes. I missed everything about him—the heft of his body, the taste of coffee on his lips, the sweet-sour smell that pervaded his crumpled cravat. I thought of Therese's comments about Josephine's lively conjugal relationship with Joseph. I'd wanted that with Beethoven. He had stirred something in me.

I knew I shouldn't be dreaming about a man who'd damned me to hell but delighting in the baby inside me. It wasn't its fault that it had been conceived against my will. But despite its kicks and jabs, I felt nothing for the tiny creature, and then one day I felt nothing at all. Lucy caught me running my hand over my stomach and asked if something was wrong. "I think it's dead," I said. A part of me was relieved.

She immediately arranged for the carriage to take us to the Hospital for the Incurables, which was built in the sixteenth century to treat patients with syphilis. The hospital now included an obstetrics department, and though I showed no outward signs of syphilitic disfigurement, no ulcerating sores that prompted people to look away, I, too, felt incurable.

The doctor who examined me had sympathetic brown eyes and the soothing manner of someone accustomed to dealing with screaming women in labor, but I wasn't screaming. I was strangely calm. Running his fingers over my bulging stomach, he applied light but confident pressure. *"È morto,"* I said softly. *"È morto!"*

Unwilling to concede, he placed his ear on my swollen belly, listening for a heartbeat he'd never hear. *"Mi dispiace,"* he said finally.

I asked if I could leave, but the doctor explained that I'd still have to go through labor. Since the birth process had already started to shut down, he warned that it would be difficult. It wasn't enough that I'd had to carry Prince Lichnowsky's baby in my stomach for eight months. The consequences of that fateful encounter remained inside me even after all life was extinguished.

"Please let me go!" I begged, grabbing the doctor's arm. How could I give birth to something dead? It went against nature. Beethoven's baby, my luminous fairyfly, had gracefully flown away. But this thing, this cruel memento, wouldn't succumb without a fight.

The doctor, gently prying away my fingers, introduced me to Sister Immaculata, an elderly nun in a voluminous black-and-white habit, a large wooden rosary dangling from her waist. I heard the doctor whisper, "Make sure she doesn't get up." The good sister tried to distract me by suggesting we recite the rosary. We were on the third mystery when Robert arrived.

"My child, I have lost my child," he cried. We'd spent so little time talking about anything, least of all the baby, that I was shocked by his sudden outpouring of grief. He tried to hold my hand, but I pushed his away. I wanted nothing to do with him.

"This is the father?" the nun asked.

"Yes," Robert replied. "Is there any hope?"

"None," I said.

My labor began three days later, with Sister Immaculata urging me to *spingere, spingere.* "Push, push." For the next eighteen hours, I writhed and screamed and shouted curses. When the baby finally emerged, I felt an odd sense of achievement. I had given birth. But then the silence, the deadly silence. Not a wail, not even a whimper.

No sound at all. I heard the sister murmur, "It's a boy. Would you like to hold it?"

"No," I said. "Please take it away." I closed my eyes in case I caught a glimpse of it.

She patted my hand. "I'm sure this is the most devastating thing you have ever experienced."

"No," I cried. "I've experienced far worse."

Days were lost in delirium. At one point I heard the doctor mutter, *"febbre puerperale"* ("childbed fever") and something about a possible transfer to the *"anticamera della morte"*—"the dying ward." I recalled the tourist phrase *"Vedi Napoli e poi muori!"*—"See Naples and then die!"

I had seen Naples.

Viewing Naples from my window apparently didn't qualify as actually "seeing" Naples, so I lived. My body, blissfully ignorant, began to produce milk for a baby already in its grave. I'd lost control over everything. My body wasn't my own. My life wasn't my own. Melancholia descended upon me like a black net. All I could do was stare out the window. As a Calabrian bagpiper played a mournful tune on the street below, I watched my strapping fisherman wrestle a slithering branzino. He seemed elated when he tossed it into the boat. I envied his simple happiness.

Lucy was concerned that I wasn't eating, but food had lost its flavor. Our cook was apparently excellent and was willing to make anything I wanted, but I'd consume a few bites and then tell her to take it away. When a month or more had gone by—time had blurred like the drone of a bagpipe—Robert asked if we could talk. He wanted me to have a child with someone else. He thought it would be good for me and also for him. He was afraid that people might question his manhood.

"What do you propose I do?" I asked, looking out the window. "Give myself to one of the fishermen?"

"Are you mad! I won't have a fisherman father my child."

He left in a huff, returning to the pianoforte, where he began to improvise on a melody that sounded like "Trippole Trappole."

I stayed current with the goings-on in Vienna through my mother's frequent letters. Having ruined my life, she accepted her responsibility to keep me entertained, and her writing was lively and filled with gossip. Though I wanted nothing to do with her, she was my main link to Beethoven. Our correspondence was fairly one sided. She wrote about all the soirées and concerts she'd attended. I described clams and tuna and sea bream.

I learned that Beethoven was a frequent visitor to Palais Deym, where the widowed Josephine had four children under the age of six. She had also inherited all of Joseph's debts. Since he'd left half of Palais Deym to the children, she couldn't sell it and was forced to rent out rooms. Josephine had been raised to play music and marry well, not run a boardinghouse with a wax museum downstairs. It overwhelmed her. "Therese tells me that Josephine's swamp fever has returned and that she can't stop crying and screaming," my mother wrote. "At least she has Louis. He visits every day to give her lessons and provide the poor girl some comfort."

I pictured them side by side at the pianoforte, Beethoven praising her playing, Josephine flushed with pride. I imagined their bodies brushing against each other, knees momentarily touching, fingers coming together. I could see his muscular hands, the dark ferocious eyes, the black scowl that could suddenly pass like a thunderstorm. I still remembered his sweetness, so precious for being unexpected. I wondered if he showed the same affection toward her. In my darkest moments, I found myself wishing that she would finally go mad and be committed to the Narrenturm. But then I recalled her kindness to me during my miscarriage and berated myself for being so cruel.

That fall, Armgard Schulenburg came to visit. I hadn't seen her since our strange encounter at Abano Terme, when she had asked me to bear Friedrich's child, but we'd corresponded periodically. She and Friedrich had recently moved from Saint Petersburg to Vienna, where Friedrich had assumed a new diplomatic post. They were taking a holiday before he began his official duties.

Armgard gasped when she saw me. Though I'd once derived a certain pleasure in my appearance, I hadn't been near a looking glass in months. "Dear Julie, you're all skin and bones," she said. "What happened?"

I told Armgard about my stillborn baby but didn't mention anything about Robert's disability. As far as she knew, we enjoyed a typical arranged marriage of minor satisfaction. She hadn't changed at all, still the precocious child, with big eyes, dimples, innocent smile. She told me how sorry she was that I'd lost the baby, reminding me that at least I could bear children. It was then I confided about Robert's problem. She was understandably confused about the dead baby's patrimony.

"You took a lover so soon?" she asked. "In a way, it's admirable. If your husband can't perform, I suppose there's no sense waiting. But from our previous conversations, you struck me as a cautious woman. The father of your child, is he still your lover?"

"The man is no more."

"He's dead too?"

"In a manner."

"Dearest Julie," she said, taking my hand. "What a terrible time you've had! But don't you see? It's fate. You and Friedrich . . . you both want children."

"It's too soon," I demurred. "I couldn't possibly."

"This from a woman who took a lover immediately after her nuptials?" She laughed, and I laughed too. I had forgotten how good it felt. I pointed out my fisherman, admitting that I watched him every day.

"Julie, you must get out," she scolded. "You will lose your mind if you remain cooped up here."

She and Friedrich had arranged to travel to Pompeii, and she insisted I come with them. "It will make you forget everything," she promised.

I was nervous about joining them. I hadn't been outside in months and had been staring at the sea so long that I felt like a siren, part human, part monster. Lucy forced me to go. "Remember how much you enjoyed waltzing with the count," she said. "You've never been excited about another man, except Herr Beethoven, and I'm sorry, milady, but he is lost to you."

All my gowns were much too big for me, but Lucy tied a ribbon around the waist of one to disguise its poor fit. My hair had grown out and now reached the top of my shoulders. She braided it and then pinned it to the top of my head. I was no longer La Bella Guicciardi, the fashionable girl with the short coiffure, but Countess Gallenberg, an emaciated woman in a loveless marriage who fancied a fisherman.

I held Lucy's hand as I walked outside. The sun was blinding and I couldn't see the carriage. "Over here," Armgard called, and the coachman helped me inside. Friedrich looked more handsome than I'd remembered, and it made me feel worse about my own diminished appearance. I was awkward and tongue tied and kept staring at my fingers. I noted that my sapphire betrothal ring matched his eyes. As the carriage passed the island of Megaride, the sun hit the Egg Castle, prompting Friedrich to explain its origins. The Roman poet Virgil had reputedly placed a magic egg beneath the stone foundation to keep the fortress safe. If the egg broke, Naples would be destroyed.

This prompted a discussion of the fraught political situation in the city, where King Ferdinand and Queen Maria Carolina were universally reviled. After Napoleon won and then lost Naples five years earlier, it was rumored that the queen beheaded all the nobles suspected of French collaboration. "As Marie Antoinette's sister, one would have thought she might have shown a little mercy," Armgard remarked. "It's well known that the king and queen despise each other. She once said she'd rather be cast into the sea than marry him."

"My dear husband Bertie was lost at sea," Lucy said, eliciting sympathy and a question from Armgard about whether Bertie was a sailor. "No, a coppersmith," she said, and we left it at that.

Once we arrived at Pompeii, we gave our bags to the porter at the Hotel Diomède, where we had booked rooms for the night, and then proceeded to the ruins. Hordes of uniformed guides immediately encircled us. While Friedrich negotiated with one, I inspected the souvenirs, which ranged from florid paintings of Vesuvius to rows of wax phalli. Seeing the puzzled look on my face, a middle-aged Englishman, cheeks flushed from the sun, explained that I was looking at votive candles.

"Votive candles?" I said, still confused. "But aren't they supposed to be used in worship?"

"Pompeii was a very sybaritic place," he replied before introducing himself as a member of the Lunar Society of Birmingham, England. "We meet each Monday on the week closest to the full moon. We call ourselves lunatics." He chuckled and then presented his nephew, who was finishing up the Grand Tour, a practice that introduced young men of means to the art and culture of Western Europe. They were accompanied by the nephew's tutor, who was secreting away a wax phallus in his waistcoat.

The Englishmen tagged along as I rejoined Friedrich and the others, who were listening to the guide rattle off Pompeii's terrifying history. After Vesuvius erupted in AD 79, burning rocks and gases rained down on the city, killing several thousand inhabitants and blanketing the city in ash. It remained abandoned until 1748, when explorers found that beneath the layers of dust and pumice, Pompeii was nearly intact. We toured the amphitheater, temples, baths, and brothels. Visible on the narrow streets were the ruts of carts and chariot wheels. Some of the villas still bore the word *"Salve"* or "Greetings." Poking my head into one, I glimpsed a female skeleton, its bony fingers clutching a piece of gold jewelry. The woman had tried to take it with her before the sky fell down.

Pompeii's most explicit items were stored in a locked room that was open to men for an extra fee. Friedrich declined out of respect for us, but something made me want to go inside. Armgard and Lucy stayed behind while Friedrich slipped the guide a few extra coins so I could join them. Satisfied that he had earned his wages by merely unlocking the door, the guide loitered outside while my English "lunatic" conducted the tour.

He pointed out small bronzes and marble sculptures of copulating couples, men and women, men and men; and a vast assortment of decorative phalli—on lamps, wind chimes, and a slab of red travertine. The tile bore the inscription *"Hic habitat felicitas"* or "Here dwells happiness."

"Living in the shadow of Vesuvius, the Pompeiians wanted to enjoy life while they could," the Englishman explained. *"Carpe diem."*

Later in the afternoon, we climbed Vesuvius, the men on mules, the women seated on small armchairs that were fastened on long poles and hoisted by several young men. We stopped midway at the San Salvatore hermitage to have a glass of Lacryma Christi, the local wine. As we continued upward, I saw the rose-colored sunset over the Bay of Naples, until everything turned darker and darker. It was night by the time we reached the summit, and strangely quiet. As we carried on by foot, we circled the crater, our shoes sinking into the thick layers of soil and ash. With only the stars for illumination, the lava within the crater blazed so brightly it seemed far too beautiful to have extinguished Pompeii. I thought back on the woman who'd grabbed her jewelry before she died.

Carpe diem.

The experience at Pompeii helped lift my despair. After witnessing the aftermath of so much death and destruction, I realized I couldn't alter the past any more than the ossified woman could have stopped the volcanic eruption. The scar on my palm had faded from bright red to pink. It would always be with me, but I wanted to feel alive again.

I told Armgard that I would accept her offer. It made sense. Neither of us could have children with our spouses, so why should we all suffer? I wasn't sure how it would work out. We didn't even live in the same countries, but Friedrich was handsome and intelligent and I'd been drawn to him from the first time we met at Prince Lichnowsky's ball. I'd have a baby with a good lineage, and Armgard would keep her marriage intact. Even if Friedrich didn't see the child very often, Armgard believed it would be enough for him. I had my doubts, but it was her marriage, not mine, and she greeted the news enthusiastically. She did, however, provide a caveat. She made me promise that I'd never become his wife. "It would break my heart," she said.

The idea had never even crossed my mind. I was still in love with Beethoven and had no plans to steal anyone's husband. I assured her that I viewed it as a business contract between two people who shared the same goal. "Three people," she reminded me, and then, remembering Robert, amended it to four.

Robert was so pleased that he even stopped playing the pianoforte for a few minutes to address it. "Schulenburg comes from a long line of field marshals and generals, and his family owns a very fine estate in Saxony."

"You've done research on him?"

"I've made discreet inquiries. I couldn't have come up with a better solution myself. *Brava!*"

After agreeing on the plan, I began to have second thoughts. "I don't think I can do this," I told Lucy as she brushed my hair and laid out my ivory silk bedgown. "I hardly know Friedrich. Maybe he's a drunk and a total degenerate."

"He doesn't strike me that way," Lucy said, helping me into the bedgown. "He seems very polite. Of course, you never know what he'll do in the bedchamber. Sometimes even the mildest of men turn into brutes."

"*Lucy!* This isn't helpful!"

"Now, now. Don't fret. You said he waltzed beautifully. That's a good sign."

After she'd left, I paced up and down, trying not to think of my wedding night. This was different. This time it was my choice. I had to admit that the situation was very strange, but in my brief sexual history, I had known little else. I'd bedded a musical genius and been raped by a prince. As for the diplomat, I would have to wait and see.

Friedrich knocked on the door, and after I told him to come in, he stood on the threshold looking extremely uncomfortable.

"Armgard says that you wish this?" he asked hesitantly.

"I think it's a reasonable course of action."

"Reasonable, only if you desire it," he said, nervously running his fingers through his blond hair. I noticed that he had a cowlick on the right side. It appeared to be his only physical flaw.

"I'm not sure where desire fits in," I lectured. "We both want a child. Think of it as a diplomatic transaction. Love doesn't have a place in such an arrangement."

He looked hurt, which surprised me, for he had always seemed so confident. "Countess, I will leave if you would like," he said with an edge in his voice. He was still standing at the door, so I invited him in and we drank some wine. I suddenly felt shy and tried to remember what Madame Violette had taught me, but I realized that he probably wouldn't need my help. A man who waltzed as gracefully as he did was no stranger to seduction.

After we'd finished half the bottle, he took my hand, gently kissed it, and then led me over to the bed. "Let me help you undress," he said, untying the satin ribbon at my waist and removing my silk slippers. I stood before him naked, feeling ashamed of my body. Armgard was younger and hadn't borne any children, while I had endured two pregnancies. Silver marks, like small fish, flickered across my stomach.

"I'm not what I once was," I said haltingly. "There was a time when—"

He put his fingers to my lips and told me to hush. "You are lovely." When I looked away, he turned my face toward him. "Julie, you are still as beautiful as the day we met."

Friedrich started to take off his clothes, but I reached up and unbuttoned his shirt and then removed his britches. The lessons from Madame Violette were coming back, but it didn't matter, for he was soon on top of me, his tall, muscular body encompassing mine. He was extremely gentle but also demonstrated a strength and assurance that aroused me. He kissed me tenderly on the lips, and something stirred inside me. And then I heard it—the *Moonlight*. I tried to block out the music, focusing on the sensations in my body. Was the droning emanating from my head or the bagpipes outside the window? The droning developed into the opening ostinato triplets before it progressed into *Trauermusik*. I thought of Prince Lichnowsky, the humiliating spanking, the total degradation of body and soul. The black net descended over me, a spiderweb of lies and betrayals. I couldn't breathe.

"Please, no!" I cried, pushing him hard in the chest. "No!"

He immediately rolled off. "Did I hurt you?" he asked. "I apologize." He was shaken and didn't seem to know what to do.

"I'm sorry," I said, covering my bare breasts with the sheet. "It's just that I haven't done this in a very long time."

"I understand. Armgard explained about your husband."

"Not only that. I'm in love with someone else—Herr Beethoven. We were to be married, but Prince Lichnowsky put an end to it."

"Lichnowsky is the devil himself," Friedrich said. "He has a reputation."

I didn't want to add to it by admitting that he'd also raped me. It was too shameful, too agonizing. I'd throw myself into the sea before I'd ever say those words.

"You are still in love with Herr Beethoven?" Friedrich asked. "Then I should be going." He kissed me gently on the forehead. As he turned to get up, I admired the broad width of his shoulders, the strong jaw, the waves in his thick blond hair.

"Friedrich," I whispered.

He looked at me with his penetrating blue eyes, kind, compassionate, forgiving. I couldn't let him leave. If I did, I'd be mired in mourning music, a petrified corpse preserved in ash. I took a deep breath, pulled him toward me, and for the next hour, the drone was a distant hum.

21

I embraced the coming of summer with an enthusiasm I hadn't thought possible six months earlier. I was pregnant with Friedrich's child, a chance to start over. The doctor had advised me to stay indoors, but with the brilliant sky and balmy weather, Lucy and I took a stroll outside. I found Naples a spectacle—outlandish, comical, a city of marked extremes. Extravagantly garbed noblemen mixed with black-robed monks, sailors, fruit sellers, fishmongers, and the ever-present *lazzaroni*. The poorest of the poor, they often slept in wicker baskets and spent their days picking lice off each other's bodies.

I soon became fatigued, so we rested in a piazza beneath the shadow of a giant obelisk and watched a marionette show. It starred Pulcinella, the pot-bellied man of the people, and his feisty wife, who traded insults and blows with equal vigor. Grabbing his cudgel, she knocked him out as women of all ages cheered. Lucy and I were among the loudest, which drew stares from the crowd. We weren't the typical women at marionette shows, though our sympathies were in alignment.

Returning home, we walked along streets paved in blocks of dark lava, colorful laundry flapping in the wind. We stopped in a *pasticceria* for a slice of cake made from ricotta, lemon, and orange-flower water. It was delicious. My senses had returned. Perhaps I could be happy here.

"Milady, I have something to tell you," Lucy said as we approached the house. "You have a visitor."

Was it Beethoven? Except for traveling to the countryside, he rarely left Vienna.

Friedrich? He had never responded when I shared the good news of my pregnancy. Armgard sent congratulations from them both. I realized it was a wife's duty to handle the correspondence, but I was hurt. Maybe I was a fool to expect more. We had an arrangement, the equivalent of a treaty, and his kindness toward me could have been mere diplomacy. But I was thinking about him more and more, wondering if the baby would have his almond-shaped blue eyes.

"It's your mother," Lucy said, putting a stop to my daydream. "She wanted to surprise you."

My mother was the last person I wanted to see. She had traded me as surely as Aunt Anna traded horses. I knew I wasn't unique in that respect. If it hadn't been Robert, it would have been someone else, although anyone else would have been an improvement. To be fair, she didn't know beforehand that Robert was impotent or that the prince would serve as a wedding-night surrogate. But she had known of my love for Beethoven and didn't flinch when I was banished to Naples.

"My dearest Jülchen," my mother said when I entered the drawing room. "You look wonderful, but where have you been? Not out walking, I hope. The city is filthy. I actually saw men living in baskets! You wouldn't see that in Vienna."

"No, I wouldn't, because I'm not *in* Vienna," I replied sharply.

"That's all in the past," my mother replied. "Besides, the wonderful climate more than makes up for a few men in baskets. Your father wished he could have accompanied me, but he is too busy doing whatever he does at the chancellery."

"How is Papa?"

"The same." She sighed. "He reads books. He doesn't get the promotions he is promised. He reads more books."

"Does he ever ask about me?"

"No. But he doesn't ask about me either, and I'm his wife."

"Not a very loyal one."

Ignoring the comment, my mother asked if I'd found a pianoforte teacher, because it was important for me to keep up my lessons. I told her, for reasons of which she was very aware, that I intended to never play again.

"You're depriving yourself of music as a form of protest?" she asked. "That doesn't sound very sensible. Karl bought me a new pianoforte from Frau Streicher. I'm learning Pamina's aria from *The Magic Flute*." She started singing, "'Ah, I feel it, it has disappeared / Forever gone— love's happiness.'"

"No truer words were ever sung."

"Julie, if you're going to be so morose, I'll regret that I made the long journey."

"I apologize." I didn't want her to leave before I caught up on the latest gossip. "Is Herr Beethoven still giving Josephine lessons?"

"Lessons—and more!" she said, taking a bite of a cream-filled *sfogliatella* that Lucy had bought earlier in the day. "This is really delicious! Naples does have its merits. Still, I think Viennese desserts are—"

"Josephine and Herr Beethoven?" My mother could flit from conversation to conversation like a butterfly. It made for charming chitchat at soirées but was otherwise infuriating.

"He's in love with her and she with him," she said, finishing off the pastry. "It makes one wonder if there's a weakness in the Brunswick line that makes certain females more susceptible to falling in love with madmen."

"Better a brilliant madman than a mediocre fool," I muttered.

My mother went on to say that Beethoven had even dedicated a song to Josephine—"To Hope"—but that Prince Lichnowsky had seen it, causing him great concern. "He pretended he was happy, telling Louis that he held Josephine in the highest esteem. But then Karl confessed that he would make sure to end things if the relationship became serious. He asked if I knew anything about it, but as my loyalty lies with my family, I said nothing."

"Your loyalty lies with your family? Really, Mama, you astound me."

"Go ahead, criticize your poor old mother, as if I haven't had my share of burdens. Princess Christiane has cancer. In her breasts!"

"I'm not sure how that affects you, unless, in addition to sharing the same man, you also share the same body parts."

"Karl is being more attentive to her, and we're not spending as much time together."

"That must be painful," I said, attempting to muster sympathy. The prince was contemptible, but my mother did love him, and I understood what it was like to yearn for someone. I asked if she'd heard Beethoven's Third Symphony. He'd been working on it when we were planning to move to Paris, but so much had happened that Paris seemed as distant as ancient Pompeii.

"I was just about to tell you when we began talking about that dreadful woman . . . I hope Vesuvius won't interrupt while I'm here."

"I believe you mean 'erupt' . . . the Third Symphony?"

"Several friends who went to the private performance at Prince Lobkowitz's said it was ghastly. I attended the public premiere at the Theater an der Wien. It was very long and very strange. And it didn't help that Louis was conducting. Standing on his toes and flailing about like someone possessed by the devil. But I will say he's created something totally original."

"He was going to call it *Bonaparte*," I said wistfully.

"Not anymore. After Napoleon decided to become emperor, Louis was so furious he scratched out the dedication. Karl told me all about it. Thankfully, he didn't mutilate yours. Before I left, Karl asked if I'd have a word with Josephine. He's hoping that she can get him to finish his opera. It's called *Leonore, or the Triumph of Conjugal Love*—not that Louis would know anything about that."

My mother explained that it was yet another "rescue opera," but this time the woman rescues the man. I wondered if Beethoven chose the libretto with Josephine in mind, though if anyone needed rescuing, I wasn't sure she'd be the first person to call upon.

"Karl will eventually take care of Josephine," my mother reiterated. "You have nothing to fear."

"I want Louis to be happy."

"With Josephine?" my mother scoffed. "Oh, Julie, don't be ridiculous. You want him for yourself, but that's never going to happen. You're just being greedy. You have a wonderful life. You're having Robert's child. It's like a rescue opera, and Robert has rescued you!"

The week we spent together wasn't entirely unpleasant. My mother had an indomitable spirit, and while I couldn't forgive her for what she'd done, a part of me still loved her. As she readied to leave, she handed me one of Beethoven's recent sonatas. "You really must start playing again," she insisted. "You will miss him less if you do."

When I kissed her goodbye, I saw that she had tears in her eyes and noticed for the first time that her beauty had faded. At forty-eight, she had white streaks in her blonde hair and deep creases around her mouth. I wondered how much longer she could keep the prince interested. When she descended into the carriage, she whispered, "Please be happy, dear," and then she waved, and the horses took off.

The sonata was the closest I'd come to Beethoven since I left Vienna, and I held the sheet music to my heart, caressing it the way I'd once stroked his cheek. The title page read "Grand Sonata for the Pianoforte." It was dedicated to Count Ferdinand von Waldstein, one of his earliest patrons in Bonn. I opened it, and Beethoven was right there, in the first chords, the constant key changes, the grueling technical challenges. It was like a heartbeat racing out of control. My own heart began to accelerate, and I put the sheet music down, picked it up, and put it back down again. It was beyond me.

I named my new son Hugo, which means "bright in mind and spirit," and he was all that—lively and energetic, with Friedrich's vibrant eyes and blond hair. The same doctor who had been at the hospital when I delivered my stillborn son supervised the delivery of my robust one. When I saw Sister Immaculata, I wept with joy, and she said, "God can work miracles." Though I'd been baptized in the Catholic faith, we had gone to church only for weddings and funerals. And after what happened with Prince Lichnowsky, I'd put God out of my mind entirely. But I did feel that a miracle had happened. When we brought the baby home, Robert couldn't stop staring at it. "I think he looks like me," he said proudly. "I know he's not mine, but I see a little Gallenberg in him."

When I wrote to Armgard and Friedrich, she immediately wrote back expressing their mutual delight. They were both eager to see the baby, but with Napoleon on the march, it wasn't safe to travel. I was miffed that Friedrich hadn't bothered to write, but several days later, I received the following note:

> *My dearest Julie,*
> *You have given me a son, and for that I will always be grateful. A man could not ask for a finer woman to mother his child. I look forward to meeting Hugo when the war is over. I am not optimistic that we will defeat Napoleon. I know few men who are as willful and determined, except your Beethoven. I often think of the night we spent together, but I remain true to our bargain that love has no place in such an arrangement.*
> *Your servant,*
> *Friedrich*

I was disappointed, yet what did I expect? I'd made my intentions clear, but however much I loved Beethoven, I'd also developed strong feelings for Friedrich. To call it love was premature, but it was more than a mere flirtation. We now had a child together. When I looked at Hugo, I saw Friedrich and my heart melted.

We hired a wet nurse named Anna who had six children of her own and twelve younger siblings. Every time I held Hugo, I was afraid I'd drop him, but Anna had no such fears. After nursing him, she'd hoist him over her shoulder, slap him on the back, and wait for a loud burp. With all the noises he made, I worried that he might develop stomach problems like Beethoven, but Anna told me that it was all perfectly normal—music in the key of ordinary life.

Three months later, Napoleon defeated the Austrians and allied Russians at the Battle of Austerlitz and set his sights on Naples. Before Robert left for work, I told him that I needed a distraction and that Lucy and I were going to visit the *presepe*, the elaborate nativity scenes set up in churches across the city.

Robert was holding Hugo in his arms, singing a lullaby he'd written for him. Now that he had a son to carry on his name, we'd been getting along much better. He was very affectionate toward the baby, delighting in his crooked little smile and perfect toes. When Hugo began waving his arms in time to Robert's music, he proclaimed him a budding conductor. It touched me that Robert loved Hugo so much, never mentioning Friedrich or the circumstances of his conception. As he handed the baby over to Anna, I told him that Lucy and I probably wouldn't be back until midafternoon.

Viewing the *presepe* was like stepping into an imaginary world that combined the sacred with the profane. Drawing on the skills of multiple artisans, from sculptors to seamstresses, the figurines were incredibly lifelike, representing a wide range of the populace. By setting the nativity scene in Naples, not Bethlehem, butchers mingled with magi, the *lazzaroni* with the Holy Family. Lucy and I visited three or four churches before the sirocco winds started to blow. Instead of stopping for lunch, we headed home early.

Hugo was sleeping, so I went into the drawing room to finish reading *The Vicar of Wakefield*, about the Primrose family, whose calamities exceeded my own. Before I reached the end, I heard noises from Robert's bedchamber. I knew he was at work, so I walked down the hallway to investigate. Opening the door, I saw Robert crouching over someone and immediately thought of the erotic images from Pompeii. I tried to sneak out, but he heard me and jumped off the bed. He was naked, his member fully erect. Before I ran out, I caught sight of his lover. It was my fisherman.

I raced down the hallway and into my bedchamber, telling Lucy that I needed to be alone. Robert, who had dressed hastily, appeared a few minutes later. He smelled of fish.

"Julie, please don't be angry at me," he said pitifully.

"I'm not angry. But I'm most definitely confused. I do recall you telling me that you were impotent. Unless my eyes deceived me, you didn't appear so."

"I am impotent—with women," he explained. "Or at least I was on my first few attempts. My mother took me to Madame Violette's, and several of her whores treated me in a most aggressive manner."

"So you had me sleep with two other men because you think whores represent *all* women?" I shouted.

"It is not like that at all. I didn't want to embarrass you in case I failed."

"How very kind of you! I suppose using Prince Lichnowsky as a substitute was another act of your generosity."

"It was," he said softly. He asked if he could sit down because he was feeling a little faint, the combination of sodomy and memories of our wedding night weakening his nerves. He kept mopping his brow with a lace handkerchief that he'd snatched from my dressing table. I'd have to throw it away.

"I *was* being generous," he continued. "Karl and I, we were lovers. Do you think you were the only one who suffered when our baby died? I wanted to raise his child."

It was then that I, too, began to feel light headed. "You were Karl's lover?" I asked feebly.

"Only once or twice."

I couldn't believe what I was hearing. Was I still reading *The Vicar of Wakefield*? Had I lapsed into a literary raptus?

"I was fifteen, and he discarded me," he explained.

I began to lose feeling in my face. I touched my lips. They were tingling, as if they wanted to move but couldn't. Raptus had turned to rictus.

"I loved him," he continued. "I kept writing letters, but he never answered them. When I tried to see him, his servants kept turning me away. Finally, I stopped contacting him altogether."

The room was swirling around me. I kept envisioning dancing fish—branzino, grouper, carp—all trapped in nets, waltzing to the music of chaos.

"A few months before our wedding, I confronted him after a concert at Prince Lobkowitz's. He warned me that if I didn't stop, he would expose me."

I didn't even know what he was talking about. "Expose you?" I managed to say.

"As a sodomite. You do realize that in Vienna I could have been jailed or even beheaded."

I had no idea. Who thought of such things?

"Do you know what it's like to live with that fear?" he said.

"So he forced you to marry me?" I asked.

"He gave me a choice."

"Either marry Countess Guicciardi or lose your head? How long did you have to think about it?"

"Longer than you might imagine," he admitted, continuing to mop his brow. "I was suffering from extreme melancholia and considered taking my own life. Beheading was just another option, but I didn't want to disgrace my mother. She doesn't know of my particular persuasion." He swallowed hard. "So now you have the whole story."

It was part of the story but not all, and it was clear that Robert didn't know my version of events. Prince Lichnowsky had blackmailed both of us, but as Robert still seemed to have affection for the man, I kept quiet.

"Are you in love with him?" I asked. "The fisherman?"

"He's beautiful." His face lit up in a way that I'd seen only when he played his own music. "His name is Ramo."

"Ramo," I repeated, as if knowing it made everything perfectly respectable.

"I suppose you'll want a divorce now," he said. "I would understand, but I beg you not to mention . . ."

He looked so forlorn that I immediately reassured him that I'd keep it a secret—one of many—and asked to be left alone. Why did happiness continue to elude me? Just an hour ago, I had been enjoying the Christmas decorations, content with my precious Hugo, and now I'd learned that my formerly impotent husband preferred a man to his own wife. And not only any man, but my fantasy fisherman. All those wasted hours staring at fish! As I paced up and down the room, I felt myself growing increasingly agitated, my heart quickening. I remembered what the doctor had said when I'd fainted at the Golden Griffin: "Many women find Beethoven's music too agitating."

Since I was already in that state, I walked into the music room and sat down at the pianoforte. I was badly out of practice, my fingers stiff and clumsy. After I ran through some scales, I attempted the first few measures of his new composition. It was supposed to be played "with energy," but I wasn't sure if I had the energy or the sufficient talent. Beethoven had once called me stubborn, but his music required more than tenacity. In challenging himself, he pushed mere mortals to the limits of their endurance, in this case, starting in the key of C major and then moving in a feverish manner away from it and back to it. I felt Beethoven's energy; the music mimicked the way he walked—fast, with a driving momentum that left everyone else far behind. When he relaxed his pace, it came as a relief and a surprise. The slow melody was delicate, affectionate—and far too brief. He was running away again.

I persisted through Christmas and the New Year, playing as the French troops marched down the Via Toledo and took possession of an undefended city. I played as Joseph Bonaparte, Napoleon's brother, arrived to assume the crown of Naples. I played while Hugo cried and a fisherman slept in my husband's bed. I played to be reunited with Beethoven, and when I'd reached the end of the sonata, I felt not only that he'd touched my heart but that I was holding his hand in mine.

22

1806–1807

Robert was chosen to write the music for Joseph Bonaparte's coronation festivities, having ingratiated himself with influential people at the new French court. With typical speed and efficiency, he churned out three overtures, eight pieces for a wind band, and numerous dances for a full orchestra. It proved so successful that he was appointed music director at the Palazzo Reale's Court Theater, ending his banking career and my hope of remaining solvent. Our combined family incomes weren't enough to supplement a musician's wages, especially now that Ramo was living with us and taking pianoforte lessons.

Robert described Ramo as his protégé, which didn't fool anybody, least of all the servants. Lucy admitted that it was strange to find Ramo playing scales instead of scaling fish but said she'd had a hunch about Robert all along. "I didn't think he'd go off with a fisherman, mind you, but I have experience with men being lost at sea."

"Not Bertie?" I asked, though everything was beginning to make sense.

"He left me for another coppersmith. Big and brawny too. Somehow you don't expect that. You expect someone more . . . ladylike."

"Oh, Lucy, I'm sorry," I said, hugging her.

"You just have to get on with things, milady. Don't fester in it."

I continued to find joy in the pianoforte. It wasn't a substitute for a fulfilling erotic life, but occasionally the music penetrated so deeply that I could feel it inside me. I returned to the *Moonlight* Sonata, hoping to find it less unsettling. It was still painful, but the pain had become part of me, like the faded striations on my belly, the blue veins coursing down the back of my forearms, the stigma on my palm. After I'd finished the first movement, I looked up to see Ramo standing in the doorway. He immediately apologized and was about to leave when I invited him in. He stood around awkwardly, not wanting to dirty the silk chair, but I asked him to sit down. He was dressed nicely—Robert must have bought him new clothes—and did not smell of fish.

"It is beautiful, what you play," he said. "Roberto, he wrote it?"

"No, no," I replied. "Someone else. His name is Ludwig van Beethoven."

He shook his head. "I don't know him, but I think he is as good as Roberto."

"Better, actually."

He smiled, revealing two missing teeth. "I thought so too, but I was afraid the lady might be offended."

"The lady is not offended at all."

Ramo confided that he hated practicing scales, complaining that it was worse than shucking clams. After spending so much time indoors, he was beginning to lose his muscular physique and healthy color. When I asked why he didn't leave, he admitted that Robert was paying him to stay. "My widowed mother, she is poor and needs the money."

"Don't you love Robert even a little?" I asked.

He shrugged. "A little."

The year passed quickly with little of the drama one associates with living in conquered territory. With the Bonapartes occupying the royal palace, the Neapolitans went about their chaotic lives as they'd done under the Bourbons. With the return of the French soldiers, prostitution was booming again, and the doctors at the Hospital for the Incurables were deluged with cases of syphilis. As the heat of summer approached, the air thick with the smell of overripe melons, I was desperate to leave the city. An opportunity arose when my mother invited me to join her in the spa town of Baden, in the foothills of the Vienna Woods. She wanted to see Hugo and to relate all the delicious gossip she'd been saving up. Robert was busy with his music and encouraged me to go.

We met my mother at a hotel near Johannesbad, one of the main bathing houses in the town center. "He looks exactly like me," my mother said when she first saw Hugo. "He has my blue eyes and light hair." Hugo, who was nearly two years old, used the opportunity to start screaming. It had been a long journey, and he was tired and hungry. "He certainly doesn't have my temperament," my mother observed. "That must be from the Gallenberg side."

Anna, who had stayed on as Hugo's nurse, put him down for a nap, while Lucy unpacked my clothes. My mother and I strolled through the Theresa Gardens, named after Empress Maria Theresa, the only female ruler of the Hapsburg empire. Baden, like Abano Terme, had been built by the ancient Romans who believed that the sulfurous water and vapors were beneficial to wound-healing and rheumatism. Now it functioned as a summer playground for the imperial family, as well as aristocrats and the musicians who sought their patronage. In addition to its beautiful gardens, it had two atmospheric castles and an ancient Roman temple.

"It's so romantic here," my mother said, plucking a rose even though guests were expressly forbidden to touch the flowers. "I wish Karl could be with me. Unfortunately, he's with his wife. Princess Christiane had both breasts removed."

"You sound as if she did it on purpose."

"It's just that I can't stop envisioning one of those horrible paintings of Saint Agatha with her breasts on a platter. But enough gruesomeness! Guess who's coming to join us? Josephine! I ran into her at a concert at Prince Lobkowitz's, and she told me she was traveling to Baden with the children. She's excited to see you."

"Is Louis still pursuing her?" I asked. Since I hadn't seen him in more than three years, I now pictured him as a compilation of musical notes.

My mother plucked another flower. "Yes," she said, sitting down on a bench and inhaling the fragrant smell. "And it's destroyed his relationship with Karl. They're not even speaking anymore." My mother stopped to introduce me to a countess she'd met at a previous outing to Baden. "Her husband died choking on a piece of venison," my mother remarked as the countess walked away.

"Louis?" I prompted.

"Karl suggested that he stop courting Josephine," she continued. "I believe he described her as being too 'fragile,' which is a polite way of putting it. Louis told him that he had no right to interfere. Chairs and punches were thrown. At least Karl hasn't rescinded Louis's stipend—yet."

Josephine and I hadn't stayed in touch since I left Vienna. Our relationship had always been complicated, and now that Beethoven had renewed his love for her, I hoped I'd be able to conceal my jealousy.

She arrived a week later with her four children. For someone who had suffered several nervous breakdowns, multiple bouts of swamp fever, and was doubling as a landlady and proprietor of an insolvent tourist attraction, she looked remarkably well. Derangement and adversity suited her. I introduced her to Hugo, who immediately announced that his birthday was coming up in August. He held up two fingers.

"He's definitely a Brunswick with that light coloring," she observed. "I don't see much of Robert, but they change so rapidly from year to year."

While the nurses took the children out to play, Josephine and I sat in her room and caught up. "I'm sure you've heard about my hardships," she explained. "Joseph left me with very little money. It's exhausting running his business. And Louis . . ."

I waited to hear what she'd say, hoping that she wasn't totally enamored of him.

"I love him deeply," she continued. "You probably think I'm silly. He's not an easy man, and many consider him physically unappealing. I'm sure you don't understand. You have a handsome husband. But he is—"

"Passionate and tender."

"Yes! Sometimes it's too much to handle, but other times it's thrilling." She lowered her voice. "We have not lain together. I would never do anything so improper."

She stood up to gather a handful of papers from her valise, holding them in the air. "These are just some of the letters he has written to me. I should add that his style is somewhat peculiar." She began to read:

> *You my Everything my supreme joy—Alas, no—even in my notes I cannot do so, although in this respect your Nature has not stinted me with gifts, yet this is too little for You. Beat only in silence oh poor heart—you cannot do otherwise—For You—always for You—only You— eternally You—only You until I die.*

She looked up. "Do you think he likes me?"

I stifled the urge to rip all the letters into a thousand pieces. How dare he write such things to Josephine when I had sacrificed everything for him! I tried to stay calm, assuring Josephine that it sounded as if he truly loved her. Unfortunately, this only encouraged her to read more.

> *Oh! beloved J., it is not the drive to the opposite sex that attracts me to you, no, only you, the whole of your Being with all its singularities—has my respect—all*

my feelings—all of my sensibility is chained to you . . .
Long—long—time—may our love last—

She looked over again for support. I nodded and said, "There is no mistaking his affection."

I'd had enough, so I suggested to Josephine that she put away the letters and take in the fresh air. She insisted I hear one more snippet.

"Listen to how he signs the letter: 'Farewell, angel—of my heart— of my life.' Isn't that beautiful? I am the angel of his heart. Have you ever heard anything so romantic?"

I wanted to scream, "Yes, in a letter to me," but I merely said, "Who knew he was capable of such poetry?"

"My family disapproves," she complained. "Even Therese thinks that I should spurn him. As for Mama, she says I'll lose my children if I marry him."

I detected Prince Lichnowsky's handiwork. He and Beethoven might not be speaking, but that didn't mean the prince was above meddling in his love affairs. By appealing to Aunt Anna, who feared social censure more than Josephine's unhappiness, he had a willing ally.

"Louis doesn't have much money," Josephine said, "but it doesn't matter. When I sit next to him at the pianoforte, something happens. It's not just his music, although I can't deny that's part of it. It's his sweetness and vulnerability. Julie, what do you think? You know him. What should I do?"

I wanted to tell her to forget him, that it would never work, because certain people would make sure that every ounce of pure love would be reduced to ash. But I couldn't, because she looked so hopeful.

"You must be true to your heart," I counseled. "But you won't have an easy time."

"I can't imagine life without him."

"No, you can't, but one day you will."

That, of course, was a lie.

Josephine and I spent the week taking long walks and soaking in the warm sulfur pool. Guests could order food and drinks from attentive waiters who stood nearby. Nudity had once prevailed, but now everyone was required to wear long linen robes that clung to the skin like wrapping on a mummy. Josephine couldn't stop talking about Beethoven, even contemplating running away with him and abandoning her children to Therese.

"You don't really mean that," I said. "You love your children."

"Louis does too. He is so kind to them, so caring . . ." She stared straight ahead. "Oh no! Look over there."

A stocky man in the standard linen robe was about to get into the pool. His hair was longer and he'd gained weight around his middle, but there was no mistaking Beethoven. He was carrying a bundle of papers and humming loudly. I had been dreading and longing for this day for three years, and now he was just twenty feet away. Seeing him in person and hearing his familiar gruff voice made him palpably real again. The physician Franz Anton Mesmer believed that a mysterious force regulated human behavior. He called it "animal magnetism." Beethoven's appeal was such that I began to move toward him, until Josephine tugged at my robe.

"Where are you going?" she whispered. "You can't let him see us. I told him I'd be in Martonvásár. He'll catch me in a lie." As she pulled me down next to her, she pointed out Archduke Rudolph, one of Beethoven's patrons and music students. The archduke was drinking a glass of sulfur water while Beethoven stood on the edge of the pool, making changes to a manuscript. As he absentmindedly descended into the water, he bumped into another guest, sending pages flying. He shouted to the archduke for help, and they both lunged after the papers, retrieving all but one page. It floated in our direction.

Josephine, pulling her bathing bonnet down over her face, submerged herself.

Beethoven and the archduke continued to chase after the paper, splashing guests and toppling food and drinks. Ignoring my impulse to shout his name, I turned my back, and as I did, the errant piece of paper brushed my hand. "For God's sake, woman, grab it!" Beethoven bellowed. "It's part of my Mass in C Major for Prince Esterhazy."

I picked up the soggy paper and, without looking at him, held it out. He was so pleased to get it back that he had no interest in finding out who had retrieved it. As Beethoven splashed his way to the opposite end, Josephine and I quickly scrambled out the side exit. As we were leaving, I saw him trying to dry the wet paper by blowing on it, puffing out his cheeks like pictures of the north wind. I sat down on a nearby bench to catch my breath.

"Are you ill?" Josephine inquired. "You look very pale."

"No, no, I'm fine. I stayed in the water too long. That's all."

"I must leave immediately," she said. "I can't risk running into him again. My family will be furious."

Later, when my mother and I were inhaling the vapors in the inhalatorium, she asked if I knew what had happened to Josephine. She had barely said goodbye, gathering up her children and servants and rushing home to Vienna.

"She saw Louis," I explained.

"He's here? Where?"

"In the Roman bath."

"I can't imagine him in any bath," she said, breathing deeply. "He always looks so unkempt. I would advise you to avoid him at all costs. You have a successful husband and a beautiful son. Now . . . when are you going to have another? I'm sure Robert wants that."

I was already hot from the vapors, and my mother's comment infuriated me. *"Robert?"* I said, raising my voice. "Who cares what he wants?"

"I'm sure he wants another baby." Droplets of perspiration were trickling down her forehead and into her eyes. She dabbed at them with a towel.

"He's in love with someone else." The words echoed in the chamber like a Greek chorus. *He's in love with someone else.*

"Julie, don't be such a prude. That shouldn't get in the way. Husbands take lovers all the time."

"Yes, but his lover is a fisherman."

"I'm not sure I heard you correctly. A *fisherman?*"

"Robert prefers men."

"Oh," my mother said, trying not to betray her surprise. Recovering nicely, she recounted how Countess Eggenberg had married such a man, and both were very happy.

"She has a lover, he has a lover, and they all adore Mozart." She paused for a moment. "But a fisherman? Is he cultured at least?"

"He takes pianoforte lessons."

"Does he still . . . fish?"

"He's now a man of leisure."

"I'm sorry," my mother said, "but what could Robert possibly see in a fisherman?"

"Enough so that he's no longer impotent."

"Robert is impotent? Then who fathered Hugo? Please don't tell me it's the fisherman!"

"No, someone else."

"With a title?"

"Yes, a count."

"Oh, thank God! Julie, you scared me to death. The vapors are making me dizzy. I'm feeling quite unwell."

The revelation that Robert was in love with a man who gutted carp temporarily distracted my mother from the news that Beethoven and

I were both in Baden. When she recovered, she insisted that we move to a hotel outside the town center. Since Beethoven kept a fairly strict schedule, it was easy to avoid him, and my mother, realizing my marriage wasn't on terra firma, warned me to steer clear of temptation. "I promised Karl that you wouldn't have anything more to do with him," she explained, "and even though the two men are estranged, the agreement still stands."

My mother tossed off the word "agreement" in such a cavalier fashion that I wanted to tell her what the prince had done to me, but I couldn't say the words. I was still too ashamed.

For the next week I stayed in my room and obsessed over Beethoven. I pictured running into him and learning about his new compositions and telling him about my progress on his sonata for Count Waldstein. I wanted to know if he still had my portrait miniature or if he'd thrown it away. I wanted to know about his hearing and if he could still play the pianoforte and if he really truly loved Josephine. I wanted a simple conversation, nothing more, but I reminded myself that nothing was simple with him. It was all a grand sonata.

I might have remained in my room if Friedrich hadn't accepted my offer to visit. With Vienna only two hours away, I'd wanted him to meet Hugo. I'd also invited Armgard, though I was secretly hoping that she'd be on holiday. When he appeared alone, I wondered whether he'd planned it that way but accepted his vague excuse that Armgard was "traveling." He had brought presents for Hugo, and tears sprung to his eyes when he saw his son playing ball with some of the other children. Embarrassed, he cleared his throat and pretended to cough.

"How should I introduce myself?" he asked. "Am I just a friend?"

"A good friend," I said, calling Hugo over. He didn't want to stop playing, so Anna had to pull him away and he began to wail.

"It has nothing to do with you," I said, trying to reassure Friedrich.

He smiled. "I know. I was a small boy myself once."

"Hugo," I said. "I want you to meet a very special friend. His name is Count Friedrich von der Schulenberg."

Hugo was still sniffling, but, remembering his manners, he bowed and introduced himself as Count Hugo von Gallenberg. Friedrich presented him with a set of colorful toy soldiers. "We could play with them if you like," Friedrich said. Hugo immediately sat down on the grass and began pulling the tin soldiers out of the boxes. "I come from a military family," Friedrich explained.

"Count Schulenburg is a diplomat," I said. "He takes a different approach to conflict."

Watching father and son on the grass, I immediately saw the physical similarity, the light hair, almond-shaped blue eyes, straight nose. Their hands were exactly the same, right down to the long fingers, and yet I recognized the oval shape of my nails. I was marveling at nature's ability to combine and duplicate physical traits when I saw Beethoven walking toward us. This time there was no escape.

"Good day, Herr Beethoven," I said pleasantly. During one of our last encounters, he had thrown me out of his apartment, so I wanted to let him know I didn't hold a grudge. By the hostile way he looked at me, however, he most certainly did. He nodded and grunted something I couldn't make out. It could have been "Countess" or a curse.

"I believe you've met Count Schulenburg," I said loudly. I didn't know how much he could hear.

"Yes, the man who waltzes," Beethoven replied.

"Nice to see you, Herr Beethoven," Friedrich said, rising from the grass. "I hope you've been well."

"I have not. I'm plagued with terrible abdominal pain, diarrhea, and occasional vomiting. The doctors hope the waters will help."

Beethoven never withheld his medical complaints from anyone, even total strangers, but despite his issues, he looked well. He loved walking outdoors, and his skin had turned a deep bronze color. I longed to touch his cheek. He pointed to Hugo and asked, "And this is?"

Hugo had put one of the soldiers in his mouth, and as I bent down to extract it, I said, "It's my son."

"I cannot hear you," Beethoven said. "Who is that child—the one about to choke on a soldier?"

"My son," I repeated, having successfully secured the toy.

Beethoven loosened his grip on his ever-present notebook and it fell to the ground. Since Hugo was already on the grass, he picked it up. "Yours," he said, holding it up.

"Yes, mine," Beethoven replied, bending down to retrieve it. Hugo's smile was so sweet that even Beethoven couldn't help smiling back.

"Play with me?" Hugo said, pointing to the soldiers. Seeing the stricken look on Beethoven's face, I quickly changed the subject and asked about his work. "Play with me," Hugo pleaded while Friedrich crouched down on the grass. "Not you—him!" Hugo said, pointing at Beethoven. Trying to defuse the situation, I picked Hugo up, but he held out his arms to Beethoven, who was about to hold him, until he caught himself.

"I suppose we won't see the resemblance to Count Gallenberg until he starts playing the pianoforte," he said. "Now I must go. I have work to do."

"He's a man of great talent but little charm," Friedrich observed.

"True," I replied as Hugo waved bye-bye.

My mother returned to Vienna, while I remained in Baden for several more days. It gave me a chance to be with Friedrich. Since our relationship had skipped the ritual pleasantries, we had achieved a level of intimacy founded on physical attraction, nothing more. We had a son, but I didn't know anything about Friedrich's parents, or how he grew up, or if he'd always wanted to be a diplomat. During dinner at one of the restaurants overlooking the gardens, we talked at length. He told me about growing up in Saxony, where his grandfather had been the royal tutor of Frederick the Great and his own father had died when he was a young boy. Friedrich was left in the care of his mother and a guardian, whose son was the Romantic poet and philosopher Novalis. He died at twenty-eight, not long after his fifteen-year-old fiancée wasted away from consumption.

"He dedicated a collection of poems to his young fiancée," Friedrich said, "so at least she'll always be remembered."

"I imagine she would have preferred a few more years over a few poems."

"True, but Novalis could only control the poems. He once wrote that 'in a work of art, chaos must shimmer through the veil of order.' Do you agree?"

"I'm not an artist myself, but I know at least one person to whom that applies."

There was silence for a few seconds while we both sipped our wine. Staring out at the garden, I commented on the red and yellow roses that remained vivid in the dusk.

"You're still in love with Herr Beethoven," he stated. Had I been that obvious? Our interaction in the garden had been short and, to a casual observer, dispassionate. But Friedrich wasn't a casual observer. He was adept at dealing with politicians, whose expressions were often difficult to discern.

"It's impossible to love a man like Herr Beethoven," I replied evenly. "I'm not that foolish."

I wasn't sure if I convinced him, since I hadn't convinced myself, but he let the subject drop. Strolling the grounds after dinner, we bumped into the countess whose husband had succumbed to a large piece of venison. She was with a much younger man, greeting us with a cursory nod. Love affairs were so common at the spas that Friedrich's appearance didn't attract any attention above what anyone would consider normal when gazing at a tall, extremely handsome man.

"Did you invite me here only to meet Hugo?" he asked.

"I'd think it would be reason enough."

"You know what I mean," he said, pulling me close. "Did you summon me because you want another child?"

Women were supposed to conceive their next baby as soon as they'd delivered the last one. Conception, pregnancy, childbirth—a perpetual cycle until age or death intervened. After Hugo, I hadn't thought of having a second. I adored him and, in light of my challenging marriage and finances, he was enough for me. I'd never considered another baby with Friedrich. I wasn't even sure if it was part of the strange bargain I'd struck with Armgard.

"I couldn't ask you to do that again," I said.

"Yes, it would be a terrible sacrifice." He smiled, pulling me even closer.

"I wasn't thinking of another child," I explained, "but I can't deny that I wanted to see you again."

"Are things with Count Gallenberg that bad?"

I felt it best to leave out the Ramo story and laughed off the comment. Friedrich led me to his room, where he slowly undressed me; unlike the first time at Pompeii, I wasn't frightened but welcomed his appreciative stare. Hugo had been the only one to touch me in the past two years, but his kisses were a child's kisses, his hugs sweet and innocent. This was not that. There was something powerful between Friedrich and me. It had nothing to do with the drama of music and its capacity to transform apathy into desire through the meticulous placement of notes on a page. It was simple attraction, which of course wasn't so simple, because it relied on its own rhythm, harmony, and heat, but despite the erotic intensity, I felt safe. After what I'd been through, I was enormously grateful.

The next morning, I woke up early and watched him sleep. He was on his back, his naked body stretched to its full length. For someone who spent much of his time in Vienna's salons, he kept himself in excellent physical shape. I liked that he was tall and that we fit well together.

Armgard was tiny, and I wondered if he worried about crushing her. I wondered if he worried about her at all. They had an odd marriage, though most marriages were odd in their own distinctive ways.

Friedrich, opening his eyes, caught me staring at him and asked, "What are you thinking?"

"That I must go," I said unconvincingly. He gathered me into his arms and we picked up where we'd left off the night before, and when we were finished, I realized that I was falling in love with him. I immediately felt guilty because I was also in love with Beethoven. Or was I? I'd experienced so little love in my life that it seemed audacious and downright greedy to love two men. Friedrich hadn't declared his love for me. Beethoven had declared it, but then took it back. So maybe I wasn't so much greedy as ridiculous and stupid.

Friedrich told me that he was leaving after breakfast to join Armgard, or maybe that was a lie. Maybe he was meeting another mistress at another spa. I'd opened myself up to Beethoven, and he'd damned me to hell. What if Friedrich did the same?

"I would like to see you again, in case things don't go according to plan," he said as we walked outside.

"I'm not sure we have a specific agenda," I replied coolly. "This is a business transaction, remember?"

"Is it?" he said, gazing directly at me.

When I didn't respond, he gave me a cordial embrace and left me in the Theresa Gardens. I plucked a rose and scattered the petals to the four winds.

I woke up at five in the morning, and, unable to fall back to sleep, I decided to take a walk through the Kurpark. No one else was around, so I sat down on the grass. The passion I'd experienced with Friedrich made me realize how much my own life lacked passion and purpose. I'd become a chess piece at the mercy of unseen hands. Marry Count

Gallenberg. Live in Naples. Move forward. Move back. It had started to rain, so I got up off the ground and as I did, I heard familiar off-key humming. I was in such a fragile state that I started to walk in the other direction to avoid him, but he called out my name.

"Is that you—Countess Gallenberg?" Beethoven shouted.

He was wearing a nightshirt under his coat and, as usual, was carrying a notebook. It was raining harder now, and my long hair was hanging in wet strands down my shoulders.

"So now you have a lover as well as a husband," he said. "You keep yourself very busy."

"It's not what you think," I replied as the rain continued to pelt.

"I don't think anything. I'm in love with Josephine, as I am sure you've heard from that gossipmonger of a mother of yours." He placed his notebook inside his pocket. He didn't want the rain to smudge his already messy notes.

"You are cruel," I said, awaiting the explosion I knew would come.

"I am cruel? I am cruel?" I could hear him attacking the keyboard. "Have you forgotten what happened?" he went on. "You agreed to marry me and then you went back on your solemn word." *A series of broken chords and a long terminal trill.* "But now I have Josephine." *Recapitulation of the opening theme.* "She is sweet and docile and not a shrew like you." *The conflict between C-sharp and C minor has yet to be resolved.*

"Don't you dare speak to me like that!" I said, wiping rain from my face. "I tried to be nothing but kind and supportive. I gave you everything I had."

"Yes, you did. You acted like a whore." *Sforzando* ("suddenly with force").

I slapped him hard across the face. He looked surprised. For a minute, I thought he was going to slap me back.

"I did love you once," he said, "but you were undeserving of that love. And now I have given it to Josephine. Good day, Countess."

I was tempted to run after him and then realized that I couldn't continue like this. It was one thing to love Beethoven's music, but to love Beethoven was sheer madness. The man only thought about himself and only cared about me in relation to how I made him feel. I didn't exist except to praise and support him. I should have been grateful that Prince Lichnowsky saved me from the horror of marrying such a self-absorbed creature, but I wasn't.

I was in such a state when I returned to the hotel that Lucy took one look at my distraught face and wringing-wet clothes and asked if she should call a doctor.

"I'm afraid I slapped Herr Beethoven."

"If I do say so, milady, I'm sure he deserved it."

"Now I feel awful. He's so sensitive, and with his hearing loss, I've only added to his pain. He called me a whore, but he didn't mean it. What should I do?"

"He called you a whore?" Lucy said indignantly. "You should never see him again, that's what you should do."

I knew that Beethoven loved walking through the Helenental Valley, and after slipping one of the housekeepers a few small coins, I learned that he was heading there the next day. I took the main path following the course of the Schwechat River. The forest was dense, the incline so steep that I was soon out of breath. I was about to turn back when I heard someone screaming a melody and glimpsed an arm flapping in the air.

"Wait!" I cried. "I want to talk to you."

"Leave me alone," he shouted as I hurried toward him. "Even nature isn't safe from your untimely intrusions."

"Please, I just want a few minutes."

"You don't have the strength or the fortitude to catch up with me," he said, picking up his pace.

I gathered up my gown and ran as fast as I could, reaching him as he neared the ruined turrets and towers of Rauhenstein Castle.

"You shouldn't have called me a whore," I said, gasping. "I demand that you take it back."

"You demand? Really, Countess Gallenberg, I'd think you'd consider it a compliment. I could say much worse."

"Such as?"

"Calling you a mediocre musician. Josephine plays far better than you do."

"I'm good too. Perhaps not as talented as Josephine, but I'm practicing again."

"Next you'll be composing. Do you think what I do is easy?"

"I would never compare myself to you."

"Countess Gallenberg, do you exist simply to torment me? You have a husband. You have a lover, and now you have a child. What else do you want?"

"I want you," I heard myself saying weakly.

He didn't hear me, so I repeated it. "I want you—I love you." After I said the words, I felt naked, embarrassed. I'd debased myself. I'd slept with one man and now I was throwing myself at another. What was wrong with me? I slumped down on the ground, holding my head in my hands. At least Josephine, for all her problems, managed to keep her dignity.

"I'm sorry," I kept repeating. "I'm sorry." I didn't know whom I was apologizing to or what I was apologizing for. Beethoven felt wronged—and rightly so. I'd gone back on my word, but I couldn't tell him what had really happened. It was hopeless.

"Are you all right, Countess," he asked. When I didn't respond, he asked me again but this time called me Giulietta. I heard a telltale catch in his throat, like a scratch tone on a cello. He couldn't hide his emotions any more than he could write a lifeless sonata.

"I'm perfectly fine," I said. "Please continue with your walk."

He hesitated for a moment before forging ahead. I lingered at the base of the ruins, feeling utterly dejected. In the course of twenty-four hours, I'd sent two men away, and the one I loved the most was humming so loudly that even the birds had gone mute in protest.

23

It was a celebration fit for a king, and Naples had a new one: Joachim Murat, Napoleon's brother-in-law, a brilliant cavalry officer and unabashed dandy. Riding into a city accustomed to splendor, he made his mark in red leather boots, white riding breeches, a blue tunic embroidered with gold, and a three-cornered hat topped with a huge white ostrich plume. Even his horse was extravagantly attired with a tiger-skin saddlecloth and gold stirrups and bits.

People were still talking about his grand entrance when we gathered at the harbor to see the fireworks display. Hugo screeched in delight at the whistling comets, dome-shaped weeping willows, and spinning girandoles. The illuminations continued until the last thread of light evaporated into the darkness, leaving the soft glow of a hundred Chinese lanterns dangling from the fishing boats.

When we returned home, Ramo was sitting in a chair rocking the second addition to our family. Maria Julie, or "Jülchen," as we called her, was now three months old, and once again I'd experienced an easy labor. By then, Sister Immaculata had died, but I remembered her comment about miracles and knew that I'd experienced another one. Jülchen was perfect. She had my dark hair and blue eyes and Friedrich's full lips and chin. She even had his endearing cowlick, the swirl of hair that resisted lying flat.

Anna, the nurse, complained that Ramo was usurping her responsibilities, but he was surprisingly adept at getting Jülchen to fall asleep. "Wriggling fish, they are much worse." He laughed as she squirmed in his arms. He then began singing "Nonna Nonna," a traditional Neapolitan lullaby that managed to reference angels, *mammone*, and rotting flesh in a uniquely hypnotic way.

"He's wonderful, isn't he?" Robert said, gazing at his lover with my lover's child. After Jülchen was born, I had written to Friedrich, purposely omitting Armgard's name. It was unclear whether she knew about our rendezvous in Baden, and if she didn't, I thought it best not to announce that we'd had a second child. She hadn't specified a limit, but it made me uneasy. We corresponded only infrequently and I didn't know her state of mind.

Friedrich had sent an elegant gold-and-blue enamel necklace fashioned with a cameo of his grandmother. He wanted me to give it to Jülchen when she was older but asked if I'd occasionally wear it. In his letter, he told me that he'd started a biography of his family in case the children discovered our secret and wanted to know more about the Schulenburgs. And then he went on:

> *You must be aware that I have deep feelings for you. I understand that we had an 'arrangement,' but even the most official treaties are subject to renegotiation. Armgard is a kind, dutiful wife, but we both know what happens when duty precedes love. The lucky ones find compatibility, but with you, I have found more, and it has made my marriage increasingly intolerable. I know there is little love between you and your husband. I beg you to leave him and start a new life with me. We already have two children. We could be happy together.*

I thanked him for the necklace and expressed my excitement about his biography, ignoring the rest. What could I say? I'd promised Armgard that I wouldn't come between them, and I was still in love with Beethoven. The way he'd uttered my name had become a beloved aria, one I played over and over again, probing for nuances and clues. I longed to hear him say it again, with the same break in his throat, the same husky inflection. *Giulietta, Giulietta, Giulietta . . .*

With Joseph Bonaparte's ascendency to the throne of Spain, I was concerned that Robert wouldn't be allowed to keep his position at the Court Theater, but Joachim Murat, having recently conquered the British-controlled island of Capri, had more pressing matters. I met the king and his wife, Caroline, at one of Robert's performances. They were seated in a throne-shaped royal box, which was surrounded by statues of Apollo and his nine muses. I didn't find Robert's opera buffa amusing, but the king laughed uproariously. Afterward, when Robert presented me to the Murats, he boasted that I was the woman to whom Ludwig van Beethoven had dedicated his most famous sonata. Robert still didn't think highly of Beethoven, but Beethoven's reputation was growing and he sought to impress Murat.

"*Beeto-vin?*" the king said. "I don't know the man, but if he dedicated anything to your wife, it is entirely warranted. I'd heard that the Countess Gallenberg was the most beautiful woman in Naples. Now I can personally vouch for it."

The queen, a dark-haired beauty with a reputation for ruthlessness, gave me a look that implied that her husband's comments had the same enervating effect as my husband's music had on me. I smiled back, and in that brief shared moment, I felt a kinship for this woman, who was Napoleon's youngest sister and seemed eager for an ally.

A few days later, I was summoned to a mysterious meeting at the Palazzo Reale, where a monumental cream-and-gray marble staircase led to multiple antechambers, the throne room, and finally the royal apartments. Two *dames d'annonce*, in white-and-yellow gowns, called out my name as I passed through the door to the queen's quarters. She was surveying a new portrait by François Gérard, who had completed a similar commission for her sister-in-law, Empress Josephine. With her four children nestled at her side, Caroline sat on a blue throne dressed in a neoclassical white satin empire gown with a seductive décolletage.

"It's beautiful," I said, admiring the way Gérard had captured both her strength and femininity.

"It's called *Caroline and Her Children*," she said slyly. "In order to gain power, it's important to project a maternal image. Otherwise, I'll be thought of as that." She pointed to the menacing specter of Vesuvius visible through the large window next to her dressing table. "Women are viewed as temperamental, volatile, subject to erupting on the slightest whim," she continued. "Motherhood counteracts our 'erratic' nature."

"In the eyes of fools," I said.

"In the eyes of men." She looked at me carefully. "Despite your eye for fashion, you don't strike me as a frivolous woman. Is that a fair assessment?"

"Yes, Your Majesty, it is."

"Josephine may be beautiful and stylish, but she cannot give my brother a child. Without heirs to the throne, the marriage won't last. There's some talk that if my brother cannot produce an heir, my husband should be put forward for the imperial succession. But of course, it is just talk."

I waited for the queen to continue. She couldn't possibly be asking me to have a child with Napoleon?

"My husband thinks you are very attractive," she went on. "To be honest, he thinks many women are attractive. Still, he mentioned you several times. I want you to become his mistress."

"His . . . mistress?" I said. How could it be that two different women would send me to their husbands' beds? Was my lack of an erotic life so obvious? I did have two children. That indicated I was having conjugal relations with someone. "I mean no disrespect, Your Majesty, but I don't know what you would gain from this?"

"Knowledge," she said, moving about the room to appreciate her portrait from various angles. "You would be my eyes and ears. My brother values my husband on the battlefield. But he disapproves of his constant womanizing and his unwillingness to share power with me. I fear a rupture, so I need to know what the king is really thinking."

She wanted me to be a mistress—and a spy? Madame du Barry, King Louis XV's mistress, had been sent to the guillotine during the French Revolution. Even though the Bourbons no longer occupied the throne of Naples, Queen Maria Carolina was said to have ordered the beheading of the nobles who'd demonstrated loyalty to the French. What if the Bourbons came back?

"I'm afraid I'm not cut out to be a spy," I said.

Turning away from the portrait, she looked directly at me. "Of course you are. You live with secrets. Isn't your husband's lover a butcher?"

"A fisherman," I said hesitantly.

"I would hate for that information to become public. I understand that your husband's salary is a small one. I would reward you generously. It would serve both our purposes. My husband has a certain animal vitality. I suppose it comes from all that carnage."

The queen wasted little time setting up the assignation, and the following week, I had the distinct pleasure of watching the king's valet meticulously finger-curl his long damp hair. I tried not to seem impatient in case he thought it a necessary prelude to lovemaking. When the valet finally created a luxuriant lion's mane, he dressed the king in his military uniform and left the room. The king wasted little time getting straight to the point. "Countess Gallenberg, my wife tells me that you'd like to be my mistress. You won't be the first or even the twenty-fifth. I collect women the way I collect art. The more I have, the more I want."

I nodded as if I understood what he was saying, but I didn't own any valuable art, and I was nervous about what he'd do to me. A man with infinite mistresses prized variety and might have unorthodox taste.

"We must make this quick," he said, moving over to the bed. "I need to make an offering at the shrine of Saint Januarius. I want my people to love me."

Given the complexities of his uniform, I couldn't imagine how he intended to disrobe in such a hasty fashion, but perhaps dodging grapeshot and cannon fire had accelerated his reflexes. Why he'd even bothered to get dressed mystified me. After I complimented his elaborate attire, with its feathers, braids, and medals, he confided that he designed his own uniforms.

"I wouldn't think you'd have the time," I said. "I don't sew and I haven't—"

"Led the cavalry into numerous battles? Nearly avoided death countless times? Had a Turkish commander fire directly into your mouth?"

"Not the last one, no."

He tried to figure out if I was being serious, and after realizing I was joking, he threw his head back and laughed, his long curls falling in perfect regimental alignment. "I presume you'd like to hear about it," he said. He solved the uniform dilemma by yanking down his pristine white britches before efficiently undressing me. "It was during the Egyptian campaign. I'd wanted to take the Turkish commander prisoner, so I rode into his tent, but he shot me in the mouth." Recounting the incident excited him; he pulled my hips toward him and penetrated me, the braids and medals on his blue tunic digging into my flesh.

"Ouch!" I said. "That hurts!"

"Of course it hurt. I was shot in the mouth! But then I spit the flesh directly into his face, cut off two of his fingers, and disarmed him." Murat moaned and then rolled off. "Napoleon promoted me right afterward."

"Congratulations," I said.

"That was good, wasn't it? As for my battlefield experience, I would love to tell you more about it one day, but Saint Januarius awaits. I hope we can do this again. You are a fascinating woman."

After the king left, I was escorted directly to the queen's chamber, where Caroline was eager to hear everything.

"He's an excellent lover, no?" she asked.

I chose my words carefully. "He is unique."

"I certainly hope he took off his clothes. I practically have a permanent indentation in my breast from his medals. Did you learn anything of interest?"

"A Turkish commander shot him in the mouth."

She sighed loudly. "Oh that. I suppose I shouldn't expect much the first time." She motioned for one of her twenty-eight ladies-in-waiting to hand me a silk purse and then solicited my advice on color possibilities for her boudoir. "The Bourbons had such terrible taste—so dark and heavy," she complained. "I want something light and airy. Pale blue, or blue and white?"

I suggested blue and white. It seemed the safest choice.

As I left the palace, I wondered what my mother would say if she knew I'd bedded a king. She'd probably shout, "Brava!" but I didn't feel a sense of accomplishment, just a nagging awareness that I'd betrayed everything I held dear. I walked to nearby Santa Chiara, lit a candle, and said a prayer. A great swell of emotion came over me and I began to sob. A young nun appeared at my side. She was a Poor Clare, a religious order devoted to prayer and contemplation. They were prohibited from having any contact with the outside world and could speak only an hour a day.

Placing her finger to her lips, she led me into a secret garden in the cloisters, where dozens of columns and benches were decorated with vibrant majolica tiles. I hadn't expected such a riot of color—blue and gold flowers, brilliant yellow lemons, lush green vines. Each tile was unique, with scenes of men hunting and fishing, couples eating and dancing, all reaffirming the beauty and vibrancy of everyday existence. I couldn't understand how the nuns could possibly embrace a life of introspection and seclusion in such a dazzling setting. But perhaps that was the point, a constant reminder of what they'd sacrificed in order to strengthen their resolve. The young nun disappeared, and, inhaling the soothing scent of lavender, I sat down on one of the benches, soaking in the unexpected beauty.

Robert continued to play Pygmalion to Ramo's Galatea with little success. Though I was naïve about such liaisons, it didn't seem wise for Robert to treat him as a prisoner. Every day he looked increasingly miserable. His pianoforte teacher had quit in frustration, leaving him so mortified that I volunteered to teach him myself. He had a good ear, and while he'd heard me play the *Moonlight* only a few times, he was able to pick out the first few bars with its moody ostinato triplets.

"You don't find the music sad?" I asked.

"It brings back memories. Sometimes we'd take out our boats at night and attach torches to the prows. The mullets would be so dazed by the light, they'd jump up, and then we'd spear them."

"Now that's sad."

He smiled widely. "Not to a fisherman. One time it was just me and my father. We were in the middle of the water, and the moonlight was even brighter than the brightest torch. Fish were jumping everywhere. We just sat there in the light, and then my father began to sing. I joined in. I've never been so happy. When I try to play this song, I hear the lapping of waves and I remember singing with my father. He died a few months later."

"I'm very sorry."

"He was a good man." He gulped hard and then suddenly grabbed my hand. "I'm dying here. I feel trapped. Help me."

Later, I asked Anna if she knew anything about Ramo's situation. They spent a lot of time together in the nursery, and I thought he might have taken her into his confidence. "I swore an oath," she said, putting Jülchen down for her nap. "I cannot tell you."

"Robert doesn't mistreat him, does he?"

"I can't say what goes on in the bedchamber, but Count Gallenberg seems very loving toward him."

When she still wouldn't tell me, I offered her a few coins from the queen's purse. It seemed appropriate that money I'd earned from my failed spying attempt would go toward uncovering information about my husband's lover.

"Ramo tells me every day that he wants to live with his family," she said reluctantly.

"You mean his widowed mother?"

Anna looked embarrassed. "No, his wife and baby. She is Jülchen's age."

Now I understood why Ramo was so attentive to my daughter. He missed his own.

"Please don't tell Count Gallenberg, but I let him sneak out to see them," she said.

"Thank you, Anna. I will deal with this."

When Robert returned from the theater that night, I asked if we could discuss something important. He immediately poured himself some wine.

"You must let Ramo go," I said. "He's like a fish caught in a net. Can't you see how unhappy he is."

"Why should he be unhappy? He's living in a beautiful home—far nicer than where he came from—and he loves music."

"He loves the sea. He doesn't want to be here."

"He's never told me that." Robert seemed offended that Ramo would even contemplate the possibility of loving the sea more than music.

"You must let him go," I said firmly.

"But I love him," Robert protested. "I have never loved anyone so much. I'm sorry, but it's true."

I told Robert that he didn't have to apologize. I knew that he had never loved me. I had never loved him. But I wondered if he couldn't find another man who might reciprocate his affection. I was going to add "preferably not a fisherman," but I didn't want to be unkind. Instead, I suggested that he might find someone more comfortable in his social milieu.

"There is only Ramo," he replied stubbornly.

He had to hear the truth. "He has a wife and child," I said.

There was a long pause before Robert whispered, "I didn't know." He sat there for a few minutes looking stunned. I pictured one of the mullets dazed by the light. Slowly, he got up and, without saying anything, walked out. In the middle of the night, I heard Robert and Ramo arguing in Robert's bedchamber. It sounded as if they'd been drinking heavily. I listened for a little while longer and then fell back asleep. At some point, I woke up to the sound of the front door slamming, but imagined it was part of a dream.

The next day, Ramo's body washed ashore on the rocks of Megaride. After leaving the house, he'd taken his boat onto the sea. It was a cold December night. The moon was full, and I pictured the fish jumping, falling upward like playful stars. Perhaps he'd wanted to relive the happy time with his father and accidentally fell overboard. He had consumed much wine. The police described it as an accident, but regular Neapolitans saw Ramo as a modern Parthenope who had thrown himself into the sea.

For obvious reasons, we didn't attend the funeral. I sold my engagement ring and had Anna deliver the proceeds to Ramo's widow. Anna said she couldn't have been more than fifteen.

Robert was inconsolable, sobbing that he would never find anyone as beautiful and pure hearted. I held him in my arms while he wept. "He was the love of my life. I don't know how I can live without him."

"People cope with loss all the time," I said, thinking of Beethoven. "You'll find a way." I wiped away his tears with my lace handkerchief and kissed him on the forehead.

Suddenly his face brightened. "At least I have my music."

"Yes," I said. "At least you have that."

24

Vienna, Martonvásár, and Naples, 1809

I'd been in exile for five years, a prisoner like Ramo, and I wanted to go home.

After I learned that Prince Lichnowsky had withdrawn Beethoven's stipend, he had no more power over me, and I returned to Vienna for a visit. My father had never met his grandchildren, and I hoped I might see Beethoven again. He'd recently presented his Fifth and Sixth Symphonies at the Theater an der Wien, and I wished I could have been there. When I lost Beethoven, I lost the thrill of listening to him make music. That in itself was punishment enough.

I found my father in the library exactly as I'd left him. Noticing two little creatures staring up at him, he broke into a bashful smile and took his grandchildren into his arms. Though Hugo couldn't yet read, he loved books, and pulling one from the lowest shelf, he sat down on the floor and began paging through it.

"Goethe," my father said. "Your son is quite the intellectual."

My mother was in the drawing room reading one of her Parisian fashion magazines. "Karl has been beastly to me," she complained. "He ended our relationship by sending one of his servants to deliver a letter.

He rescinded his love, along with my annuity. We needed that to live. Who'd ever expect that I'd be in the same spot as Louis?"

"My sacrifice was for nothing, then."

She picked up the magazine again and began flipping through it. "I don't recall anything about a sacrifice."

"I wanted to marry Louis, remember?"

"Now that would have been a sacrifice. But tell me about the man who fathered your children—the one who isn't a fisherman."

When she learned his name, she couldn't have been happier. "Count Schulenburg? Why, all the women in Vienna are in love with him. And to think that you're his mistress. That's quite a coup."

"I'm also the mistress of the king of Naples."

"Very amusing, Julie."

I didn't bother to elaborate and there wasn't much to tell. After our brief encounter, I'd seen little of Murat, who had other mistresses and a kingdom to rule. When I asked my mother about Josephine, she told me that she was hovering near death "thanks to Karl." In what had become a familiar gambit, the prince had convinced Aunt Anna to persuade Josephine to leave Vienna. He wanted to make sure she wouldn't see Beethoven. On a quest to find a tutor for her two boys, she and Therese traveled to Switzerland, eventually hiring a young man who my mother claimed was the son of the "Lord of the Isle of Worms."

"I presume this is all in jest," I said.

"Would I make up such a story?" my mother replied indignantly. She showed me a letter that she had recently received from Josephine, whose health was suffering due to the cold temperature and arduous travel. "I fear I am dying," she wrote. "Please tell Louis that I love him."

"Did you convey the message to him?"

"I most certainly did not. Countess Erdödy had been generous enough to let him stay in one of her rooms. After he learned that she was paying a male servant to take care of him—and if anyone needs caring for, it's Louis—he got into a huge fight and moved out. He's now living above a brothel."

Climbing the stairs to Beethoven's apartment, I heard the strains of what would become his fifth pianoforte concerto above the raucous noise of drunken carousing. Nervously, I knocked several times on his door. Once again, I'd taken care to look my best, but Lucy reiterated that my problem wasn't a lack of attractiveness. It was the misfortune of having fallen in love with a man who couldn't see beyond his next composition.

"May I come in?" I asked when he finally opened the door.

He wasn't sure who it was until I pulled down the hood of my cloak. "Will you not leave me in peace?" he bellowed. "I'm convinced that you would pursue me to the gates of hell and back."

The expression on his face didn't match his words or tone of voice. He didn't appear happy to see me, but neither did he seem unhappy. It was more curiosity mixed with apprehension. I looked around the room. By now I'd seen enough of Beethoven's apartments that I shouldn't have been shocked. I thought back to the Novalis quote about chaos shimmering through the veil of order. Here the veil had been ripped away. Half-empty bottles of wine vied for limited space with a wedge of Italian cheese, a Veronese salami, business letters, and scribbled compositions. Beneath the pianoforte was a chamber pot. It needed emptying.

"I fired my housekeeper," he said unnecessarily. "I blame my current situation on Countess Erdödy. She supplied me with a servant! That's why I left her home."

"It sounds as if she was only trying to help, but as you misinterpret even the most well-meaning gestures, I suppose this is the result. You're living above a brothel in a state of pandemonium."

"Did you come all the way from Naples to insult me? If so, you may leave. I have suffered enough."

Realizing that I needed to change tactics or he could easily throw me out, I commented on the painting of his grandfather leaning against the wall. "I see that the kapellmeister is still with you."

"Yes, I bring him everywhere," he said, warming up. "I wanted to be a kapellmeister too. When I was offered the position in Jérôme Bonaparte's court, I almost took it, but certain patrons offered to give me a yearly stipend if I agreed to stay."

"Was Prince Lichnowsky one of them?"

"No," he said gruffly. "My true friends—Archduke Rudolph and Prince Lobkowitz. Prince Kinsky too, although I don't really know him."

"Then you are indeed very lucky. You have something every composer wants—uninterrupted time."

"Not quite. You are here." I was still wearing my cloak, but since he hadn't asked me to sit down, I got straight to the point.

"I've brought a message from Josephine." I realized this undercut my own cause, but if Josephine were truly dying—and with Josephine one never really knew—I felt obliged to pass it along.

"I have no interest," he replied, and then immediately wanted to know what she had to say.

It crossed my mind that I could lie and tell him that she'd married the son of the Lord of the Isle of Worms, but it sounded too preposterous.

"Josephine still loves you," I said, all the while thinking, *I love you too.*

"Still loves me?" he sneered. "Then why did she leave Vienna? People don't abandon the people they love, but from your perspective, they obviously do."

It seemed like the perfect time to tell him about Prince Lichnowsky. He no longer relied on the prince's stipend and neither did my mother. But if the prince and Beethoven had come to blows over the prince's suggestion that he stop seeing Josephine, I couldn't imagine what

Beethoven might do if he knew the prince's influence had also extended to me. Besides, I couldn't tell him about the rape. Without that, the story was incomplete.

Changing the subject, I told him about a concert I'd recently attended at the apartment of Nikolaus Zmeskall, a friend of Beethoven's and a prominent violoncellist. "Baroness Ertmann played my sonata. She performed it brilliantly."

Beethoven grunted. "That sonata was never meant for you. I intended it for Prince Lichnowsky's sister."

The sonata meant everything to me. It was the only thing I had of him.

"That isn't true," I said, raising my voice. "I was there when you played it for the first time."

"How do you know it was the first time?" he countered. "I could have been working on it for months. Besides, you can't make too much out of one dedication. For me, it is meaningless—both the dedication and the sonata. In fact, of all the sonatas I've written, it is the one I detest the most, and I will go on detesting it until the day I die."

"Do you hate me that much?" I stared at his face, trying to find the man I once loved, the man I still loved, though loving him was becoming more difficult. The boyish glee that made it easier to overlook his foul temper had dissipated. He was now thirty-eight, and while I still saw flashes of the childlike qualities that were once so endearing, I also saw the middle-aged misanthrope.

"You have given me hope," he said quietly. At this, my heart rose, waiting to hear an expression of love, even of mild affection. "That Josephine will come back to me."

I'd never met anyone so capable of breaking my heart. I wondered if it was a critical part of being a musical genius. To be able to touch the emotions in such a visceral way had to involve an ability to rouse both passion and pain in one's personal relationships. But I didn't know other musical geniuses. I knew only Beethoven.

Later that week, I was playing with the children when my mother announced a surprise. "Look who I encountered on the Graben!" she said elatedly. Friedrich gave me an apologetic look while Armgard rushed over to kiss me.

"I can't believe you haven't called upon us," she said, wagging her finger. "You are indeed very naughty."

I made an excuse that I'd been ill and had been planning to contact them when I'd fully recovered.

"And your little boy?" she asked. "Where is he?"

Lucy brought both Hugo and Jülchen into the room, and Armgard immediately started to cry. Hugo's resemblance to Friedrich was striking, and I understood why it was hard for her, but apparently that wasn't the only reason.

"Who is this?" she asked, pointing to Jülchen, who was almost a year old.

"Her name is Maria Julie," I explained.

"But how . . . why?" she asked.

I looked over at Friedrich. As I suspected, he hadn't told her. Armgard began crying even harder. "Fritz, how could you do this to me? How could you keep it a secret?" She turned to me. "And you! Are you just trying to humiliate me because I can't bear children?"

"Armgard, I do believe this was your idea," Friedrich said.

"I wanted you to have one child—not two."

"I don't believe you specified a limit," he replied.

"Would anyone like some sweets?" my mother said. "We just bought the most delicious strudel."

"I know what it's like to lose a child," I said tentatively.

"But at least you had a child to lose," she said. "This was a terrible idea. What was I thinking?" She looked at my necklace, the one belonging to Friedrich's grandmother. It was so pretty that I'd taken to wearing it. "Isn't that Oma Lena's?" she asked. "What is she doing with it?"

"I think it best we leave," Friedrich said, escorting Armgard out but not before she ripped the necklace off my neck.

"Why was that lady crying?" Hugo asked. "Did something happen to make her sad?"

"Yes, darling, but it doesn't have anything to do with you, so why don't you go into your room and play."

The next day, one of the servants announced the arrival of Count Schulenburg, who wanted to return the necklace and apologize for Armgard's behavior.

"I understand why she'd feel that way," I said. "She loves you very much."

"You are well?" he asked awkwardly.

"Well enough."

We stood in the drawing room staring at each other, not knowing what to say. I didn't even have the presence of mind to invite him to sit down. He finally broke the silence. "Jülchen is beautiful. But why shouldn't she be? She looks exactly like her mother."

"She looks like you too. The same mouth."

We were now gazing at each other's lips, and once again I felt the familiar pull toward him. I immediately shifted my eyes to the window. "I think it might rain," I said lamely.

"Julie, are you really interested in the weather?" I'd forgotten what a nice voice he had, deep and resonant, a diplomat's voice, one accustomed to smoothing over differences and striking compromises, one adept at the art of suggestion.

"No."

"If you are free this afternoon, I suggest we meet here." He handed me a card with the name and address of an inn on the Taborstrasse, on the outskirts of the city. "It's very discreet."

I wondered if he had taken other lovers there. One couldn't expect marital fidelity from a man of his stature and sophistication.

"All the more to stake your claim," my mother advised. "He's extremely attractive, and his wife is the most tiresome creature. Imagine sobbing in front of your husband's bastards. Such poor manners!"

Friedrich and I spent the afternoon in bed. We hadn't been together since Baden and, at first, I was shy, but he quickly put me at ease. He was a very skilled and sensitive lover, arousing such passion that I was almost overwhelmed. I hadn't realized that women could feel this way. Prince Lichnowsky had left me frightened and vulnerable; Murat had left little impression at all. My experience with Beethoven was mired in tragedy and loss. With Friedrich, I no longer felt like a Poor Clare trapped in a cloister, but a woman who could touch and be touched, arouse and be aroused. Lying in his arms, we talked about our lives, carefully avoiding any mention of the future. He described the pleasures and difficulties of writing his family biography. I told him about Hugo's love of books and Jülchen's first steps. He was hungry for stories of the children.

During the next month, we met at least a half dozen times, and each time my feelings for him intensified, but he didn't mention anything more about sharing our lives together. Since I'd already rebuffed him twice, I assumed he'd given up, but one afternoon as I nestled by his side, he broached the subject again.

"Why do you persist in staying in your marriage?" he asked. "Is it for financial reasons? I'm not a prince, but I can make you very comfortable."

I didn't want to tell him that we had little money, that Robert, in addition to everything else, was a poor provider. I also didn't want to humiliate myself by asking for help. And then there was Armgard. I couldn't accept the responsibility for destroying their marriage.

"It's still Beethoven, isn't it?" he asked.

"No," I lied. "I just don't think we are suited to one another." It wasn't true. Even he knew that. "I'm sorry," I said.

"I am too." Without saying another word, he put on his clothes and left the room. I wondered if I'd ever see him again and also if I'd made a terrible mistake. I did love him. I loved him in a different way than I loved Beethoven, but that kind of love was as rare and as difficult as the man himself. A few days later, I wrote Friedrich a note telling him that I was ready to make a life with him. There was no reason why I shouldn't be happy. I was only twenty-seven, young enough to start over again. I was still holding the letter when Lucy came into the room.

"We need to go to Martonvásár immediately," she said. "The royal family have already left for Hungary. Napoleon's army is marching toward Vienna."

The city was in chaos, hundreds of carriages jamming the access roads. Austria had invaded Bavaria, spurring Napoleon's army to move toward the capital. I knew that Friedrich would find a way to safety. But Beethoven? He was so stubborn that I suspected he wouldn't leave. I pictured him cowering in a corner, covering his head with a pillow. His ears were too fragile for the ugly, discordant sounds of war.

The red tulips at Martonvásár were in full bloom, a sight that normally would have delighted me, but with Napoleon on the move, they resembled fields of blood. The lemon trees that Josephine and Therese had planted for loved ones had sprouted considerably. Beethoven's was now among the tallest.

Aunt Anna and Franz were the only family members living in the house, and without the usual theatrics, it was dreary. I was happy when Josephine and Therese finally arrived, not only because Josephine was still alive, but because she could always be counted upon to break the monotony. She'd brought along the mysterious tutor, Baron Christoph von Stackelberg. Knowing that he'd lived on the Isle of Worms, I'd imagined him as soft bodied and legless, but he carried himself like a field marshal, with a face like a beautiful weapon—razor-sharp cheekbones, brows like rapiers, eyes the color of cold gray steel.

"Pepi is in love," Therese confided in the garden. "It's not a good situation. I liked Christoph in the beginning, but he pushed me aside. He wanted to be alone with Pepi in order to . . ." She patted her stomach, whispering, "Mama doesn't know. It will kill her when she finds out."

During dinner Therese regaled us with stories of their harrowing journey from France through Italy. Crossing Mont Cenis, they had to convert their carriage into a sled by replacing the wheels with runners. "The path was so narrow that we nearly plummeted down the mountain when a caravan of mules passed by," she said. Josephine was very quiet, and I wondered if Christoph had prohibited her from speaking. Earlier, I'd heard him reprimand her two boys for talking out of turn.

"Baron, forgive my ignorance, but where is the Isle of Worms?" my mother inquired.

"It's one of the islands off the coast of Estonia," he explained, "but we grew up in Faehna Castle, near the country's capital. I'm one of fifteen brothers. My father died some years ago."

"Are you the oldest?" Aunt Anna asked in a transparent attempt to find out if he'd inherited the estate.

"No. And even if I were, I've decided to devote my life to education. I'm a keen admirer of Rousseau, particularly his novel *Julie, or the New Heloise*. I presume you haven't read it."

"Indeed, we have," I said. "We revere books in our family."

"I don't," my mother said. "But I'm very busy with my charity work."

"Then let me give you a summary," he offered. "It's the story of an impossible love affair between an aristocratic girl named Julie and her tutor. Despite the father's objections, the couple consummate their love, and Julie's mother dies of sorrow."

"How uplifting!" my mother said with a roll of her eyes.

"It actually is," Christoph insisted. He went on to explain that Julie died a saint, having discovered the benefits of tranquility as opposed to the chaos of erotic passion. "Rousseau was trying to return to the concept of chaste love. For a couple, that is the essence of happiness."

In light of Josephine's condition, it was difficult not to view Christoph as a hypocrite, and his arrogance didn't end with Rousseau. He also fancied himself an expert on livestock, lecturing Aunt Anna on all the reasons women shouldn't handle animals. "The female essence interferes with breeding patterns," he cautioned.

A day later, Hugo ran screaming into the house after discovering a bloody sheep's head nailed to the stable door. We quickly narrowed down the possible culprits. Christoph explained that on the Isle of Worms, it was a traditional method of preventing livestock epidemics. "With a woman touching the animals," he said, "one can't be too careful."

When I relayed the horrifying incident to Josephine, she didn't seem surprised.

"Christoph's methods can be extreme," she said, "but he's a brilliant scholar and a fine influence on the boys. Fritz is very troubled. He's never gotten over his father's death, and Christoph has helped him become a man."

"By decapitating a sheep?"

"Christoph is learned and wise."

"What of Louis? I gave him the message that you still loved him. Do you?"

"I do, but it is too late. Christoph is better suited for me. I need someone strong. I'm too weak to handle Louis."

"You are stronger than you think. Look at what you've already endured."

"I can't endure much more. Christoph will guide and teach me. I believe it is God's will."

The Siege of Vienna ended under a barrage of artillery fire at the Battle of Wagram, with combined losses of more than eighty thousand men. In October, Emperor Francis signed a peace treaty with Napoleon, ceding vast territory and leaving his country mired in debt.

By then, I'd already returned to Naples. If I needed another reminder that life was volatile, Vesuvius erupted, showering the city in fine white ash. It spewed lava for the rest of the year, leaving me feeling profoundly unsettled. We had very little money and our landlord was threatening to evict us. We'd already let Anna go, and we owed Lucy several months' wages. Instead of trying to find a solution, Robert bemoaned his lack of patronage. "At least Beethoven had Prince Lichnowsky," he said. "Who do I have?"

In a mordant way I appreciated the situation. Forced to give up Beethoven, who lacked a title and money, I'd wound up with Robert, who had a title but no money and, even worse, modest talent. I asked my mother for help, but she, too, was struggling. My father wasn't cut out for business, leaving my mother to ply her feminine wiles. Her latest quarry was the Russian diplomat and widower Count Andrey Razumovsky, whose string quartets performed Beethoven's compositions at his palace on the Landstrasse. The count had an impressive collection of art and rare books, and my mother hoped that she could compensate for her advanced age with a feigned knowledge of both. "I realize I'm no longer a great beauty," my mother wrote, "but I have wit and charm. Those attributes are very useful when you lose your currency as a woman. Remember that, Julie."

I was now five months pregnant with Friedrich's child, which didn't make me the most desirable mistress for the king, but with the war, I hadn't been required to play that role for some time. Once again, however, I found myself in Murat's bedchamber while a new valet fixed his hair. The queen was still suspicious of him and wanted information, but since he tended to confess everything to her anyway, my spying services were unnecessary.

"I enjoy talking to you," Murat said. "I can bed anyone, but most women are boring, except for my wife. She scares me!"

He talked about Napoleon's condescending attitude toward him and how he couldn't understand why he was being kept away from the main fighting.

"I was once a field marshal," he complained, "and now what am I?"

"A king?" I was beginning to agree with Napoleon's assessment that he was brilliant on the battlefield but that was the extent of it.

"I wanted to be the king of Spain, not Naples. Napoleon doesn't care what anyone else thinks. He is power mad."

"That's what Herr Beethoven feared," I said.

"*Beeto-vin?*" Turning to his valet, he chastised him for flattening a ringlet. "They must all be even!" he scolded.

"The composer," I reminded him. "He'd written a symphony for Napoleon and then took it back."

"He took it back? I like this man. Perhaps he'll write a symphony for me. What do I need to do?"

"Win a very decisive battle."

"What about Austerlitz?" He slapped his valet's hand, taking command of the curling operation himself. "I helped Napoleon win his greatest battle yet. That's not big enough for this *Beeto-vin?*"

"It would be, except you vanquished the Austrians."

Murat was silent for a few seconds as he glanced at his hair. "I think I understand. I would have to fight on the side of Austria *against* Napoleon."

"Yes, Your Majesty, I believe that would help."

"I can practically hear the music in my head. It's big and brash and sounds like a marching band. I will call it *Murat's Victory!*"

When I met with the queen, she was preparing to go to Paris with Murat to discuss her brother's planned divorce from Josephine. He was looking to marry someone from the reigning houses of Europe and wanted to hear their suggestions. "My brother is leaning toward an

Austrian marriage, but my husband thinks a Russian alliance would be more beneficial," she said. "He worries that an Austrian bride would remind people too much of Marie Antoinette. Did he tell you anything about that?"

"No, we talked mostly about Herr Beethoven creating a composition for him."

"I've heard of this Beethoven. He's on our side?"

"I can't say that he is."

"What else did my husband tell you about this piece of music?" Caroline began pacing up and down in front of the large window in her boudoir.

"He wants it to be called *Murat's Victory*."

"A victory against Napoleon? This doesn't sound good. Perhaps Beethoven would want to write something for my brother?"

"He already did, but I'm afraid he scratched out the title."

"And this is the man Joachim wants to write his victory march? This concerns me greatly. I will see how things develop in Paris. Thank you." She left as the volcano spewed a large plume of smoke.

In December I gave birth to a baby boy christened Friedrich. I wrote to his father to share the news but said nothing of the love letter I'd written but never sent. We were desperate for money, and I didn't want him to think it was the reason I was now reconsidering his offer. I'd already sold much of my jewelry and was about to beseech the queen for a loan when I received three hundred florins from my mother.

I worried that she might have told Friedrich of my financial predicament and read through her letter very quickly. I learned that Josephine had given birth to a daughter within weeks of my little Friedrich. Since Josephine wasn't married to the "Estonian Worm," as my mother called him, the Brunswicks pretended the baby didn't exist. "Josephine has now become the family's Mary Magdalene," my mother wrote. "Even though your husband prefers men and your children are bastards, you're far better off than Josephine." It was only at the end that my mother addressed the money: "I hope you don't mind, but I was talking to Frau Streicher about your difficulties. She must have mentioned it to Louis. He gave me 300 florins to send to you. In light of his animosity, I was quite surprised. However, you must not thank him. He wants to remain anonymous."

I knew Beethoven was a generous man. He had frequently helped out friends, but I was not a friend. I was someone he'd once loved but no longer did. I wondered if Josephine's involvement with Christoph had changed things. Had his thoughts turned to me? At the moment, however, my thoughts turned to more practical matters. Three hundred florins. I could finally pay the rent.

25

The queen and I were discussing marriage, which struck me as amusing, for both our unions were challenging in very different ways. Relations between Napoleon and Murat had grown increasingly hostile, with Murat vacillating between his loyalty to the emperor and his allegiance to Naples. Unlike Murat, who dreamed of a united Italy, Caroline sided with her brother, who wanted Naples to remain under French authority. She feared a head-on clash between the two men she loved the most.

"I admire my brother, but I do love Joachim," she said. "It must be very difficult to be married to someone who doesn't desire you. Joachim desires many women, but I know he desires me the most. Why don't you get a divorce? Find another husband."

"I love someone else."

"Don't tell me it's that musician, that Beethoven—the one Joachim thinks is going to compose his victory march."

"It is."

"And when was the last time you saw him?"

"Two years ago," I admitted. It seemed impossible. He was forever in my mind.

"That doesn't sound very sensible. He's a musician. You will be poor for the rest of your life."

"You still love the king, Your Majesty, yet you've described his weaknesses in great detail."

She looked out at the long terrace with its potted lemon trees and expansive view of the Mediterranean. "Joachim plays with the children out there," she said wistfully. "They adore him. I do too. We share a passion for so many things. We collect art. Canova is our favorite, but we also have a fondness for Ingres." She looked over at me. "I know you're thinking, *How silly!*"

"I wasn't thinking that at all. Art can be the highest form of love. If I didn't believe that, I couldn't go on."

The queen had a surprise for me. She had used her considerable influence to make Robert the director of ballet music at the Royal Theater San Carlo, the oldest and largest opera house in Europe. Ballets were routinely performed between acts, so the position carried much prestige and meant a larger salary. Robert would also be given the opportunity to compose original works.

"There is only one little problem," she said, smiling.

"Yes, Your Majesty?"

"The Beast."

Domenico Barbaja, or "the Beast," was the former Domenico Barbaglia, a munitions dealer and Milanese coffee shop waiter, who had created a sensation by adding cream and chocolate to coffee. He called it the "Barbagliata." After Napoleon became king of Italy and the French legalized gambling, he switched his main focus from cocoa beans to games of chance, leasing the gambling concession at La Scala opera house. Barbaja then moved to Naples, where he quickly conquered the gaming world. Murat appointed him manager of the Theater San Carlo with a mandate to oversee gambling in the theater's foyer and to produce entertainment that could rival the thrill of winning and losing money.

We met the impresario at the theater, where he was surveying his newly installed trattoria, allowing audiences to eat before, after, or during performances. For lighter fare, there was also a gelato stand and a coffee shop featuring the Barbagliata.

"What could be better?" he said. "Music, gambling, and my very own specialty coffee drink."

"Nothing, Signore Barbaja," I replied.

"I am the Beast," he said.

"Yes, of course, Signore Beast."

"No, just Beast! *Beast!*" Laughing, he said, "Joke!" and then thrust a Barbagliata at me. "Drink," he ordered.

I took a sip. "Good," I said, not wanting to possibly offend him by speaking in full sentences.

Despite his beastly manners, he had a pleasant face distinguished by large penetrating eyes. It was rumored that he was practically illiterate, although his lack of education hadn't hindered his financial success. His palazzo on the Via Toledo, exquisitely furnished through his gaming profits, was one of the finest in Naples.

After I'd finished my Barbagliata and Robert had consumed a bowl of pasta, which Barbaja insisted he eat the true Neapolitan way, by swallowing it in successive mouthfuls, he took us on a tour of the theater. The seats were covered in sumptuous blue upholstery while six tiers of boxes, all brightly gilded, ascended straight up to the frescoed ceiling. Mirrors reflected the candlelight from dozens of gold torches.

Robert was excited about his new position, telling me on the way home that he already had an idea for a ballet. "I'm going to base it on Samson and Delilah. The story has everything—war, politics, love, betrayal."

"And hair."

"*Hair?* Oh yes, Samson derived his strength from his hair. The wigmakers will love it."

"I'm not sure the king will," I reminded him. "If you haven't noticed, he does bear some resemblance to Samson. He's a great warrior—with long curls."

"So?"

"After Delilah cuts off his hair, the Philistines capture, blind, and enslave him. Murat's situation is currently very shaky."

Robert wasn't listening to me. He was already in his own raptus.

"I can hear it now," he said dreamily. "Delilah's *Dance of Seduction*. It builds to a wild crescendo, with violoncellos mimicking the sound of scissors, and then Samson stands before the audience—bald!"

I knew something was wrong when I saw my father's handwriting. He'd never written a letter to me before. He explained that my mother was ill, requesting that I return to Vienna as quickly as possible. The first thing I noticed upon arriving was the number of Napoleon's soldiers congregating on the wintry streets. The sound of French vied with German, but since the French had already taken the city, they'd won the musical duel.

Despite the occupation, however, Vienna had changed very little, maintaining its carefree character in good times and bad. My mother shared a similar trait. Though Hungarian-born, she was a true Viennese—frivolous, cultured, decadent, a woman who would rather sing than stay in bed. My father had told me that her heart was inflamed and that the doctor had prescribed rest. I found her playing Mozart at the pianoforte. "He makes me so happy," she said, scowling suddenly. "The C-sharp is sticking. I must tell Frau Streicher."

After greeting the children, in whom she showed minor interest, she asked if I'd accompany her to a benefit for the Society of Noble Ladies for Charity. She hadn't been outside in two weeks and felt like a caged bird.

"Mama, you're ill," I said. "You're supposed to rest."

"Julie, don't be so melancholy. Going out will do me a world of good. Besides, it's the Viennese debut of Louis's fifth pianoforte concerto."

"Will Louis be performing it?" I said, excited.

"I knew that would pique your interest. Unfortunately—at least from your vantage point—Carl Czerny, one of his students, will be playing it. I believe Louis's performing days are over. His hearing has gotten much worse."

I knew how much Beethoven loved to perform. No one could bring his unique blend of passion, stubbornness, and sheer force of will to his own compositions. He didn't lull or seduce listeners; he commanded them to pay heed. Now there'd be no more duels, no more virtuosic fireworks. My heart ached for him.

"He visits me, you know," my mother continued. "He never stays very long, but he's a comforting presence."

I wondered if my mother's weak heart was causing her to have visions. I couldn't imagine Beethoven visiting her. The two didn't even like each other.

Friedrich and Armgard were seated several rows in front of us. Turning to say something to Armgard, Friedrich saw me and nodded. I was left staring at his wavy blond hair, remembering how I'd brushed it behind his ears and played with his cowlick after lovemaking. My mother whispered, "It's not too late."

The women had labored for weeks on the costumes and props for the *tableaux vivants*, "living pictures," that replicated well-known scenes from paintings or sculpture. They'd become very chic with the publication of Goethe's novel *Elective Affinities*, in which the characters perform several of them. From her sickbed, my mother had learned that one of Vienna's most beautiful young countesses would portray Queen Esther in Poussin's painting *Esther Before Ahasuerus*. When the curtain rose, Esther, having fainted, was lying in the arms of three servants, while the king, who in real life was an eligible young count, looked on. Though the poses were supposed to be held for only a few moments, Esther didn't move. It turned out that she'd actually fainted from the strain of starving herself to duplicate Esther's ethereal complexion. The king, rising from his throne, carried her off the stage.

The room was still buzzing about the dramatic climax when Czerny, a serious-looking man with dark curly hair and spectacles, approached the pianoforte. After the orchestra played an exuberant opening chord, Czerny entered with a brilliant cadenza, combining the kinds of runs and trills that only Beethoven would have had the audacity to include at the beginning. After the jubilant opening, the second movement, with its muted strings, was so lyrical and gentle that tears came to my eyes. Friedrich excited me with his touch, but only Beethoven had the power to touch my soul, to make life, with all its beauty and sorrows, feel infinitely worthwhile.

The concerto was greeted warmly in accordance with Beethoven's stature, but as soon as Czerny took his bow, people returned to gossiping about the young countess. Friedrich left before we had a chance to speak, but from a distance I saw Prince Lichnowsky. He'd lost much of his hair and appeared emaciated. "Syphilis," my mother whispered. "They all have it." I was immediately alarmed about her own health, but reading my mind, she assured me that she didn't suffer from the disease. "We did other things," she said cryptically. "He liked watching."

She then introduced me to Count Razumovsky, who asked how she was feeling, and she responded, "Extremely well . . . catarrh, nothing serious." My mother's gaunt face gave truth to the lie, but he told her that he looked forward to showing her some of his newest paintings.

"Your mother has such an excellent eye," he said, casting his own toward the beautiful young countess.

Several days later, I took a carriage to the Landstrasse to consult Nannette Streicher about my mother's faulty C-sharp. Inside the warehouse, a man was painting wet gypsum onto the face of another man lying on a table. Straws protruded from the man's nostrils, and cotton covered his eyes. He wore a deep scowl.

"Hello," I called. Startled, the man sat upright and ripped off the cast; it fell to the floor, breaking into several pieces. Behind the oil and gypsum, I recognized Beethoven.

"What happened?" Frau Streicher asked as she walked into the warehouse.

"I'm afraid I intruded at a bad time," I apologized. "My mother is having problems with her keyboard."

"Countess Gallenberg, this is Herr Franz Klein," she said. "I commissioned him to do Louis's life mask." With the growing field of phrenology—the study of the skull as an indicator of character and mental abilities—life masks were increasingly in demand. Klein, who had honed his craft at morgues, was one of Vienna's foremost anatomical artists.

The oil had seeped into Beethoven's eyes, and he kept blinking to clear his vision. *"You?"* he said when he could finally see.

"I was at the charity event," I blurted. "The concerto, it was thrilling."

"I'd heard it wasn't well received."

"That's because it was the wrong audience. They were there to see the *tableaux vivants.*"

He looked at me blankly.

"You know, living pictures. They copied Poussin's—"

"I have no interest in what they copied." He continued to blink.

"Louis, why don't I take you inside and help you clean up," Frau Streicher said. She promised to return in ten minutes or so.

"I'm sorry if I ruined everything," I told Herr Klein, who was attempting to piece together the mask.

"Ruined? Do you know how difficult it is to deal with someone of Herr Beethoven's volatile nature?"

"I do."

The gypsum had hardened enough so that it had captured Beethoven's likeness, even the scars and pockmarks. The scowl, however, was greatly exaggerated. It was a portrait of Beethoven at his most churlish. "I'm sure no one will ever get him to sit for a life mask again," Klein said. "This is how people will remember him." He left without saying goodbye, carrying Beethoven's "head" beneath his arm.

When Frau Streicher came back, she told me that Beethoven had left in a very agitated state. "It was all my fault," I said. "I feel terrible about it."

She told me not to worry. If it hadn't been the broken life mask, it would have been something else. "He needs to keep stirring the pot."

"I guess that's why he still isn't married," I said, attempting to learn about any possible romances.

"He's certainly difficult," she replied, "but he's had no shortage of women."

No shortage of women? Did they ever step inside one of his apartments? Did they find his stomach ailments charming? Not only was he exceptionally prolific, but he was also going deaf. How did he find the time for these women? The same was true for Murat. He could fight bloody battles, rule a kingdom, quarrel with Napoleon, and still have multiple mistresses and a wife. At least Beethoven didn't have a wife. It was one less thing for me to worry about.

Frau Streicher began to reel off names: "Amalie, Antonie, Bettina, Josephine, Theresa . . ." Was she doing it alphabetically? "He seems to do best with married women," she continued. "That way he can remain infatuated without bearing any responsibility. I believe he's still in love with your cousin. Have you seen her yet?"

I told her I hadn't but that I planned to pay a call later in the week. Leaving the warehouse, I kept repeating the names as if reciting an incantation. *Amalie, Antonie, Bettina, Josephine, Theresa . . . Giulietta, Giulietta, Giulietta . . .* At least *G* came before *J—Josephine.*

Palais Deym was no longer a glittering fairy palace but a rundown boardinghouse and tourist attraction. I found Josephine in tears while Therese paced up and down the bedchamber.

After giving birth to an illegitimate baby, Josephine had privately married Christoph. Nine months later, another daughter, Theophile, was born. Therese explained that Christoph had convinced Josephine to buy an estate in Moravia. They couldn't afford it and were now involved in a costly lawsuit. But that wasn't the worst of it. Christoph's philosophy of education was on par with his fanatical ideas on breeding livestock. If the children touched anything that didn't belong to them, he bound their hands. If they rolled on the floor while playing, he tied them to the bedpost.

He was equally harsh with Josephine, forbidding music, dancing, parties, and laughter. Maintaining a set of rules that he referred to as "the Code," he celebrated order, cleanliness, tranquility, sobriety, and, most recently, chastity. "We have violent quarrels," Josephine explained between sobs. "He has ruined me physically." I noticed bruises on her arms.

"Did he do that to you?" I asked.

"No, I fell on the stairs," Josephine said unconvincingly.

"He's a monster," Therese said, confirming my suspicions. "He tells her that she has an evil character and that if she disobeys him, he will take away all her children."

"What am I going to do?" Josephine pleaded. "My mother and brother hardly speak to me, and I've lost the one man I ever loved."

"You mean Joseph?" I said hopefully.

"I loved Joseph, and if he hadn't died, I wouldn't be in this terrible position," she said, "but I'm referring to Louis. I love him. I've always loved him."

In many ways, they were lit by the same fire, a willingness to defy fate. Beethoven had the structure of his music, the concentration, the will. He was a titan struggling with the gods, while Josephine was pure undiluted passion. In a way, I envied her. I was too cautious, too unwilling to give myself over to total abandonment. I'd done it once with Beethoven, and the results had been so devastating that I was afraid to risk it again. Yet despite our differences, Josephine and I were both in loveless marriages, both with money woes, and both enamored of the same man.

When my mother could no longer get out of bed, I arranged to send the children to Martonvásár. Before they left, I wanted to give Friedrich the opportunity to meet his namesake. Friedrich arrived at the appointed time with gifts—a book for seven-year-old Hugo, a doll for four-year-old Jülchen, and a gold-and-lapis signet ring for three-year-old Friedrich. "It has the family crest," he pointed out. "When he's old enough, you can make up any story you want."

This time he didn't play with the children, even little Fritz, who grabbed his leg and was clinging to it. I wanted to tell Friedrich that I was sorry for everything, but he didn't give me a chance. Instead, we talked politics. With Napoleon about to invade Russia, Murat, fearful of a French coup d'état, wouldn't leave Naples.

"It's rumored that he suffered a nervous breakdown," Friedrich said. "But I believe he's recovered and will now command the cavalry of the Grand Armée. I'm sure he's plotting his wardrobe as we speak, but you would know more about that."

"I'm not sure what you mean."

"It's well known that you are his mistress—or one of them."

"It isn't what you think."

"It no longer matters."

It mattered to me. I was almost thirty and had been in love with only two men. Beethoven became easily infatuated. I did not. I knew that if I let Friedrich leave without saying anything, he would be lost to me forever.

"I wish—" I started to say.

He immediately cut me off. "I know," he replied. "Fritz is a fine boy, Countess."

When the doctor examined my mother, he told me there wasn't much he could do, but trying to be kind, he added, "Perhaps a miracle will happen." I believed him because I needed to. It was inconceivable that this fifty-six-year-old woman, the love of my life, the bane of my existence, would cease to exist.

As my mother's condition worsened, my father became increasingly remote. It was too painful for him to even be in the same room with her. I knew that he loved her very much, but I could also see what drove her to seek excitement with other men. For the next two weeks, I watched my mother waste away. I watched as her cheeks hollowed and her beauty disappeared. I watched as she grew thinner and frailer, and yet I couldn't accept that she was dying. At one point, she wanted to be moved into the music room, and Lucy and I set up the divan as a bed. She sighed deeply and asked me to play the *Moonlight* Sonata. "Soon I'll be gone and no one will remember me," she said in barely a whisper. "I will just be the mother of the girl to whom Beethoven dedicated a sonata. You will be famous for all eternity."

"I doubt it. Nobody will know the truth behind Giulietta."

"I can't see," she said suddenly. "What is happening? I want to go home." She began reliving her childhood. She called out for her mama and papa. She was breaking my heart, so I sat down to play the *Moonlight* but couldn't stop crying.

I felt someone tap me on the shoulder. I looked around to see Beethoven. At first, I thought he was an apparition. I reached out to touch his arm. He was real. My mother hadn't been imagining his visits after all. We changed places, and he began playing the first movement. He played it more beautifully than I had ever imagined, infusing it with the loss we'd suffered together, but also the loss of his own mother and now the loss of mine. He knew suffering. He knew heartache and pain, and he also knew how music could transcend it.

"It's beautiful, Julie," my mother murmured. "The music, it is just so beautiful."

When he finished, he took my mother's hand and kissed it, and then, turning around, he kissed my hand too.

My father was too distraught to come into the room. The death watch was all mine. I climbed into the makeshift bed, holding her tight. I whispered that she'd been a wonderful mother and that I loved her very much. As she closed her eyes and her breathing grew more ragged, I continued to hold on. Time ceased to exist. I watched as she appeared to fade away, her skin turning colors like an autumn leaf, yellow slowly turning to brown. She gave one last gasp and I put my ear to her chest, listening to the final beats of her heart. When I looked again, she was no longer there. She had drifted to another place. Mama, my mama. Gone.

26

Naples and Vienna, 1814

After my mother's death, I returned to Naples and tried to put Vienna behind me. But the queen had other plans. In the autumn, she summoned me to Palazzo Reale on the pretense of showing me her latest portrait. Unlike Gérard's earlier painting, in which she was depicted as a loving mother, here she stood alone, dressed all in black, a woman of power and authority.

"Ingres did it," she explained. "I also commissioned him to do this." She pointed to a painting of a harem concubine languishing nude on an opulent divan, her forthright gaze drawing the viewer into the erotically charged scene. "It's called *La Grande Odalisque*. I wanted it as a pendant to *The Sleeper of Naples*." Unlike *La Grande Odalisque*, with the model's body turned away from the viewer, *The Sleeper of Naples* faced front, her breasts and private parts exposed. She was languid and fleshy, with large child-bearing hips.

"The painting carries a great deal of sentiment," she confided. "Joachim bought it for me about five years ago. I had lost a child . . ." She composed herself and talked about Murat's fondness for Orientalism before getting to the point. "I'd like you to go to Vienna. I need someone I can trust there."

The Murats were in a perilous spot. After a series of catastrophic defeats, Napoleon had been exiled to Elba, and Murat was in danger of losing his throne. No one trusted the queen, who'd betrayed her own brother, or the king, who'd switched sides so many times he'd alienated both the French and the allies. The European powers were gathering for the Congress of Vienna to restore peace and reconstitute territories. With the help of Prince Klemens von Metternich, Austria's minister of foreign affairs and a former lover of the queen, she had promoted a treaty to keep Murat on the throne. She wanted assurance that she wouldn't be double-crossed.

"You're asking me to spy?" I said incredulously. "If you recall, Your Majesty, I wasn't very successful the last time. Besides, I'm practically a stranger in Vienna now."

"Your sister-in-law, Countess Fuchs, is married to an imperial chamberlain and is well acquainted with Wilhelmine, the Duchess of Sagan. She is Metternich's current mistress, and I know from personal experience that he's very indiscreet. You will report back whatever you hear."

I nodded in agreement. I had no choice. As I left, I glanced at *La Grande Odalisque*. Her dark eyes hinted at a world of intrigue.

Never before had so many emperors, kings, princes, assorted dignitaries, secretaries, couriers, and lackeys gathered in one city. Three hundred carriages had been provided for the most important guests, creating throngs of onlookers, who packed the narrow streets. The hotels were filled to capacity, with local residents, including my father, renting out rooms to house the overflow.

My mother's bedchamber was unoccupied, so Lucy and I moved in there. It was exactly as she'd left it, clothes still hanging in the wardrobe, Galimard perfume on the dressing table. I opened the bottle and inhaled the familiar smell of rose, orange blossom, and amber before dabbing some on my wrists. When I walked into the library, my father, startled, looked up. "I thought it was your mother," he said sadly.

He was lost without her. Though he inquired about Robert's new ballet and the children's studies, he seemed relieved when I told him that I had an appointment with Robert's sister. Leaving the library, I nearly collided with the Prussian diplomat who had taken over the music room. Seeing the pianoforte again, I remembered holding my mother for the last time and Beethoven's unexpected kindness. I pictured him out walking, notebooks bulging from the pockets of his coat, felt hat perched on the back of his head. Prince Lichnowsky had died that spring, leaving Princess Christiane a contented widow.

Robert's sister, Countess Eleonora von Fuchs, eagerly shared the news of all the exciting social events happening at the Congress. There were parades, masked balls, medieval jousts, banquets, hunting parties, concerts. "Louis opened the festivities with his opera," she said. "He revised *Leonore* and it's now called *Fidelio*. He's had great success with it."

"His hearing, has it improved?" I asked.

"He sometimes uses these strange hornlike contraptions. Ear trumpets, I think they're called. I'm not sure they help much. Despite all the praise he's been receiving, he seems very melancholy."

She excused herself to retrieve a letter she'd received from him. I had no idea he even knew her. Was Beethoven on intimate terms with every countess in Vienna? "It's so sad," she said upon returning. "He talks about having to keep composing so he won't die of hunger."

"He's dying of hunger?" I asked, alarmed.

She continued to skim the letter. "He doesn't want his brother to die either. He's referring to Karl. I believe he has consumption. Listen to this: 'Society cannot deal with a person who suffers from a thoroughly wounded heart.'"

I'd wounded his heart once, but since then he'd surely suffered multiple injuries from his catalogue of countesses. Realizing that I needed to stay focused on my assignment from the queen, I contrived an invitation to the Duchess of Sagan's party the following evening.

The duchess's pink-and-white salon was located at the Palais Palm, to the right of the staircase. When I mistakenly turned left, Eleonora grabbed me as if I were about to step in front of a runaway carriage. "No!" She gasped. "That's Princess Bagration's salon." The duchess and the princess, known as the "Naked Angel" for her low-cut gowns, were rival hostesses and experts at seducing powerful men in order to gain power themselves. They had many men in common, including Prince Metternich, Caroline's former lover, who had been voted president of the Congress.

A slight man with fair hair and fine features, he was now gazing at the beautiful duchess like a besotted adolescent. After Eleonora introduced us, he tried to make the duchess jealous by flirting with me. "I'm acquainted with all the great beauties in Vienna," he said. "Why haven't we met before?" I explained that I'd been living in Naples, and he immediately asked if I knew the Murats.

"I've only met them once or twice," I lied.

"He knows Caroline," the duchess said. "He told me she's like a man in bed."

"And what of the king?" I asked, feigning innocence. "I know nothing of politics, but will he keep his crown?"

"Speak to Talleyrand." He laughed, referring to France's representative at the Congress. "He wants Ferdinand returned to Naples. He's a Bourbon and the rightful king."

"Are you in agreement?" I asked.

"Quite honestly, my dear, I don't care what happens to Murat. He's a preening fool, but Caroline . . . we had some memorable times together."

"He's a brilliant man," Eleonora whispered as we walked away. "But a total fool for a pretty face. Did you know that he had a child with Princess Bagration?"

When I looked confused, she said, "The Naked Angel—the one to the left of the stairs."

I soon found out that Metternich and other key members of the Congress spent their days drinking and bedding their mistresses. Many had brought multiple women with them, the younger the better. If they were anything like Metternich, I'd probably learn more from the mistresses than from the men.

I overheard someone mention the "Saxony problem," referring to Prussia's desire to annex the kingdom and keep it for itself. The Prussians had jailed the Saxon king, but he'd sent a representative.

"He's very charming," I heard the duchess say. "Quite the ladies' man. I caught him heading into the Naked Angel's suite the other night."

I strained to hear his name, but the discussion switched to the upcoming medieval jousting competition. "Who's representing Saxony?" I asked my sister-in-law as we readied to leave.

"Count Friedrich von der Schulenburg," she said.

It was obvious that Friedrich would be involved with the Congress, but he'd bedded the Naked Angel? I hadn't seen him in two years. What right did I have to be jealous? When I returned to my father's, I started to tell Lucy all about it, but she warned me to keep my voice down. "There's a Prussian in the music room," she reminded me. "I caught him with his ear to the kitchen."

"Who's in the kitchen?"

"A representative from Britain."

I saw Beethoven again at a concert at the Hofburg's Grand Redoutensaal. Eleonora had made other plans, so I paid five florins for one of the better seats upstairs. He opened the program with his popular Seventh Symphony, but his hearing had obviously deteriorated to such an extent that another conductor, Michael Umlauf, led the musicians. Beethoven stood next to him, distracting the audience with his lively and frequently off-tempo movements. Once the music started, however, nothing else mattered. From the loud opening chord, which transitioned into the slender, naked sound of an oboe, he carried me into his joyful, melancholic, visceral world. He'd written music for dancing and music for mourning, capturing the cresting and falling, the ecstasy and struggle of everyday life.

The audience greeted the symphony with enthusiastic applause, after which Beethoven premiered *The Glorious Moment*, a treacly cantata he wrote celebrating the gathering of sovereigns in Vienna. It was a crowd-pleaser, the perfect piece for the occasion, as was the finale, *Wellington's Victory*, a salute to Lord Wellington's triumph over Napoleon at the Battle of Vittorio. I thought of Murat and his proposed victory hymn. It was looking less likely now.

Making my way downstairs, I was pleased to see Beethoven surrounded by so many admirers. Even if he couldn't hear clearly, he could tell by their faces that he was loved and adored. Here was the "public Beethoven," the one that didn't belong to me, but even after all this time, I still felt a relentless longing. When combined with his music, it was almost too much to bear.

I saw Count Razumovsky talking to Russia's Tsar Alexander and reintroduced myself. We'd met through my mother two years earlier at the charity event with the *tableaux vivants*. He offered his condolences, praising my mother's knowledge of Renaissance art and medieval manuscripts. I nodded and smiled. The tsar was a spiritual fanatic who had a wife, a "mystical" spouse, and scores of flesh-and-blood mistresses, including the Naked Angel.

"She's shown me all of Metternich's love letters," the tsar confided. "We read them in bed together. Such a silly man."

"Did you come across anything about the Murats?" I inquired. "I live in Naples, so I am just curious."

"Murat is a madman and deserves to rot in hell," Count Razumovsky said. "The Russian campaign was brutal. Moscow was nearly burned to the ground. So many beautiful things lost in the fire."

When the count turned away to converse with another delegate, the tsar thrust a handkerchief into my palm. It was embroidered with his initials and a crown of thorns. "I am in spiritual and physical pain," he whispered, emphasizing the physical part.

"I'm so sorry," I said, returning the handkerchief.

"No, keep it," he insisted, pressing it into my hands. "As a remembrance."

I was leaving the Redoutensaal when I felt a familiar hand on my shoulder. "You must miss your mother," Beethoven said before I even had a chance to congratulate him.

"I do miss her," I shouted. "But she was not an easy woman."

"No, she was very difficult," he agreed. "Selfish. Impossible. But I think of her sometimes."

We walked over to a quieter area, and I told him how much I liked the Seventh Symphony. "At some points I could almost feel you dancing," I said.

"I don't dance," he reminded me, although he didn't have to. The ball at Prince Lichnowsky's was burned into my memory.

We were interrupted by a striking man in women's clothes and heavy maquillage. He moved with the sinuous grace of a tiger. I recognized him as the famed Parisian ballet dancer, Louis-Antoine Duport. "I could barely contain myself," he told Beethoven. "Your music . . . it is dance itself!" Soon he was joined by others who wanted to congratulate Beethoven. When Beethoven saw that I was leaving, he reached for my hand. Our palms touched, and then our fingers drifted apart until I was left holding nothing.

Afterward, I visited Josephine at Palais Deym. I thought she'd be interested in hearing about the concert, but she was too distressed. "Life has become unbearable," she sobbed. "I can't endure it any longer."

The previous spring, she had given birth to a daughter, Minona. I was confused because the last time I'd seen her, she'd told me that Christoph had taken a vow of celibacy and moved out of the house. Josephine explained that Minona was a singer in the Ossian poem that Goethe quoted in *Werther*. "'It is night,'" she recited in between tears. "'I am alone, forlorn on the hill of storms. The wind is heard on the mountain.'"

It was the same verse Therese had read to her before she married Joseph. "Christoph has taken Minona, along with Marie Laure and Theophile," she cried. "I don't know where they are."

She explained that after Christoph had finished searching for enlightenment, he wanted to return to Estonia. When Josephine refused to accompany him, he went to Vienna's chief of police, Baron Franz von Hager, falsely claiming that she'd allowed an incestuous relationship to exist between the step-siblings. The police took the three Stackelberg children away before Josephine even had a chance to say goodbye.

"Now I have lost everything," she wailed. "My children. My good name. Christoph told the police that I was immoral and wicked. Now he's trying to kidnap the Deym children as well."

I didn't know what I could do. I realized that I'd promised Joseph that I'd look out for her, but Josephine was beyond my help. When I left, I could hear her reciting the Ossian poem in a despondent singsong voice. "'It is night. I am alone, forlorn on the hill of storms . . .'"

By December, I had attended so many fetes that I could barely fit into my gowns. I had nightmares of hams, partridges, pigs, hares, pickled tongues, pies, pastries, and gateaux. Prince Metternich had taken a liking to me, and I'd been invited to his Monday salons. Since Murat's representative had been excluded from the Congress, I hoped to find out as much as I could about the king's chances of survival, but Metternich wanted only to talk about the Duchess of Sagan. "I think she's taken up with that lunatic tsar," he confided. "She is breaking my heart. No one has ever suffered such grief."

"I'm sure that's the case," I agreed, "although I daresay Murat is facing a difficult situation."

He ignored me and continued. "Everyone here is in love. Even Talleyrand, who walks with a limp. He's bedding his nephew's wife— the duchess's half sister!"

"Murat has many lovers," I persisted.

"I despise the Russians, especially the tsar," he said. "Do you know what I found in the duchess's bed? A handkerchief embroidered with a crown of thorns. It's Alexander's calling card."

"Murat's calling card is his luxurious hair."

"I would like to kill Alexander," he said vehemently.

"Isn't this a peace conference?"

Metternich laughed and told me that I was a most amusing woman and then invited me to meet him the next afternoon. "The duchess will go mad with jealousy," he said. Metternich was living in a dream world. The duchess was also having an affair with two British diplomats, to whom she divulged everything she learned from Metternich. She was also frequenting brothels with them. If he couldn't keep track of his main mistress, I wasn't sure he'd be much help gaining information about Murat. I made an excuse, which he readily accepted. There were many women in Vienna.

On December 31, I attended a ball at Palais Razumovsky, where seven hundred guests wandered about the splendid neoclassical structure, complimenting the count on his enviable collection of masterpieces. Beethoven had been invited but declined. I was disappointed. I still felt his hand slipping from my grasp.

The count's massive riding school, where he often showed his powerful black stallions, had been transformed into a ballroom with coronets of exotic flowers and hundreds of candles in crystal sconces. The ball commenced with a polonaise before moving on to several lively mazurkas, and then, after a performance by the Imperial Ballet, the orchestra struck up a waltz. I'd been mingling with members of the Russian delegation, trying to gather more information about Murat, when I saw Friedrich on the dance floor. He was waltzing with a beautiful young woman who looked vaguely familiar. I kept picturing her in Biblical garb and then it struck me: "Esther" from the *tableau vivant*. "King Ahasuerus" was dancing nearby.

From the way Friedrich looked at her, I knew they were in love. He had looked at me the same way when we'd shared our first waltz. She, like Armgard, was petite, her head barely reaching his chest. Friedrich saw me and after the music stopped, he walked over. "May I have the next dance," he asked. The orchestra started to play another waltz.

"Aria da capo," I said. "The song ends as it begins."

"Or begins as it ends," Friedrich replied.

With his elbows held high and away from his body, he placed his right hand on my left shoulder blade; his left hand held my right. In the thirteen years since I'd waltzed with him, the dance had become more intimate, our hips drawn together.

"You're in love with her, aren't you?" I asked, feeling the warmth of his skin beneath his clothes.

"Who are you talking about?" he said, sweeping me across the floor.

"Esther," I replied, trying to remain calm.

"Esther?" He looked perplexed.

"Esther and King Ahasuerus. Remember, the *tableau vivant* before the Beethoven concert?"

"How did you know?"

"I just knew. Is she your mistress?"

Friedrich nearly lost a step. "Yes, she's married to—"

"King Ahasuerus."

"Julie, must we do this now? We're dancing." He pressed his body even tighter, and I could understand why so much had been written about the sinful effects of the waltz. Right then I felt as naked as the Naked Angel.

After the music stopped, Count Razumovsky announced that a lottery would take place. I expected Friedrich to find Esther, but she'd disappeared with her husband. The men drew prizes, awarding them to the women of their choice. Someone received a sable cape to great applause. "I don't want to monopolize all your time," I said to Friedrich, to which he replied, "You aren't."

We took seats in an adjacent room and talked for a long time, about Armgard, whose health was poor; the death of my mother; his family biography; the children, our children; the key players at the Congress—Metternich, Talleyrand, Britain's Castlereagh. He asked why I'd come. I told him I was visiting my father, and he said, "And also spying for the Murats."

"How did you know?" I asked.

"There are few secrets here. Baron Hager is gathering intelligence on everyone. He employs housekeepers to ransack wastebaskets and pilfer letters. Don't trust anyone."

"Then you shouldn't trust me. Even without the police, I happen to know that you were seen entering the Naked Angel's bedchamber a mere two weeks ago."

He laughed. "Diplomacy, my dear."

I pressed him to tell me what he knew of Murat's chances of retaining his throne. "Next to nothing," he replied. "Metternich has little loyalty to Caroline. Murat will be lucky to keep his life, let alone his kingdom."

At two in the morning, the doors opened to the dining room, where fifty tables were set with gold porcelain bearing Razumovsky's monogram in the shape of flower garlands. Despite quarrels over territory, the representatives of the Congress were united in their love of fine cuisine. There were plates of sturgeon from the Volga; truffles from Perigord; oysters from Cancale; oranges from Sicily. Fruit trees from imperial hothouses lined the room. People plucked ripe peaches, biting into the soft golden flesh, the sweet juice mingling with the scent of exotic flowers swaying from the ceiling.

Friedrich had arranged for us to be seated next to each other, and we drank too much wine and laughed as the French and English delegations fought over the merits of Brie versus Stilton. After dessert, we strolled through the palace, peeking into the music room, where the count's own string orchestra had played Beethoven's notoriously difficult quartets. We walked through galleries filled with Raphaels, Rubenses, van Dycks, and Correggios.

In the distance, I heard muffled cries from numerous bedchambers. The nature of the Congress permitted and encouraged such amorous activities. I'm not sure what happened next. I might have kissed Friedrich, or he kissed me. All I know is that he pressed me against the wall, kissed me again, and lifted up my gown. Everything melted away, the horror of my rape, my despair over Beethoven, my disappointment with Robert. I remembered Caroline showing me *The Sleeper of Naples* and realized that I'd been asleep for far too long.

I was still clinging to Friedrich when I smelled something burning. I immediately thought that they were presenting hundreds of flambés to the remaining guests, but then someone shouted "Fire!" and I heard the percussive pop of explosions. Running from the room, we were immediately engulfed in thick black smoke. The fire was already well under way, moving with sickening speed through the palace. Flames darted from the walls and ceilings. The smoke was so thick I could barely see. Friedrich picked me up, dodging burning beams that fell to the ground, igniting the marquetry floors.

We made it outside, inhaling the bitter-cold air. My eyes burned so much that I could barely open them, but when I did I saw Palais

Razumovsky, the receptacle of all that was fine and beautiful, burning to the ground. A few brave servants remained inside, trying to save some of the art by flinging it out the window. Farther away, I heard shrieks that didn't sound human. I looked over at Friedrich. "The horses," he said grimly.

The wind picked up and with it the scent of burning flesh. Half in a daze, I began walking around in the blackened snow as if surveying a battlefield. A woman's painted torso, charred and disfigured, was lying in the sludge. Several busts by Canova had landed not far from where we were standing, their heads cracked open, noses broken.

Count Razumovsky, wearing the sable cape from the lottery, was seated on the ground, head in hands, weeping. The fire brigade arrived, but it was too late. Floors buckled, the roof collapsed. Emperor Francis appeared and patted the count on the shoulder. Tsar Alexander offered the same gesture. No one spoke. Except for the crackling of the fire, it was dead quiet. Even the horses had stopped shrieking.

Friedrich placed his coat around me. I was dressed only in my ball gown, and my exposed arms were turning blue. He saw me home to my father's, but we were too stunned to even speak. My gown was mottled with singe marks and reeked of burning embers. After Lucy helped me undress, I tossed it into the hearth. It, too, went up in flames.

27

E ven the destruction of Palais Razumovsky didn't stop the festivities, and a January snowstorm brought yet another party. I met
Eleonora inside the grand court of the Hofburg, where pairs of plumed
horses with ribbon-plaited manes were attached to thirty-two freshly
gilded sleighs. Some were shaped like winged chariots, others like swans.
All had gold embroidery and spherical bells decorating each harness.

I was teamed up with the Prussian diplomat who was living in my
music room. We hadn't spoken since I'd arrived in Vienna, and after
he inquired if I played the pianoforte, a trumpet signaled the start of
the procession, and a huge sleigh containing a small orchestra led the
way to Schönbrunn Palace. Gliding across the snow, we encircled a
frozen lake, where two Dutch skaters dressed as milkmaids performed
a waltz, then a young British attaché laboriously traced the monogram
of every sovereign into the ice. Next, we filed into the palace theater
for a production of the opera *Cendrillon*, based on Charles Perrault's
fairy tale *Cinderella*. At intermission I saw Beethoven wearing a look of
utter desperation.

"I've made a terrible mistake coming here," he said. "The opera is
terrible, and it's not just my hearing."

I had no idea how he'd made his way to Schönbrunn. I hadn't seen him at the Hofburg, but he told me that he had arrived earlier in a carriage.

"I must go," he said abruptly. "One day you can tell me how the story ends."

"She marries the prince."

"What a surprise!" he said, retrieving his hat and coat. I grabbed my cape and followed. Beethoven glanced at several skaters doing pirouettes and then at me. He didn't know what to do. One of the drivers asked if he could help, and Beethoven growled, "Take me home." He climbed into one of the winged chariots, and I got in next to him, covering our laps with a large fur. The horses were frisky, and as we flew over the ice-crusted snow, Beethoven lost his hat and I started to laugh. He laughed too, and I saw that his teeth were as white as ever and that he still could look boyish and merry.

The sleigh dropped us off at the Hofburg, and we walked to the Black Camel, where Beethoven was a regular. The waiters, anticipating trouble, already looked nervous. After greeting the owner and several fellow musicians, Beethoven found a quiet table in the back and then ordered red wine and calf's liver for both of us. I had dreamed of this day for so long that I couldn't believe it was actually here. I studied his face, trying to memorize the colors and contours so I could bring them back to Naples. His hair, wild from the sleigh ride, was streaked with gray but still thick and abundant. He was forty-four but looked much younger. His skin, flushed from the sleigh ride, was plump as a baby's, his eyes fearsome as ever. When the food came, he ate with gusto, gravy splattering onto his cravat and down his waistcoat. Mopping it up with his serviette, he displayed his hands, muscular, strong, still capable of ripping a pianoforte in two.

I didn't know what there was between us, but I still felt it, and I sensed that he did too. It was hard to put into words. As impossible as it seemed, I knew that we belonged together, and yet I also knew that our mutual attraction could quickly turn to anger. I reminded myself to be gentle with him.

"You are well?" I said, realizing it was a ridiculous question, because he was increasingly deaf and would undoubtedly regale me with stories of his numerous stomach complaints.

"No, I'm not. I've had to fight with my benefactors to get the remaining shares of my annuity. It has caused me great suffering. Lobkowitz has yet to come through with his portion. What a princely rogue he turned out to be! Do you know what I call him? Prince Fizlypuzly!" He laughed and ordered more wine.

"I hear *Fidelio* was a great success," I said, attempting to enunciate clearly. "People told me how much they admired it."

"You don't have to move your mouth in such an ugly way. I'm not yet totally deaf. Some voices I hear better than others. I can hear yours." He went on, "Yes, people seemed to like *Fidelio*. I received many compliments on it, but then, I receive many compliments in general. Women are always flattering me."

"You are very fortunate, then."

He shrugged. "Women are drawn to me because of the music. It exerts a spell over them."

"But you haven't found a wife?"

"No," he said sadly. "I would like to be married. Giving up on love is close to giving up on life." He pointed to a couple several tables away. "Look at the adoring expression on the woman's face. That is beautiful to me. My needs are simple. All I want is a pretty woman who will sigh at my music. A milkmaid, perhaps. Unfortunately, the women I meet are usually from noble families."

"A milkmaid? What on earth would you say to a milkmaid?"

"Bring me some milk."

"That's ridiculous! We both know that you don't really want a woman who milks cows."

"You don't know," he said, becoming agitated. "You get some things right about me but many things wrong. You've always made me dizzy and continue to do so."

Emboldened by the wine, I debated revealing the secret I'd been holding for more than a decade. I wanted to tell him that I loved him, that I would have married him, that I sacrificed everything in order for him to keep his stipend. Six hundred florins a year. That's how much I was worth. Most of all, I wanted to ask him the question that had been gnawing at me since that shattering day eleven years ago. *Given the choice between me and your stipend, what would you have chosen?*

I was afraid to hear the answer, so I kept quiet. Loving him had changed my life, but my impact on his was minimal. He had already written eight symphonies, twenty-seven pianoforte sonatas, ten violin sonatas, eleven string quartets, five pianoforte concerti, songs, choral works, an opera, and more. He had been loved by and undoubtedly loved many other women. His life was grand and important. Mine was not.

I listened to him complain about his music publishers and his stomach issues. He didn't ask me any questions, but I'd come to expect that. Even in the best of times, he usually talked only about himself. I asked if he'd seen Josephine, and he told me never to mention her name again. "She's had a very difficult time," I said. "Her husband kidnapped three of her children."

"You've seen her?" he asked.

"Not since the fall. She's currently in Martonvásár. Her weak nerves."

I wasn't sure if he had heard me or if he'd grown disinterested in the subject. Nevertheless, I pushed ahead. "Christoph Stackelberg was very cruel. He hit her. Then he took a vow of chastity."

"What?" he said. "You're whispering." Looking embarrassed, he pulled a funnel-shaped object from deep inside his pocket, inserting the narrow end into his ear. "My ear trumpet," he added. "I don't think it helps."

I leaned closer to him. "Chastity! Chastity! He took a vow of chastity."

"Why should I care what vows he takes?"

"I just thought you might be interested because of Josephine's daughter—Minona." It had recently crossed my mind that perhaps she might be Beethoven's.

"Countess Gallenberg, are you spying for that archvillain Baron Hager? Is poor old Beethoven under suspicion? Every time I think you can be trusted, you reveal yourself to be a corrupt, dishonest woman."

"That is unfair and untrue."

"You don't seem to appreciate the pain I suffer. I just described the agony I endured to get the shares of my annuity. Are you deaf?"

"I am not deaf, and if you think I'm so untrustworthy, so inherently evil, then you should leave right now."

Beethoven hesitated, recognizing that at the very least it was impolite to abandon a woman in a public place. He took a large sip of wine.

"Go!" I ordered.

Beethoven rose from his chair, banging into the table and knocking over the wine bottle. As he lumbered out of the room, the waiters gave him a wide berth. One came over to see if I was all right. "Don't mind him," he said. "He's a difficult man. It's his deafness and also his personality. Last week he threw a plate of schnitzel at me." He pointed to a red mark above his eye. "See! I could have lost my sight. If you suffered only verbal abuse, he must think highly of you."

I paid the bill and, shaking with anger, I went outside. It was still snowing, the angels atop the buildings buried up to their wings. Instinctively, I closed my eyes and stuck out my tongue, catching a few snowflakes on the tip. I heard someone loudly clearing his throat and saw Beethoven standing a few feet away. "You are acting very strangely," he said. "Why are you sticking out your tongue?"

"Catching snowflakes. You should try it."

"I have better things to do."

"Like loitering in front of the Black Camel?"

"I was waiting to take you home. Anyway, it's a good night for a brisk walk."

"No, it is not. It's very cold and it's snowing."

He went ahead anyway, and I followed him toward the Graben and Stephansplatz. My hands started to grow numb, and I pulled off my gloves and began to rub my palms together. He removed his own gloves, and taking my hands in his, he began to massage them. His hands felt warm, the heat penetrating my skin. We were standing beneath a streetlamp, and he noticed the scar on my palm—my stigma. He'd been in such a rage that day, I doubted he remembered, but he held my palm up to his lips and kissed it.

When we reached my father's house, I wanted to invite him in, but it was already filled to capacity with diplomats. "Good night, Countess," he said. I watched as he hurried away, his unruly hair covered in snow. I hoped he would turn around, wave, smile—anything— but he didn't. I went inside, where the Prussian diplomat was playing the *Moonlight*—badly.

"Do you like Beethoven?" he asked innocently.

"I love him. But tonight, I'd really prefer Mozart."

The following day, I received an envelope covered in ink blotches. I recognized the handwriting immediately and read the enclosed letter.

> *My dearest Giulietta,*
> *Thank you for almost everything.*
> *Your*
> *Beethoven*

Almost everything? What did that mean? What hadn't I given him? Next to his name, it appeared that he'd drawn a heart with some curlicues. Or was it an ink stain? I showed it to Lucy, who said, "It looks to me like a blighted potato—see those squiggles. Worms!"

"Why would he draw a potato?" I asked, annoyed.

"Why would he do anything?" She ended the conversation by getting into her nightclothes and promptly falling asleep. While she snored, I reread the letter, parsing every word. I had to admit it was something a child could have done. But Beethoven was childlike. It was the reason he could be so ghastly rude to everyone and still be forgiven.

After snuffing out the candle, I lay awake for hours. *Thank you for* almost *everything.* Was he thanking me for paying for the meal? Had he wanted dessert? Was the heart really a potato? Or was the "almost everything" a reference to our unborn child? Why did he have to be so cryptic? He was heroic in his music. Why so tentative in love? Most importantly, why couldn't I put this impossible, quick-tempered, mercurial man behind me?

Because I couldn't.

28

I'd already returned to Naples when Napoleon escaped from Elba. The Congress was still in session, and his latest gambit caught everyone by surprise. In Paris, Napoleon set himself up in the Tuileries and began to rally the troops. Any information I'd gleaned about Murat's future was now superfluous. He'd rashly declared war on Austria and then set off to reunite Italy and seize the crown for himself. Routed by the Austrians at the Battle of Tolentino, he was forced to retreat, riding into Naples in disgrace. With the imminent return of the Bourbons, Murat had to flee, leaving Caroline to negotiate a deal with the British.

She was preparing to leave when I visited her at the Palazzo Reale, where she was staring out the window as the sun danced across the Mediterranean. "The view is so beautiful," she said sadly. "I don't know if I'll ever see it again."

She'd offered up her fleet in exchange for British protection and was escorted to the HMS *Tremendous* docked in the harbor. The British immediately reneged on the agreement, and as the richly attired Bourbon court rode into the city, she watched the end of her husband's reign from a Royal Navy frigate. Stripped of her power, the former queen was left vulnerable to the people's rage. Fishermen surrounded the *Tremendous*, screaming "Whore" and "Pig." They sang songs, not of white butterflies, but of lust-filled she-monsters.

Caroline endured several more days of listening to the sirens' vicious melodies before the *Tremendous* finally set sail. She joined her children in central Italy while Murat embarked on yet another wild scheme to retake the Neapolitan crown. By then, Wellington had defeated Napoleon at Waterloo, and the former emperor was exiled to the island of Saint Helena.

Murat was eventually caught, thrown into prison, and, after a cursory trial, condemned to death. When confronted with a firing squad, the former king was said to have refused a blindfold, kissed a cameo of his wife, and then directed his executioners to spare his face. He gave the final command himself.

In order to purge his kingdom of Murat loyalists, King Ferdinand had resorted to brutality, and it was not uncommon to see police beating men senseless. I feared that my relationship with Caroline might leave me vulnerable to reprisals, but Domenico Barbaja wasted little time ingratiating himself with the former and now current king. The two men, one from the House of Bourbon, the other from a coffeehouse, had much in common, from their crude manners to their insatiable appetite for women and food. They found a kindred spirit in Barbaja's latest discovery: twenty-three-year-old Gioachino Rossini. Not only was he a musical prodigy famous for his buoyant music, but he was also a gastronome, whose culinary tastes were as heavy as his operas were sparkling and light.

Rossini had already made a name for himself in Milan and Venice but was largely unknown in Naples. Barbaja offered Rossini a highly lucrative salary to compose two operas a year. He also gave him an apartment in his palazzo, where the impresario lived with his mistress, the Spanish opera star Isabella Colbran.

Barbaja opened the new season with *Elizabeth, Queen of England*, which Rossini had composed to highlight Colbran's ravishing voice.

All the noble families came out for the premiere, with the king occupying the Royal Box. Next to him was his former mistress and new wife, a position she'd attained not long after Queen Maria Carolina, the mother of his eighteen children, died of apoplexy. The king was eating spaghetti with his fingers, long strands dangling from his stuffed mouth.

The opera was a huge success. Colbran's voice, with its striking agility and three-octave range, was ideally suited to Rossini's florid style. After she sang her thrilling final aria, the audience couldn't stop applauding and screaming. As we congregated in the foyer afterward, I met a man named Henri Beyle, who would later write under the nom de plume Stendhal. "It was so exciting I almost fainted," he said. "Excuse me, but my heart is beating so fast I must sit down."

Robert, who had just completed his latest ballet, *Hamlet*, congratulated Barbaja before introducing me to the portly Rossini. After Robert told him that Beethoven had dedicated a sonata to me, Rossini mentioned how much he admired him and hoped that one day they could meet.

"What is he like?" he asked.

"Brilliant, difficult—like his music," I said.

"Why all this talk about Beethoven?" Barbaja interrupted. "Soon, everyone will be clamoring for my Rossini."

I've tried to erase the memory of my final years in Naples, so I'll provide only a brief summary. King Ferdinand was a despot who sold national property and cut funds for hospitals, fire brigades, and other essential services. He abolished the French system of trial by jury, and public executions became common, mutilated bodies displayed for all to see. Civil marriage and divorce were prohibited, blasphemers committed to lunatic asylums.

A plague hit Naples, the poor suffering from raging fevers, with purple spots and carbuncles visible on their skin. Authorities built ditches around the city, stationing sentries at the farthest perimeter. Anyone who crossed the line was shot to death. In the midst of the plague, a fire broke out in the storage room at the Theater San Carlo. Without a fire brigade, Italy's oldest and most beautiful theater quickly burned to the ground. The king ordered it rebuilt as fast as possible. It was one thing to have his citizens die of *pestilenza*, but he couldn't live without music.

The plague officially ended in June 1816 with cannon gun salutes and church processionals. Not long afterward, a poor harvest resulted in famine. With lack of food came debilitating fevers, despair, and increased lawlessness. The superstitious Neapolitans believed it was God's vengeance for the death of Murat, who was now remembered as a great and wise king.

Barbaja rebuilt the theater in just nine months. For the theater's inaugural, he staged a performance of an allegorical cantata, *The Song of Parthenope*, along with the ballet *Virtue Rewarded*. It starred dancer Louis Duport, the man who was dressed as a woman at the Congress. He performed his pirouettes en pointe and leapt across the stage as if suspended from wire. Though married to a former ballerina, he and Robert embarked on an affair. Robert told me that he'd found the muse he'd been seeking all his life, though Duport was by then in his midthirties, his career winding down.

Rossini was in love too—with Barbaja's mistress, Isabella Colbran, who left the impresario for the composer. The situation might have been complicated if the political climate hadn't been worse. Barbaja's close association with the increasingly unpopular Ferdinand placed him in a dangerous spot. Under pressure from the revolutionary *carbonari*, whose goal was to institute a constitutional government, members of the theater were arrested for insubordination. Even more problematic for Barbaja, gambling was outlawed. Music was fine and good, but gaming was music's lifeblood.

With the newfound popularity of Italian opera, Barbaja began making plans to bring Rossini and Colbran to Vienna. He talked about leasing a theater, hiring Robert and Duport to help run it. If Robert was thinking of leaving Naples, there was no reason for me to stay in the city or even in the marriage. I'd remained with him while the children were small. He was a devoted father, a rare quality among the men of my acquaintance, but Hugo and Friedrich, fifteen and eleven, were away at boarding school, and Jülchen was already twelve. She wouldn't be happy—the two were very close—but I couldn't tolerate my deceptive marriage any longer.

Before leaving for Vienna, I walked down to the harbor, staring at Megaride for the last time. During the past sixteen years, I'd faced the death of a child, the loss of my mother, and endured famine and plague and fires. I lived with a man who didn't love me, and at times I was so unhappy I could have filled the Bay of Naples with my tears. At thirty-eight, I was no longer La Bella Guicciardi, but at least I hadn't thrown myself into the sea.

I packed carefully, placing Beethoven's last letter inside my chemise. Over the years I'd read it obsessively and knew every curlicue and blotch. I must have traced the little drawing with my index finger a thousand times.

Thank you for almost everything.

PART THREE

29

I felt something graze my temple. My hand flew up to my face as a woman brushed past me in the doorway. "Even if you've fallen on hard times," she warned, "don't become his housekeeper." Another woman followed. "And don't be his cook either."

I picked up the flying object, a leather-bound volume of Homer's *Odyssey*. The cover was flecked with candle wax and ringed with coffee stains.

"Is Homer your preferred weapon?" I asked Beethoven. "Or do you alternate with Shakespeare?"

He stared at me through his spectacles. Deep horizontal lines slashed his high forehead and ran vertically on both sides of his mouth. His ruddy complexion had turned sallow, and his hair, now totally gray, was so long and wild he could have been one of the witches in *Macbeth*. He was wearing a navy dressing gown spotted with more candle wax, one foot in a velvet slipper, the other bare. His big toe was black and blue.

"I kicked the housekeeper," he explained. "She was a troglodyte, a hound from hell. The cook was no better—a vile arch swine!" His voice sounded sharper, more grating. "Why do I attract such beastly creatures? Is it too much to ask for someone to have a pleasant face and sufficient brains for cooking and mending?"

Six years had gone by since we'd seen each other, six years of dreaming and hoping, and not once during that time, not once on my worst day, did I picture such a reunion. Nannette Streicher had warned me that he had become intolerable. After spending several years supervising his household, she'd eventually given up. Convinced that the servants were stealing, slandering, and trying to poison him, he'd fire them and then ask her to hire more. She grew exhausted dealing with him. "As a musician, he has no equal," she had said, "but as a human being, he is mistrustful, parsimonious, and at times quite vicious. Be careful—he'll suck the life out of you."

I was still standing in the doorway holding the book. I'd carried the note he'd given me and had planned to compliment him on his little drawing of the G cleft merged with a heart. Brushing a pile of papers off a nearby chair, he gathered his dressing gown around him and sat down. "I've recently suffered a severe attack of rheumatism," he announced.

"May I come in?" I asked. When he didn't respond, I walked into the apartment, which resembled all his previous places in its titanic disorderliness. I placed the book on the dining table next to an open sketchbook and a plate of half-eaten red herring. Two pianofortes were in the room, along with the portrait of his grandfather propped up against a wall.

"I've returned to Vienna," I said loudly.

"Yes, I suppose you've been on an odyssey," he replied sarcastically. "At first I thought you were *ein Geist*."

"A ghost? Do I look that different?"

"Please speak in a loud voice. This is one of my better days, but I cannot hear when you mumble."

"Do I look that different?"

"Yes. Older." The years hadn't tempered his tactlessness. He looked down at his hands, which still retained a youthful appearance, the skin taut, the thick fingers strong and powerful. "The rheumatism attacked my joints," he continued. "I was in great pain."

All the available chairs were filled with his detritus, and I was afraid to move anything, so I walked over to examine the curious contraption on his pianoforte. Made of black metal, it was shaped like a cupola and rested on the instrument's soundboard.

"It's my hearing machine," Beethoven explained, getting up to show me. "Nannette's brother built it. I received it about six months ago."

As I bent down to look inside it, Beethoven immediately started banging on the keys. The sound resonated so loudly that it hurt my ears. "Ouch!" I cried.

Beethoven laughed. "That will teach you not to go near my things without asking first."

The pianoforte had a red mahogany finish inlaid with marquetry and ormolu and gracefully turned legs. "Broadwood made it especially for me," he said, referring to the English pianoforte manufacturer. He pointed to the inscription on the wrest plank above the company label: "This instrument is a gift from Thomas Broadwood (London) to honor the great Beethoven."

"Would you play for me?" I asked, hoping that music would lift his current mood.

"I'm not going to dedicate anything to you, if that's what you're getting at," he said. He sat down at the pianoforte, placing his head midway between the keys and the hearing machine, and began to play the first movement of a new sonata. I didn't know what to expect. I hadn't heard him perform in almost a decade. He had great difficulty discerning the notes. At times they were too soft, other times too loud, but even so, the music flowed like a waterfall—light, ethereal, as fine as angel hair. The first movement lasted only about seven minutes, but he refused to play anything more.

"I love it," I said. "So delicate."

"It doesn't stay that way."

"I didn't think so."

I asked him about the Broadwood, and he told me that he liked the sensation of his fingers sinking into the keys. It was almost as if he could "hear" the music vibrating through the frame.

I wanted to learn more, but he began ranting about the servants again, giving me a description of all the ills he'd suffered due to their stupidity and incompetence. "Now I have no one to cook for me. I've been unwell, and I need something to eat. I'm going to a tavern around the corner."

I could hear the March winds scraping against the windowpanes. I told him it was foolish to venture outside, especially since he had been ill. Ignoring me, he threw a coat over his dressing gown and headed for the door wearing only one slipper.

"Stop!" I yelled. "This is madness."

He turned around. "Would you have me die of starvation?"

Beethoven looked so helpless that even though I had no idea how to cook, I volunteered to make something for him.

"Bread soup!" he said, clapping his hands. "Before the cook turned into Satan, she bought all the ingredients and made the broth. You don't have to do a thing."

"I just toss the bread into the broth?"

"Didn't your mother teach you anything?" he scolded, taking off his coat and escorting me to the small kitchen. "No, I suppose she didn't." He dragged over a chair and sat down. "Just follow my instructions."

I wondered if I'd gone insane. Lucy had always worried that I'd wind up in the Gugelhupf, and perhaps I'd been committed for loving Beethoven. I added a cup of farina to the broth while he shouted, "Stir! Stir!" Beethoven examined the consistency. "I don't like it lumpy. See! There are two lumps right there."

"If you're such an expert, why don't you make it yourself?"

"It tastes better when someone does it for me. But it has to be the right person, not that beast of a cook who tried to kill me."

After I fried the onions in lard, I added chunks of day-old bread, a sprinkling of mace and nutmeg, and a tablespoon of butter. I was about to add the eggs when Beethoven jumped up again. "No!" he cried. "Bring them to me. Ten on a plate." He held each egg up to the light, cracked it open, and sniffed for freshness. Satisfied, he dropped the yolks into the soup and instructed me to whisk them.

When the soup was finally ready, I ladled it into a bowl and brought it to him at the dining table, where he was waiting impatiently.

"You must eat too," he said.

"No, thank you. I'm not hungry."

"I insist!"

I poured a little soup and, pushing the herring aside, sat opposite him. He looked from my bowl to his. "You haven't taken enough. In honor of your unexpected arrival, I will split my portion exactly in half." I didn't like bread soup, but as our future depended upon it, I ate it reluctantly. Beethoven quickly finished off his serving, telling me that it was the best he had ever tasted. "Perhaps you'd like to be my cook," he teased. He opened a bottle of wine and poured us each a glass.

I was eager to hear what else he was composing, pointing to the sketchbook next to the herring. "It's my great Mass—the *Missa Solemnis*, in honor of Archduke Rudolph's installation ceremony as the archbishop of Olmütz."

"When will that be?"

"It already happened—over a year ago. I'm a little late, but it doesn't matter. It's an eternal work." He scowled. "But I'm deeply hurt that you care only about my music."

"It's your life. Why wouldn't I care?"

"Yes, I suppose it is my 'life,' as you put it. How's your musician? Still churning out that execrable *Scheisse*?"

"Yes, he's still composing, but we've decided to separate."

"The great love story ends unhappily? Perhaps his *Scheisse* will now become easier to digest." He scraped the last remaining bits of soup from his bowl. "Vienna is a terrible place to live. You should have stayed in Naples. You know what they call the chief of police, Count Sedlnitzky? Metternich's poodle!" He screeched with laughter. "The Viennese are such *Ass*-trians."

More than anything, I wanted to leave. I wanted to climb into bed, pull the covers over my head, and pretend it was all a bad dream. Beethoven had always been difficult, but the latest incarnation bordered on insanity. I wondered how much his deafness contributed to his behavior. He seemed to be able to hear me, but it was hard to tell because he was ranting so much.

"I have a son," he announced. "He's really my nephew, but I call him my son. He's at boarding school here. After my brother Karl died, I took him away from the Queen of the Night."

When I gave him a puzzled look, he said, "She's the evil mother in *The Magic Flute*. I thought you knew Mozart."

"Your son—I mean, nephew—is appearing in *The Magic Flute*?" I had to repeat it twice, at increased levels of volume.

"Of course he's not appearing in *The Magic Flute*!" he shouted. "The Queen of the Night is my brother's widow—a bestial whore! You know what she's gone and done? She's had a bastard daughter and named her Ludovica. After me!"

"Maybe she just liked the name."

"Ludovica—*Ludwig*. She did it to taunt me, but I will get even."

Listening to his ugly tirade, I remembered our dream of living in Paris and pictured myself making bread soup in Montmartre while he attacked the government, housekeepers, and whores. I cleaned up the dishes while he finished off the wine.

"I don't know if you've heard, but Josephine is ill," he said suddenly.

"Have you seen her?"

He shook his head no.

I put on my coat. "I must be going."

We stared at each other as if searching for a way to rekindle the love we'd once felt. It was so long ago that it felt like swimming against the current back through time. He reached for my hand. I'd put on my gloves, but with the skill of a young virtuoso, he dexterously plucked each fingertip until my right hand was bare. He turned it over to look at my palm. "My eyesight is bad," he said. "But your scar—I think it's gone."

I wanted to tell him that the wound had become an invisible stigma. It was still just as painful. He didn't lift my hand up to his lips but simply held it. His own hand felt warm and strong and so full of life that I could feel his heart beating through the vein at the base of his thumb.

"I would dearly love to see you again," he said.

I looked at his wild hair, windswept even indoors, at his white whiskers, unruly eyebrows, and stained dressing gown. I glanced down at his feet, one still unshod, and at the dining room table, herring next to the *Missa Solemnis*. A voice said, *You are as mad as he is.*

Another voice said, "Yes, I would like that too."

30

Josephine was propped up in bed, eyes bright and sparkling, skin the color of alabaster, lips bloodred. If not for the leeches at her throat, she could have passed for any number of fashionable ladies who used cosmetics and starvation to approximate the outward effects of consumption. But Josephine's wraithlike appearance wasn't a nod to prevailing notions of beauty. My mercurial cousin, my ally, my foe, was dying from the disease.

Outside Palais Deym, a few straggly tourists were debating the price of tickets to Müller's Art Gallery, while inside, a dozen transient boarders were loitering in rooms that had once resounded with Beethoven's music. Gone were the prisms dangling from the chandeliers, along with most of the crystals. Men had snuffed out cigars on the marquetry floors, leaving angry scorch marks.

The doctor waited patiently for the engorged leeches to drop off Josephine's neck. When they'd finished feasting, he placed them in a washbasin, where they wriggled and squirmed and eventually expelled her tainted blood. Twenty-year-old Viky—the once tiny baby I had known as petite Victoire—pleaded with him to try something new.

"There's nothing more," he said, patting the leeches dry before placing them in a jar. "We tried traditional bloodletting, but it weakened her system too much. Some women are prone to the disease. Your mother suffered from melancholia and experienced a number of sad passions. That's why we call consumption the affliction of the broken-hearted." The doctor tapped the leech jar. "Come on, little ones. We have a busy day ahead."

"It's Julie," I whispered to Josephine. "I'm sorry you are unwell." Two pink spots blossomed high on her cheeks, a telltale sign of fever.

"Don't be sorry, dear Julie," she said, yielding to a coughing spasm. Viky held a handkerchief to her mouth. It was quickly saturated in bright-red blood. We waited until she fell asleep and then went into an adjacent room to talk.

If consumption was the "affliction of the broken-hearted," Josephine had suffered her share of grief. I knew that she'd already lost three of her children to her second husband, Christoph, but there was more bad news. Viky confided that a mathematics tutor Josephine had hired as a role model for her son Fritz had seduced her and left her with child. Since the police had already branded her "immoral," she gave birth in a remote mountain hut and convinced the tutor to take the infant. The baby died two months later.

Josephine's relationship with her mother never recovered from the various scandals. Aunt Anna blamed Josephine for blackening the family's name, and Josephine insisted that everything could have been avoided if she hadn't been forced into an arranged marriage. While she had grown to love Joseph, he wouldn't have been her first or even tenth choice. She loved Beethoven right from the moment she laid eyes on him—at approximately the same time I did.

"And now she doesn't even have any money," Viky explained. "Fritz amassed huge gambling debts and pressured Mama to pay them off."

"What of Franz?" I asked about Josephine's brother.

Viky explained that Franz believed that she'd squandered the money he had already provided and that he needed to conserve his resources for his own family and farm animals.

"And Therese? They were always so close."

"She begged Mama to leave Vienna and move into Grandmama's house in Pest. When Mama refused, Aunt Therese accused her of fulfilling her own dire fate. Herr Beethoven has been kind. A few months ago, he had someone deliver four hundred florins."

I remembered the money he'd sent to me in Naples. It was one hundred florins less than what he'd given Josephine. I was appalled that such a thought even crossed my mind, but with a woman's worth quantifiable in numbers, it was hard not to think that way.

"Does he come to visit often?" I asked.

"No. I haven't seen him at all." Josephine had started coughing again, and Viky excused herself to tend to her mother.

I was staying with my father until I could find a place to live. He was now sixty-nine years old, frail, and, like Beethoven, had poor hearing. Unlike Beethoven, however, he didn't need his ears to pursue his passion for reading. After we exchanged the usual pleasantries, he retreated behind a well-worn copy of Shakespeare's plays. Since I hadn't lived in Vienna for many years, I had few friends in the city and decided to visit Robert's sister, Eleonora. She'd been kind to me during the Congress, and, with her husband's death and her children married, she was alone.

Eleonora looked nearly as ill as Josephine, but then I realized that she, too, had adopted the consumptive style. She had even painted blue veins on her skin, marbling her complexion like a trompe l'oeil artist.

"What brings you to Vienna?" she asked. "Robert tells me nothing."

He had obviously failed to tell her about our separation. "He's been very busy with his music," I explained. "You know how much it means to him."

"And to everyone! Wasn't he composing a ballet based on *Macbeth*?"

"It was a great success, especially the sleepwalking scene. One critic called it 'truly soporific.'"

"It must be difficult to live with such a brilliant man. My mother always said it would take a special woman to be Robert's wife."

"Yes, and I've failed miserably," I confessed. "That's why I've returned without him. We've decided to separate."

"*Separate?*" Eleonora exclaimed. "Everyone thought you were the perfect couple. Poor Robert. I hope it hasn't affected his work."

"I'm happy to report that he's as prolific as ever. He's already written the music for *Alfred the Great* and *Joan of Arc*, and he may be coming to Vienna with the impresario Domenico Barbaja. They hope to bring Rossini with them."

"Rossini! That's very exciting news. I've only heard his operas in German but would love to hear them in Italian. Prince Metternich adores Rossini!"

The prince, who'd hosted the Congress and was about to be named Austria's chancellor, had suppressed free speech and cracked down on the press and intellectuals. Dissidents were tossed in jail without charge. When I expressed my disapproval, Eleonora was quick to defend him. "We can't have another French Revolution," she said. "He's doing it only for our own good, and personally, I've never met a dissident. If one of them winds up in jail, I'm not sure I'd even notice."

We reminisced about the Congress, a turning point in Vienna's musical life. "Everything is so different now," she lamented. "All of Louis's major patrons, except Archduke Rudolph, are dead. Nobody has a private orchestra anymore. The fire at Palais Razumovsky signaled the end of an era."

I pictured Friedrich and me shivering in the snow as flames shot from the roof. I wished things had been different, but the ending had been so explosive, so definitive, that only Beethoven could compose an alternate coda. Still, I couldn't help asking Eleonora if she knew what became of him.

"He remains the Saxon envoy. He recently arranged a marriage between the emperor's daughter and the nephew of the Saxon king. He's the perfect man to play Cupid."

"And Armgard? Are they still married?"

"You seem to know quite a lot about him," she teased. "You're not leaving Robert for him, are you?" We both laughed. "Yes, he's still with that tiresome woman. He had the most beautiful mistress, but she died of consumption. I heard he was grief-stricken. Such a dreadful ailment. I feel a little guilty embracing the fashion, but it's so attractive, no?"

Josephine couldn't stop coughing, blood bubbling around the corners of her mouth. After each convulsion, she'd collapse against the pillows, her dark lashes fanning out over hollowed eye sockets. Viky mopped her brow and tried to make her as comfortable as possible.

Josephine's son Fritz had been released from his army regiment to attend the death scene and arrived drunk and in need of money. He immediately badgered his mother for a loan.

"Fritz, please," Viky begged. "Can't you see that she's dying?"

Fritz could barely stand up, and Viky escorted him into another room while I sat with Josephine. Delirious with fever, she was singing songs and mumbling snatches of verse. "'I am alone,'" she murmured. "'Forlorn on the hill of storms.'"

"You are not alone," I said. "I'm here with you."

"Louis," she cried. "I love him, you know." She was having difficulty breathing, choking on her own blood. Her shoulder blades jutted out like a sparrow's wings each time she gasped for air.

"My dear Josephine," I said, holding her hand. She continued to cough, her breathing more labored. I hadn't said a prayer since Santa Chiara, when the cloisters opened up to a bounty of color, a rainbow in a garden of austerity, but dropping to my knees, I asked the Blessed Virgin to bring her soul to heaven. She had suffered enough.

When I learned that Josephine had died, I took a carriage to the Landstrasse to tell Beethoven. "She loved you," I said. "She told me many times."

"Many women love me," he said coldly.

"I don't know who these women are, but I can tell you that Josephine truly loved you. She kept loving you through all her troubles, and you didn't even bother to visit her when she was dying."

"I told you I was ill," he said. "I couldn't go."

"Yes, you did tell me. But if you had a concert, I can assure you that you'd have gotten out of your sickbed to show up."

"Don't you understand?" he shouted. "My mother died of consumption. All I remember is the blood. For years afterward, I'd check my phlegm for traces of it. I was terrified that I'd die too. I couldn't see Josephine dying like my mother."

I gave him the details of the funeral and left. Beethoven had such a forceful personality that I forgot how fragile he could be. It was all there in the music, the moments of ferocious defiance mixed with the very naked need to love and be loved.

Several days later, I joined a small group of mourners at the parish church of Saint Maria Rotunda. The soft light from the circular windows highlighted the frescoes of the Virgin Mother on the barrel-vaulted ceiling. Beethoven wasn't there. Neither were Josephine's two other children by Joseph. I wondered if the Stackelberg offspring even knew that their mother had died. After the requiem Mass, Josephine's coffin was taken to Währing Cemetery on the outskirts of the city. It was raining hard, just as it had at Josephine's wedding, and I knew that Therese was thinking, *Doom*. As we returned to the carriages, I glanced back at the cemetery. A short, stocky man, hat in hand, was going in to say goodbye.

31

Domenico Barbaja was in true beastly form when I met him at the café at the Golden Ox Hotel. "Look at this," he said, thrusting a cup of coffee in my face. "There's cream on top!"

"It's called a *mélange*," I said.

"I don't care what it's called," Barbaja replied. "It's going to compete with my Barbagliata." He called over the waitress. "Do you know that I invented this drink?"

"You invented Viennese coffee?" she asked. "Did you also invent Wiener schnitzel?"

"I deplore the Viennese," he said to me. "What they need is fresh Italian blood, and soon they're going to get it!"

Barbaja had won the lease on the prestigious Kärntnertor Theater and had hired Robert and Louis Duport. More importantly, he was bringing the popular Rossini to draw in the crowds. The newspapers detailed every aspect of their glamorous lives, speculating on the various ways the impresario and his star attraction would reinvigorate the city's musical scene. "Metternich is thrilled," Barbaja said. "He loves Rossini, and thanks to him, I was able to secure the fifty-thousand-florin cash deposit. He convinced the banker Salomon Rothschild to guarantee the money. As a Jew, Rothschild can't own property in Vienna, but at least he'll always have a good seat at the Kärntnertor."

I was waiting to hear why Barbaja had wanted to see me. We hadn't been on the friendliest terms, and with Robert still in Naples, I hoped he didn't have other things in mind.

"You've always been a beautiful woman," he said. "But you also have great style and taste."

I chided myself for agreeing to meet him. He was going to proposition me even as he slurped his *mélange*.

"You'll be happy to know that one of my first priorities is to completely redo the ladies' lavatory," he continued. "The current one is repulsive. Why should a woman spend all her time dressing up to attend the theater only to piss in a cesspit?"

"Did you invite me here so I could offer decorating tips on the lavatory?"

"No, but if you'd care to offer your advice, I'd love to hear it. But I have something more important to discuss. To maintain Austria's cultural legacy, I'm obliged to stage a minimum of three German operas per week. You are close with Herr Beethoven. Do you think you could ask him if he'd compose something for us? Nothing political! It should be light and pleasant à la Rossini."

"I can assure you that will not go over well."

"Why not? Rossini is the most successful composer in the world. Beethoven could learn something from him. Rossini writes for the audience, Beethoven only for himself. People want to have a good time at the theater. The women are dressed up. They want to laugh and feel pretty. It's like the lavatory."

"You're comparing Herr Beethoven to a lavatory?"

"What I'm saying is that he doesn't fit the current mood. Even Metternich says German opera is dead, and he's the chancellor of Austria."

When my daughter Jülchen heard that Robert was returning to Vienna, she couldn't have been happier, advising me that I should reconcile with him. She informed me that a woman of my advanced age—I was thirty-nine—couldn't expect to find another husband. With Hugo and Friedrich away at school, I had Jülchen all to myself. Now a headstrong thirteen-year-old, she insisted on substituting her childish nickname for the more grownup Giulietta. When I explained that it was the name on my sonata, she accused me of living in the past. She refused to take pianoforte lessons, and after I made the mistake of telling her that she'd never find a husband, she took to her room and wouldn't come out until I apologized.

We lived near Stephansplatz, not far from my father's, and I tried to make the apartment as bright as possible. With Vienna's narrow streets, the buildings pressed in on one another, and the plum-colored walls felt dreary and old fashioned. I'd had them painted pale green with white doors and moldings. I thought it looked modern and fresh, but Giulietta said she preferred plum.

Beethoven had moved to Baden without saying goodbye. I was too preoccupied with settling into our new apartment and dealing with Giulietta to spend time obsessing over him. Our visit had left me shaken and filled with self-doubt. Had I spent decades in love with a monster? But whenever I thought back on the way he'd removed my glove, I had to catch my breath. He had once called me bewitching, but he'd bewitched me as surely as Parthenope had bewitched all those sailors she'd lured to their deaths. I was never going to be the milkmaid he dreamed of marrying, never the volatile, incandescent Josephine. Beethoven was always reaching for more in his music, while I was always reaching for more in Beethoven. Two decades was a long time to be in love with a man who was forever exceeding my grasp.

One afternoon in October, Kitty, our new housekeeper and cook, announced that a strange man wanted to see me. Kitty was Lucy's sixteen-year-old niece, and while she came with few qualifications, she was good company for Giulietta. Red-haired and freckled like her aunt, she also had her talent for chatter. "I believe the man has part of a tree in his hair," she said. "I was going to tell him to remove it, milady, but he scares me."

Beethoven was waiting for me in the drawing room, where he was seated on the edge of a chair, running his fingers through his wayward locks. "I've been reading about your husband in the papers," he said in lieu of a proper greeting. "And this Barbaja. Tell me about him."

I picked up a large twig from the Persian carpet and sat down. "His nickname is the Beast," I said loudly.

"You once referred to me as a werewolf. Do you compare all men to ferocious animals?"

"Not all."

"I liked your bread soup," he said. "I'd hoped you'd come to visit me again, but you didn't."

"You were gone for the summer and never bothered to write." I had to repeat the sentence three times.

"True," he said distractedly. "Do you know that I was picked up as a vagrant?" He was yelling because he couldn't hear himself and because he was incensed that he had been mistaken for a tramp. He explained that he'd lapsed into a raptus while going for a walk and become disoriented. Hungry, he began knocking on people's windows to see if he could get some food. "Before I knew it, the police threw me in jail!" he shouted. " I had to share the cell with a thief! And he smelled like week-old herring. I thought of you."

"You thought of me because of herring?"

"No, I remembered when we were both at Baden and you followed me up to Rauhenstein Castle, and I thought you were going to kiss me. Don't ever try that again."

"Do I look as if I want to kiss you?"

"I don't know, but it would be most improper. I've slept with whores." When I didn't immediately respond, he bellowed, *"Whores! I've slept with whores!"*

Lucy and Kitty had been eavesdropping outside. Kitty's hand flew up to her mouth as Lucy dragged her away.

"I'm deeply ashamed," Beethoven confessed.

I sat next to him and took his hand. "Don't be. It's what happens when men don't have wives. It frequently happens when they do have wives."

"I would never sink so low if I had a wife."

To cover up the awkwardness, I returned to his original question about Barbaja and the incursion of his Italian troupe. "He is quite uncouth but a brilliant impresario," I said. "He totally transformed the San Carlo."

I still didn't know the extent of his deafness. His eyes were focused on my face and lips as if willing the sounds into existence. He nodded occasionally to indicate that he understood, but I'd seen my father play the same trick.

"And Rossini?" he asked. "You know him?"

"Yes. He's very good. Not like you. But good. Are you afraid that people will forget you?"

He looked surprised. "No, I certainly am not. I'm still working on my Mass and some variations on a waltz." He went on to explain that the publisher Anton Diabelli had asked fifty composers to write a single variation. "His original composition is nothing more than a beer-hall ditty," he complained. "Horrible, really. But I've already composed two dozen variations and plan to do even more."

"Variations . . . on a waltz?"

"I realize I am not a good dancer, as you know very well."

I remembered his pathetic attempt at waltzing at Prince Lichnowsky's ball. It still pained me because it led to the revelation of his hearing loss and everything else that followed.

"And what about Count von Walzer?'" he asked.

"You mean Friedrich Schulenburg? I haven't seen him in a very long time."

"You love him," Beethoven said bluntly.

At that moment Giulietta came into the room. She shared my coloring, but for the first time, as if seeing her through Beethoven's eyes, I saw Friedrich. Beethoven looked at her and then at me. He knew.

"This is my daughter, Giulietta," I said.

"Ah, yet another Giulietta. You've inherited your mother's fondness for doomed love."

"I've been reading *Romeo and Juliet*," she said. "To die for love, what could be better?"

"She is very young," I explained after she'd left the room.

"Perhaps she'll fall in love with Rossini," he said.

32

*R*ossini, Rossini, Rossini. One couldn't walk down the Graben or sit at a café without hearing those soaring vowels. Unlike Beethoven, who wrestled with every note, Rossini was viewed as a magician, spinning melodies out of silkworm thread. Beethoven might have been a genius, but Rossini—*Rossini!*—was the man of the hour.

He arrived in the spring with his new bride—and Barbaja's former mistress—the coloratura Isabella Colbran. Barbaja didn't seem to mind. He had plenty of mistresses, but there was only one Rossini, and he was busy staging five of his operas for an upcoming festival at the Kärntnertor.

Robert lived with us while he found an apartment. It made Giulietta happy and, despite everything that had passed between us, I had grown fond of him. "Are you still infatuated with Louis Duport?" I asked, remembering their dalliance in Naples.

"No, it's over. Besides, he has a wife in Paris."

"He's in love with her?"

"Louis is in love only with himself."

"He's a very famous ballet dancer. I suppose that's to be expected."

I noted that Robert had maintained his looks. While most men nearing forty had thickened around the middle, he was fit and trim. He asked if we could give our marriage a second chance. He recognized that he hadn't been an ideal husband, but he was willing to change. "It would please Giulietta," he said. "And me as well." He knew other men who, despite their proclivities, had succeeded, and he promised to be faithful.

I was touched but knew it wouldn't work. I couldn't begin to understand what he wanted in a lover. Then again, I didn't understand how I'd wound up as chaste as a Poor Clare. Of the men in my life, Beethoven wouldn't kiss me, because he'd slept with whores; Friedrich had disappeared; and Robert wasn't attracted to women but now seemed willing to take me to bed.

"I wouldn't expect you to be faithful," I told him. "But my answer is no."

Robert seemed both disappointed and relieved, though he could have been feigning disappointment to soothe my pride. He asked if I wanted a divorce, but I assured him that it wasn't a priority. "Thank you," he said genuinely. "As a married man, people won't suspect, or if they do, they won't gossip as much. I do love you, Julie. Just not in the way you deserve."

Metternich held a gala dinner for Rossini at his country villa to celebrate the opening of his opera, *Zelmira*, which was greeted with orgiastic enthusiasm. Rossini, who had just returned from visiting Beethoven, was distraught at finding the man he considered the greatest composer of his generation living in squalor. "The place was so dirty and disorderly," Rossini said, shaking his head. "And his face—it looked unbearably sad. He was gracious enough to compliment me on *The Barber of Seville*. He told me that I should never attempt anything other than comic operas. Coming from anyone else, I would take it as an insult, but I'm sure he didn't mean it that way."

I was sure he did but could only imagine what must have been going through Beethoven's mind. He was fifty-one, Rossini thirty; the younger man had a new wife, an adoring public, and the ability to write one opera after another. Beethoven was alone, respected but not loved, and increasingly deaf. Rossini attempted to solicit contributions for him but was met with total indifference.

"Beethoven is an impossible man," Metternich said. "No amount of money will change that. It is indeed unfortunate that he's deaf, but let's not allow one person's bad luck to ruin this glorious evening."

Metternich offered to give Barbaja a tour of his villa, inviting Robert and me to accompany them. The man once considered the "Adonis of the Drawing Room" was still attractive, but his hair was now white, his cheeks concave from the extraction of several molars. Two daughters had died of consumption, but he kept his grief private, and his various passions—for women, art, and music—appeared to sustain him. He was proud of his sculpture hallway with Canova's *Psyche Revived by Cupid's Kiss* as the centerpiece. "It's such a tender and voluptuous creation," he said, "but for the prudish, I'm obliged to hang my dressing gown around Cupid and toss a sheet over Psyche. I trust none of you are offended."

"Do you have any Canovas?" he asked Barbaja.

"I may have a few lying around somewhere." He shrugged.

"I had the opportunity to admire several fine ones at the Palazzo Reale," I volunteered. "The Murats were great supporters of the artist."

"Now I know why you look so familiar," Metternich said. "You were in the employ of the Murats. The housekeeper at your sister-in-law's worked for the secret police. That's how I learned you were a spy."

When Metternich turned to Barbaja, Robert whispered, "*What?* You were a spy? And you implicated my sister?"

"Whores, spies," Barbaja said. "Women!"

Metternich explained that Caroline Murat, his ex-lover and the former queen of Naples, was now the Contessa di Lipona.

"Lipona?" I asked.

"An anagram of Napoli," he explained. "Pure fantasy. She created it herself. The Bonapartes can never go back to France. They might stir up sympathy, and we've had enough bloodshed. Caroline moved to Austria at the emperor's invitation. She wanted to come to Vienna, but I couldn't have that. We're occasionally in touch. She's very lonely."

"I composed the music for Joseph Bonaparte's coronation," Robert said proudly. "How is he faring?"

"Better than Caroline," Metternich replied. "He's living in New Jersey."

Metternich had supervised the planting of an immense rose garden and urged us to see it. While Robert and Barbaja lingered inside to discuss business, I strolled down the various walkways, admiring the velvety red and bright-pink flowers. Beautiful young women sauntered past, attracting the attention of men of all ages. The *chemise à la grecque* had been abandoned for a more voluminous silhouette, corsets cinching the waist. I'd adapted the new style, donning a blush-colored silk gown with horizontal stripes, short puffed sleeves, and a bonnet decorated with flowers, but I missed the freedom of the loose-fitting gowns. Giulietta accused me of being too nostalgic. Perhaps she was right.

I saw Friedrich in the distance. I should have known he'd be here. Since the fire he'd become a dream figure, someone with whom I might have shared a life, the way I might have married an actor I admired on stage or someone I'd glimpsed on a rainy night in front of the Kärntnertor. I didn't expect him to look my way. At my age, I'd become invisible.

I turned to go but heard him call my name. He quickly caught up to me. "Julie," he said in his rich baritone. "I thought—"

"That I was a ghost?"

He shook his head, gazing in a way that revived me. "You were never a ghost. Even when we were apart, you were always real to me. I assumed you wouldn't be at a party for Rossini."

"One is capable of loving the work of two different composers," I said. "Besides, I'm here in my official capacity as Robert's wife. He's working with Signore Barbaja at the Kärntnertor."

"Yes, I know. It's difficult to escape Rossini. He almost makes one long for Napoleon."

Friedrich looked every bit as handsome as the first time we'd waltzed together. His blond hair remained thick and wavy, his blue eyes more hooded but just as expressive, and his mouth, with its full lower lip, summoned my dormant desire.

"You knew I was in Vienna and didn't bother to contact me?" I asked.

"I could say the same of you, but the truth is I've been in mourning. Someone I loved died." Friedrich had always been skilled at shielding his emotions, but his voice swelled with grief.

"I am sorry," I said.

"We'd been together for many years. Her name was Sofia."

I remembered her as the young countess I'd seen in the *tableau vivant* and then later at Palais Razumovsky. I wondered if Armgard had grown accustomed to sharing him.

I saw Robert stride toward us. The two men had never met, and after I introduced them, Friedrich tried to put everyone at ease by discussing Metternich's skill at landscape design. I noticed Robert examining his face for similarities to our children. Neither, of course, said anything about it.

We walked together toward the conservatory, where round tables overlooked the immense gardens. Armgard had been searching for Friedrich and wasn't happy when she saw us together. The girlish appearance that had once been so appealing no longer suited a woman in her late thirties, and she looked like a rouged *poupée*. She took Friedrich's arm and led him away.

At dinner, Metternich offered Rossini a toast, extolling his virtues as the man who wrote music that went down as easily as an oyster. "Establishing Italian opera in Vienna has been one of the most wonderful episodes of my life," he said. "In comparison to the Italians, the German voice is quite pitiful."

The guests laughed and applauded. Since the majority were German-speaking, it could have been perceived as an insult, but they were so smitten with Rossini that I was surprised they hadn't all moved to the composer's hometown of Pesaro.

"We Viennese want to be calm and happy," Metternich went on. "We want our music to delight and astonish. We want beautiful singing. *Bel canto.* And more than anything we want to welcome Rossini!"

While Robert was talking to Barbaja, Friedrich came up behind me and whispered, "I would like to meet again."

"That would be unwise," I said. "You are still grieving. You don't know your own heart."

"I know my heart all too well. I once grieved for you."

"Friedrich, the carriage is waiting," Armgard called.

"Good night, Countess," he said.

On the ride home, Robert and I were quiet for the longest time. I imagined him thinking about Friedrich and feeling bad that our children were Gallenbergs in name only. I was surprised when he turned to me and said, "Julie, he's your only chance for happiness. You deserve it more than any woman I've ever met. Don't let him slip away."

33

A nd there he is," Caroline said, pointing to a huge equestrian portrait of her late husband, Joachim Murat. Dressed in his signature white-plumed hat, colorful riding breeches, and a blue jacket festooned with gold buttons and braids, he looked exactly as I remembered him—flamboyant, fearless, and slightly absurd.

After Metternich told me that Caroline was lonely, I learned where she lived and made plans to visit. I couldn't forget the jeers and ugly songs when she had left Naples. It reminded me of the story of Marie Antoinette's last days. Caroline, at least, had kept her head and, from a quick look at her surroundings, much more.

"I adored him," she said, staring dreamily at Murat's portrait. "Next to my brother, he was the greatest man I ever knew."

The Contessa di Lipona had apparently forgotten that she'd frequently disparaged his judgment and intellect, but that was before she'd been exiled and turned into an anagram. She had created a museum to his memory, decorating the room with portraits, medals, busts, Turkish swords, sabers, and a diamond-studded dagger. Even his tiger-skin saddlecloth, with the animal's head still attached, was draped over a blue silk bergère, as if he'd just dismounted it.

"I miss him so much," she said.

Napoleon had died of stomach cancer the previous year in exile on Saint Helena. "He suffered greatly," Caroline said. "I hope that isn't my fate."

Caroline's face was still pretty, her luminous skin free of lines, but she had gained much weight, and with her short stature, she looked pudgy and alarmingly low to the ground. If she'd been in her prime, I suspected she would have been in Metternich's bed instead of in the small market town of Frohsdorf.

"Metternich has treated me in the most callous manner," she complained. "I was once his lover. It's true that we mainly traded sexual favors for political gain, but I thought he was sufficiently fond of me to ensure my comfort and freedom. My sister, Pauline, remains at the Villa Borghese, so why am I relegated to this backwater? Yesterday I was so bored I went with the cook to buy onions! I can't decorate anymore, because I've run out of money and my mother—Madame Mère—won't give me a single franc."

Caroline had paid dearly for Schloss Frohsdorf, a large baroque château with an English garden, expansive parklands, and more rooms than anyone who hadn't been a queen could desire. "Do you know that I was forced to sell two of my Correggios to the Marquess of Londonderry? Joachim had bought them in Spain and they held much sentimental value. At least I still have my Canova." She gestured toward a bust of Murat, his deeply carved curls spilling down his back.

"Metternich has a Canova—*Psyche Revived by Cupid's Kiss*."

"It's a copy," she snapped. "Joachim purchased the original from the artist himself. I introduced Metternich to Canova. He knows nothing about art."

A tall, good-looking man entered the room to inquire if we needed anything. Caroline introduced him as General Francesco Macdonald, Murat's former aide-de-camp and minister of war. I wondered whether he was Caroline's lover or paid companion. It was hard to tell by the way they interacted. He seemed obsequious, more like a servant, or maybe he was merely shy.

"It's nice to have company," she said obliquely. "My son, Achilles, is about to leave for America. My other children are rarely here. I so miss the court intrigues and love affairs. I wish I'd appreciated them more at the time."

"It was difficult. We were at war."

"Yes, but war brings lust to the surface. Peace is dreadfully dull, especially in Frohsborg."

"I believe it's Frohsdorf."

"*Borg . . . dorf*. It's all ugly sounding, which is why I never learned German. But what about you? I hope you've brought some delicious gossip."

I tried to be entertaining, regaling her with stories of Vienna's passion for Rossini and the Beast's outrageous antics, but it only made her long for Naples. Switching topics, I announced that Robert and I had separated, but Robert had made such little impression that she asked, "Who is that?" When I started to explain, she said, "Now I remember . . . *les mœurs des grecs*. He was in love with a man who made macaroni."

"He fished."

"Didn't your husband also fall in love with Duport? I saw him perform in Paris on several occasions. His pirouettes took my breath away. He then ran off with a mistress of my brother's and had to escape Paris dressed as a woman. I thought this was very inventive until I saw him dressed like that on several other occasions, and I didn't know if it was intrigue or habit. That's why I've steered clear of creative men. One never knows who or what they'll bring to the bedchamber. But please tell me more about you? What about your musician? Beethoven?"

"It's been difficult," I admitted.

"Does he wear women's clothes? Does he prefer men? Does he have any delicious peccadillos you would care to share?"

"He's losing his hearing."

"That's not very interesting. I think you should reconsider your options. Schulenburg is your best choice." I was surprised she knew anything about him. When she saw my startled look, she laughed. "It was common knowledge at the Congress. My spies told me."

"I thought I was your spy."

"Did you think I'd rely solely on you? I had many spies. I should tell you that I slept with Schulenburg. It was a long time ago. He's a very good lover, as you undoubtedly know, but he was immune to my charms. I could never get him to divulge one secret, whereas Metternich would disclose the most private information the minute he jumped into bed. It was amazing how much he could reveal with his tongue so preoccupied. I do miss those days."

I was jealous that Friedrich had slept with Caroline, though I realized it was all in the past and in the line of duty. My visit seemed to have done little to cheer her up, and she announced that she was fatigued and wanted to retire to her private quarters.

"I'm suddenly feeling very old." She sighed. "Forty. How did it happen?"

"I'll be forty this year too," I reminded her.

"Yes, but you've managed to keep your beauty. Use it while you can. Otherwise, you'll wind up like me."

General Macdonald suddenly appeared and, taking her arm, escorted her into one of a dozen bedchambers in her palatial garrison.

Frohsdorf was close to Baden, so I'd arranged to meet Beethoven, who was still struggling with poor health. Since moving from England, Kitty hadn't had a chance to see the countryside, and, as a favor to Lucy, I'd taken her along. She had roamed the gardens and parklands during my visit with Caroline, and the bright autumn sunshine had brought out even more of her freckles.

"Isn't Herr Beethoven the one who sleeps with whores?" she asked. "Why would you want to visit a man who sleeps with whores? And if you did, why go to Baden? You could easily find men like that in Stephansplatz."

"Herr Beethoven is a brilliant musician. I will have no more talk of whores."

The carriage pulled up to a low one-storied house on the Rathausgasse. It was painted imperial yellow, with green shutters and trim, and on one side, several tall chestnut trees had turned golden. Encountering the owner, a cranky locksmith, I inquired as to Beethoven's whereabouts, and he immediately asked, "Are you a relative?"

"No," I replied. "A friend."

"If you were a relative, I'd ask you to reimburse me for damages. Some are beyond reimbursement, such as the noise he makes when he beats time on the kitchen table. The plumber next door moved out. But look at the window shutters! He scrawls notes on them."

"Then you should feel very privileged," I said. "Can you please tell me where he is?"

"Out. Probably for a walk. That's why it's so peaceful here."

"Did he say when he was coming back?"

"Do you think we have that kind of relationship? No, he didn't. He's deaf, you know."

"Yes, I know. When he returns, will you please tell him I'll be waiting in the Theresa Gardens."

A few moments later, I heard loud humming and a crashing sound, as if someone had stumbled over a hedge. It was Beethoven back from wherever he had been.

"You're here," he said, looking confused.

I nodded, not bothering to point out that we'd already arranged the meeting.

"You need to scream," the locksmith instructed. "He's deaf."

"Yes, thank you. I know."

"I'd like to take a walk," Beethoven announced. Anticipating the possibility, I'd brought along a pair of lace-up booties so I wouldn't be hiking in pastel pointed slippers. Kitty was happy to explore the nearby gardens but warned me to be careful of going into the woods with a man who slept with "you know who."

Beethoven and I took the road west to the ruins of Rauhenstein Castle, inhaling the earthy smell of fallen leaves mixed with the sweet scent of ripened apples. Neither of us spoke. At one point he reached for my hand, and we walked like that for ten minutes or so. Once again, I was moved by his simple gesture. Words tended to create trouble, not only because he had difficulty hearing them, but because his true language was music. But when we were together, side by side, everything felt natural and right. Suddenly, his grip tightened. He was squeezing too hard. Dropping my hand, he pulled a pencil out of his pocket and began scribbling in his notebook.

Once we'd reached the ruins, he spread his coat on the ground and we sat down. "I've taken nearly thirty baths so far," he said. "They don't help. I have gout along with my stomach problems. I'm in constant distress."

He told me that more and more people were writing down their comments, his ear trumpets proving less effective. I wrote "I'm sorry" on a piece of paper.

"I understand that Metternich is bringing Rossini to the Congress of Verona. He calls him the 'God of Harmony'!" he said.

I remembered when Beethoven had been the star of the previous Congress, when the mawkish *Wellington's Victory* had been such a success. It clearly bothered him that Rossini had captured the public's attention, but Beethoven hadn't been forgotten. He had been asked to provide the music for the opening of the Josephstadt Theater, and his opera *Fidelio* was being staged at the Kärntnertor. Though the theme was overtly political—a woman dressed as a man frees her husband from prison—the censors left him alone.

"Did you hear what happened when the Burgtheater put on *King Lear*?" he asked. "They refused to let Lear and Cordelia die. When one of the actors complained, he spent three days in jail."

"But why should it matter if Lear dies?" I wrote.

"Because he was a king!" he replied, exasperated. "Metternich's strategy is to protect all monarchs, legitimate and fictional."

"It's such a beautiful spot," I wrote, changing the subject. "I love the ruins."

"I've brought my son, Karl, here several times. It's one of my favorite places."

We continued to sit in the shadow of the medieval castle, the ramparts high above us.

Beethoven told me he'd been reading Kant and quoted a line he'd inscribed in his diary: "The moral law within us, and the starry sky above us." It reminded me of the drawing I'd done years ago, the one in which I'd placed his face in the stars in a reference to *Romeo and Juliet*. "'He will make the face of heaven so fine.'" He'd ripped it up into tiny pieces when I'd been forced to marry Robert. He still didn't know why, and I was tempted to ask the question that still tore at my heart. *Given the choice between me and your stipend, what would you have chosen?* But I couldn't without divulging a darker matter, and I wasn't ready. I didn't know if I'd ever be.

We sat in silence for the longest time. I was happy to be in his presence, though I'm not sure he even noticed me. He was writing furiously in his notebook, looking out at some fixed point beyond the trees, and then scribbling again. I thought of the small boy staring at the sky through the telescope, the boy who believed he did everything best alone. He was right. He needed musicians after he wrote the music, but while thinking and composing, he needed no one. I didn't want to leave Kitty too long, so I announced that I had to go. I hoped he might offer to walk back with me, but he didn't. I shouldn't have expected it. Being with Beethoven was like being alone too.

Friedrich wanted to speak to me about an urgent matter. When he arrived at the house, Kitty offered him some refreshments, but he brusquely sent her away. I had never seen him so angry. "I heard from Metternich that you visited Caroline Murat," he said. "You realize that you're already in the police records for spying at the Congress. Now you've raised further suspicions. What were you thinking?"

"That she was a friend, and I hadn't seen her in a long time."

"That she was a 'friend'? Honestly, Julie, I never thought of you as naïve, but no one trusts the former queen, especially Metternich. That's why she's not permitted to live in Vienna. Caroline has no friends."

"Being a former lover, I suppose you would know. But I'm sure it was all done in the name of 'diplomacy.'"

"Stop it, Julie! And listen to me." He grabbed me by the shoulders. His grip was hard, and I pushed him away. "You also visited Beethoven at Baden?" he asked.

We were still standing. I hadn't had time to ask him to sit down, but I sensed it wasn't going to be a cordial visit.

"Is there something wrong with visiting a friend?" I said, raising my voice. "Were Metternich's spies there too?"

Friedrich tried to control his temper to little effect. "Metternich's spies are everywhere," he said. "Up until now, they've left Beethoven alone because he has influential friends. But you certainly don't want Sedlnitzky cracking down on him because of your carelessness."

"I don't see—"

"No, you don't. Caroline still represents a threat. She could be dangerous."

I laughed at the seeming absurdity of a lonely middle-aged woman representing a threat. "She's hardly in a position to raise the troops."

"It doesn't matter what you think. Only what Metternich thinks. And now you've been seen consorting with her for any number of questionable reasons and then meeting Beethoven. Who knows what you were doing with him!"

"It sounds like you're more interested in what I was doing with Beethoven than Metternich is."

"Don't be coy, Julie. It doesn't suit you."

I heard Giulietta call my name, and she rushed into the room to model a silk gown Lucy had almost finished. She was wearing the necklace Friedrich had given me when she was born. It was now one of Giulietta's favorite pieces. She was about to twirl around when she saw Friedrich, who tried to conceal his surprise. He took a step back and didn't say anything, just stared at the daughter who looked so much like him.

"Excuse me, but do we know each other?" she asked, not waiting to be introduced.

"You met many years ago when you were just a baby," I said quickly. "Count Schulenburg, may I present my daughter, Countess Giulietta von Gallenberg."

He was clearly caught off guard, his anger overtaken by disbelief and then something I recognized as paternal pride. Giulietta was his daughter, his blood.

"The gown suits you," he said softly. "The blue sets off your eyes. And the necklace . . ."

"A friend of Mama's gave it to her when I was born," she said. "I had to wait until I was older before I could wear it. It's pretty, isn't it?"

She moved closer to Friedrich so he could take a look. His hand shook slightly as he examined the cameo of his grandmother. "I don't know who she's supposed to be," Giulietta continued. "Some anonymous woman, I guess. But her profile looks a bit like mine. Don't you think?"

"It does," he said. "Very much."

Giulietta excused herself and was off to find Lucy, who needed to make a few adjustments to the bodice.

"I, I saw . . . ," he stammered, taking the nearest chair.

"You saw yourself."

"I saw us," he replied. "It must have been hard for your husband."

I sat down opposite him, staring into the face of my children's father. I loved his face. Even when Friedrich was angry, he possessed an innate serenity, a "veil of order."

"He loved all the children and they him," I explained. "I'm just sorry you couldn't have been more a part of their lives. Hugo loves art. He says he wants to write a biography of Leonardo da Vinci."

"He's obviously picked up his mother's fascination with impossible geniuses," he snapped. His face grew red. I detected a twitch in his left eye. Chaos was simmering. "Why is Beethoven still in your life?" he said with mounting intensity.

"I'd hardly say he is in my life. I've seen him only a few times since I've returned from Naples."

"Then he's in your heart. He's been in your heart since the day we met, and you've let him ruin any chance you've ever had for real love."

"And that would be with you?" I said bitingly. "It wasn't as if you were pining away for me. You had a mistress for many years. A woman you loved deeply."

"Yes, Julie, I admit that I'm capable of love. Is that so terrible?"

I knew it wasn't. A man who hadn't severed ties to Armgard was good and decent. He'd stayed true to his marriage vows as best he could. He'd grieved for a woman he loved.

Friedrich stood up and announced that he had to leave. He had an important appointment with the British ambassador and couldn't be late. He told me that he'd personally informed Metternich that I had no interest in politics, and that as long as I steered clear of Caroline, I shouldn't have trouble with the police. There was no talk of wanting to see me again.

34

Beethoven was pouring a pitcher of cold water over his head, letting it dribble down his bare chest and seep between the floorboards of his latest apartment on Kothgasse. A housekeeper was on her hands and knees mopping up the overflow. "The downstairs neighbors have already complained about flooding," she said. "I've told him to stop, but he says the water sharpens his brain."

After he'd finished, he handed the empty pitcher to the housekeeper and put on his dressing gown directly over his wet britches. He looked at me. "I think I shall call you Countess von Geistenberg, because you are always appearing out of nowhere like *ein Geist.*"

"I am hardly a ghost," I shouted. "You asked to see me."

"He can't hear anything today," the housekeeper said.

"Old witch, are you talking to me?" Beethoven muttered. "Go out and do the shopping. Here's the list." He sat down at the dining table and put his head in his hands. "She is fatter than Fat Lump," he moaned.

"Who is that?" I wrote in the notebook I'd brought with me.

"My evil sister-in-law."

"I thought she was the Queen of the Night."

"That's my other sister-in-law. Fat Lump is married to my brother Johann. She had a child with another man. I call the girl 'Little Bastard.'"

"Fat Lump and Little Bastard? You certainly have a way with nicknames."

Beethoven was about to present a copy of the *Missa Solemnis* to Archduke Rudolph and offered to let me look at it. As I carefully paged through the manuscript, I noticed a message above the Kyrie, a prayer that implores God's mercy and occurs near the beginning of the Mass. Beethoven had written "From the heart—May it return to the heart." Pointing to the phrase, I shook my head to indicate that I didn't understand, but he didn't bother to explain.

Beethoven had also completed his variations on Anton Diabelli's waltz. "I was going to dedicate it to the wife of a friend," he explained, "but now I may dedicate it to someone else. Her name is Antonie Brentano. She has also suffered her share of illnesses, and I've tried to comfort her."

My heart sank. "You have feelings for her?" He didn't hear me and it didn't matter, because I already knew the answer. Her name would grace the title page of *Thirty-Three Variations on a Waltz*. I suddenly thought of the portrait miniature I'd given him twenty-two years earlier, the one I'd advised him to hide in a desk drawer. With all his various moves—and women—I wondered aloud if he still had it.

"Many women have given me miniatures," he replied to my question. "I have dozens of them." Furious, I went over to his writing desk, opened the drawer, and began searching through the piles of paper. It wasn't there.

"Stop!" Beethoven shouted. "You're making a mess."

"Things are already a mess," I wrote. "You have hurt my feelings very much."

Ignoring the last statement, he went on to tell me about his new secretary, Anton Schindler, who lived nearby. "The man is a ragamuffin and an arch scoundrel and about as competent as Mozart's idiot Papageno."

"Then why do you keep him around?"

"He works for free. He told me that he had the most unpleasant encounter with your husband. I needed the score of *Fidelio*. It's in the Kärntnertor's music library. Your husband had the nerve to ask what happened to my copy. He told Schindler that I probably lost it due to all my 'wanderings.'"

"Did you lose it?"

"I did lose a trunk containing letters and notebooks, but I don't believe *Fidelio* was in there."

"Maybe my miniature was in the trunk?"

"I am talking about *Fidelio*, not your miniature. Later, Schindler and I went out to eat, and I pretended I hadn't seen you since you married Gallenberg. We were in a public place, and after you told me that Metternich thinks you're a dissident, I had to be careful. I said that you came to me crying after your marriage to Gallenberg, but that I spurned you."

"I would have preferred being called a dissident," I wrote.

"To make up for his rudeness, Gallenberg extended an invitation to dinner."

"Dinner where?"

"At your house. I hope that red-haired, spotty-faced ruffian you brought with you to Baden knows how to make bread soup. I would also like perch and macaroni. Tell Spotty-Faced Ruffian about the ten eggs for the soup. Not eleven. *Ten*. I will also be bringing Schindler and my nephew, Karl. They will eat anything."

My father hadn't been outside for several weeks, so I suggested we take the carriage and enjoy the temperate weather. Out of curiosity we drove to the Rotenturmstrasse, where the Deym children were selling their eighty-eight-room palace along with the cabinet of curiosities. Josephine's daughter Viky had died of scarlet fever earlier that year. In a rumor befitting Herr Müller's daughter, it was whispered that she'd been buried alive, her body discovered outside the coffin with an arm chewed off.

The spectacle outside Palais Deym was equally gruesome. Wax figures and mannequins were spread across the cobblestones, Marie Antoinette's head separated from her body, the pregnant woman with her removable parts spilling out onto the street. I closed my eyes until we passed the disturbing scene.

We continued on to the Hofburg, where my father wanted to take me to the National Library. The State Hall, with its soaring frescoed dome, marble columns, and gleaming mahogany bookshelves, was one of the most beautiful rooms I'd ever seen. Thousands of books begged to be touched, the tactile leather mixed with the rich smell of Moroccan bindings. When my father sat down to rest, I took a few minutes to tour the other rooms. At the far end of one, I spotted a familiar head of hair, thick waves flipping up over his collar. I tapped Friedrich on the shoulder.

"Aren't you supposed to be doing official business?" I asked.

"We diplomats sometimes get time off," he replied.

He stood up, looking down at me. He was wearing glasses but immediately removed them.

"Are you still working on your family biography?"

"Yes." He smiled. "It's not easy, especially when you're negotiating treaties and arranging marriages. I want to apologize for being so harsh the last time we met. It was unnecessary."

"You were only trying to be helpful."

"Please don't misinterpret this, but I would like to provide for the children. I feel it's my responsibility."

"Robert is doing well enough," I said.

"He cannot be making much. I'm not asking for anything in return."

"I can't accept your generosity, but why are you being so kind?"

"Why? Because I am greatly fond of you." He reached over and lifted up my chin. "My dear Julie, I've known you for a very long time." I remembered when he'd led me out of the maze. He'd looked into my face the same way.

"My father is waiting for me in the State Hall," I said. "I must be going."

I walked past the rows of books, each with a story to tell. Our story, Friedrich's and mine, had always been complicated. I'd promised Armgard I'd never break up their marriage, and I couldn't go back on my word. And even if I hadn't made such a vow, the timing never worked, and then there was Beethoven. Always Beethoven. Perhaps Friedrich had been right that Beethoven had ruined my chance of ever finding real love. Perhaps Beethoven was the maze.

Beethoven arrived for dinner looking surprisingly elegant in a blue frock coat with yellow buttons, spotless white knee breeches, and a matching vest. His hair was still unruly, but I was touched that he had taken care with his dress and told him so.

"The Master has trouble hearing." I looked up at a tall, thin man who was looming over him. He introduced himself as Anton Schindler—"lawyer, musician, and secretary to Herr Beethoven." Schindler had pasty skin, straight black hair, round spectacles, and wore a dour expression that matched his severe black clothing. I was surprised to learn that he was only twenty-eight. The boy next to him was Beethoven's nephew, Karl, whose delicate features and sweet expression were the exact opposite of his uncle's. I assumed he took after the Queen of the Night.

Giulietta, who had expressed little enthusiasm for the dinner, had decided to join us after glimpsing Karl. She had borrowed my rouge, and her cheeks were flushed to an unnatural degree.

"My eyes are terrible," Beethoven said. "I hope I'm not going blind."

"I thought his ears were the problem," Giulietta whispered to me.

"My doctor forbids me to read or write," he continued. "I cannot strain, because I get violent headaches."

"That is indeed terrible," Robert said, directing the comment toward Beethoven's ear horn. "How can you compose?"

"How can you?" Beethoven replied.

"What he means is how can you compose with all your responsibilities at the Kärntnertor," I translated.

Robert nodded. He had yet to understand the full nature of Beethoven's cunning.

"I'm hungry," Beethoven announced. "I'm very much looking forward to that bread soup."

When everyone moved into the dining room, Lucy motioned for me to come into the kitchen, where Kitty was collapsed on the floor in tears. "If I may say so, milady," Lucy said, "this dinner is one of the most ill-conceived notions."

"It wasn't my idea," I snapped. "And what is wrong with your niece?"

"I'm not sure I'm up to the task," Kitty cried. "He's a very famous man who likes whores. Do whores cook well?"

"Could you please forget about the whores! How is the bread soup coming along?"

"It's almost done, and I have the ten eggs on a plate, just as you instructed."

We sat around the dining room table while Beethoven went through the ritual of cracking open the eggs. No one spoke. Holding the eggs up high, he let them plummet into the pot like synchronized cliff divers. Giulietta was so impressed that she applauded. After Lucy went back into the kitchen to whisk them, she and Kitty served the soup. I held my breath while Beethoven tasted it.

"This is excellent," he said. "Your cook should be commended."

He also enjoyed the perch, macaroni, and especially the wine. Despite his eye ailment, he was in a jovial mood, even inquiring about Giulietta's pianoforte lessons.

"I don't take them any longer," she said. "Mama says I won't get a husband, but I don't care."

"She doesn't care if she gets a husband," Karl repeated loudly.

"I'm inquiring about your music lessons, not your marital prospects," Beethoven replied. "Everyone should play the pianoforte. I hired Czerny for Karl, but he wouldn't practice."

"I hate practicing," Karl replied.

"Me too," Giulietta said, smiling agreeably over their mutual dislike of the pianoforte.

Robert brought up the possibility of Beethoven composing an opera for the Kärntnertor, praising him for the successful revival of *Fidelio*. Since Robert was seated at the far end of the table, Beethoven couldn't hear him at all. "Normally I would request that you write down your questions," Schindler said, pulling a notebook from his pocket. "But knowing that Countess Gallenberg might be a dissident, I think it best that we don't implicate the Master."

"Mama, you're a dissident?" Giulietta asked.

"Herr Schindler has been misinformed," I said, getting up to retrieve one of my own notebooks and handing it to Robert. He wrote down his question and passed it on to Beethoven, who began reading from another page.

"What is this?" he said. "'He poured a pitcher of icy water over his head . . . So careless, he lost my portrait miniature.'" Occasionally I kept notes along with writing down my questions. I'd totally forgotten about them.

Beethoven was so angry it took him a few seconds to compose his thoughts, until he finally shouted, "Have you been spying on me?"

Robert took the notebook back from Beethoven and began scribbling furiously in it. "I explained that your spying days were over," he said.

"Mama!" Giulietta exclaimed. "You were a spy?"

Schindler stood up and motioned for Beethoven to leave. "Sit down, you Samothracian scoundrel!" Beethoven said. "Countess Gallenberg is a woman of impeccable morals."

"One cannot be too careful, Master," Schindler replied.

Robert and I switched places so Robert could be closer to Beethoven, who explained that he'd been thinking of composing an opera around the legend of Melusine.

"Doesn't she turn into a mermaid?" Giulietta asked.

"Only on Saturday nights," Robert explained. "The rest of the week, she's a normal woman. I was once thinking of choreographing a ballet based on it, but now I'm considering a revival of my *Hamlet*."

"You cannot!" Beethoven shouted. He couldn't judge his volume at all. "Since Hamlet is a prince, he'll have to live. Metternich's censors will insist upon it."

"That would be a challenge," Robert said.

Beethoven was having fun now. "To be or to be . . ."

Robert took him seriously. "So perhaps he does live," he mused. "And Ophelia too. This could be perfect for Rossini fans. And you, Herr Beethoven, what are you writing now?"

"A symphony."

Robert nodded.

"With a chorus," Beethoven added.

"A symphony has never been done with a chorus," Robert wrote.

"I have set Schiller's 'Ode to Joy' to music," Beethoven explained. "I've wanted to do it for thirty years. The poem is important to me."

"I believe the Master is getting fatigued," Schindler interjected. "I'm afraid we must go."

"I would like to congratulate the cook," Beethoven said. "Where is Spotty-Faced Ruffian?"

I went into the kitchen and asked Kitty to come out. "He's not going to ask me to be his whore, is he?"

"Kitty, don't be ridiculous."

"I've been looking for a girl like you," Beethoven said as Kitty's eyes widened. "I've never found anyone who has mastered the art of bread soup in addition to macaroni. You also strike me as a very smart girl, not like the beasts I seem to attract."

"Beasts?" Kitty said, staring at me.

When I explained that Kitty was Lucy's niece and that they wanted to remain together, he relented, muttering, "Pity."

After Beethoven had left, taking the extra food and wine with him, Robert and I reviewed the evening's events.

"I'm sorry, Julie," he said. "I know you think highly of him, but he wants to do a symphony with a chorus."

"No worse than doing a happy version of *Hamlet*. If Beethoven says he's doing it, he will do it."

"Perhaps, but not at the Kärntnertor."

35

He's demanding an extra twenty-four violins, ten violas, twelve basses and violoncellos, doubled winds, and all the theater's solo singers and choral personnel," said Louis Duport, waving a letter. "Between the orchestra and chorus, that's close to one hundred sixty people. No one has ever attempted anything like this before. And Beethoven wants the concert held in early May. That's less than three weeks away."

"Impossible," Robert exclaimed. "Tell him no."

We were seated in Duport's office adjacent to the theater, where the walls were decorated with watercolor drawings of the dancer in some of his favorite ballets—*The Loves of Venus and Adonis, Acis and Galatea*, and several featuring his most famous role: Zephyr. "I did *Venus and Adonis* in Saint Petersburg," he reminisced. "The Russians were wild for me."

If the drawings weren't enough to remind visitors of Duport's status as one of ballet's *premiers danseurs*, he was dressed today in one of his many costumes—a colorful brocade caftan and a pair of loose orange silk trousers. It was warm in the small room, and the caftan seemed to be weighing him down, or else it could have been from dealing with Beethoven, who oppressed people on a regular basis.

"Beethoven was scheduled to do the concert at the Theater an der Wien," Duport explained. "But he wanted the violinist—Ignaz Schuppanzigh—to act as concertmaster. The musicians refused to work with an outsider, so here we are."

"And where is that?" Robert asked nervously before I jumped in.

"You must hold the premiere here," I suggested. "It's his first new symphony in a decade. It will be a coup for the Kärntnertor."

Robert gave me an angry look before attempting to dissuade Duport from involving the theater in something potentially catastrophic. "There's no question that Beethoven is a musician of great distinction," he said, trying to remain calm. "But he is erratic, headstrong, and prone to fits of temper."

"What great artist doesn't possess those qualities?" I replied, addressing Duport. "You were the greatest dancer in the world, and they said the same of you."

"It's true," Duport said, removing his caftan before beginning a series of *rond de jambes*. "I was the greatest dancer in the world." He dipped into a *grand plié*.

"You still are," I enthused. "Duport and Beethoven. Two great names linked forever."

Duport stretched his leg over his head. "I don't foresee any negative consequences," he said.

"You don't?" Robert said, his voice rising. "Beethoven is a madman, and he's deaf! What could possibly go wrong?"

"May I remind you, Robert, that I make the decisions here," Duport said. "I will write to Herr Schindler immediately."

Escorting me outside, Robert asked if I had had anything to do with Schindler sending the letter. "I did advise him to write," I admitted, "but he would have done so anyway."

"And it was purely by coincidence that you appeared today?"

"I always love visiting the Kärntnertor."

"I don't think you appreciate the complications. If Duport has to deal with Beethoven, he will end up in the Narrenturm. His nerves are too fragile. Did you see him warming up? He dances whenever he feels overwhelmed. Yesterday, he spent the day reliving his role as Zephyr—the west wind. I practically had to stop him from flying out the window."

"Then let Signore Beast handle it."

Robert nervously cleared his throat. "Barbaja is currently under house arrest in his villa outside Naples."

"House arrest?"

"The police claim he was trying to burn down the San Carlo to cover up false expense accounts."

"Why am I not surprised?"

"Julie, I understand that you mean well, but if anything goes wrong—and everything will—just know that you will be responsible for the disaster that will go down in history as Beethoven's Ninth Symphony."

Why couldn't Beethoven stay in one place? I could have been working for the secret police for all the effort that went into tracking him down. He was now back in the Landstrasse, in lodgings known as the "House by the Beautiful Slave Girl." A terrified housekeeper was cleaning up a platter of leftover roast. Catching her nibbling an end piece, Beethoven bellowed, "Swine! I will have you arrested." An adjacent room was piled high with the orchestral parts for his upcoming May 7 concert. They included the overture to *The Consecration of the House*, parts of the *Missa Solemnis*, and the Ninth Symphony. Beethoven was in a rage over nearly everything. Since he had to cover the cost of the concert, he wanted to raise ticket prices to assure a profit, but Duport insisted on keeping the standard rate. The censors refused to let him perform the *Missa* in a secular setting, so he had to compromise by presenting only three hymns. The singers complained that he didn't know how to write for the human voice and that they couldn't hit the high notes. Everything was out of reach, which of course was exactly the way he had designed it.

"I am cooked, roasted, and stewed," he fretted. "That arch scoundrel Duport hasn't even given me adequate rehearsal time. I'm going to call it off. There will be no concert."

"You will not call it off," I wrote in my notebook. "Everything is all set."

"The Master should be wearing a black coat," said Schindler. I hadn't noticed him before. He was like a shadow attached to no one.

"He has a dark-green one," I replied. "The theater is dimly lit. No one will see, but we need to do something about his hair."

Schindler waved a pair of scissors. "I will cut it for him."

"You obtrusive appendix! Get away from me!" Beethoven yelled. "Do you think I'd trust you with scissors? Leave us! Countess Gallenberg will cut it."

Beethoven sat in a chair while I stood behind him brushing his thick hair. It was clean from his habit of pouring cold water over it but contained so many snarls it was like untangling knotted yarn. When it was finally all smoothed out, I brushed it while Beethoven moaned with pleasure. "Except for my mother, I don't remember anyone brushing my hair like that. It feels wonderful."

It was an intimate moment, perhaps the only one we would ever share again. Finally, I picked up the scissors, cutting off five inches and adding layers. I brushed the front pieces straight back to accentuate his widow's peak and tried to tame the side pieces that flipped up over his ears. When I held up the looking glass, he smiled and said, "You have made me too respectable. I am a mad genius, haven't you heard?" I bent down and kissed him on the forehead. "Thank you," he said. He closed his eyes and kept them shut. When he opened them again, he appeared to be in another world. "I wish my mother could come to my concert," he said. "I think of her every day. She was the only woman who ever loved me."

"Mother love is different," I wrote in my notebook. "It never goes away. Romantic love is—"

"Impossible," he said. "At least for someone like me."

I took his hand and led him over to the bed. He was hesitant at first, and I feared he might push me away, but he lay down and I curled up next to him. We held each other, nothing more.

He was hungry for the warmth of another human being, and I was hungry for his warmth. And in different ways, we were both hungry for our mothers, he for the pleasant memories that were either true or a trick of his imagination, I for the memories that were best forgotten but ultimately forgiven. We were all flawed. I'd never met anyone who made me understand and accept that better than Beethoven.

I could have stayed in his arms for the next several hours, but Schindler was returning at any moment, and Beethoven had a major concert coming up.

"How much can you hear?" I wrote in my notebook before I left.

"Nothing," he said. "Everything."

It was a brisk walk from Stephansplatz to the Kärntnertor, where a sizable crowd was already entering the theater. Beethoven's nephew, Karl, was overseeing the box office. Giulietta gave him a warm smile. Robert and Duport were talking to a short, heavyset young man with spectacles and a bad wig. They introduced him as Franz Schubert, who was twenty-seven and would be dead four years later of syphilis. The Kärntnertor had commissioned him to write an opera, but Barbaja had canceled it in his enthusiasm for Rossini.

The theater, which held one thousand people, was shaped like a horseshoe and had two levels of seats on the main floor and five tiers of galleries. It was filled to near capacity. Robert escorted us to a box in the middle gallery, where my father was already waiting. His hearing had continued to fail, but I wanted him to be there. The boxes were reserved for nobility, but Robert had made an exception for Lucy and Kitty, who were more excited to be in a prestigious box than at the concert itself.

"Beethoven had a chance to do only two rehearsals," Robert said. "He tried to conduct, but Umlauf instructed the orchestra and singers to keep their eyes trained on him. As I suspected, it's turning out to be an utter debacle."

I looked across at the empty imperial box. Though Beethoven had hand delivered the invitations himself, the emperor and empress had already left Vienna for the season. As I continued to search the crowd, I saw Friedrich and Armgard in discussion with someone in a nearby box. It appeared to be full. We had four extra seats, so Robert invited them to join us.

"A simple misunderstanding," Friedrich said sheepishly. "Armgard didn't think we were attending and invited friends."

"I'm very happy that you're here," Robert replied. "It should be an exciting evening. Now if you'll excuse me, I have to check on a few things, but I'll be back for the symphony."

"Countess Gallenberg." Friedrich nodded, taking a seat directly behind me. Armgard stared at Lucy and Kitty before asking if we were related. "The boxes, as you know, are reserved for the upper classes," she said haughtily.

"They're from the English branch of the Brunswick family," I replied as the orchestra and chorus surged onto the stage. Beethoven, in his green-black coat, silk stockings, and buckled shoes, stood slightly behind and to the right of Umlauf. They both gave the downbeat, and Beethoven lurched slightly as if about to conduct but controlled himself. After the overture, the orchestra and chorus performed the three hymns from the *Missa Solemnis*. When I heard the plaintive Kyrie, I remembered the inscription he'd written above its title: "From the heart—May it return to the heart."

The theater was extremely warm, and members of the audience were fanning themselves. The performance had already lasted an hour, and some people left. Robert slipped in next to me for the start of the symphony. I watched Beethoven. He shifted his weight from side to side, flicking his hair back with his left hand. Once again, he and Umlauf gave the downbeat, but this time Beethoven was a little less restrained in his movements, not exactly conducting but not standing still either.

The first movement began slowly, tentatively, almost as if the orchestra were still tuning up, until Beethoven unleashed his stormy theme. Terrifying in its darkness and despair, it conjured a starless night with no hope of a sunrise. Beethoven knew that desolate world. He had contemplated taking his own life. Yet the terror he invoked, the anguish and loss, was universal. I could hear Therese muttering, "Doom." I could picture Josephine spitting up blood. I saw myself in the dying ward at the Hospital for the Incurables, my dying mother's autumnal skin. Ashes to ashes, dust to dust. It all seemed overwhelming and futile, but then Beethoven yanked us into the loud, bacchanalian second movement. People swayed to the dancelike rhythm, a celebration of earthly pleasure. Breaking into applause when the unruly timpani exploded, the audience shouted so loudly for an encore that Count Sedlnitzky's police agents demanded quiet.

The crowd was still shouting when Beethoven shifted moods once again, moving from the world of the living to a place beyond the stars. The music was so sublimely beautiful, so inherently seductive that I immediately thought of Parthenope luring Odysseus to the rocky shore. Beethoven was writing his own story, revealing the various aspects of his nature, from anguish to optimism. Above all, he was posing the question that has vexed philosophers for centuries: Knowing that we are going to die, how are we to live?

Beethoven had been contemplating the Schiller poem all his adult life and believed it supplied an answer. It was as simple as human voices rising up together, united in brotherhood.

Joy, bright spark of divinity,
Daughter of Elysium,
Fire-inspired we tread
Within thy sanctuary.
Thy magic power reunites
All that custom has divided,
All men become brothers
Under the sway of thy gentle wings.

Beethoven, the curmudgeon, the misogynist, the most impossible of men, was preaching the gospel of joy. He was beseeching us to come together, to embrace the universal struggle at the heart of existence. The chorus grappled with the music, attempting to hit notes beyond their normal register. Some simply mouthed the words, but despite the mistakes and omissions, they were all reaching for something "above the canopy of stars." He had set the poem to a simple march, one that could get stuck in the ear and remain there forever. It was a "song of praise," a "kiss for all the world." The music spiraled faster and faster, an outburst of childlike glee that ended with the little piccolo, the instrument with the highest range, soaring heavenward.

The response was loud and rapturous, with members of the audience jumping to their feet, shouting, *"Vivat!"* Beethoven didn't turn around. It was possible that he didn't hear the applause, just as possible that he wanted to live in the music a little while longer. Caroline Unger, one of the soloists, tugged his sleeve and he faced the crowd. He bowed slightly, taking in the outpouring of almost delirious admiration. He pushed his hair back with his hand and looked around at the people on the main floor, the five tiers of galleries, the standing-room-only section at the very top. He drank it all in.

People stood, clapped, stamped their feet, waved handkerchiefs. Beethoven received five standing ovations, two more than what was customary for the imperial family. Count Sedlnitzky finally yelled, "Silence!"

Beethoven brought so many people together that night. In my box alone, there was Robert, my husband of twenty years; Friedrich, the father of my children; Giulietta, my beautiful daughter, who belonged to both men; my father, straining to hear; Lucy and Kitty, loyal and true. In that moment, I was no longer Countess Julie von Gallenberg. I was Joy, Daughter of Elysium.

36

J oy lived for less than two days. Beethoven's profit from the concert was a disappointing 420 florins, and he was so apoplectic that
Schindler sought my advice. We met at the Golden Pear, a coffeehouse
around the corner from Beethoven's apartment. Schindler looked miserable, his eyes more lifeless than usual, his spindly fingers clasping a
glass. "I usually abstain from alcohol," he said, "but the Master has
driven me to such extremes that I am drinking during the day. I trust
you will tell no one."

Schindler then related what happened when Beethoven was presented with the ticket office receipts: "He fell to the floor of his apartment and refused to get up. He called Duport an arch scoundrel and
every other name you can imagine."

"I presume Herr Beethoven was still not on the floor, although with
his talent for name-calling, he could do it from anywhere."

"It was the next morning, and he was in a chair," he said, "but
please be respectful. It is the Master we are talking about."

"Yes, Herr Schindler, I understand."

"That is why I wanted to talk to you. I believe you understand him
very well."

"I'm afraid I do not, but please continue."

He told me about a planned celebratory dinner at a restaurant in the Prater, where Beethoven had become so abusive that Schindler had walked out. "Herr Umlauf and Herr Schuppanzigh came with me, leaving the Master alone with his nephew, Karl," he explained. He pulled out a letter. "Listen to what he wrote to me: 'I have a certain fear that some great misfortune will befall me through you.' How could I cause the Master great misfortune? I have been nothing but loyal." Schindler looked to be on the verge of tears. "You must think me ridiculous," he said.

"No, I don't." While Schindler fawned over "the Master," I felt there was more to his slavish devotion than proximity to greatness. He loved him. That was obvious.

"Would you kindly put in a good word?" he asked. "Even though I worry that your scandalous reputation may be deleterious to his career, I know that he has great respect and fondness for you. He's in the apartment right now."

Beethoven was in bed, groaning with abdominal pain, while scribbling down ideas for a set of bagatelles he was writing to repay a debt to his brother Johann. "Why if it isn't Countess von Geistenberg," he said.

"Are you feeling unwell?"

"Unwell? Yes, I suppose one could call it that. That arch scoundrel, that 'Dancing Napoleon,' cheated me out of my money, and I made such a small profit that the whole enterprise was not worth my time."

"You received numerous ovations, and the applause was rapturous," I wrote. "It was a great success."

"Tell that to Dancing Napoleon. I've arranged for a second performance at the Grand Redoutensaal, and you know how he insults me? He insists that I substitute part of the *Missa* for a Rossini aria. *A Rossini aria!* He thinks it will help bring in the crowds. The crowds were not a problem at the Kärntnertor. The theater was practically sold out, and I still made no money."

I picked up my pencil. "It was an expensive concert to mount."

"Whose side are you on, Countess von Geistenberg?"

"I am here because of Herr Schindler. He's very upset at the way you've treated him."

"He is a dreadful hanger-on. I despise him almost as much as I do the *Ass*-trians and that double-crossing dancer. What was Duport's famous role? The west wind? The man is an ass wind, a French fart."

This wasn't going well. Schindler would have to repair relations on his own. I inquired about his nephew, Karl, but that elicited even more outrage. "I'd hoped he would become a musician like me, but he doesn't have the discipline. He's too much like his bestial, immoral mother. I'm afraid that he's drinking too much and frequenting whores. I must speak to him again. I will threaten to cut him off. My son, my son—how can he treat me like this?"

I pressed so hard on my pencil that the lead broke off. It was for the best. There was nothing I could write that would change his mind. He was treating Karl as if he were a composition, attempting to impose a thematic structure on the young man's life. I wondered how much of his obsession with his so-called son had to do with the baby we'd lost. I supposed it didn't matter. People were a mystery to Beethoven. He could conjure them in notes and harmonies and rhythms, but in his everyday life they were ghosts.

Schindler was waiting for me outside. "What did he say?" he asked anxiously.

"I'm afraid he's still not in the best frame of mind."

"There is no hope."

"There is always hope, Herr Schindler, but . . ."

He took off his glasses and wiped his eyes. He was crying openly now.

My father's health continued to deteriorate. His hearing had worsened, and he was increasingly unsteady on his feet. The previous week he'd fallen and couldn't get up. The housekeeper had found him on the floor with a broken wrist and a deep gash beneath his eye. I continued to visit every day, but he seemed even less willing to engage. I frequently brought books, but one day he told me that he didn't want them anymore. I knew what that meant. He was giving up.

At the end of September, he announced that he wanted to return to Reggio, where his family had lived for centuries. His pension was moderate, and Vienna was expensive. He wanted to make sure he had enough money so that I would have a small inheritance, and he didn't want to be a burden.

"You have a kind heart," he said, "and I know you will care for me, but I've caused you enough pain. You loved Beethoven, and I ruined your life. Please forgive me."

"Of course I forgive you, but you didn't ruin anything."

I couldn't bear to think that he was suffering over something that had happened two decades earlier. I tried to reassure him that I was happy and that everything had turned out for the best. I didn't believe it, but as I grew older, I tried to draw happiness from wherever I could find it. In Naples I'd seen mutilated bodies hanging in public squares; I'd watched Josephine suffer a cruel death; I knew of people who'd lost their loved ones in useless bloody battles. How could I possibly complain? I hadn't found true love—or at least true reciprocal love. But maybe it was greedy to want that.

I hugged my father tightly, tears spilling down my face. "Papa, I love you so much."

Over the next week, the housekeeper and I helped him pack his belongings. He didn't want to take many things, presenting me with my mother's hard-won medal of the Order of the Starry Cross and a necklace and ring he had saved for Giulietta. "I'm leaving you my books," he said.

When the carriage came to take him to Reggio, he left with only two small valises. I told him I would visit soon and hugged him tightly. As Giulietta and I stood on the street waving goodbye, I feared I would never see him again. He had composed his own ending.

Eleonora's Christmas tree was festooned with colored ribbons, gold stars, apples, walnuts, candies, and little cakes hand-painted with decorative angels. Dozens of candles were carefully attached to the boughs, some sputtering dangerously close to the pastries. "You have outdone yourself yet again," Robert said, praising his sister. The Christmas tree was a relatively novel idea, and Eleonora was known for having one of the finest. With all the effort that went into it—her servants had spent days attaching string to the walnuts—she gave an annual Christmas party so people could admire it.

"I invited Louis," Eleonora said, "but I doubt he'll appear."

I saw Metternich in a corner chatting with Duport, who, after the strain of dealing with Beethoven, had spent time in Karlsbad in lieu of a straitjacket and was now seemingly on the mend. Barbaja, no longer under house arrest, had extended his concession with the Kärntnertor, and the Viennese were looking forward to a packed season of Italian operas.

Wandering from room to room, I sipped a cup of mulled wine and nibbled on gingerbread biscuits. Eventually, I found myself in front of the tree again. A hand snatched a candle before it torched a bough. "No more fires," Friedrich said. I looked around for Armgard, but he appeared to be alone. "I never had a chance to talk to you after Beethoven's concert," he continued. "I wanted to let you know that I finally understand why you love him so much. Who could possibly compare? Certainly not I. I've been successful in politics. I'm writing a book." He smiled. "One day I'll finish it. But Beethoven is a true genius.

I hope you find happiness with him." I'd never seen Friedrich so vulnerable; it stabbed at my heart.

"Things are different between us now," I explained. "It isn't what you think . . ."

Before I had a chance to finish, I heard someone call out, "Countess von Geistenberg," and saw Beethoven coming toward us. "Count von Walzer," he said. "A pleasure to see you again."

Friedrich looked confused. "Count von Walzer?"

"He's joking," I said.

"I call her Countess von Geistenberg because she is always appearing ghostlike in my apartment," Beethoven explained. "I wake up and there she is. I go to sleep and there she is."

"You must excuse me," Friedrich said curtly. "I have another party to attend." He joined a small group, including a pretty young woman who looked up at him adoringly. They left a few minutes later.

"This is terrible," Beethoven said, spitting something out in his hand. "I've been poisoned." He had plucked one of the painted pastries off the tree and popped it in his mouth. "I need some wine." After he downed two glasses, he asked if we could talk in private, so we moved into the library. He wasted little time getting to the point. "Could you lend me three hundred florins? I am trying to preserve my bank shares for my ungrateful son. I will repay you with interest."

I remembered Beethoven's generosity when I needed money in Naples, but I was barely scraping by. After I wrote down my apologies, I offered to ask Eleonora on his behalf, but he patted my arm and said, "It's all right. I'm leaving now."

"Can't you stay a little longer?" I asked, but he couldn't hear me.

Robert was talking to a young ballet dancer from the Kärntnertor's troupe. He had recently told me that he had fallen in love and thought it was time to find his own apartment. The dancer, who bore a strong resemblance to Ramo, had brought a pretty ballerina to the party. She was flirting with a recently widowed baron. I was happy for Robert. I'd always hoped he would find love apart from his all-consuming passion for music, but I'd come to enjoy our late-night talks about the goings-on at the theater.

As people imbibed more punch, I heard the frenetic clinking of glasses and loud laughter. People sang; others danced. I stared at the blazing Christmas tree. My father was gone, Robert was in love, Friedrich was off with a beautiful young woman, and Beethoven was probably drinking or composing or both.

When I arrived home, I looked in on Giulietta, who was sound asleep. I sat down on the bed and watched her eyelids flutter as if she were watching her own dreams. I kissed her lightly on the cheek and then found Lucy and Kitty in the kitchen admiring several freshly made bread puddings. "My mother taught me the recipe," Kitty said. "Most people have plum pudding for Christmas, but we preferred this one." I told her that it looked very tasty, and she said that she'd made an extra one for Beethoven. "Seeing how he really liked my bread soup . . ."

"How thoughtful of you," I said. "Shall we deliver it to him now?"

"Now, milady?" Lucy said. "It's almost midnight."

Kitty looked skeptical. "Who knows what we'd find . . . not that I'm suggesting anything."

I told them I thought it would be a kind gesture and called for the carriage to take us to his apartment. After knocking several times, I tried the door. He'd left it unlocked. I saw an empty bottle of wine on the table next to the pianoforte. He appeared to be passed out, but when I looked closer I saw that his ear was pressed to the keys. He was composing. I tapped him on the shoulder. Startled, he turned around to see three women bearing one bread pudding.

"Kitty made it especially for you," I wrote. "It has bread in it."

I could tell that he was touched but tried to cover it up. "Ah, the three magi," he said. "You'll have to eat it with me, then." Kitty had never seen such a disorderly apartment, and it was almost too much for her. She edged closer to the door, but Beethoven cleared off the dining table with a swipe of his hand, and we all sat down and ate the bread pudding. "Spotty-Faced Ruffian, you have done it again!" he cried. "This is excellent."

He told us that London's Philharmonic Society had offered to pay him to compose a symphony and that he was looking forward to traveling there. It was late when we finally left, but he was going back to work. There was still so much to do.

37

1825

When I was younger, I had a recurrent dream of being on a runaway merry-go-round, the carved animals springing to life and taking me with them. I wanted them to stop, but I'd lost control. The next two years were like that dream. The tempo had shifted, and I couldn't slow it down. Accelerando—"to gradually grow faster."

Beethoven had become increasingly agitated, disturbing the neighbors with his loud playing and even louder arguments with Karl. The landlord threw him out, and he had to move yet again. Even Schindler couldn't tolerate the abuse any longer and had deserted him. Beethoven seemed largely oblivious to the chaos. I wondered if his deafness acted as a kind of protective caul. Not only did it allow him to focus completely on his own inner voice, but it afforded him an entire world that he could rule with impunity.

He was now working on three string quartets for a Russian nobleman, Prince Nikolai Galitzin. The first had been performed at the Musikverein, where the violinist Ignaz Schuppanzigh organized regular Thursday night chamber concerts. Beethoven had been late finishing the composition, giving the musicians inadequate time to practice, and the concert hadn't been well received. Beethoven blamed Schuppanzigh, whom he'd nicknamed "Falstaff" for his excessive girth. "Falstaff turned out to be a false friend," he complained. "Karl said his stomach was too fat and got in the way of his violin."

Schuppanzigh's stomach was the only thing he and Karl appeared to agree upon. Poor Karl could do nothing right. He was smart and kind and tried to be as helpful as he could with his demanding uncle, but he wasn't Beethoven. Knowing that he could never live up to those lofty standards, he wanted to leave university and become a soldier. "A soldier?" Beethoven raged. "Why doesn't he become a servant? I wanted him to do something worthy of the Beethoven name, but he's disgracing it."

Beethoven eventually allowed him to leave university to study business at the Polytechnic Institute, but by then much damage had been done. Karl was a sweet, sensitive soul who took Beethoven's reproaches to heart. Beethoven was treating his "son" much the way his father had treated him, but while Beethoven was strong and resilient, Karl was not. More and more, his spirit appeared broken.

In the spring, Beethoven complained once again of severe abdominal pains. His doctor prohibited wine, spirits, and coffee, but since Beethoven subsisted primarily on all three, it was difficult for him to give them up. Before he moved to Baden for six months to write and recover, he asked if I'd do him a favor. Karl wanted to remain in Vienna to be free from his overbearing uncle. "He wants to stay behind in order to frequent whores," Beethoven told me. "I hope he doesn't get a disease and die. My son—with whores! It's unimaginable! Perhaps you'd spy on him for me. I believe that's your expertise."

"I will not spy on Karl," I said, "but since I'll be in Vienna for most of the summer, if he needs anything, please have him contact me."

"If anything happens to him, I will hold you responsible," he said half-jokingly.

Walking outside, I found Schindler pacing up and down the Krugerstrasse in front of Beethoven's building. "Did he say anything about me?" he asked pitifully.

"I'm afraid he didn't, Herr Schindler."

He looked more spectral than ever, as if proximity to Beethoven had drained his very essence.

"What am I to do?" he asked.

"Whatever you did before you met him."

"There was no before."

"Then let's hope there will be an after."

I was saying it to myself as much as to him. The concept of "after Beethoven" seemed as foreign as saying "after the world ends" or "after I die." Beethoven was such a force of nature that even nature wouldn't be the same without him.

With Beethoven in Baden, I learned that my father was dying, and Lucy and I set out for Reggio. When we arrived, my aunt told me that my father hadn't wanted anyone to notify me. "He didn't want to trouble you," she said. That broke my heart. He was pushing me away even as death embraced him. My aunt led me up to a bedchamber, where my father was so weak he couldn't speak. His eyes, wide open, stared straight ahead.

"Papa, it's Julie—I'm here."

I sat down on the bed and threw my arms around him. I'd never had the opportunity before, but now he couldn't push me away. I kissed his forehead and cheeks and told him how much I loved him. I told him that he'd given me the greatest gift, a love of books, and that I'd never forget him. I told him that I'd keep his memory alive through my children. I told him how much Mama had loved him. I told him everything that was in my heart and more, until Lucy finally pulled me away. I'd told him so many things that afterward I felt foolish, until I remembered he probably hadn't heard me and that I needn't feel foolish at all.

I could see that he was dying. His skin was changing color just as my mother's had, and his breathing was labored. I wouldn't let him die alone. I sat in a chair and kept vigil for the next twenty-four hours, and still he wouldn't die. I drank coffee and willed myself to stay awake for another day and night, and yet he persisted in clinging to life. Finally, Lucy convinced me to leave. "He won't die while you're in the room," she whispered. "You need to leave so he can go in peace. It's his journey now."

"Goodbye, Papa," I said, kissing him for the final time. He died two hours later.

I was in mourning for the rest of the summer. I paged through my father's books and wept. It was no coincidence that both my father and Beethoven lived in their own private worlds, their hearing loss richly symbolic of their inability to hear me. I was my father's daughter in many ways. If my mother had robbed me of Beethoven, my father had given him to me. I was accustomed to loving absent men.

In early October, Lucy asked if she could talk to me about something important. I hoped she wasn't announcing her retirement. With Robert newly in love and my father gone, I couldn't afford to lose anyone else. Lucy was one of the few who knew my pained romantic history. She was my companion in every way. Direct as always, she laid out the problem: "Kitty doesn't want to return to Yorkshire and die in Hutton-le-Hole."

I wasn't sure what I'd been expecting, but it certainly wasn't that. "What are you talking about?" I asked. "Why should Kitty die in a hole?"

"It's Hutton-le-Hole, milady. It's where we're from. It's a very pretty place, if you like scenery, but there's nothing to do except roam the moors and dales."

"I don't understand. Why does Kitty have to leave? I haven't dismissed her."

"You might when you hear what happened."

At that I became nervous. Kitty was a kind-hearted girl, but she didn't have much common sense. "Please bring her to me immediately," I said.

Kitty had been crying so much that her eyes were the same color as her red hair, and she was holding a packed valise. "I will miss you so much, milady, and all our fascinating talks about Herr Beethoven and his whores. Nobody talks like that in Hutton-le-Hole, although I did know one whore. Her name was Betsy Brown. She lost a leg falling down a well."

"Will someone please explain what happened?" I asked impatiently.

Kitty couldn't stop crying, so Lucy relayed the details as best she could. "I've only just heard the story. Otherwise, I would have alerted you sooner."

"Auntie Lucy, you are making me feel worse," Kitty said, sniffling.

Lucy took a deep breath. "Giulietta . . . she's in love."

After the dramatic buildup, the news came as a relief. Giulietta was seventeen, and even though she hadn't shown interest in any young men, it didn't surprise me that she might be infatuated with someone.

"Is that all?" I said. "Giulietta is in love?"

"It's not that she's in love," Lucy explained nervously. "It's the man she's in love *with*."

"It's Karl van Beethoven," Kitty said, picking up her valise. "I'll be leaving for Hutton-le-Hole now."

"Karl!" I said amazed. "How did this happen?"

Lucy explained that the two had been seeing each other since the beginning of the summer. "Giulietta made me promise to keep it a secret," Kitty said, starting for the door. "Sometimes she went to his apartment, or they met in the Prater. I usually accompanied her but kept my distance."

I told Kitty that I wasn't going to dismiss her and that I would deal with the situation myself. Shakespeare hadn't given the feuding Montagues and Capulets enough ferocious dialogue to match the verbal abuse that would spew from Beethoven's lips. I'd have to keep it from him.

When Giulietta returned home, I brought her into my bedchamber and closed the door. I suspected that Kitty had tipped her off, because she'd already adopted a defiant stance. "I understand that you've been seeing Karl," I said, struggling to remain calm.

"I love him," she said firmly.

"Does he love you?"

"He says he does, but things are a little confused because of Herr Beethoven. He's the cruelest and most hypocritical of men. He composes a hymn to universal brotherhood, yet he doesn't have the smallest bit of compassion for his own nephew. He won't even let Karl visit his mother, although he sneaks away to see her as much as he can. He's ruining Karl's life. Karl needs me. I can help him."

I knew from experience how this story would end.

"We are going to marry," she announced.

"Has he asked you to marry him?"

She admitted that he hadn't, because he was still attending school and didn't have any money apart from what his uncle gave him.

"What do you think will happen?" I asked. "His uncle will cut him off. Karl will be left with nothing. How will you live?"

"We will get by."

"I'm afraid that I'm going to have to forbid you to see him."

"You can't forbid me. We will run away together. You have no idea what it's like to be in love. You're as cold and cruel as Herr Beethoven. You broke Papa's heart and made him leave home."

"There's a lot you don't understand."

"I understand that I love Karl and that we will marry."

After Giulietta left in tears, I thought back on the way Prince Lichnowsky and my mother had plotted to prevent me from marrying Beethoven. That was much worse. Or was it? My mother had acquiesced to her lover because she needed his money, and for whatever reason, she had feelings for him. In this case, there was no money involved, but was I thwarting a love affair to please Beethoven?

I went to the Kärntnertor to discuss the situation with Robert, who immediately asked, "Does every woman in the family have to fall in love with a Beethoven?" He agreed that such a marriage was unsuitable based on any number of reasons, from Karl's lack of a title and money to his madman uncle.

"I'd hate to have Beethoven as my relative," said Duport, who'd been listening in. "He'd probably insist on composing the music for the nuptials and then accuse everyone, even the bride and groom, of swindling him."

"I will take care of this," Robert said. "It will be better if it comes from me."

Giulietta wasn't speaking to either of us when she left with Eleonora on the Grand Tour. I felt guilty that we were sending her off to travel but hoped she'd be distracted enough to forget about Karl. If she didn't, I made a promise that if she still felt the same when she returned, I'd abide by her wishes.

"The trip will be good for her," Robert said as we waved goodbye. "She'll get to see the world."

"Neither of you understand love at all," she shouted as the carriage pulled away. "I *will* marry him."

I'd hoped to enjoy a respite from Karl, but whenever I saw Beethoven, I heard of little else. His preoccupation with his "son" was becoming a kind of sickness for which there was no cure. If Karl devoted too much time to his studies, he wasn't devoting enough time to his uncle. He couldn't do anything right.

Beethoven had moved into the "House of the Black Spaniards," named for the black-robed Benedictine monks who'd established a monastery there in the seventeenth century. For Beethoven the name had a deeper meaning. In Bonn, people had often referred to him as 'the Spaniard' because of his dark skin.

"Who'd guess that someone would name a house after me?" he joked one afternoon.

"Or that a musician would occupy a place where monks spent their days in silence," I wrote.

"I spend my days in silence," he reminded me.

I started to write "I'm sorry," but he took away the pencil and walked over to the window to show me the open view over the Alservorstadt glacis. The apartment was everything he'd always wanted; it was bright and airy, with five rooms to spread his clutter. I noted that he slept in the same room with two pianofortes. Along with the Broadwood, which had recently been repaired due to his brutal keyboard assaults, he also had a Viennese Graf outfitted with his hearing machine.

Stephan von Breuning, his old friend from Bonn, lived nearby with his wife and twelve-year-old son, Gerhard. Frau Breuning had hired a housekeeper named Sali, one of the few servants to meet Beethoven's approval, mainly due to her pretty face. He also enjoyed spending time with Gerhard, whom he affectionately called "Trouser Button" for the way he stuck close to his father—"like a button on a trouser."

He wanted me to stay and meet them, but he began criticizing Karl again, accusing him of debauchery, theft, and all manner of vile offenses. "'Few sons are like their fathers,'" he said, quoting from the *Odyssey*. "'Most are worse, a very few excel their parents.'"

"I suppose it depends on the parents," I wrote on a nearby slate.

"Please don't go," he implored. "You will like little Trouser Button."

"I'm afraid I can't stay. Perhaps another time."

Karl was scheduled to return from running an errand. I didn't want to hear the ugly explosion that was sure to follow.

38

Robert and I took our seats in the Musikverein to hear Beethoven's third Galitzin quartet in B-flat major. After the disastrous reception to the first one, Schuppanzigh had decided to present the concert not as part of his normal subscription series but as a special event. That way he could attract his usual audience of music elites as well as those seeking novelty. A new Beethoven quartet had the potential to appeal to both. Beethoven was awaiting news of the quartet's reception in a nearby tavern. I suspected he was drinking heavily.

Giulietta had returned from the Grand Tour, having fallen in love with a young poet she'd met at the Trevi Fountain. He besieged her with bad poetry, describing her as his muse. She began referring to herself as "Dante's Beatrice," which was far better than "Karl's wife." Joining us for the concert, she immediately encountered her former and now nearly forgotten love. Karl was polite but reserved, informing her that he'd been busy with his studies and his uncle. He wished her well and moved on. Giulietta interpreted his indifference as heartbreak. "He's devastated and will never recover," she moaned. "How could I have been so cruel! I should have married him when he asked me."

"He didn't ask you," I pointed out.

"It's true, but I have ruined his life."

"You haven't, my darling," I said, patting her hand. "I'm sure he will find someone else."

Duport sat down next to me. "Why am I even here?" he wondered aloud. "Just thinking of Beethoven affects my nervous system." Duport was wearing a cloak fashioned from pieces of leopard skin, along with fuchsia Turkish pants and a chartreuse turban. His eyes were lined in kohl. "I hope he's written something pleasant," he said. "My head is already pounding."

The string quartet was Beethoven's most ambitious, with six distinctive movements, each almost a short story. He was testing the limits of musical language, manipulating the narrative by switching moods and tempos. The slow first movement led to a high-speed scherzo, which was followed by a light, leisurely andante. The fourth was a rustic waltz, a throwback to simpler times when peasants danced the ländler. The audience loved it, but Beethoven moved quickly into a cavatina, the equivalent of an operatic aria, in which he replaced the human voice with strings. It was one of the most beautiful compositions I'd ever heard, a profound and heartfelt expression of love. The room was eerily still, everyone mesmerized. And then it happened: the *Grosse Fuge*.

The opening was so startling that I nearly let out a small cry. Where was Beethoven taking us? The music was shocking, discordant, teetering on the edge of chaos—not even on the edge. It *was* chaos. I could scarcely believe what I was hearing. It was as if he'd hurled a rock at a looking glass, piercing our hearts with the jagged shards. I'd never listened to such music. No one had. I looked over at Duport. The color had drained from his face. The movement lasted nearly sixteen minutes, ending with a series of drawn-out trills. Listeners were baffled, astonished, depleted.

"That's what happens when you're deaf," Robert said. "It's a miracle he was able to compose for as long as he did."

"I don't think I'll ever recover," Duport said. "I need a drink very much."

"What did you think, Mama?" Giulietta asked, making a face to indicate what she thought of it.

The music was beyond me, not only three steps ahead, but universes apart. It summed up my relationship with Beethoven, two people on two different planets. "This is what I think," I said slowly. "If Beethoven's hearing machine could fly, he'd be the first man to reach the moon."

"Trouser Button, this is Countess von Geistenberg," Beethoven said, introducing me to Gerhard von Breuning. Gerhard's searching eyes made him seem far older than twelve. He appeared not to miss a thing. He went outside with Sali, the housekeeper, and Beethoven immediately wanted to know what I thought of his quartet.

"I liked it very much, especially the cavatina," I wrote in my notebook. "It moved me to tears."

Beethoven nodded. "But what about the *Grosse Fuge*? That's what I care about."

"It was . . ." I searched for a word that wouldn't incite him. "Otherworldly."

"That's not exactly what I was aiming for, but otherworldly is, I suppose, an accurate description. But did you *like* it."

Beethoven didn't take well to criticism, especially from me. He didn't respect me as a musician, and why should he? I was a good pianoforte player but hardly a great one, and I'd let my playing lapse. He did, however, respect my intelligence. I parsed my words carefully. "It's difficult to like, especially coming after the heavenly cavatina," I wrote. "It was very jolting. Like a foreign language I couldn't understand."

"You wanted a happier ending just like the other cattle-asses?" he sneered. "I suppose you applauded after the fourth movement. The waltz! You are too romantic, Countess von Geistenberg."

"Perhaps."

"You think I should substitute the fugue for something else? That's what some other people are telling me."

"It's your choice, of course." I couldn't imagine Beethoven changing a composition to please anybody. "But if it were my quartet, I might end it differently."

"But it's not your quartet," he said, taking a seat at the Graf.

He seemed less prickly than usual, more open to discussion, though once again he complained that he was feeling poorly, and I noticed that his eyes had a yellow cast. "How do you know when something is finished?" I wrote. I'd always been curious about how he arrived at his endings, and since we were already discussing the ending to his string quartet, it seemed a good time to ask. I pulled up a chair next to him, waiting as he read the question.

"When I've said everything I want to say," he replied, as if the answer couldn't have been more obvious.

"But how do you know when you've said everything?"

He tapped his heart. "I just know."

Placing his head close to the hearing machine, he began amusing himself with a fantasia as he'd done in the old days. Suddenly, he transitioned into the first movement of the *Moonlight*. I don't know what compelled me to do it—he could have easily stopped playing or rapped my knuckles—but I gently rested my fingers on his right hand, letting him take me up and down the keyboard. It was as close to Beethoven as I'd ever get. Traveling hand in hand, we flew straight into the heart of the music, moving to the steady rhythm of the funeral march. When we'd finished the first movement, I kissed his fingers. He gazed at me intently. He didn't know what to say.

"You're not going to hit me with a knitting needle, are you?" I scribbled, recalling one of the first times we met.

He shook his head. "I would never do that to someone who plays as well as you do."

"You were the one playing. I was just following your lead. We were waltzing together."

"I don't dance."

"Yes, you do . . . just in a different way."

"I loved you once," Beethoven murmured. I expected him to rail against how I'd betrayed him, but that's all he said. *I loved you once.* I had to tell him the whole story. It was time. People often placed bells inside coffins in case their loved ones had mistakenly been buried alive. I'd buried so many secrets that I'd built my own coffin. I reached out and rang the bell.

I began writing in my notebook and kept writing and writing. "I would have married you. I loved you. Prince Lichnowsky forced me to marry Robert. He sent us away to Naples." The words poured forth, faster and faster. I wrote about the prince's affair with my mother, about Robert's preference for men, and then, with a slight hesitation, about my wedding night. "The prince raped me." I'd finally said it, or more accurately, written it. I promised myself that I'd never utter the words, and as it turned out, I didn't have to. I handed the notebook to Beethoven, who read with increasing disbelief. It was difficult to absorb. Even I knew that, and I'd lived it.

"Why didn't you tell me?" he said at last. "Why did you keep it a secret?"

"Because the prince threatened to withhold your stipend."

He was quiet again as he stared at the words. I stifled the urge to scream at the top of my lungs. Instead, I began to write: "If given the choice between me and your stipend, what would you have chosen?" There it was. The question.

He turned to look at me. "The money," he said. "I would have chosen the money."

Of course. I knew. I had always known. If I'd faced up to it earlier, I probably would have let him go and been the better for it. But the question tied him to me. The question kept my love for him alive.

"What would have been left of me without my music?" he asked plaintively. "I'm sorry."

I began to cry, not from sadness but from sheer relief. I finally knew the truth, and so did he. No more secrets.

"You would have done things differently?" he asked. "You loved someone else—Count von Walzer?"

"Yes, I did love Friedrich," I wrote. "Still do. But that ending has already been written."

"You've said everything there is to say?" he asked.

"Almost everything."

"Oh, my dearest Giulietta," he said, putting his arm around me. I placed my head on his broad shoulder, and we sat together at the pianoforte, two old friends, comfortable in silence.

39

Karl tried to kill himself. I shouldn't have been surprised. Some people can only endure so much. Not everyone was as stoic as Beethoven, even when their name was Beethoven. Schindler told me the news. He was back in Beethoven's life, attempting to control access as well as the narrative. Jealous of Karl and everyone else who had a claim on Beethoven's affections, he blamed the young man for bringing the problem on himself.

Dressed all in black, his matching hair painted on his head, Schindler sat in my drawing room almost gleefully relating the tale. "Karl didn't give a thought to how the Master would suffer due to his selfish act," he said, shaking his head at the young man's alleged insensitivity.

"How? Where did it happen?"

"He put a bullet in his head at Rauhenstein Castle," Schindler explained.

Rauhenstein . . . the picturesque ruins outside Baden, one of Beethoven's favorite places. He had destroyed it for his uncle, shattered it to pieces. It was Karl's *Grosse Fuge*, an attack on the past, on tradition. "Is he all right?" I asked.

"No, the Master is very distraught."

"I was referring to Karl."

Schindler explained that he'd asked to be taken directly to his mother but was now in the General Hospital. The doctor had successfully removed the bullet from his forehead, but he was placed under police custody. Attempted suicide was a crime, and since Karl didn't appear to be insane, the only other motivation was an absence of spirituality. While recuperating in the hospital, Karl was required to take religious instruction.

"How embarrassing for the Master!" Schindler complained. "He has always been so interested in the religious education of the common man, and now this misfortune."

"I'm not sure Herr Beethoven was ever interested in religious education."

"I'm afraid you don't know him as intimately as I do."

Schindler was insufferable, perhaps one of the few people who actually deserved Beethoven's ire. "Is Herr Beethoven at the hospital?" I asked. "I'd like to go and visit him."

Schindler shook his head no. Not a single hair moved. "With the police monitoring Karl, we don't want to add to the poor Master's problems by introducing a dissident. I will let you know when it's proper to pay a visit."

Several days later, Schindler invited me to Beethoven's apartment, placing his finger to his lips to indicate that the Master was resting. He explained that Karl was doing well or as well as could be expected for someone whose faults had assumed demonic proportions. Taking his cue from Beethoven, he was now the young man's chief critic, a role that bore all the signs of a desperate lover attempting to annihilate a rival.

"Karl slanders his uncle's true friends and leads such a rakish life that it's a surprise he didn't try to kill himself sooner," he said smugly. "I don't know how the Master bears it."

When Beethoven emerged from his bedchamber, I was shocked by the change in his appearance. Despite his numerous ailments, he'd always projected the image of a vigorous man ready to take a brisk country walk. Now he could barely walk to the chair. His shoulders hunched forward, his gait unsteady, he had a yellow hue to his skin, and his hair had seemingly turned white overnight.

Schindler wrote something down in one of the notebooks and showed it to him. "Do I want Countess Gallenberg to leave?" Beethoven shouted. "No, I want you to leave. Now." Schindler, head hanging down, moved toward the door. "Pick up shaving soap," Beethoven instructed, "and a new chamber pot."

"I'm so sorry about Karl," I wrote, "but Herr Schindler says he will recover."

"He will, but I may not. You know what he told the police? He said he tried to kill himself because I harassed him. I wanted only the best for him. He is my heir, the only male Beethoven in the family. If he had died, who would carry on my legacy? Who would cherish the portrait of my grandfather? Trouser Button?"

"Your legacy will carry on with or without a male heir," I wrote.

"The stupid boy still wants to become a soldier. I hope he learns how to shoot. He couldn't even put a bullet in his head—not that I wanted him dead. I love him dearly." He began to cry but then just as suddenly stopped. "Someone told me the most amazing thing. If you crush green nut rinds in lukewarm milk and place the liquid in your ear, you might be able to regain your hearing. Wouldn't that be wonderful?"

I was continually amazed that no matter the depths of Beethoven's despair, he still had the ability to muster hope—and to bring the attention back to himself. He had recently finished a new quartet in C-sharp minor and was working on yet another. He also spoke of composing another symphony—his tenth.

"I'm going to write a new finale for the B-flat major," he said. "I'll publish the *Grosse Fuge* separately."

"Why?"

"You told me you didn't like it," he said, feigning hurt.

"Since when has my opinion ever mattered to you?"

"Believe it or not, I do take to heart what you say, but in this case, I'm thinking of a lighter ending. A smile, perhaps."

"Or a sneer?"

"I don't know. I haven't written it yet."

Giulietta had been visiting relatives in Korompa and hadn't heard about Karl. When she returned at the end of August, she was distraught. "He tried to kill himself because of me," she cried. "I need to beg his forgiveness."

"It had nothing to do with you," I explained. "He was under great pressure from his uncle. The situation became too intense."

"I will never forgive myself," she continued. "You forced me to leave him, and he died of a broken heart."

"He isn't dead. He's doing well. Herr Beethoven finally agreed to let him become a soldier."

"A soldier? Oh . . . I don't see myself as a soldier's wife."

"I don't see you as Frau Beethoven in any capacity," I said, putting my arm around her. "What happened is very sad, but it's not your fault."

The French aeronaut Elisa Garnerin was scheduled to perform for the first time in Vienna later that evening. As a distraction, I suggested to Giulietta that we go to the Prater to watch the spectacle. Since the late eighteenth century, female balloonists had taken to the sky, first as decorative accompaniments to men and then as soloists. Mademoiselle Garnerin came from a family of prominent aeronauts, her uncle having designed and launched a spectacular unmanned balloon for Napoleon's coronation ceremonies. Beautiful as well as fearless, she was known for singing and playing the harp, as well as setting off fireworks while airborne.

Mademoiselle Garnerin had already ascended into the basket of her striped balloon farther down the Prater. With a white canvas parachute draped around her shoulders, she floated for a time in the sky. Lucy and Kitty were convinced that something awful was going to happen. "Women shouldn't be in balloons," Lucy said. "Leave that to foolish men."

As we craned our necks looking upward, I heard a familiar voice and turned to see Friedrich. Giulietta scarcely paid any attention to him, and I whispered that she was a little upset because a friend was ill. Overhearing me, Giulietta announced that Karl was in the hospital.

"I am sorry," Friedrich said.

"He tried to kill himself because of me," she explained. "I broke his heart."

"That's not true, Giulietta," I said. "We discussed this earlier."

"We were going to get married."

Friedrich looked at me. "Marriage? To Beethoven's nephew?"

"Just a fantasy," I assured him.

"Look, here she comes," Kitty cried.

Mademoiselle Garnerin had cut the cord fastening her to the balloon. At first, the parachute didn't open and she seemed to plunge straight down, but then it released, spreading out like a huge parasol. We watched as she drifted past us, a woman buoyed by the wind, flying.

Karl was determined to join the army, so Beethoven found an officer willing to accept him into the infantry. In appreciation, Beethoven dedicated his C-sharp minor quartet to him. Released from the hospital after six weeks, Karl had to wait until his hair grew over the scar from the bullet wound before joining his regiment. In the interim, he and Beethoven moved to the small hamlet of Gneixendorf, where they lived with Beethoven's brother Johann and his wife, Therese, otherwise known as Fat Lump.

I received no news of him for the next several months and realized how much he'd come to define my life. My love for him had gone from girlish adoration to full-fledged passion to something "above the canopy of stars." Beethoven was and would always be the magical tiles in the cloister, the Mediterranean on a stormy day, mourning in the moonlight, morning at dusk. He meant the world to me.

In early December, Beethoven returned to the House of the Black Spaniards with a terrible chill. Schindler came to visit and shared the details, though I regarded them with suspicion. I didn't know Johann or Fat Lump, but Schindler's description made them out to be archvillains and worse. "The Master had one simple request," he explained. "He wanted Johann to leave all his money to Karl instead of to his wife, which seems more than fair."

"I don't think that sounds fair at all," I said as Kitty served him some of her bread pudding. "Fat Lump, I mean Therese, is his wife."

"The point is that the two brothers got into a violent argument, and the Master and Karl left as quickly as possible. In an open milk wagon. The Master developed an inflammation of the lungs. He's now under a doctor's care."

"I must see him immediately," I said.

"Perhaps we could bring him some of the bread pudding," Kitty suggested. "Remember how much he liked it?"

"Not to cast aspersions on your baking," Schindler said, polishing off the dessert, "but as the person in charge, I want to spare Countess Gallenberg the distressing sight of seeing the Master in such a pitiful condition." He informed me that he would keep in touch.

I wrote Beethoven several letters but didn't receive a reply. He might have been too ill to respond, or Schindler might have intercepted them. Finally, at the end of December, Schindler sent word that I could pay a brief visit. The doctor had just left, and Beethoven was alone with Schindler and Sali. "I made sure no one else would be here," Schindler whispered. "I need to protect his reputation. I'm sure you understand."

Beethoven immediately asked where I'd been. "I thought you had deserted me," he said.

"She didn't want to tire you," Schindler wrote on the slate. To me, he added, "The Master recently had his stomach drained. Much liquid poured out."

"Leave us," Beethoven said, pointing to the door.

Beethoven looked terrible. Even his normally vibrant eyes had completely lost their luster, yet he treated his illness as just a temporary distraction. In his mind he had overcome much worse, and nothing stopped him from composing, even deafness. He had completed another string quartet and substituted a new finale for the *Grosse Fuge*. "You will like it," he said before launching into a series of complaints about his benefactor, Prince Galitzin. Beethoven had yet to receive the money from him, and he was currently in Persia with the army.

"Everyone seems to be going into the army," Beethoven grumbled. "My Karl is about to leave for his regiment in Moravia. I suppose I should be grateful that it's not Persia, but now I'm all alone. Well, not quite." He pointed to a forty-volume set of Handel's works that a British admirer had sent him. "I've been studying them," he said excitedly. "One can learn much from Handel."

It touched me deeply that he still wanted to learn and that despite his conviction that his own work would be eternal, he showed humility and a deep respect for his musical forebears. I didn't know how long I had before Schindler returned, so I pulled out the note I'd carried with me for twelve years. It was wrinkled from the many times I'd unfolded it. I watched as he read it.

Thank you for almost everything.

"I gave you what I could," he said slowly. "It was not enough. I know that."

"You gave me a sonata," I wrote on the nearby slate.

"It's not my best, but people will play it forever."

I kissed him lightly on the forehead.

"You will always be my dear, enchanting girl." He had tears in his eyes, and then his lids closed and he fell asleep. I heard Schindler coming up the stairs, so I quickly wiped the slate clean. If one looked hard enough, the word "sonata" lingered in a wisp of chalk.

For the next six weeks, I awaited news of Beethoven's condition, but Schindler had finally achieved a position of power and was loath to relinquish it. He provided me with only the tiniest crumbs of information. I learned from Robert, who'd heard from two musicians, that Beethoven had undergone several more painful operations to drain his stomach. I heard from Nannette Streicher that one of his doctors had let him drink iced wine but that he drank too much and his abdominal pains grew worse. All throughout, a steady stream of visitors made the pilgrimage to the House of the Black Spaniards to say goodbye.

Many times, I waited outside his building, staring up at the windows. I've often asked myself why I didn't simply walk upstairs. It would have been hard for Schindler to stop me, but as I watched the people come and go, I realized that I wasn't part of Beethoven's public world. Our relationship had been conducted largely in private. I knew him better than most, but no one knew who I was, or if they did, I was "Count Gallenberg's wife" or "Josephine Brunswick's cousin" or "the countess whose name was on a sonata." It was too late to rewrite the narrative, and perhaps it was better that way.

One day I intercepted Schindler as he was leaving to run an errand. The hood of my cloak covered most of my face, and he didn't recognize me. "It's Julie," I said, hoping to create a level of intimacy that would make him more likely to grant my request.

He reeled back as if I'd struck him. "I . . . didn't expect to find you here," he said.

"I didn't want to intrude. I know that you have a difficult task handling all the people who want to see the Master."

"It is indeed very difficult," he agreed. "The Master is beloved by so many."

I told him that I completely understood but asked if he'd find it in his heart to let me visit the Master alone. He shook his head no. "The Master has already received the last rites. He doesn't have much time left. I think it would be too upsetting. Better that you remember him the way he was." He started to walk away.

"Please," I said, tugging on his sleeve. "I know how much you care for him. I know that you, too, are grieving."

He continued to walk down the street, a little taller for the power he wielded. "Herr Schindler, I beg of you," I called out. When he turned around, he saw that I'd dropped to my knees. "Just a few minutes alone with him," I pleaded.

"Please, Countess. People will think I am mistreating you."

"You are."

He walked over, extending his arm to help me up. "You may come on the afternoon of March 26 at four o'clock."

The sky was uncommonly dark as I hurried to the House of the Black Spaniards, snowflakes visible from the carriage. When I arrived, Sali told me that Schindler and Breuning had gone to the graveyard at Währing to find a proper site. A musician who had traveled from Graz to pay his respects was the only other person there. He remained with Sali in the kitchen.

Beethoven's bed had been moved to face the window, his Broadwood pianoforte keeping watch like a warrior guarding a pharaoh's tomb. Beethoven was unresponsive, eyes open but unseeing. He had lost so much weight that he was already a skeleton, his cheekbones protruding high in his otherwise sunken face. His hair, that glorious messy white mane, was spread out like a halo, matted but incandescent. Taking a seat next to the bed, I listened to the music of death, a loud percussive rattle that persisted in a steady rhythmic way, a funeral march with no alternate ending.

"Goodbye, my friend—my love," I whispered. "I wish you joy."

The snow was falling faster now, wrapping the glacis in a thin white veil. Hailstones clattered against the window and then a clap of thunder like timpani. Lightning flashed across the room. Beethoven's right arm flew upward as if he were trying to seize the lightning bolt and use it as a baton, but just as quickly his arm fell limp.

Sali came into the room, and I quickly left. I couldn't bear to see him die. Turning around one last time, I noticed his arms resting comfortably on his chest.

Beethoven's hands . . . the last thing I remembered.

40

Robert and I walked from the House of the Black Spaniards to Trinity Church. After the storm three days earlier, spring had suddenly arrived and the bright sunshine had brought out an estimated twenty thousand people for Beethoven's funeral. The authorities had closed down school for the day, and children were out playing. Two boys were flying a kite.

The crowd was so large that we could barely move. Up ahead, I could see Beethoven's coffin, which was made of polished oak and covered in an ornate embroidered pall. Robert had attended the lying-in-state ceremony at Beethoven's apartment and told me that it was a good thing that I'd stayed away. An autopsy had distorted Beethoven's face, and friends, eager for a souvenir, had cut off locks of his hair. A garland of white roses rested atop his scraggly lion's mane.

As we turned a corner and headed toward the church, a brass band played Beethoven's *Funeral March* from his Sonata in A-flat Major. He had written it a year before the *Moonlight*, dedicating it to Prince Lichnowsky. The crowd jostled the pallbearers carrying the coffin. It was only two hundred paces from Beethoven's house to the church, but it took us ninety minutes to reach it. A military guard was stationed at the door to turn away uninvited guests. We squeezed past the hordes to find seats in the nave.

After the priest officiated at the requiem Mass, we followed the hearse and the large procession to Währing Cemetery, where Josephine had been laid to rest. An actor delivered the funeral oration written by the playwright Franz Grillparzer. "He was an artist—and who shall arise to stand beside him?" Beethoven's coffin was then lowered into a narrow grave. People threw dirt on the coffin and wept openly. I couldn't cry. My grief was private. Nannette Streicher caught my eye and nodded. Schindler whispered, "My heart is broken." Duport wondered if he would rate such an impressive funeral. Robert wondered the same.

When the ceremony had ended, people began to walk home. It was still bright and sunny, and if Beethoven had been given the chance, he would have walked too.

41

My life had been about one man for so many years that I felt unmoored. It was hard to accept that it was finally over. Beethoven had such purpose, such a gift. Robert didn't have his gift but shared his purpose. He was busy composing two ballets for his lover. They would premiere in Vienna the following year. Even Giulietta had her own life. She was planning to join her brother Hugo in Rome, where he was studying art.

"Will you be seeing your poet?" I asked. She hadn't spoken about him in at least a month, and I hadn't noticed any correspondence.

"I'm no longer in love with him," she said. "He's not a very good writer. Who wants to be a muse to an untalented poet? It would only reflect badly on me. No, I want to have an exciting life."

Noticing my downcast mood, she offered to stay, but I urged her to go. "Just be happy, my dearest."

"Were you happy, Mama?"

"At times."

"Did you love Herr Beethoven?"

"I did, but it wasn't meant to be."

"Why?"

"Because he didn't need my love—enough."

A week after the funeral, Friedrich arrived at my apartment. He wanted to express his condolences and to show me a letter that he'd received a few days earlier. His housekeeper had described the man who'd delivered it as looking like a vampire. It sounded like Schindler, but I couldn't imagine why he'd be writing to Friedrich.

I looked at the handwriting. It belonged to Beethoven, but it was barely a scribble, executed with great effort.

> *My dear Count Schulenburg,*
> *I've requested that my secretary, Anton Schindler, deliver this letter after my funeral—presuming the Ass-trians even bother with one. Countess Gallenberg once asked how I knew when a composition was finished and I told her, "When I have said everything I want to say." I still have much to say but little time left, so I will be brief. It is my dying wish that you visit the Countess and request the honor of a waltz. It would please her very much. It would please me too. Now I have said everything.*
> *Your most envious servant,*
> *L. v. Beethoven*
>
> *From the heart—May it return to the heart.*

I began to weep, tears falling on the letter, smudging his already blotchy handwriting. Soon my crying turned to sobs. *Damn him!* He was breaking my heart from the grave.

"Forgive me," Friedrich said, "but I'm confused."

"Don't you see? Beethoven finished the composition. He wrote the perfect coda."

We stood there gazing into each other's eyes.

"Now what should we do?" I asked.

He held out his arms. "Waltz."

EPILOGUE

1856

The next twenty years were among the happiest of my life. Friedrich and I never married, but we remained deeply in love. I was content to be his mistress even after Armgard died. We spent summers at his family's estate in Saxony. When he decided to move there permanently, he asked me to go with him, but I couldn't leave Vienna. Beethoven's music was everywhere.

Friedrich died three years ago. I was seventy and not well enough to travel, but the children—our children—were at his bedside.

Robert took over the Kärntnertor Theater, lost most of his money, and moved to Rome. By the time he died, he had written the music for more than fifty ballets. My son Hugo published a well-received biography of Leonardo da Vinci; my daughter, Giulietta, had many adventures; and my son Fritz became an army officer. Lucy died not long after Beethoven, but Kitty remains with me to this day.

I recently sold my pianoforte. I have rheumatism in my fingers and can no longer play. I had hoped my grandchildren might want it, but the newer instruments have more power and a greater range. To them, it's the equivalent of a harpsichord, a curiosity piece from the past.

I wish someone had painted my portrait so I could show them that I, too, was once young. I don't even have my portrait miniature. Beethoven kept it. Even with all his moves and the total chaos of his living conditions, he'd made sure it was safe. When Schindler and Stephan Breuning were going through his belongings after his death, they discovered it in a secret compartment in his writing desk. It was auctioned off with his other things. Trouser Button won the bid.

It comforts me to think that whenever Beethoven looked at my youthful face, he saw the "dear, enchanting girl" who loved him with all her heart. That was my sonata. I hear it even now.

AUTHOR'S NOTE

The Woman in the Moonlight is fiction based partly on fact—an improvisation on a theme or as Beethoven might have called it, a fantasia.

I first heard of Countess Julie Guicciardi when a friend mentioned that Beethoven had dedicated the *Moonlight* Sonata to her. The friend didn't know anything more but thought it might make an interesting story. I was immediately intrigued. Years ago, I'd studied piano and voice and had once thought of becoming a singer, but ultimately, I traded one keyboard for another and developed a different voice. Still, music had been my first love, and I hoped Julie would help me rediscover it.

First, I had to discover Julie, a task made all the more difficult by the dearth of biographical materials. There were no memoirs, diaries, and only a few letters. Known as La Bella Guicciardi for her fetching looks, she seemed to have evaded nearly everyone who wanted to capture them for posterity. I could locate only one lithograph, a marble bust, and a charming portrait miniature that Julie's son had identified as that of his mother. In the intervening two centuries, however, other women's names have been put forth, so even the portrait miniature is in dispute. Consequently, Countess Guicciardi, whose name graces the most popular piece of classical music in history, has receded into the past as a ghost.

At one time, however, she was thought to be Beethoven's greatest love. Anton Schindler, in his 1840 biography, *Beethoven: As I Knew Him*, anoints her the "Immortal Beloved"—the name given to the anonymous woman to whom Beethoven had penned a passionate letter discovered after his death. Schindler was one of the people who found it in a secret compartment in Beethoven's desk. It was tucked away along with the wrenching "Heiligenstadt Testament," in which Beethoven grieves over his lost hearing and confesses that he contemplated suicide. Two portrait miniatures, including the one Julie's son identified, were also hidden away in the desk.

The mystery of the "Immortal Beloved" has intrigued music fans and scholars since the undated letter was first discovered. Julie was eventually disqualified when an analysis of the paper's watermark pinpointed the year as 1812, after Julie had moved from Vienna. Today, the general consensus is that the "Immortal Beloved" is either Antonie Brentano, a friend and the dedicatee of the Diabelli Variations, or Julie's cousin, Josephine von Brunswick, to whom he wrote at least fifteen ardent letters. I've excerpted several of these in the book.

Schindler's reputation has been seriously damaged since his biography was first published. It was discovered that he forged documents and greatly exaggerated his role in Beethoven's life. Nevertheless, he wasn't wrong in suggesting a romantic entanglement between Julie and the composer. Many scholars agree that she is the "dear, enchanting girl" who temporarily lifted Beethoven's despair as he confronted his hearing loss. Here is a portion of an 1801 letter Beethoven wrote to his childhood friend Dr. Franz Wegeler:

> *My life is once more a little more pleasant, I'm out and about again, among people—you can hardly believe how desolate, how sad my life has been since these last two years; this change was caused by a dear, enchanting girl who loves me and whom I love. After two years, I*

*am again enjoying some moments of bliss, and it is the
first time I feel that marriage could make me happy, but
unfortunately she is not of my station and I certainly
could not marry now.*

Years later, while reminiscing with Schindler, Beethoven con-
firmed his affection for Julie, as well as his dislike for Count Robert
von Gallenberg, the man she married in November 1803. The couple
then moved to Naples, where Gallenberg, an aspiring composer, took
a job at a merchant bank. Did Julie fall out of love with Beethoven?
Did they suffer a rift? Schindler, with the utmost discretion, weighs in:

*It is a matter of some delicacy, and out of deference for
those still living can be only lightly touched upon. It
cannot be said for certain whether it was a question of
faithlessness on the part of the woman alone, as has been
claimed, or whether intrigues from another side severed
the alliance and prompted the young lady quite suddenly
to become the wife of the famous composer, Count von
Gallenberg.*

Julie's marriage and move to Naples seemed the logical end to the
story, but by then I'd become so captivated I couldn't stop researching.
In reading André de Hevesy's 1927 book, *Beethoven: The Man*, I came
across a reference to Julie in Vienna's police records. A "society spy"
reported that she'd arrived in the city in October 1814 and that she was
an emissary "of the Murats." Joachim Murat, the heroic cavalry officer,
was then the King of Naples, married to Napoleon's youngest sister,
the formidable Caroline. Beethoven's "dear, enchanting girl" was more
complicated than I'd imagined.

Julie's appearance in Vienna coincided with the opening of the
Congress, the international forum that redrew the continent's political

map after Napoleon's defeat. Beethoven gave a concert before the assembled monarchs, courtiers, consorts, and spies. I have no evidence that Julie and Beethoven saw each other during that time, but it provided another opportunity to bring them together.

The police records also noted that she was the mistress of Count Schulenburg, the Saxon diplomat who was the other man in Julie's life. Not much has been written about Friedrich von der Schulenburg or about Julie's husband, Robert Gallenberg, who composed more than fifty ballets. Fairly or unfairly, he has been described as a man of mediocre talent, but his proximity to several of the most colorful musical personalities of the period made for rich material. As a ballet composer at the Royal Theater San Carlo in Naples, he worked under the impresario Domenico Barbaja, a former munitions dealer and coffeehouse waiter, who invented the drink that ultimately became the cappuccino. Barbaja discovered Gioachino Rossini, the beloved composer of such popular operas as *The Barber of Seville* and *William Tell*.

In 1822, when Barbaja took over the lease for Vienna's Kärntnertor Theater, he hired Gallenberg and Louis-Antoine Duport, the famous Parisian ballet dancer, to help run it. Vienna was then in the midst of a Rossini craze. At that point, Beethoven was almost totally deaf and working on his Ninth Symphony. After negotiations with the Theater an der Wien broke down, he premiered the work at the Kärntnertor. I'd never expected the story of Julie and Beethoven to come full circle. While I can't definitely place her at the concert, it was considered a major event, held at a theater where her now estranged husband was employed. I can't imagine she'd have been anywhere else.

As far as I know, Julie gave only one formal interview, to the Mozart biographer Otto Jahn. It took place in 1852, a few years before her death. Even allowing for the nineteenth century's gentle approach to interviewing a lady about her love affairs, Jahn didn't elicit much information. She told him that Beethoven had been her teacher, that he was prone to excitement, and that he accepted linens in lieu of payment.

She then described him as "ugly" and even declared that the *Moonlight* Sonata wasn't originally meant for her.

Beethoven had given her his Rondo in G Major but, according to Julie, took it back when he needed to dedicate a piece to Countess Henriette Lichnowsky, the sister of his foremost patron. The Rondo in G Major had been written several years earlier and doesn't have anywhere near the depth of emotion expressed in the sonata. It seems more likely that Beethoven wanted to give Julie something special. But of course, that is pure speculation. Otto Jahn died before completing his biography of Beethoven, and his notes fell into the hands of Alexander Wheelock Thayer, a librarian and journalist from Massachusetts. His book *The Life of Ludwig van Beethoven* became the first scholarly work on the composer, and Julie's opaque interview became the definitive one.

Throughout the book, I've changed some facts about Julie's life. For example, she wasn't an only child and had upwards of six children, not three. I have no evidence that her mother was the mistress of Prince Lichnowsky, though his reputation for debauchery was well known. Countess Lulu von Thürheim, who was acquainted with the prince through her sister-in-law, Princess Razumovsky, wrote a memoir in which she describes him as a "cynical degenerate" and a "shameless coward."

Josephine Brunswick did indeed live above Müller's Art Gallery. The tragic facts of her life have been well documented in books and articles.

During Beethoven's lifetime, the *Moonlight* Sonata was known as the Piano Sonata no. 14 in C-sharp Minor, op. 27, no. 2. It wasn't until five years after his death that the poet and music critic Ludwig Rellstab compared the first movement to "a boat visiting the wild places on Lake Lucerne by moonlight." Many have scoffed at the romantic title, most notably the Swiss pianist Edwin Fischer, who writes in his book *Beethoven's Pianoforte Sonatas* that he'd discovered a sketch in

Beethoven's handwriting in a Viennese archive. Beethoven had copied out a few lines from Mozart's *Don Giovanni*, in which Don Giovanni has killed the Commendatore. Beneath the lines, Beethoven had transposed the passage into the *Moonlight*'s key of C-sharp minor. It was Fischer's belief that the first movement wasn't romantic at all but a funeral hymn.

I've "lived" with Beethoven for four years, listening to him, learning about him, but I'm hardly an expert. I am, however, sure of one thing. As Julie led me to Beethoven, he led me back to music. I couldn't have asked for a more brilliant, volatile, infuriating, endearing guide.

ACKNOWLEDGMENTS

I've benefitted greatly from the music scholars, biographers, and editors who've devoted much of their careers to researching Beethoven's life and work. I couldn't have done this book without them.

I'd like to thank David Blum for the original idea, Carmen Johnson for her encouragement and sensitivity, and her team at Little A for their enthusiasm and diligence.

I'm grateful to the following people for their friendship, support, and advice: Glynnis O'Connor, Ira Resnick, Jamie Delson, Jenny Gilbert Delson, Nancy Morrisroe, Elaine Altholz, Mary Beth Kaslick, Carolyn Swartz, Penelope Rowlands, Gerry Buckley, Harry Lang, Jennifer Crandall, Richard Story, Dorothy Stern, Sandy Tillett, and Tom Crawford and the American Classical Orchestra.

A special thank-you to my husband, Lee Stern, for his love and infinite patience. I can't think of anyone I'd prefer to come home to after a difficult day with Beethoven.

SELECTED BIBLIOGRAPHY

Albrecht, Theodore. *Letters to Beethoven and Other Correspondence.* 3 vols. Lincoln: University of Nebraska Press, 1996.

Atteridge, Andrew Hilliard. *Joachim Murat: Marshal of France and King of Naples.* New York: Brentano's, 1911.

Barea, Ilsa. *Vienna: Legend and Reality.* London: Secker and Warburg, 1966.

Beethoven, Ludwig van. *Beethoven: Letters, Journals, and Conversations.* Edited and translated by Michael Hamburger. New York: Thames and Hudson, 1984.

Beethoven, Ludwig van. *Beethoven: The Man and the Artist, as Revealed in His Own Words.* Edited by Friedrich Kerst and Henry Krehbiel. New York: Dover, 1964.

Bradley, Ian. *Water Music: Music Making in the Spas of Europe and North America.* New York: Oxford University Press, 2010.

Breuning, Gerhard von. *Memories of Beethoven*. Edited by Maynard Solomon. Translated by Henry Mins and Maynard Solomon. Cambridge: Cambridge University Press, 1995.

Clive, Peter. *Beethoven and His World: A Biographical Dictionary*. New York: Oxford University Press, 2001.

Comini, Alessandra. *The Changing Image of Beethoven: A Study in Mythmaking*. New York: Rizzoli, 1987.

Cone, Polly, ed. *The Imperial Style: Fashions of the Hapsburg Era*. Based on the exhibition Fashions of the Hapsburg Era: Austria-Hungary at the Metropolitan Museum of Art. New York: Metropolitan Museum of Art, 1980.

Cooper, Barry. *Beethoven*. Master Musicians. New York: Oxford University Press, 2000.

Dallas, Gregor. *1815: The Roads to Waterloo*. London: R. Cohen Books, 1996.

Day, Carolyn A. *Consumptive Chic: A History of Beauty, Fashion, and Disease*. London, New York: Bloomsbury Academic, 2017.

DeNora, Tia. *Beethoven and the Construction of Genius: Musical Politics in Vienna, 1792–1803*. Berkeley: University of California Press, 1997.

Dusinberre, Edward. *Beethoven for a Later Age: The Journey of a String Quartet*. London: Faber and Faber, 2016.

Edwards, H. Sutherland. *The Life of Rossini*. London: Hurst and Blackett, 1869.

Eisenbeiss, Philip. *Bel Canto Bully: The Life and Times of the Legendary Opera Impresario Domenico Barbaja*. London: Haus Publishing, 2013.

Fischer, Edwin. *Beethoven's Pianoforte Sonatas: A Guide for Students & Amateurs*. London: Faber and Faber, 1959.

Fischer, Hans Conrad, and Erich Kock. *Ludwig van Beethoven: A Study in Text and Pictures*. London: Macmillan, 1972.

Goethe, Johann Wolfgang von. *Elective Affinities*. Translated by R. J. Hollingdale. London: Penguin Books, 2005.

———. *The Sorrows of Young Werther*. Translated by Thomas Carlyle and R. D. Boylan. New York: Dover Publications, 2002.

Grant, Michael. *Eros in Pompeii: The Erotic Art Collection of the Museum of Naples*. New York: Stewart, Tabori, and Chang, 1975.

Guerzoni, Guido. *Waxing Eloquent: Italian Portraits in Wax*. Edited by Andrea Daninos. Translated by Catherine Bolton. Milan: Officina Libraria, 2012.

Harris, Judith. *Pompeii Awakened: A Story of Rediscovery*. London: I. B. Tauris, 2007.

Hazzard, Shirley, and Francis Steegmuller. *The Ancient Shore: Dispatches from Naples*. Chicago: University of Chicago Press, 2008.

Hevesy, André de. *Beethoven: The Man*. Translated by F. S. Flint. New York: Brentano's, 1927.

Hibbert, Christopher. *Napoleon: His Wives and Women*. London: HarperCollins, 2002.

Jones, Timothy. *Beethoven: The 'Moonlight' and Other Sonatas, Op. 27 and Op. 31*. Cambridge: Cambridge University Press, 1999.

Kahn, Robert S. *Beethoven and the Grosse Fuge: Music, Meaning, and Beethoven's Most Difficult Work*. Lanham, MD: Scarecrow Press, 2010.

Kelly, Thomas Forrest. *First Nights: Five Musical Premieres*. New Haven: Yale University Press, 2000.

Kinderman, William. *Beethoven*. Berkeley: University of California Press, 1995.

———. *Beethoven's Diabelli Variations*. New York: Oxford University Press, 1989.

King, David. *Vienna, 1814: How the Conquerors of Napoleon Made Love, War, and Peace at the Congress of Vienna*. New York: Harmony Books, 2008.

Klapproth, John E. *Beethoven's Only Beloved: Josephine!* Charleston, SC: CreateSpace Independent Publishing, 2011.

Kraus, Wolfgang, and Peter Müller. *Palaces of Vienna*. New York: Vendome Press, 1993.

Landon, H. C. Robbins. *Beethoven: His Life, Work and World*. New York: Thames and Hudson, 1992.

Large, David Clay. *The Grand Spas of Central Europe: A History of Intrigue, Politics, Art, and Healing*. Maryland: Rowman and Littlefield, 2015.

Lockwood, Lewis. *Beethoven: The Music and the Life*. New York: Norton, 2003.

Mai, François Martin. *Diagnosing Genius: The Life and Death of Beethoven*. Montreal: McGill-Queen's University Press, 2007.

Marek, George R. *Beethoven: Biography of a Genius*. New York: Funk & Wagnalls, 1969.

Martin, Russell. *Beethoven's Hair: An Extraordinary Historical Odyssey and a Scientific Mystery Solved*. New York: Broadway Books, 2000.

Mathew, Nicholas. *Political Beethoven*. New York: Cambridge University Press, 2013.

McGuigan, Dorothy Gies. *Metternich and the Duchess*. New York: Doubleday, 1975.

Morris, Edmund. *Beethoven: The Universal Composer*. New York: HarperCollins, 2005.

Norway, Arthur H. *Naples: Past and Present*. London: Methuen, 1901.

Ockman, Carol. *Ingres's Eroticized Bodies: Retracing the Serpentine Line*. New Haven, CT: Yale University Press, 1995.

Parsons, Nicholas. *Vienna: A Cultural History*. New York: Oxford University Press, 2008.

Rice, John A. *Empress Marie Therese and Music at the Viennese Court 1792–1807*. New York: Cambridge University Press, 2003.

Rolland, Romain. *Beethoven the Creator: The Great Creative Epochs, from the Eroica to the Appassionata*. Translated by Ernest Newman. New York: Dover, 1964.

Sachs, Harvey. *The Ninth: Beethoven and the World in 1824*. New York: Random House, 2010.

Schindler, Anton. *Beethoven As I Knew Him: A Biography*. Edited by Donald W. MacArdle. Translated by Constance S. Jolly. Chapel Hill: University of North Carolina Press, 1966.

Seward, Desmond. *Metternich: The First European*. New York: Viking Penguin, 1991.

Skowroneck, Tilman. *Beethoven the Pianist*. Cambridge: Cambridge University Press, 2010.

Solomon, Maynard. *Beethoven*, 2nd ed. New York: Schirmer, 1998.

Sonneck, O. G., ed. *Beethoven: Impressions by his Contemporaries*. New York: Dover, 1926.

Steblin, Rita. *New Facts about Beethoven's Beloved Piano Pupil Julie Guicciardi*. Bonn: Verlag Beethoven-Haus, 2009.

Stendhal. *Life of Rossini*. Translated by Richard N. Coe. New York: Criterion Books, 1957.

————. *Rome, Naples and Florence.* Translated by Richard N. Coe. Surrey, UK: John Calder, 1959.

Sterba, Editha, and Richard Sterba. *Beethoven and His Nephew: A Psychoanalytic Study of Their Relationship.* New York: Pantheon, 1954.

Suchet, John. *Beethoven: The Man Revealed.* New York: Grove Press, 2012.

Sullivan, J. W. N. *Beethoven: His Spiritual Development.* New York: Vintage Books Edition, 1960.

Swafford, Jan. *Beethoven: Anguish and Triumph.* New York: Houghton Mifflin Harcourt, 2014.

Tellenbach, Marie-Elisabeth. *Beethoven and His "Immortal Beloved" Josephine Brunsvik: Her Fate and the Influence on Beethoven's Oeuvre.* Translated by John E. Klapproth. Charleston, SC: CreateSpace Independent Publishing, 2014.

Thayer, Alexander W. *Thayer's Life of Beethoven,* rev. ed. Edited by Elliot Forbes. Princeton, NJ: Princeton University Press, 1973.

Tinterow, Gary, and Philip Conisbee, eds. *Portraits by Ingres: Image of an Epoch.* New York: Metropolitan Museum of Art, 1999.

Tyson, Alan, ed. *Beethoven Studies.* New York: Norton, 1973.

Zamoyski, Adam. *Rites of Peace: The Fall of Napoleon and the Congress of Vienna.* New York: HarperCollins, 2007.

ABOUT THE AUTHOR

Photo © 2019 Lee Stern

Patricia Morrisroe is the author of *Mapplethorpe: A Biography*, *Wide Awake: A Memoir of Insomnia*, and *9 ½ Narrow: My Life in Shoes*. She was a contributing editor at *New York* magazine and has written for many other publications, including *Vanity Fair*, the *New York Times*, *Vogue*, the London *Sunday Times Magazine*, *Travel + Leisure*, and *Departures*. *The Woman in the Moonlight* is her first novel. For more information, visit www.patriciamorrisroe.com.